WIDOW

WIDOW

THE RIFT BRIDE BOOK III

ADA DART

PAINTED BLIND
PUBLISHING
LITERARY ALCHEMY

PAINTED BLIND
PUBLISHING
LITERARY ALCHEMY

Widow: Book III of The Rift Bride
© 2023 Ada Dart
ISBN: 978-1-957469-09-6

Text: Ada Dart
Book & Cover Design: M. F. Sullivan

Ada Dart Online: adadartromance.com
Painted Blind Publishing: paintedblindpublishing.com

*I have already written on the natures of Riftborn
such as my husband, Malin;
and of altered, like my mate Eleison,
my memoir has had much to teach.*

*But what of the Hunter's Guild,
that treacherous organization of which Glenn
—father of my beloved daughter Rosina—
is a disgraced member?*

*And more frightful, still:
What of the Rift demons,
the blood-drinkers called dharmines?
Creatures like my servant, Ba'al-Dinon—
If, indeed, he is a dharmine at all?*

PART I

THE SAME MONTH as my husband's assassination, I was already pining for him. He had been away three weeks on some sort of unavoidable business trip down to Azstoria, and while I was without him, my loom sat undisturbed. Eleison had gone away with him to keep him company, and to guard his life as the dharmine guarded mine.

It was that very servant, Ba'al-Dinon, who was least troubled by our Master's absence.

"He will always return to you, Thecla," my Dinon said to me while, my eyes stubbornly turned from the beauty of his face and neatly plaited pale hair, I gazed through the window of my weaving room.

"I've warned you about being too familiar," I said absently, watching the nurses in the garden below. Her dark curls bouncing with every step, Rosina toddled along behind the boy who was half her sibling after being raised on the same breast. Behind me, the dharmine exhaled with strange pleasure at the faint reprimand he had endeavored to earn. "And, anyway—"

"There you are!"

I straightened upright, twisting at the waist to find Aleister leaning into my weaving room without even having knocked. "Your manners are terrible," I told him, earning a grin and a knowing glance at my footman.

"Tell me something I don't know...and, anyway, it's not like you're doing anything. The whole of Karrisregion can hear it when you're busy working at your loom, cranking out those blasted tapestries of yours. Look, dear—you can't just sit there pining when you know he's back tomorrow."

"They're both back tomorrow," I reminded him. "Eleison as well as Malin. But even one more day is too long to wait. I miss them both so terribly!"

"Well, all the more reason to busy your mind. Come on down! Play Aether with us."

My mouth twisted. Aether was a gambling game, largely based on one's skill at bluffs and card counting. "I've never been particularly good at Aether. To tell you the truth, I barely understand it."

His eyes lighting with the promise of a lucrative mark for future gambling predations, Aleister strode in with another somewhat too appreciative look at my servant before drawing me from my bench with a hand around my forearm.

"Come along, now, Thecla...I'm not giving you a say in the matter, no matter how you were planning on using your manservant to relieve your boredom..."

Sputtering, I glanced back at thinly smiling Dinon. He looked more as if his plans had been interrupted than mine had been. "Enjoy the game, Madame..."

While Aleister marched me through the door, he muttered to himself, "Now, then, we'll need a fourth player..."

While he dragged me along, I wracked my brain for suitable protests. I hadn't had a headache in well over a year by then, thank goodness—a conscious year, anyway—but that of course meant it was an unreasonable excuse. Menstrual pains? No, not yet. I was due for it soon if at all that month, but didn't like to lie about it in case I cursed a fetus surreptitiously developing within my womb.

For oh! That was what lay in the heart of my pining for my husband. Every day he was away was precious: sacred time we might have spent in the task that was at once a joyful celebration of love and a hopeless, desperate race against time.

I was still then plenty young, not quite twenty-seven, and could have had many child-bearing days ahead of me if I wished it. Yes—if I had begged Eleison to neglect his shots for a season or two, or pursued Glenn for another of his stock, I could have had all the children I desired. An endless litter of precious boys and bonny girls.

But it was only one child I longed to carry in my womb: to birth into the world and raise alongside the one for which the ventil within my heart had acted as my strange surrogate. I wanted only Malin's child...yet, it was Malin's child which continued, month on month, refusing our calls to take entry to the world.

By then, in a silent way, we were both beginning to worry; but Malin insisted, time and again, each time the cramps disappointed me or the blood disturbed me, "Never mind, my love, never mind. When the time is right, the child will come."

How could he be so confident? I always wondered that, as I wondered much else about my mysterious husband and territory master. The greater part of his secrets, all those which affected me, had been lain bare in his confession once he won me back from the depths of animal unconsciousness. Now, with nothing of the sort between us, I felt as close to my husband as I did to my altered mate. I could hear the vast clockwork arrangement of his mind tick-tocking away every second I lay in his bed, nestled in his arms with my head on his pillow. Malin was always thinking, and when his thoughts vibrated at their deepest and darkest— when I saw in his eyes, his dark, dreamy eyes, that he was whole leagues of spacetime away—I knew then that he ruminated upon his final secrets: whatever thoughts he held within himself that he had deemed too detrimental to be shared with me.

Once, his secrets had bothered me. I wished to know him, to know everything, as though he and I were of one mind—and many times, it seemed that we were.

Yet, with the emergence of the ventil, more in me had changed than my abrupt transition from young wife to new mother. Far, far more. My husband's patient love and forgiveness had transformed my entire way of being with him. As he trusted and forgave me, I trusted and forgave him—felt, indeed, there was never anything to forgive between us. In the clearest, most honest sense, Malin and I were devoted partners; and, as his partner, I trusted fully that when the truth became relevant, I would learn it.

Still…I not infrequently worried his brooding involved me or our unfulfilled hopes of conception. Especially after all we had been through in the time surrounding the birth of Rosina, I wanted my presence to bring my husband nothing but the constant pleasure I felt he deserved. Deserved, in spite of all he had done.

All he perhaps continued to do.

"I say"—Aleister drew me from my pensive mood as, on the first floor of the sprawling country estate, his attention dragged at the sight of a few wilting roses normally kept fresh in their vases— "the flowers are dying quickly this year! Is the garden blighted? I couldn't help but notice just this morning the violets outside aren't faring very well, either."

Frowning—having hardly noticed it, given how preoccupied I'd been with Malin's absence—I paused by the vase to study it with no small displeasure. "I'll have to talk to Charlotte," I said, casting a reflexive glance around the place to see many servants much too busy to remember to change out some flowers unless it were Malin himself who gave the command. "You're right, dear; it is quite unbecoming, isn't it?"

At once, Aleister burst into merry laughter, his boyish eyes a-twinkle with delight. My brow furrowing, I found myself prickly. I confess that, even all this time later, my humble beginnings sometimes haunt me with the ghost of inferiority, and I am prone to taking even innocent jokes the wrong way if they should strike me in a mood that's inopportune. "What is it," I asked, self-consciously smoothing my dress. "Is it something I said?"

"Well—yes, in a way." Still glowing with mirth, Aleister slipped his hand around my elbow again and resumed guiding me out to the gardens. "When I think of the feral little peasant-girl you were when Malin brought you here, and even after, it's quite funny to me to think you the sort of lady who worries her lip over the state of some roses in the atrium. Ah! Aha, there he is—there's our fourth!"

Owing to its bluffing nature, Aether was a game requiring partners—I had assumed that Kalypso and Aleister had tended to that matter already and that I merely rounded out the game, but, given the eagerness Aleister showed to set eyes on Glenn as we stepped into the mudroom, that didn't seem to be the case. Not that Aleister needed a reason to be eager to see Glenn...I had more than once felt my servant dharmine, who spoke so often in my heart's private chambers, offer to pluck the duke's eyes from his skull on sensing my displeasure for his lingering gaze.

But what ownership had I over the hunter who dwelled in our house as an exiled murderer—a wanted man? Even though, seeing him in the middle of removing his hat, my heart leapt in my throat to speed my blood with delight, that was simply the natural effect of the man's rugged good looks. His sleeves were buttoned at his wrists, allowing only the slightest hint of the tattooed Rift beasts trailing across his arms and body; but the one upon his neck, the luptich bursting from an array of mithrae and other Rift flowers, shared the look of quiet intensity that always set about his face.

Especially when our eyes linked.

"Thecla," he said, lowering his eyes quickly again, "Duke Montagne. Good morning."

How Glenn could sting me with just a word, or lack thereof! There I stood, the mother of his only child—that same delightful daughter he had just been in the garden visiting, no doubt—and still, after a year of living in our house, he could hardly seem to stand the sight of me.

When I was a girl first arrived at the estate, such behavior would have offended me. Did offend me, in fact, when Eleison exhibited the same wariness to set his gaze on me too long. Yet, experienced as I now was, I could discern that this aversion to holding my stare was in no way a sign of distaste: far from it. Glenn, to whom Malin's name of 'Farrow' was an unworthy blemish beside my own, had not yet been capable of accepting the nature of my relationship with my husband. Malin longed to embrace him as a brother in my love—if not as closely as he had embraced Eleison, then at least with as much preternatural compassion.

All the same, poor Glenn had not yet accepted his own transformation—the one that was reflected in the golden luptich-glow of his altered eyes. How could I ask him to accept that Malin Farrow, the territory master of Gudrune and his sworn enemy, was willing to share his wife's treasury of love with him? He had certainly changed over the past year, Glenn; he still had a certain restlessness about him, but he no longer appeared inclined to flee the property and either take to a life in the wilderness or tear out the throat of the man who had offered him safe haven from the undue price placed upon his head. Accordingly, Glenn was now welcome to treat the manor as his home; to wander its grounds the same as any one of us, so long as he did not leave the property.

But what pains he took to avoid Malin! Glenn was now his own prisoner, captive to his biases and unnecessary shames. In truth, I barely saw him outside his apartment at all; it was only the absences of Malin and Eleison that had permitted his excursion to the garden at a time when his door was usually sealed to all but Rosina and myself.

Of course...Aleister's enthusiasm to see him may have been a contributing factor toward greater isolation during the summertime visits of the courtiers.

"'Good morning,' he says in a tone fit for a funeral." With a tut and a shake of his head, Aleister kept me back so that together we would fill the doorway to the house and slow, if not entirely prevent, Glenn's escape from our conversation. "Come now! It's a beautiful day—weren't you just under the lovely blue sky yourself? How can you wear such a *frown*, Glenn?"

"I'll try to smile more," Glenn responded dryly, making no effort to disguise his displeasure as he would have if, say, he should bump into Malin or Eleison in the upper hallways. "Excuse me—"

"Please Aether with us," I blurted, embarrassed by my own inelegance but urged to by his shifting into motion, a gesture that spoke of his intent to find any means to squeeze past us and flee back to his rooms. Hesitating, looking intently at me, Glenn allowed himself to drink in the features of my suddenly flaming face. With a girlish stutter as few men could have still inspired in me even then, I endeavored an enticing little smile and suggested in a more delicate tone, "Aleister's right—it *is* a beautiful day, and I've been quite cooped up, myself. He and Kalypso are hoping to play Aether today—but we'll need one more, and I could hardly pick a better partner than you, Glenn."

His wry look communicated an unspoken rejoinder to that claim, but luckily Aleister leapt in to agree, "Yes, indeed. You look like a man who knows his way around a deck of cards, Glenn. A gambling man like myself, I'd wager."

With a meek shrug and the barest twitch of his beard as he ignored the urge to smile, Glenn confessed, "I've played a game or two in my life."

"Mm, trying to ring me dry already...of money, I mean." With a light chuckle, Aleister ignored the glance Glenn and I exchanged. Freeing me, the duke instead stepped forward to drop a hand on the hunter's shoulder. "Come along, Glenn! We won't accept 'no' for an answer, will we, Thecla? Have to take all the chances we can get...Lord knows, as soon as Uncle's back in town"—that was, of course, Malin; not Aleister's real uncle but only a close mentor of many years—"you'll be locking yourself in your blasted apartment again, denying us your enlivening presence."

"I'm not sure I'm exactly a—uh, bastion of joy even when he's not here...but, sure." While I tried not to let the excitement show too much on my face, Glenn allowed himself to be pushed back out the door by Aleister and said as he stepped out into the open air, "I'll play a few rounds with you three."

"There we have it! A regular miracle—ah, almost as miraculous as the good staff here..."

The roguish duke's eye had landed upon a pitcher of vibrant, cool-looking cocktail that had been supplied at the wrought iron table where Kalypso reclined in a bathing suit and lacy cover-up, sipping a drink that had no doubt been refilled at least once already since her brother left her. "*There* you are," cried the spoiled girl, thumping the glass back down upon the little table and perking to see the hostage we brought with us. Somewhat less shrewishly now, she sat up straight and lowered her sunglasses to offer a coquettish bat of her eyes.

"Well," she said to Aleister as he drew out a seat for me, "here I was about to give you the third degree for leaving me here so long I've gotten drunk before the game begins—but now I see you must have had to apply some lock-picking skills to get our two recluses out into the sun. Well done, Aleister!"

"I didn't realize my isolation was a topic of such conversation," said Glenn, politely bending to kiss Kalypso's offered hand before he slid into the seat across from mine.

"Much less so since Madame Farrow here has taken to absenting herself from high society these past few weeks." Aleister spoke to the table at large, but his eyes were fixed upon the lemon-golden fluid of the cocktail he poured into one of the waiting glasses. "Ah, that's the stuff—Thecla, dear, here you are...and—"

"No, thank you," said Glenn, turning the glass nearest him facedown upon the tray.

With a scoff, Aleister poured himself one instead. "Why, a teetotaler in our midst? No wonder you lock yourself up all the damn day..."

As Aleister winced for his sister's semi-surreptitious kick in the shin upon his profanity, Glenn snorted. "How would I survive? No...it just seems sort of early, doesn't it?"

"Tosh—it's *summertime*, good man! You can't start the day drinking *water*, how dull. Nor can you play Aether sober. It's an unfair advantage."

"That's right," agreed Kalypso with an eager nod, "we won't accept your mind games, Hunter—at least one drink, that's the requirement to play with us."

"I'm already starting to think this was a mistake," said Glenn with a not unamused glance between the siblings. Letting his gaze flicker to me and seeing there no small measure of hope, he sighed and turned his glass upright again. "Just one," he allotted while Aleister and his sister cheered.

"That's the spirit! Now...shall we review the rules? You said you hadn't much of a head for this game, didn't you, Thecla?"

A bit embarrassed to confess such a thing before Glenn, I laughed lightly and shook my head. "I must have had—oh, seven different friends in Lescaut try to teach me how to play it over the years." Even my father tried once. Rigel could teach me anything under the sun...but he just couldn't manage to make me understand Aether in a way that made sense.

Aleister, bless him, did the best job of anyone…but, if not for the unique advantage that quickly became apparent, I wouldn't have done much better than I did at seventeen, when last I played and swore off the blasted game forever.

"It's twelve cards apiece," said Aleister breezily. "We'll play for—let's say—300 points for this first game."

"Are we playing with negatives," asked Kalypso, her eyes bright as she once again hid them behind her sunglasses.

While Aleister took up the deck in the center of the table and commenced shuffling with a hand as practiced as any professional card-dealer's, Glenn protested, "That's hardly fair when Thecla doesn't know how to play the game well."

The Duke Montagne got in half an eyeroll before he stopped himself with a sigh of agreement. "I suppose you're right…though I don't know if we can expect her to learn the game while we're mollycoddling her…all right, so"—shooting out cards one at a time, Aleister turned his attention back to me—"I don't have to explain to you how the partnerships work, do I? Either you or Glenn will set down cards in a given round. Whoever's turn it is has to go against both players of the opposing team—so there's overlap, you see. When Kalypso has played her second turn, I'll take her place as the opponent."

"Since you're the dealer," I asked meekly, "right?"

"That's right, dear, very good." Shooting cards to each of us—and himself—one at a time, Aleister went on. "At the beginning of a player's turn, you're given a chance to trade up to three cards in your hand with cards from the Aether: that's this cache." He briskly dealt three cards into a pile at the center, then set the last— two of spades—upright. "There! So spades will be our opening suit for this round, you see?"

"Wait," I implored, gathering my hand and espying a paltry number of spades for my liking, "what's the purpose of trading with the cache?"

"It's strategic." In a kind tone somewhat more patient than Aleister's, Glenn interjected to explain, "Mostly, you'll want to trade your cards into the cache in hopes of getting higher cards... but there are times when it's better to trade down. That's when the bluffing comes in."

I scoffed. "Why in the world would I want to trade down?"

"Because if you have an excess of high cards," Glenn explained, "and you want to disperse some of them to me so we can keep our opponents from winning tricks, you can lie about the cards you're trading into the cache in hopes that they'll skate through to me."

"Does that ever work?"

Aleister laughed with the arrogant sound of a man already sure of his victory. "Of course it works, darling! That's why it's part of the game, and why it's important to decide when you announce the cards you're trading in—for you *must* announce the cards you're trading in—if you think it's worth lying about them. Let's say you want Glenn to get three large cards, or you want me to get three small cards—either way, that's a reason to lie."

Eager to assist in my education given her inebriated state, Kalypso leaned forward with an eager nod. "That's just right! Oh, but you must be *careful*, of course, Thecla, because if Aleister or I have one of the cards you've lied about, then we'll know for sure to call your bluff and make you clear the aether."

"She means flip the cards face-up," Glenn clarified. "Your opponents can challenge your trades into the aether anytime, but it's better to do it only when the cards in question are in your hand."

"And we can't communicate with our partners in any way," I asked, astonished people could get good at this game.

"Some players do, of course, but that's called 'cheating.'" Chuckling to himself, Aleister fanned out his cards, scanned them left to right, then settled back in his seat with a sip of his drink. "Anyway, if someone calls a bluff and it turns out it wasn't a bluff, the team that called the bluff loses the number of points equivalent to the cleared aether. The same goes for if you were bluffing and your opponent catches you—then, you lose your team the equivalent points."

Weary already, flashing back to far too many parties from my teenage years, I said, "I think I understand...and then it's one card per trick, isn't it?"

"By Malin, she's got it." Ignoring Glenn's unamused eye-flick off into the distance at his choice of oath, Aleister sorted out the cards in his hand and explained, "Yes, Thecla, that's just it. You must try to follow our opening suit of spades here if you can; and if you can't, you can play a trump card. What's trump, Kalypso? I'll let you decide."

"Let's say hearts." After announcing this, she explained to me, "Dealer's team always picks trump."

"And that's all there is to it," said Aleister with a shrug. "Person sitting clockwise to the dealer goes first—that's you, Thecla, dear—along with dealer's partner."

"But wait! What if I haven't either the suit or the trump?"

"Then you're going to want to lay down something quite small, of course...or if you must, something large while praying we're also out of suit cards and trump cards. Any other questions?"

Was it too late to get Charlotte to take my place? My head fairly swam; it was simple enough, but when we got into the business of trumps and suits, and when one watched how *quickly* the tricks could turn in this game, I always began to lose track. Still, with Glenn across from me and, for the first time in what must have been months, willing to interact in a capacity unrelated to the rearing of our daughter, I was dedicated to putting everything I had into not just understanding the game, but winning it.

"Very well," I said, straightening up with a little wave of my hand. "Then let's start—I'm the sort of person who learns best by doing."

WHILE I CAN HARDLY SAY I took to the game much better than I had on previous attempts to learn it, with Glenn as my partner in Aether, it was difficult to lose. He was a truly excellent liar whose poker face—Aether face, I suppose—could not be matched by even Eleison's. Perhaps it was the beard, which disguised any slight twitch of cheek muscle that could have betrayed emotion as he set cards, generally one at a time, into the aether, then busied himself with his turn. Twice, Aleister misjudged him and called these trades as bluffs, subsequently eating the cost of the card while revealing to me that I had no need to trade into the cache in pursuit of whatever Glenn had discarded—they really were small cards in those instances. And when Aleister learned his lesson and stopped calling, Glenn began passing me real cards under guise of small ones, a few of which I, by luck, had in my own hand and therefore was able to identify as fiction.

Not that this helped me at first. I couldn't help showing frustration when I lost a few high cards to trumps during my early tricks; and when the round was over and Glenn became dealer, the position moving counterclockwise along the table, I opened quite poorly.

But, come Aleister's second set of tricks in the round, when the first thing he did was sighingly set down a couple of cards while lamenting, "You gave me such a sorry opening hand, Glenn—that's a three of clubs and a two of diamonds," the familiar itching of the dharmine prickled along the edges of my brain.

He's lying, my Rift beast of a servant insisted in the privacy of my mind, his refined voice crystal clear to me even though his form was nowhere to be seen.

Was he absolutely sure about that? Because, if he wasn't—

I'm telling you, Madame, Dinon uttered in that dreamlike tone of his, edged with only the lightest sense of urgency. *Hurry, now—you must call him before—*

"You're a terrible actor, Aleister," I said, freezing the duke's hand before he could finish pulling two corresponding cards from the aether. "Let's see these low cards, if Glenn's deal was really so stingy."

Scoffing, his lips twitching as if in embarrassment or irritation, Aleister managed a small laugh and said, "Really, darling, I know it's only a few points to take from your team, but—"

"Oh yeah, he's definitely lying." Glenn chuckled, jerking his chin at Aleister. "Flip them."

With a grumble under his breath, Aleister did as commanded and revealed the King of Hearts, along with the Ace of Clubs. "All right," he muttered, snatching up the pencil to subtract the corresponding points while Kalypso tutted at him, "all right, so maybe she's learning..."

"Good one, Thecla," said Glenn, the corners of his glittering gold eyes crinkled with mirth—with real approval.

Unearned approval that made my face burn with humiliation.

"It was just luck," I stuttered, idly toying with the idea of telling off the dharmine and sending him away—then having the burden of the decision lifted from my shoulders altogether when I spied a familiar head of dark red hair, its customary updo perfect as always, descending the staircase from the manor into the yard.

"Charlotte," I called, waving a hand and assessing the empty pitcher on our table. "Would you come here for a moment, please?"

Whisking toward us without delay, Charlotte paused by our table to curtsey and say, "I was just looking for you, actually, Madame—nice to see you out and about. And you, too," she added with a nod to Glenn.

"Hello, Charlotte," said Glenn, his tone much more agreeable than it had been at the start of the game. "Beautiful day, isn't it?"

As he said this, his eyes flashed across me, of all things, and I couldn't help the silly little smile that spread across my face as Charlotte agreed in her usual business-like tone. "I suppose it's lovely enough now, but a month from now, a day like this will be hellish...mark my words, Master Stone."

"What a dreary mind you have, Charlotte," protested Kalypso while Aleister agreed with a knowing roll of his eyes. "How could even you protest this splendid weather?"

"Perhaps I'm just jealous I haven't the leisure to enjoy it," she said, looking poised to speak on before Aleister leapt in.

"What a lot in life! Poor woman. Well, if you refill our pitcher"—he put it in her hands, which expertly responded despite her mind's unready condition to receive the object—"and you come back with your mouth smelling like pineapple, I promise, I won't tell anyone."

With a sardonic sort of glance at the duke, Charlotte looked back at me; I confess, spoiled brat as I had become, I was egged on by Aleister's mirth and had no mind to wait for her to express her thought before I said with a playful slap of her elbow, "Yes, Charlotte, have a sip, it's the middle of summer! The other servants are always so busy that it's a miracle you have any work of your own left to do—oh, but that does remind me—"

Sitting up and laying my cards facedown upon the table, I looked over my shoulder across the expanse of our gardens. Although the sky was a beautiful and the day temperate, I found myself cringing at the sight behind me. Leaves that had once been proud and vivid green in the first spring of my staying at the Karris house now seemed twisted as if by malnourishment, their edges crisped—perhaps by the attack of some insect. What flowers there were that year seemed sickly, stems bowing beneath what ought to have been a natural burden to bear. Half the plants, though, had no flowers to speak for at all; the roses, in particular, seemed to be suffering enormously under whatever stress kept the garden from flourishing. Only the hedge maze seemed capable of withstanding the mystery blight, and I couldn't help wondering when it would be next.

"I was going to ask you to replace the roses in the front hall," I remarked, frowning to take this all in, "but now I can't help but wonder—just what on earth is the matter with the gardens, Charlotte?"

"You'd be better off asking young Master Kyrie that," she said, referring to Eleison's younger brother. With the transference of the estate's property to my mate along with the new courtesy title of Lord, the Karris house's former groom had been promoted to its primary custodian; while he still spent an inordinate amount of time with the horses of which he had grown very fond, Kyrie was now by and large responsible for monitoring the condition of the property as a whole: gardens included. That said—when we were about the country house and Charlotte was running the staff, it was also her business to know, and I found myself frowning at her shirk of responsibility until she went on with a frown of her own.

"Though I will say," she elaborated, glancing around, "after the Rift Event two weeks ago, there's been reports of a dharmine making its way through the region, killing cattle and attempting to prey on merchants in the guise of a weary traveler."

With a gasp of fright, Kalypso pressed a hand to her throat. "No! Oh, how awful—tell me it's only a rumor, Charlotte. I won't sleep at night if one of those vile creatures is lurking about!"

Across the conversation Aleister joined in agreement with his sister, Glenn and I exchanged a knowing glance. Still feeling the heavy presence of Ba'al-Dinon upon me, his pressure in the edges of my mind like the weight of a half-tame tiger cradled in the bosom of his mistress, I had only to turn my attention to him. Without needing to inquire further than the conversation enfolding me, I felt him claim within my soul, *Not I, Madame, not I—the wild one she means is an agent of the Rift.*

Oblivious to either Glenn's questioning study of my face or my own slightly glazed eyes as I made mental communion with my man-shaped pet, Charlotte said to Kalypso and her brother, "I can't do more than speculate now, I'm afraid, as Ignatius and his staff have located no trace of the beast around our property. However...if I were a dharmine headed through Karrisregion, and

I came upon this property full of perfectly edible beings with flesh and blood for me to feast upon—"

"Oh stop," begged Kalypso with a theatrical shriek, clutching Glenn's arm in a way that annoyed me far more than threatened me. "Stop it at once, Charlotte, you're frightening me so that I'll *faint.*"

Looking quite amused, at least insofar as her glittering eyes and suddenly strained cheeks revealed, Charlotte said meekly, "I only mean to note that the presence of a dharmine has been known to have an ill impact on the health of sensitive beings such as plants and small animals."

"What do you say, Glenn, old boy," asked Aleister, sounding just a bit wary, himself. "Think there's anything to this? You're the expert, after all."

"I'd hardly call myself an expert on dharmines in particular," he admitted. "There are hunters who spend their whole careers specializing in their eradication; I've always been more of a generalist. However..." With a nod and quite a solemn expression, Glenn extricated his arm from Kalypso's steely grip and leaned back in his seat to assess the garden behind me—or perhaps to stare at me. Hard to tell, given how discreet he was. "I've heard that dharmines cause crops to fail...and cause women to lose their children."

My hand flew to the broach at my collar as my throat tightened in fear. "You don't say," I managed after a second. "I hadn't heard that one. I knew about the disease, of course—the blood-sickness of a dharmine's bite is what killed my father. But you really mean to say a dharmine's mere presence can—"

"It isn't like there's any scientific literature on the subject," Glenn consoled me gently, seeing his surreptitious warning had frightened me in a way he obviously regarded as more sincere than Kalypso's poor excuse to squeeze his bicep. "It's just wives' tales, really, Thecla...but, if you and—"

I was very nearly proud of him—he worked so hard to avoid even speaking Malin's name, let alone acknowledging my relationship with him—until, true to form, Glenn corrected course before I could be pleased by any sign of progress.

"If you're really hoping for another child," he amended, picking up his cards again, "you probably shouldn't pick up the habit of walking around the grounds by yourself at night."

"Well," Charlotte began, feeling she had one more chance to address the reason she interrupted our game in the first place, "there's no need to worry about that anytime soon—"

Thecla.

Dinon's voice pierced my fright, the vibrations of his attention coming to me like movement through water. Even as I wondered if I should be fully refusing to feed him a scrap of my energy during such a sensitive time of easily disrupted efforts, I felt myself leaping at the stimulation of his call.

For, as dangerous as the dharmine was, and as depraved and disturbing as he could be, there was no avoiding the heat he inspired in my soul.

It was second only to the heat inspired by the sound of lurching carriages and prancing hooves carried on the distant wind, sounds amplified by Dinon's plea for my attention.

Sitting upright with my hands landing upon the edges of the card table, I gasped.

"Malin—"

As the atmosphere changed, Aleister smiling, Kalypso muttering, "Oh, and that fine Eleison fellow," and Glenn's casual affect clamming up into immediate tension, Charlotte said with a new look of unbridled humor, "That's what I've been trying to tell you for five minutes, Madame...Master Farrow just called to ask me if you were inclined to tear yourself away from your weaving anytime soon."

All but flinging myself from the chair and half-remembering to smooth my gown into acceptable shape, I permitted my face to split in a tremendous smile of sheer pleasure and only too late realized it. Seeing the joy my beloveds' returns sparked in my soul, Glenn fished his pocket watch out of his waistcoat and set his cards down with a hefty sigh.

"I'd better get some rest, actually," he told Kalypso and Aleister in unapologetic announcement of his flight. "Looks like you're both back to square one...good game, though."

"Oh *phoo*! Don't let Uncle send you running off..."

Aleister's protest fell on deaf ears: with a lingering look at me, Glenn was already en route to a side entrance of the house where he risked neither bumping into the return party, nor finding himself alone with me and my pleas that he try to perceive the territory master in a more flattering light.

It didn't matter. As annoying as Glenn's sullen avoidance could be, the sudden awareness of Malin and Eleison—back upon the Karrisregion property after three long weeks!—made me carefree. Unburdened by the need to protect his feelings, I let myself smile as wide as I felt while rushing up the stairs to the house in what I fear must have been a quite unladylike manner. Yet the whole house knew by observation or reputation how deep my love ran for my husband, as well as for my mate: and those of understanding who noticed me dashing through the corridors to the front hall smiled a little themselves, servants and visiting courtiers alike, in the fashion of fond parents witnessing a daughter's young love. Each step I darted, my excitement grew.

And, as I emerged in the front hall at the very same moment the doors were opened to permit Malin and Eleison's entrance into the house, that excitement reached a crescendo and came bursting from my soul.

There they were, the songs of my heart, the harmony that filled my days with joy and my nights with heat: dark Eleison, his flame-crimson eyes lingering with a nod upon Dinon's anticipatory hold of the door, his suit a little rumpled with the wear of sleeping in the carriage on the way back home; and tall, intriguing, pale-haired Malin, whose black gaze snapped straight to me as a game hunter pursued the motion of an ornamental bird fated for his rifle.

"Thecla," my husband cried, his arms opening to me as I came rushing to him first, "oh, my darling—at last—"

While he swept me into his arms, strong despite his age some thirty years advanced of mine, I melted into his embrace and couldn't stop my little moan at the ferocity of his kiss. It stole the breath from my lungs to leave my smile wild—and me, higher than any favorite substance of Aleister's could have made me. When I pulled back with a laugh and a gasp, the intensity of Malin's eyes sweeping over me sent a great flush across my face and throat: a heat that extended to the tips of my ears and my suddenly tingling fingers. I felt helpless, naked under a gaze whose only competition was the lazy animal smile of the mate into whose embrace Malin passed me.

"I'm so glad you're both home," I enthused, still breathless, barely getting more than a few seconds to collect myself before Eleison fit his hand to my cheek and craned my mouth up to his.

His name a wet murmur upon my lips between the heat of our kisses, I pressed close enough to him to be left in shock from the almost aggressive pressure of his body's desire for mine: he was already aggravated and ready to take me.

"Did you miss us, baby," Eleison asked, his words a growl released when he lifted his lips just enough to ask the question before another hungry kiss.

"Every second," I whispered, reaching with my left hand to caress Malin's chest and draw him to me for the next claim of my mouth. "Every second, oh, yes, I've been so lonely! You must never both leave me at the same time again, I beg you—"

"Mm, poor little dove." His eyes hooded with lust betrayed also in the small, erotic smile that he most often wore when watching Eleison make love to me, Malin fit his massive hand to the back of my neck and let his thumb play along the sensitive skin behind the lobe of my ear. "You must feel so neglected...ah, but we missed you, too."

"We were just talking about you," Eleison said with a crooked grin and a knowing sidelong glance at Malin.

Blushing a deeper scarlet to wonder at that, I stuttered, "Good things, I hope."

"Perhaps we can tell you in Eleison's apartment upstairs," Malin suggested with a mirthful flick of his eyes around the busy hall. "You can decide whether it's good or bad, Madame...and if bad, you can discipline us accordingly."

Woozy already with the mere promise of receiving their love, I managed a smile and, nodding, slipped an arm around Malin's when Eleison released me. "No amount of even the strictest discipline is sufficient to correct your devious mind, my husband... Dinon"—I called over my shoulder to my pet, who looked over from the door with an innocent expression designed to hide from the other members of the house his keen awareness of my every thought—"oversee the servants' unloading of the carriages, please; Charlotte has been waylaid by a few of our guests."

"With pleasure, Madame."

"Have you fed him today," asked Malin in a whisper with a sort of intimate, heat-sparking rumble in the base of his throat.

"And come find me when you're through," I added to the dharmine in response to my husband's question. "I'll have more for you to do while the masters of the house get settled back in their proper places."

"Your wish is my command," Dinon said, his dreamy eyes crinkling with a knowing smile as he bowed to me. "Welcome home, Lord Eleison, Master Farrow. Your household has greatly missed you both."

THERE WAS NO DOUBT THAT, in the fifteen months or so since Malin had awarded Eleison the Karris estate, our lifestyle had changed substantially. Though formally the apartment that had once belonged to Malin was now Eleison's master suite, one would have been hard-pressed to find a night where all three of us were not intimately ensconced within its private chambers far away from the busier wings of the house. It was our true home within the country estate, and as we crossed the threshold, a new atmosphere descended upon us. The men both sighed in relief, Malin releasing his hold on me to slide his jacket from his shoulders; I took it from him happily, my heart racing with good reason.

By the time I turned from hanging it near the entry, my predator was upon me for the feast.

I almost had time to gasp before Eleison crushed my mouth to his, his powerful hands tight around my biceps. His forceful lips persuaded mine to open in a trice and soon his tongue, hot and wet and hungry, stabbed into my mouth to command mine to its pleasure.

"It's certainly not a competition," Malin said while watching with unabashed lust, his lips slightly parted in hypnotic admiration as Eleison dragged me toward the bedroom, "but I almost think Eleison missed you more than I did, Thecla...impossible though that would seem, he's been in quite a strop since we left for Azstoria."

"Poor baby," I murmured, looking fondly up at my mate even as he used one hand to open the bedroom door and the other to force me inside. His lip curled to bare his teeth in an expression of frustration meant more for Malin than for me.

"It's only because your damned husband has been torturing me the whole time we've been gone...'Who do you think she's fucking while we're away?' 'Do you suppose she's getting it from that hunter right now?' 'I hope she's still saving her cute little ass for me...we'd better hurry back as soon as possible before she finally makes the mistake of letting the dharmine plow that greedy cunt of hers.'"

While I gasped in hot-faced humiliation and deep arousal to hear Eleison reiterate questions I had no doubt my imaginative libertine husband had asked, my gaze turned accusingly to meet Malin's. "You wicked old man," I told him while he took me in his arms, an embrace almost sufficient to distract me from the sound of Eleison's belt buckle jingling open. "And I was so *good* the whole time you were out—what must you think of me, to ask Eleison such things?"

"I think you're a deliciously insatiable little slut," Malin told me with amusement, his hands running up and down my waist, his eye briefly flickering from me to Eleison and then down the bodice of my gown. "Don't act like you haven't been desperate for a cock for three weeks...you didn't even try to seduce the hunter?"

I bit my lip, glancing back at Eleison to realize he was not undressing but instead doubling over the leather strap of the belt in the same hand bejeweled with a sigil ring that served to mark him as cavalier of Gudrune, his formal position in the territory master's court. "How could I even think of sex when I was so busy pining after both of you? I've been so heartbroken in your absence—why, I haven't been able to touch my loom—"

"You haven't been weaving? Naughty girl."

Agreeing with Malin's tender-toned, playful condemnation, Eleison snapped the belt to make me jump in my husband's arms. "So you've turned into some indolent little aristocrat while we've been out of the house, huh? That's almost worse...hold her for me, Malin."

While I cried out in excitement I did my best to turn into mock-fear, I thrashed in my husband's arms in similar display of false protest. Even as, grinning with evil glee, Malin yanked me down to the bed with him and pulled me over his lap, I squirmed and kicked and even twisted to bite at one of the hands that held me.

"What a hellcat she is today," Malin said in approval, smiling through gritted teeth as he applied real exertion to keep me still. While I kicked blindly out behind me, Eleison caught one of my legs and used his knee to pin the other to the edge of the bed. I squirmed on until Malin used one arm to push my upper-half down and, with his other hand, drew my skirts up high enough to expose the lacework of my panties.

Both men's respiration hitched at what they clearly regarded as a most enticing vision. Before any cruel use ensued from Eleison, Malin's broad hand slid affectionately up my thigh and over the shape of my rear, his fingers taking advantage of every crack and crevice and divot which invited his exploration from outside the form-fitting Chantilly.

"Oh, Thecla," my husband sighed, squeezing my flesh to make me moan in anticipation, my play-fighting given pause, "Thecla, my love—I missed you every second I was away. Would you look at her, Eleison...what a hot little bitch we have." As, all the more deeply flush at the appellation, I let my thighs shift further apart, Malin's fingers trailed down to tease my already hot mound through the veil of the fabric. We moaned together, my husband's tantalizing fingers slipping just under the edge of the lace to steal a direct assessment of the hot, damp flesh desperate for his touch. "Maybe she really did restrain herself...come here, feel how wet she is already."

Malin's hand lifted away to leave me whimpering, but soon Eleison had bent down, his firm thumb taking its place. From the other side of the lace, he teased me cruelly, that thick, articulate digit pressing just between the lips of my vulva and trailing down to rub back and forth along my veiled clit.

"She really is a needy slut, huh, Malin...but you know better than anybody..."

Eleison straightened, his touch receding, and the belt snapped in his hands to make me gasp.

"If we reward her with a fucking right away," my mate said in a voice dark with lust, "she'll start thinking it's okay to neglect her creative pursuits when we're apart...hold her still, now."

As I yelped in anticipation, squirming into action again, Malin chuckled and let his hand drop upon my thigh. With his other forearm heavily pressing upon my upper-half, I was immobilized to do all but look over my shoulder at the exact second Eleison's heavy swing brought the belt across the cheeks of my ass.

The sharp snap of the stinging leather made me cry out: a girlish noise of pained protest that made Malin tut in a low, mocking tone betraying his already irresistible arousal. "Poor pet," he commented as the second snap came, making me whimper and futilely kick with the new strip of stinging heat Eleison applied along my upper thighs. "I almost feel guilty...you probably thought you were going to be worshiped the second we walked in the door, eh, you adorable trollop..."

If this wasn't worship, I didn't know what worship was. Every time we all three played together, I was gladder and gladder I had begged Malin to lead me into the depths of his sadomasochistic proclivities. Whether it was from Malin or Eleison, the stings and swats of a good thrashing had risen to among the sweetest of life's hedonistic pleasures—second only to that pleasure of having such rough treatment made up to me afterwards, with tender kisses and murmured words and the sweet caresses.

"You're such wicked brats," I protested, my toes curling as a quick volley of blows cracked upon the nates of my ass to gather the heat of pleasure along my sympathetic sex. "Oh, oh—! Here I've been all alone, loyally waiting for your return, and you've been off—oh, fondling each other and thinking wicked things of me while having fun in Azstoria—"

"We did a fair bit more than fondle each other," Malin reflected with a tone of amusement that made me squawk in envious desire at the next lash of the belt. Now the separate stings were merging into one: one glorious, throbbing flame to which the ache of my cunt synchronized itself in anticipation of what was yet to come. I noticed my arousal while, in an intermission between blows, Malin roughly jerked my panties down to my knees and let his fingers glide back up to steal a caress of my achingly wet labia. Gasping, moaning, I arched back against him as he murmured in a tone of appreciation, "Why, even on the way here, I confess I spent the last hour or so winding poor Eleison up to fuck you...in other words, you should thank me."

"You sadistic libertine," I chided with a groan while his hand lowered again to my thigh, drawing it wide from the other to allow the men to study my pussy with a palpable pair of possessive stares. "Thank you, for debauching my mate the same way you've debauched me? It's you who should be stripped and beaten, you cad—oh! Oh—"

This next lash was heavy and almost slow; a more playful, almost tender slap of the belt's weight down against my upper thighs and exposed labia. Groaning, my toes curling, I shivered and arched my rear up higher to promote Eleison's access.

As the next blow landed, Malin bent down to breathe a dark whisper into my ear.

"Now, you naughty little slut...is that any way to speak to Daddy?"

The word had, I should perhaps be embarrassed to confess, an obscene effect of arousal upon me: a kind of wicked magic that stemmed from the knowledge that, while my mother had fled from him at the end of her life, Malin really *had* been my stepfather at the time of my birth, at least in a legal sense. Since Malin foreswore all parental claim and didn't even meet me until adulthood, I had only ever known my true father: and Rigel had always been 'Papa' to me, the more common paternal title around the town of

Lescaut. In the map of my psyche, therefore, the word 'Daddy' had not been mapped to any one person or thing in particular until, after the truth emerged and Malin and I had reconciled, that wicked husband of mine had begun slipping the term into our sex life with an almost insidious calculation by which he proved its power over me. Knowing its strength, he used it sparingly; it had a way of inspiring in me a state of total submission and almost unbearable arousal, and was therefore found on his lips when he most wanted to enjoy full control of my body, mind, and soul.

"No, Daddy," I whispered back as a new, slightly sharper lash bore down across me, the edge of the belt wrapping enticingly between my cheeks to lay its sharp fire along very sensitive flesh, indeed. "Oh," I gasped, "no, sir—I'm sorry, I got carried away again..."

"That's all right, angel...Daddy knows how your mouth runs away with you sometimes, you naughty thing...Eleison..." Straightening up, the volume of his voice increasing again, "Give me the belt, old boy. No sense in making you do all the hard work. You must be eager to get out of that suit, anyway..."

As I softly moaned, Eleison chuckled and passed the strap over with an ominous jingle of its buckle. "She's all yours...hold on, I need to get cleaned up anyway. I'll be back."

While his footsteps carried him off with unapologetic haste to the washroom, Malin trailed the edge of the belt across the existing red welts along my upper thighs. Though Eleison had, over the past twelve months, grown much more comfortable with the idea of these rougher sex games, my mate still almost always held back from going full bore as I craved him to. The borro in his altered heart, possessive as it was, seemed perpetually torn between protecting me and hunting me to be quite literally devoured.

But Malin had no such qualms. To my husband, pleasure and pain were sensual siblings: a mere matter of interpretation, each as worth basking in as the other. And oh, how that opinion showed whenever, free of Eleison's internalized wont to fuss over me, Malin had me alone with a rod, or a belt, or the simple flat of his well-practiced hand.

"Oh, Thecla," sighed the master of my heart, his longing for me like a tangible force in the room as he lifted the belt away from my rear. "I've missed you so."

The first heavy snap from Malin's arm made me groan and shudder, my legs stretching to assist in the arch of my back. "I've missed you, too, Malin," I whispered back, my fingers sinking into the fabric of our bed's coverings to brace myself for the next blows. "Oh, ah—oh, my husband, I've longed for you every day—"

Without Eleison in the room, my need to pretend to fight was somehow lessened. Now I wanted only to submit: to be utterly yielding to my master, whose gentle left hand trailed over the welts incurred by the strikes of his right. With each pat, the cool metal of his wedding band around his finger stood out to me above any other ring upon his aristocratic hand; I shuddered and gasped, gritting my teeth against the heavier blows even as I begged, "Can't you take me with you next time?"

"Next time—yes, perhaps next time. But Thecla, darling, you know how I worry on these longer trips...you're safer at home, unless we're on a pleasure trip of some kind."

There was no doubt I understood his reticence to allow all three of us to travel together for any purpose of announced state business. I myself had been present for the meeting at Glenn's house in Valquist, where the Hunter's Guild schemed to assassinate my husband and indeed hoped to recruit me to their cause in what they perceived to be a moment of my heart's weakness. They had no idea of the devotion of that heart, even in its pain: of the intensity of its true cause, which was absolute love and loyalty for the man who now dropped the belt and pulled me upright to press to my mouth a kiss so hungry and deep it seemed with every stroke of his tongue that he had already penetrated me.

There was no doubt my husband, with Eleison's help, could take care of himself: but, even with the Hunter's Guild's operations having been banned in Gudrune, we all knew what a tempting target the three of us could make for any insurgent. It was no doubt that the craving of the Guild to eliminate my husband from the political landscape had only increased, and there was much proof of that with the kinds of protests and even demonstrative attempts at terrorism which the former Guild had been lodging in Saalast. With a shudder for the thought, I pressed closely to him, my hand tracing over the scar running along the outer edge of his left eye. As his fingers deftly navigated the hooks at the back of my brocaded gown of red silk, I nipped at his mouth and whispered, "I wish you could stay safe at home with me, husband...I wish we could enjoy a quiet country life—oh—"

"But how could I give my pet the luxury she deserves," he asked, his lips vibrating along the skin of my throat as every murmur came between slow, steady kisses. "How could I give you a life of pleasure and ecstasy if we were poor farmers? How could you love an old man like me, if—"

"Stop." He pushed my dress away to leave me in bodice and thigh garters along with my hosiery—and the ankle-high boots he leaned forward to remove, a gesture which only further drew his eye to the dark triangle between my thighs. "Stop it, Husband. I wish you wouldn't call yourself 'old'. You're not—not in your heart..."

"Easy for you to say now, when I have money to help me keep my health…" His lips pressed along the exposed skin of my thigh and hip while his hands ran along the column of my leg, his eyes turning toward me. "Just think if we were back in Lescaut… how would a beautiful girl like you ever think to give me time of day?"

"I think about that all the time," I confessed to him with a laugh, meriting an amused twitch of his lip and unscarred brow. As he rose to his feet and took me in his arms to lay me down in the bed, I went on while gazing up at him through heavy-lidded eyes, "Sometimes I like to fancy you a priest, or a tutor, and me an innocent young thing who catches your eye…or, better still, you're the innocent one, and I'm a wicked, greedy girl who seduces you off the noble path and persuades you to debauch yourself in my arms. Oh, Daddy—"

"Poor angel! Does it hurt…" While I winced and sadly nodded as my stinging backside connected with the cool sheets, my husband slid a hand up my thigh and around my rear. He handled me thoughtfully, aware of every part of me, yet with such a sense of ownership and entitlement that my stomach tightened with the empty ache of desire. "Well," he said, "let this be a lesson about spending too little time on your work in my absence…and about denying yourself the fun you deserve."

The same hand that squeezed my welted ass now trailed around to permit the dip of his fingers between my thighs, unobstructed by lacework or propriety. I moaned at the demanding exploration of my slickness, offering myself to him unquestioningly. While his index finger gently probed the already saturated slit aching to be filled, then trailed up to brush teasingly back and forth along my clitoris, he murmured, "You should have been letting your hunter fuck you every night in my absence...or perhaps a few of the courtiers. I think quite a few of the duke's friends fancy you—what man couldn't?"

"That's the truth," Eleison agreed, returning to the room with his shirt unbuttoned and a generally more leisurely inclination to his stride. "But that's where you and I are opposed, Malin...I think of her getting it from the courtiers and imagine knocking out their teeth before sending them all out the door."

With a laugh back at Eleison, making no move to stop teasing my pussy as my mate bent to dip a deep kiss into my mouth, Malin asked, "Now, Eleison, darling, why be jealous of Thecla letting the courtiers enjoy her pretty body as much as we do? You're not jealous of *me* anymore, are you?"

"Of course I am," Eleison said while I laughed merrily and Malin tutted. Straightening up from me then, my mate thrilled me by catching Malin by the back of his neck and craning his head back from his focus on my body. "The difference is that I consent to being made jealous by you."

Eleison bent, a ferocious kiss passing from his mouth into Malin's permanently ready one. I moaned to catch a glimpse of hungry tongue exchanged between them, my body more aflame with yearning than even the beating had made me. How well I understood what Eleison meant! Of course, I was always a little jealous when they paid attention to anyone who wasn't me, even if they were only paying attention to one another...but it was an intensely erotic kind of jealousy, inspiring arousal I couldn't have avoided even if I'd wanted to. It was no wonder that Eleison didn't want to experience that kind of arousal with just any man, since, so far as I knew, Malin was the only male to whom he had ever committed his affections. Yet one wouldn't know that to see them kiss or make love: they were natural together, their affections as much a celebration of romance as anything they gave me.

And, as with me, Malin was relentless in the way he pushed and played with Eleison's boundaries.

"You consent to being made jealous by me," Malin teased, reaching up from me to unbutton Eleison's trousers, "but your cock consents to it all, doesn't it, darling...Thecla, come here, look at how hard your mate gets when I make him think of how eagerly any man in this manor would fill your perfect pussy at the snap of your fingers."

"Oh yeah," ribbed Eleison, his red eyes glinting as I sat up to moan at the springing forth of my mate's proud cock, "I think we'll evict the courtiers tomorrow..."

"Now, Eleison, they're harmless...Thecla had ample opportunity to enjoy an orgy without us, but she was such a good girl...and who could blame her?" Looking with lust of his own upon Eleison's sizeable prick, Malin relented to his natural urges and gave Eleison an appreciative stroke or two. "When she's spoiled by a cock like this, few other men on Earth could compare...why don't you show your mate how happy you are to have him home, precious?" His hand pausing to support Eleison's heavy erection by its base, Malin brushed my hair back and looked approvingly as, with great eagerness, I smiled between both men and leaned into press my lips to my mate's offered cock. His dark eyes somehow soft, almost tender in their intense desire, Malin stroked my hair and praised, "That's it, give him a kiss...there you are, what a good girl..."

"You smell like Malin," I observed, my eyes raising to my mate's face while I opened my mouth to ache the tip of his prick with the swirling of my tongue. "You really were teasing him very cruelly in the carriage ride home today, weren't you, darling."

"Now, darling, you know that when you're not around to do it while I watch, I can't resist sucking this gorgeous cock. It's just a shame he's still too shy to let me fuck him..." With a chuckle and another pump of Eleison's cock, his hands brushing against my lips as I engulfed my mate's engorged glans, Malin said, "All things in their season...I'll persuade you yet, Eleison."

"Ah, well...I don't want to—don't want you to waste your cum on me." Eleison was a little breathless as he made up an excuse, his eyes fixed on mine as I slowly drew him deeper into my mouth. "Thecla wants it so badly, after all..."

Oh, yes. It may have been a convenient excuse, and a reference to our efforts to conceive; yet, I had found over the past months that I was most excited by the pleasure of my men. Being whipped by them or, in the case of Malin, whipping them; watching them make love to one another; enjoying their rough use and coarse speech: all these were great hedonic pleasures which increased my ecstasy beyond measure. Yet nothing made my body pulse with wanton heat like the final eruption of the male orgasm: the sudden, almost painful rigidity of a cock in my womb or mouth, the bursting forth of pearl-white semen amid almost boyish, nearly shocked cries of pleasure—ah, now this was the sweetest aphrodisiac to me, and the experience of Eleison or Malin's ultimate pleasure had a way of igniting new, greater fire in the depths of my belly. No doubt, with many other men such a predilection would have been a cruelty guaranteed to leave a woman unsatisfied: but Malin, an artist of desire and particular devotee to my pleasure, took great joy in applying his mouth, his fingers, and occasionally a Rift ivory toy or two he had acquired for me to amuse myself when he was away on business. He enjoyed my pleasure nearly as much as I enjoyed his—and I must say 'nearly', for I alone know how the heat grew in my belly simply to have a man's hard cock in my mouth, let alone to receive the substance of his pleasure.

"You're getting very good at that, Thecla," Malin said approvingly, maintaining his support of Eleison's prick while the fingers of his other hand raked through my hair. "It's sweet how enthusiastic you are...adorable, how eager you are to fit the whole thing in your mouth."

Even as he said this, I, having made it halfway, gave in to a cough as Eleison's thick head bumped into the back of my throat. I drew back, laughing, raising the back of my hand to my lips to sputter, "I'm eager, but I don't know how such a thing is possible with a man of Eleison's scale."

"Oh, now—it's all just practice. Here...Eleison, why don't you lie down and make yourself comfortable while I give Thecla a little lesson."

"Glad to be of assistance," my mate said with a chuckle, stripping off his open shirt to extend his glorious frame along the bed. While I bit my lip just to see him, to my left, Malin unbuttoned his waistcoat and tossed it aside before rolling the sleeves of his shirt to his elbows.

"Now, princess, the most important thing is enthusiasm, and you have it in spades...the next two most important elements are relaxation and endurance, and both of those come with time. Come here, angel...let Daddy show you."

"You two are so fucked up," Eleison said with a laugh that was half embarrassed and half aroused, his hand landing on his forehead to slightly shield his eyes.

"Don't act like you don't enjoy it," Malin rebuffed him, lightly swatting Eleison's prick to elicit a low growl—and a subtle twitch along the length as though of pleasure. "Now, Thecla, allow me to demonstrate…"

My breath hitched, my body flooded with heat as, with me by his side, Malin parted his lips to quite expertly envelop Eleison's cock. Gasping in pleasure to observe my husband fellating my quickly panting mate, I stroked Eleison's thigh and paid studious attention to Malin's use of mouth and hands. Rest assured, I was as sincerely devoted to learning as I was to enjoyment of the scene. While my wicked old libertine's free hand slid down to cradle and rub along the sac of Eleison's testicles, his left hand, as it had for me, supported my mate's girth and worked to pump what his mouth could not yet engulf.

"You see," said Malin upon lifting his head from a few bobs of Eleison's length, "it can be difficult, especially at first, to take the whole thing in, as you know. In that case, it's best to use your hand to supplement. Here, angel, help me, put your hand just—yes, that's right, good girl. Now, try to keep rhythm with me…"

While Malin's mouth went back to work and I couldn't fight back my moan at the sight, I smoothly slid the grip of my hand fore and aft with the pace of his steady bobbing. Eleison groaned a fair bit, himself, a shaky breath rising from his lips as he said, "At least you're a good team, I'll give you that…"

While chuckling, Malin pushed on, touching my hand to encourage me to adjust my angle slightly. Given better access, Malin was able to take him deeper, and Eleison cursed at a shock of intense pleasure that came upon him when given entry to Malin's throat. Being in the midst of a lesson, Malin didn't let him enjoy it long before drawing back to address me again.

"You're normally quite careful about this anyway, but note, darling, how I always endeavor to cover my teeth with my lips…

goodness knows I don't mind a bit of menace, but some men might, so it's better to hedge one's bets until one knows what type of man one is dealing with. And do you see how I'm careful to caress his scrotum, and give it a little support? That always helps—why don't you give it a try, here—"

Lifting his fingers from Eleison, Malin now used both hands to draw my hair back from my face and smiled encouragingly as I followed his instructions. First, I tenderly cupped Eleison's testicles in the palm of my hand, letting my fingers curl to gently massage and tickle them; then, my tongue darting across the lips I tucked inward over my teeth, I drew my mate's turgid prick over my tongue and into the back of my mouth. After a few seconds, I found a rhythm, and while my somewhat hampered tongue squirmed and wriggled against the girth of his shaft, I coordinated the efforts of my hand to tend to the innumerable inches of his length I was not yet able to swallow down.

The men, however, did not seem to think my still unhewed skill a detriment at all. As Malin cooed in approval, "There you are, pretty girl, oh, good job, just like that," Eleison groaned in support and said, "You've always been a natural, baby, but—ah, fuck, that's nice, what a cute mouth, so talented—"

Yet, once again, as I drew him into the uppermost chamber of my throat, it was only a second or two before my esophagus was convulsed by the threat of an unwelcome reflex.

"Blast," I cursed, drawing back to cough while Malin, still holding my hair, bent to kiss my cheek and then my saliva-coated mouth.

"No, no, what a good job you're doing, Thecla, don't be frustrated—that's where all the practice comes in. You have to get use to it...have to open yourself to it completely, and learn to view the occasional bit of choking as part of the challenge...it's hardly as if I don't still gag once in a while, especially on a cock like Eleison's. Just relax...here...Eleison, hold back her hair..." As Eleison's great hands reached down to take up Malin's work, my husband's now trailed down the back of my bodice and ran over my backside. "You practice like I've shown you, angel," Malin murmured in my ear, his voice roughly edged with lust, "and Daddy will help you relax."

As his kisses lowered down my neck and along my spine, intent on my haunches and the flesh between, I raised my eyes to Eleison while getting back to work. His prick, so angular when it was especially hardened by pleasure, pulsed as it was once more engulfed by my mouth. While my tongue swept up a few drops of his eager precum, his hand stroked my hair back from my brow with great, warm tenderness. "Ah, Thecla," my mate sighed down at me, his nostrils flaring, "baby, baby, I missed you—hah—"

Malin's lowering kisses had produced a low moan in the base of my throat, and the resulting vibration had a delicious effect on Eleison's pleasure. He twitched in my mouth, his fingers tightening slightly against my scalp, and his eyes bored into mine as though I were the only being in the world: the only woman, certainly. Given how imperative our mating bond was to his state of mental stability, that might as well have been the case. I had learned the year prior that the natures of such bonds were more nuanced and varied than the basic understanding allowed; in truth, there were several varieties, and it seemed Eleison and I were connected by the most powerful. In the Rift—whatever lay upon its other side— the beasts dwelling within us were natural enemies, predator and prey. Yet, expressed within our hearts, tempered by human love, we were more intimately connected than two altered of the same species could ever have hoped to be.

And it was that love, however jealous, that allowed Eleison's eyes to spark with greater lust at my second moan, which marked the press of Malin's generous mouth down the soft, wet valley between my legs.

"Such an eager girl," Malin remarked with a murmur, his thumb sinking against my labia to pull it wider and give his shameless eye an opportunity to drink in the uninhibited sight of me. "My God, Thecla...you really do love sucking cock, don't you, angel...your pleasure is so beautiful to me."

At the next contact of his lips, his tongue snaked out and set to familiar, rapid work against the sensitive center of my ecstasy. I cried out, gagging just a little around Eleison's length and raising my head with a cough of embarrassment as a strand of drool connected my lip to the crown of his pride. "Oh," I laughed, "I'm sorry, I'm making such a mess—"

"Trust me, baby," Eleison growled, his nostrils flaring as I set to work with renewed vigor, "you're doing just fine...ah, fuck—"

While Malin sank his thumb into my aching entrance, barely teasing in and out, he drew his mouth away to encourage me. "No man will say 'no' to a sloppy blowjob, darling...and if he does, he has a problem." As Eleison laughed in agreement, Malin descended back to work, the rapid flick of his tongue against my clitoris enough to make me want to scream with pleasure. I very well may have were it not for Eleison's cock in my mouth; instead, I could only whimper with delight while appreciating every inch off his hot, heavy sex and the responsive way it throbbed against my tongue with every bob.

Malin was right: practice made perfect. And though I wasn't perfect at the art of worshipping Eleison's cock just yet, there was no doubt my husband's sage advice had made me far better than

I'd been. Though I choked slightly a few times, my gradual focus on my own pleasure drew my consciousness from the anxiety I felt about gagging; on the third such flutter of my throat, though I paused, I didn't let myself draw back, and made quick recovery that allowed me to ease him in just a little more. Eleison groaned, a low borro-growl interwoven with the sound, and Malin chuckled while working his thumb more deeply into me.

"How's she doing, Eleison?"

"Good—really good, uh, fucking great—"

"Well, I was going to ask if you wanted to fuck her first, but I don't want to interrupt you..."

"Oh," I gasped, raising my head with a writhe and a moan, "please, Eleison—Malin, oh, I've ached for you both for weeks, I've been so miserable—I need you, one of you, both of you—"

"My spoiled little princess...you're so used to getting two cocks a day, I can't believe you survived. Did you play with your toys, at least? No?" Tsking at the sullen shake of my head, Malin landed a playful slap upon my hindquarters. "Whyever not?"

"Because it isn't the same if you're not around to watch me, Daddy...or help."

With a low chuckle, Malin lightly pinched my sensitive clitoris to make me gasp and tremble; then, stretching out alongside me, he drew me into his arms so that I lay on my back against his chest. "Then let me help you now," he said, the words hot in my ear while his great hands slid along my body. One gently massaging my breast and teasing a finger around my peaked nipple, his other landed on my thigh and spread it wide enough for his knee to hook between my legs. By this means, he spread me open effortlessly, holding me captive for Eleison's use as my mate knelt upright at his behest. "Come, Eleison, darling...be the teaser stud we need, plow her field for me to sow..."

"You read too much flowery erotica," Eleison teased my laughing husband. I basked in the good humor of the men, in Eleison's smile—in the happy lips Malin pressed to my forehead, kissing me tenderly while his fingers slid down between my labia and pushed the swollen flesh wide to make Eleison's penetration even easier. The chuckling only faded when my mate was between my legs—our legs—his cock in his hand and his eyes sweeping from my face down the length of my body.

"Thecla," he sighed, "you're so fucking beautiful, baby...and you really are wet, huh?"

Pausing before even touching his sex to mine, Eleison instead reached down to join Malin in teasing me. While my husband spread me, my mate probed a pair of thick, male fingers just inside me, sliding into the depths of my channel while I gasped to be cleft opened for the first time in three weeks. Eleison's breath hitched as if in a repressed gasp of his own, his fingers working in and out while he watched pleasure slacken the features of my face, then furrow my brow. "That feels good, huh, baby...I know you love it when we touch you together...ah, what a slut..." While his fingers curled inside me, intensifying the sensation with a coaxing motion that seemed to send bolts of pleasure rushing straight up into my brain, Eleison said with a quick glance at watching Malin, "We really should fuck her together sometime...it'd be a tight fit, but think how she'd cum for us."

His chuckle a low rumble of pleasure, Malin nuzzled against my ear and nibbled there while Eleison removed his fingers to take his cock in-hand once again. "What do you think, princess," my husband asked me while Eleison gave himself a stroke, then pressed the crown of his cock just against the readied entrance of my body. "Wouldn't you love to feel how delicious and full your cunt would be when stuffed with my cock and Eleison's at once?"

Gasping in sudden understanding, I looked over at my husband with a whimper. "At *once*! Oh, but how—oh—!"

Eleison's thick head stabbed roughly into my tight embrace, and fireworks burst behind my eyes. I lost all train of thought. I could only stare into my husband's dark gaze as though in shock, my mouth open, my brows knitting while Eleison's thick tool murdered me with a pleasure that intensified by the inch. Laughing with wicked pleasure, Malin slid his hand back from my labia to focus on playing with my clitoris as Eleison stretched me open.

"Oh, we'd have to take it slow the first time, Thecla... but, once you get used to the sensation, I suspect you'll be addicted. Just think...my cock and Eleison's rubbing together in this insatiable cunt..." With a light spank of my clitoris that, combined with Eleison's thrust to the hilt, made me arch my hips in a sharp gasp of choking ecstasy, Malin smiled through teeth gritted against his own overwhelming pleasure at the sight. He spoke on, grinding his pelvis against the peach of my ass. "I think you'll love it..."

"Oh—oh, I didn't know such a thing was—was possible—"

"Something tells me you were made for it," Eleison grunted, glancing down to watch himself disappearing into me beneath Malin's gently petting fingers. Those same fingers rose from me only to slip around Eleison's testicles and further deepen his pleasure; while Malin worked to coax greater urgency from Eleison, my mate and I moaned together. "Ah, fuck—Malin—"

"Get her nice and wet for me, Eleison...soak her with your cum, ah, you know I love her nice and messy. Isn't my wife such a cute, dirty little whore..."

After whatever teasing had transpired in the carriage and the blowjob I had been giving him mere minutes before, Eleison's cock was already as hard as granite: harder. I swore, the weight of his high-pressure thrusts stabbing roughly into my essence and pounding a beat of blinding pleasure from my body. Indeed, each pound increased my own feeling of urgency, which had happened once or twice before. In such instances, I had grown quite worried something embarrassing had been about to transpire and had begged them to stop. As then, I now found myself stuttering in shy uncertainty, "O—oh—oh, Eleison, wait, maybe you should pause for a moment—"

"Don't stop, Eleison," Malin commanded while my mate hesitated. "She's about to cum—keep going."

"Oh, but—but"—I gasped as Eleison threw himself into it more intensely, pushing my legs high to hammer his cock into me so deep and fast I fancied I could feel my channel swelling tight around him—"no, I think this might be something else, ah—"

"Mm, no, darling, just let it happen—" His kisses along my neck incensing my pleasure all the more greatly, his fingers sliding down from Eleison's cock to resume playing with my clitoris, Malin murmured against me, "Trust me, you'll see...just relax, relax, let Eleison pound your gorgeous pussy nice and full, and you'll—"

"Oh, sweet fuck—!" I gasped from the bottom of my soul, clutching Malin's face in one hand and the bedsheets with the other as an orgasm like I'd never experienced seized my entire frame. Eyes wide, the pleasure sweetened by humiliation at the anticipated result, I instead burst with convulsions of pleasure that wracked my body and raced my heart. While my inner chamber clamped rapidly around Eleison's rapidly pounding cock, my legs shook and jolted up against my body as though to kick out of his hands: and Eleison, groaning, only slammed harder into me, more deeply into me, his own pleasure rising into an orgasm while the fluid of my ecstasy gushed wildly around his cock in one, two, three pulses of squirting pleasure that left my mouth and cunt both sputtering in a kind of disbelief. While Eleison slowed a little to enjoy his release deep inside me, grinning as he did, Malin patted my clitoris and encouraged me on. "Yes, yes, oh, angel, that's it, oh, good girl...that's right, Thecla, cum for your mate...cum for your lover, my hot little slut...oh, yes, doesn't that feel good, see, I told you...Husband knows best..."

"Oh," I groaned, my legs still quaking as my mate released his hold on them, his cock twitching stiffly within me at each jet of semen he released, "oh, Eleison, oh, darling—"

"Thecla," Eleison gasped, leaning down to grip my face and plunge his tongue into my mouth. "Thecla, Thecla...fuck, I missed you."

We moaned into the heavy kiss, the low snarl of animal love that rose from my mate's chest making me tremble with quickly renewing want. "I missed you, too," I gasped, sucking love from his lips as he slowly, carefully extricated himself from me. "Eleison, oh, darling...I missed you every day, every minute, oh—oh—"

His eyes still on me even as his cock was free, Eleison slumped to my right side and kept up the kisses. While his hand stroked along my body, then pressed to my cheek, each draw of my lips into his seemed hungrier, more passionately devoted: seeing this, Malin kissed the side of my neck once more and tenderly slid me into Eleison's strong arms, where I nestled against his naked, sweat-warmed body to surrender myself to his powerful love.

Behind me, the bed squeaked while Malin got up. His belt jingled with the removal of his trousers, his eyes fixed upon us when I glanced back in excitement at the sound. "You two really are gorgeous together," my husband commended, his eyes studying the interweaving of Eleison's body and mine. "You make love to her in the way she deserves, Eleison."

"From what I've seen," he said as I wiggled out of his grip to help my husband undress, "you're pretty good at it yourself."

"That goes without saying," Malin replied teasingly, smiling warmly down at me and cupping my face in his hand. His fingers curled around my jaw as I returned his smile, working to unbutton his shirt while we gazed into each other's eyes. "But there are levels of passion—of fierce, rough, uninhibited handling—that are beyond me at my age...sad as it is to say."

Yes, sad—not that Malin couldn't make love to me as roughly as he craved, but that he was morose about his age, which was one of the very qualities I loved about him. But I saw it in his face, just for a flash of a few seconds: a true, profound sorrow, a deep existential mourning that altered the dark eyes fixed intimately upon mine.

Then, they firmed. His entire expression hardened against the thought, newly driven. As I pushed his shirt away, Malin bent to kiss me savagely, his tongue taking complete control of mine. Moaning low, I melted into the command of his body, entirely submissive to him in the space of a second, and allowed him to manipulate me into position. As he stood beside the bed, he sank his fingers into my hair and pushed my head down, his other hand fitting to the back of my shoulder to turn me over. I obliged, eagerly sliding over the bedside to offer myself to him with my legs straight upon the floor and my forearms balanced upon the mattress. After stuffing a few pillows beneath my hips to make it easier on me, Malin resumed his grip in the locks of my hair and bent down to kiss my ear while the straining column of his prick buried itself deeply within me.

"Oh," I cried, "God—"

"That's it, my perfect wife..." His tongue teasing along my jaw as though to soften my flesh for the nibbling of his teeth, Malin shuddered with pleasure to feel how wet I had been left by Eleison's use. "That's it—pray to God, pray to the Good Lord, my angel, that today will be the day your husband gets you pregnant... ah..." His free hand shifting to grip my hip and keep me angled for a greater depth of penetration, Malin nuzzled against my ear with nose and lip and murmured into my very soul, "You're such a horny slut today, I know you must be fertile...oh, darling, that's right, open your womb to me, let me put a child in you tonight... God, oh, Lord, see past my many sins, let my love for this perfect woman bear fruit—"

I was far from perfect—in truth, I was as sinful, as much a murderer, as either man that shared my bed—but Malin's prayer and the unsullied view of me it revealed moved my soul and tightened my throat with emotion. Even as the pleasure built within me at his strokes, I took far greater pleasure at the embrace of our souls, a phenomenon of intimacy that, to my mind, was undeniable. Eleison and I had a powerful mating bond, a physiologically recognized effect of one altered individual upon another: whereas, in a similar but different way, Malin and I were spiritually interfused, a union that grew more profound and complete every single day we so much as shared a glance. It felt as though something intangible about us overlapped in a way that truly *was* perfect. As though we were mates not of body, but of soul.

And I saw that reflected in his eyes as I turned my head to admire the intensity of his admiration for me, a pure adoration that magnified as his forehead rested against mine and his strokes against the sensitive spot at the upper edge of my channel provoked the hot, taut readiness of my womb for a second orgasm.

"Pour yourself into me, Malin," I begged, reaching back to grip his hip as though to encourage him deeper. "Oh, God, my sweet husband—fuck me with your big, bare, wonderful cock, yes, oh, fuck me full, fill me with your children—we'll have so many, darling, oh, only give me the first, give me your heir to bear in my body and cradle in my arms—let me make you a father, darling...oh, God— let me give you my body completely, completely! Let me give you myself from my soul to my womb. Malin—my master—let my body be your true territory—husband! Oh—my husband, yes—"

The orgasm he gave me was softer and more unexpected than the one provoked by Eleison, but it was somehow no less intense: instead of being a great explosion, it seemed extended in duration, sweetened by his thumb as it pressed into one of the welts given me by the belting before sex. The sweet sting, the look of my husband's eyes, my own words, the deep and rapid hammering of his cock: it all culminated in an ocean that came over me not like a sudden wave but a rising tide, whose steadiness was so inexorable that I could not help but drown within its depths. Absolute tenderness softening my handsome warlord's normally stern features, Malin parted his lips to kiss me, to bury his tongue in my mouth as deeply as his cock was buried in my sex: and so it was that by this dual penetration, as my own long orgasm was reaching its end, Malin reached his climax and burst within the hollow of my love.

And at last, my heart was home again!

TO SAY WE SLEPT WELL that afternoon would be a gross understatement. I myself, who had not been traveling, was pulled so heavily beneath consciousness that I later that day found myself reminiscing about my period of coma in Azstoria. The truth was that, in the men's absence, I had slept restlessly at best, disturbed by every little sound and thought to a point of such exasperation that I had occasionally called the dharmine to for his services. His abilities were so many I ought not to have been surprised he held sway over my sleep, yet it was always a strange shock when he accomplished the task, his fingers sinking into my brain as though he were a ghost. With this strange internal caress, I would be out like a snuffed candle.

Now, it was he who roused me from my heavy slumber between the men. As silent as a reflection in a looking glass was the softly smiling servant bending over me when my eyes opened. Without moving his lips so his voice would not disturb my lovers, that strange creature whom my husband had bound to my service eased his words into my mind.

Will Madame be taking her bath before dinner?

Slowly coming out of the anesthesia of slumber, I responded by silently raising my hand. His silver eyes flitting toward the motion, he let his smile widen and took me by the wrist to kiss my fingertips and help me up. Malin, stirred slightly by my going, murmured through some dream, "Don't miss dinner, angel...I have something for you..."

While I smiled and stroked his brow, I grew aware of the thunder of running water in the distance—and the disappearance of my servant. In silence, I slipped from the bedroom without concern for modesty, having coached myself to consider Ba'al-Dinon little more than an animal. A mere Rift beast in man's clothing.

Yet, as I stepped into the bathroom and he turned to smile at me, the long silver braid of his hair swaying against the back of his suitcoat, it was difficult to think of him as anything *but* a man.

"You look quite refreshed, Madame," he observed, extending a hand to help me into the bath while his eyes shamelessly trailed across my body. "Have you had a pleasant rest?"

Such an innocent tone to his breathy words, as though he were asking about the weather; yet I well knew more lay beneath them, and I found myself slightly hot around the face well before I sank to my neck in the water and sighed in pleasure. I needed think of nothing but comfort at such a time as this: Dinon's skillful hands gathered my hair up before it touched the bath, bundling it upon my head with aptitude in far greater excess than any terrestrial servant could have shown.

"It was very pleasant, Dinon," I told him as those same strong hands sank into my hair to firmly massage my scalp. My eyes closing, I added in a sullen confession, "Though I wish you might have warned me in advance of this morning that my spouses would be returning home early...I might have spent the first half of the day in a better mood, at least."

"Now, Madame, you've told me before you don't wish to know the future...I take that seriously, as I do all your commands." As he was *forced* to take all my commands, he meant; my husband, a Riftborn as I was, had secret skills of influence over even the most sapient of Rift beasts, and had applied these abilities to controlling the dharmine who had followed me as a shadow for what was by then a great number of months. Yet, to say Dinon was cowed, or even tamed, was a bold assertion—bordering on incorrect. The dharmine merely gave the impression of a creature biding its time, much as the cat consigned to the house knows a day will come when an unlatched window will allow a resurgence of its feral tendencies. This much, my so-called servant showed as, his fingers quite literally sinking into the muscles of my neck, he said coyly, "There is much, at any rate, I would never dare tell you of your fate, or the Master's, even if I could...these matters are so delicate. As delicate as the threads weaving your tapestries."

"You're trying to tempt me to inquire about something," I accused him, resisting the curiosity he so expertly stirred in my heart and mind. "I really had ought to thrash you for such impudence, Dinon...but that would only encourage you, I suppose."

A chuckle rising from his lips, the dharmine lowered his head slightly and remarked, "All your attention is the same to me,

Madame...but some forms of it are especially sweet." Straightening up, sliding his jacket from his broad shoulders to fix back his sleeves and fetch the waiting bar of honeysuckle soap, he went on, "I only meant to say that there may come a time that you beg me for a forecast of destiny's template...and you will be incensed with me to find me unforthcoming for your own good."

With a sigh of exasperation, I shut my eyes again. "Perverse creature! Disobedient servant...when I tell you to adorn my right hand, you bedeck the left in jewels. Tell me this, then, instead of teasing me about my future: Is there truly a dharmine in our midst, or at least upon the property? Aside from you, I mean."

Having collected the lather of the soap, Dinon began with my neck, applying the foam along my skin from my jaw to my collarbone with slow, thoughtful reverence. "There is indeed a servant of the Rift circling this property, Madame."

"Can you send it away?" For some strange reason, I'd had the increasing impression over the past year that Dinon was far more than an ordinary dharmine, though this may only have been what he wished me to think. But it was an idea that was difficult to shake: dharmines took the forms of human, most often the dead but also the imminently doomed. Yet there was nothing very human in Dinon's comportment; though he was certainly humanoid, his beauty and manner had more in common with nursery tale beings such as sylphs and faeries than any earthly man. For this reason, and others pertaining to his many strange abilities I had never heard mentioned in tales of dharmines, I found myself inquiring, "You *do* have some sway over these other Rift servants, don't you? A means to persuade them, at least...you might find and speak to it. Send it someplace other than my gardens."

"Your roses are superior to any man's crops in my eyes,

madame," Dinon said, his passive observation of my selfishness blanching my cheeks while his lathered hands dipped beneath the water to run along my breasts and leave me holding back a soft gasp of pleasure. "However, the situation is not so simple."

"Then perhaps you might simply exterminate it before it lays waste to some drunken courtier wandering the grounds at night."

"Fain would I obey my mistress without question in this command," he went on, his palms sliding along my arm and down to my left hand before fetching up the soap to gather more lather, "but I dare not harm a dharmine."

Scoffing as I permitted him to tend to my right arm, then rose from the water to allow him to run his fingers along my stomach and down my back, I demanded, "Is the Rift your master even still, dog?"

"No, Madame. Only you and the Master have command over me."

"And my husband, then—has he ordered your impotence in this commission? Ah—"

I sucked in a breath, dizzied as his fingers glided over the swell of my rump and dipped into the cleft. "Your husband has never commanded such a thing of me," said Dinon, unruffled as always, his eyes unapologetically affixed to me while his other hand's expeditions took it up my thigh and along the sensitive mound that never ceased craving masculine attention. My hand falling to brace against his shoulder, I looked down into the eyes of the servant who smiled slyly up at me.

"Then what stays your hand from this predator on our grounds, slave?"

His fingers probed their lather between my sensitive nether lips, the caress a whisper along the suddenly aching nerves of every needy fold. "I only told you a moment ago, Madame," Dinon teased, his cleaning pausing to allow his finger to work slowly back and forth along the jewel of my sex, that little hillock of flesh that fired my blood and flooded my body with ecstasy. Staring up into me as though daring me to tell him stop, he caressed me slowly while continuing, "And I would elaborate, but you told me you wished to know nothing of the future."

"You are insufferable. Just what does the future have to do with a dharmine ruining my roses now?"

"Wait and see," urged my servant, his hand sliding away from me and down the length of my leg while I sighed in deep annoyance.

"What blasted good are you? I can't get a straight answer out of you on the best of days, but you're being obnoxiously vague... then tell me this—"

With a hard look that gave even the dharmine's hands pause, I demanded, "Is it true what Glenn said today?"

Effortlessly returning to motion with a chuckle and a demure aversion of his eyes, Dinon replied, "Madame, I assure you; had I any influence over your ability to bear a child, I would have used such abilities only to your greatest benefit."

It sounded like an answer; but, upon reflection, I had to wonder.

When I was clean and had been given a few minutes alone with my thoughts and the hot water, Dinon returned to help me from the bath and towel me off, then offered my choice of a few suggested gowns for dinner that night. How strange, I always thought! He was so well-acquainted with the future that surely he knew what I would choose to wear on any given night—but perhaps that was just it. If not for his providing me with the illusion of choice, I may have resentfully rejected even that decision freely made in another circumstance. As he knew what I would do, my servant knew me too headstrong, too stubborn, to permit myself to be a total slave to predestination. It was only as I had posited to Parvati, Overseer of the continent, during my ill-fated visit to Valquist the year prior: that, in truth, free will and destiny were in no wise mutually exclusive, but rather intricately woven threads.

Ugh...threads.

"You know your husband would love you if you never wove a tapestry again, Madame," Dinon said, obtrusively breaking in on my thoughts and showing off his knowledge of them while he brushed my hair at my dressing-table.

"I do so wish you would speak only when spoken to, Dinon."

"I know you detest when I invite myself into your thoughts, Madame, but, in truth, I am always there...as synchronized to you as the clock's pendulum to the flow of time." Setting down the brush and fetching up a flower-shaped ornament of red glass and small gold pistils, Dinon tucked it into place above my right ear while going on, "There are times when it seems necessary to preserve your mood by altering the course of your consciousness; I speak only for your own good, and today, I assure you—"

"I heard you," I said in withering displeasure, finding that it was myself with whom I was most displeased. "Yes, Dinon, I heard you the first time...and while it is of course pleasant reassurance to know Malin would love me if my loom sat forever covered in dust, I *want* to weave again."

"Then do it," was his encouraging yet deeply annoying reply. "If you want to weave—if it is what makes you happy, what satisfies you that your existence is put to a purpose—then weave."

Very easy for him to say. Yes...very simple. I wanted to blame

Malin and Eleison's absence, but the truth was that I had hardly touched my loom since the baby and I had left Azstoria and gotten settled in at home. My usually fast-paced output had trickled down to one slow-moving tapestry which was three-quarters finished and, to my preoccupied mind, a mere reminder of the tapestries in the series still to be completed. What once had seemed a great pleasure now felt like a dreary obligation: a weight upon my shoulders that not only filled a sizable portion of my mind but shamed me with my failure to constantly attend to it. And why should it have felt that way? Dinon was right—Malin had never been the one to suggest I spend my time weaving for him. It had only been me.

So where did this pressure come from, then? Why was I fit to collapse under the stress of the only creative outlet I had, a hobby that had once been so liberating to me? Perhaps it was the stress of trying to conceive a child with Malin, or rather the disappointment at our repeated difficulties.

Or maybe it was something else that kept me from my creative pursuits. Though I was certainly not as sensitive to the mystical nuances of reality as was my servant, perhaps my familiarity with weaving permitted me to discern something in the greater tapestry of which I was merely another small figure.

Charlotte knocked upon the door of my boudoir just as Dinon finished adorning me, though she made no move to enter when I bade her let herself inside. Seeing my servant, she simply remained in the doorway, warily observing us both.

"Dinner is nearly ready, Madame; Master Farrow and Eleison are already at the table."

"Very good, Charlotte, thank you." Rising, I told Dinon, "Straighten the bedroom and wait for my next command, as usual."

While my servant bowed, I smiled to Charlotte and swept across the floor to walk to dinner in her company. "Shall we?" I gestured, and she bowed at the waist in a formal custom so ingrained I doubted I would ever see its disappearance no matter how friendly we became—and we were indeed by then very friendly. Although my relationship with Charlotte had been somewhat complicated by my discovery of its true history, the truth was undeniable: she had saved my life and been responsible for the softening of Malin's heart when, as the midwife who found my runaway mother, she rejected promise of payment for foul commissions and instead delivered me healthily into the world. Though at first I had been incensed to think she had known the truth of Malin's long-ended relationship with my mother, I had come to view her good dead as being one that outshone any failure to keep me informed.

And, at any rate, she kept me plenty informed of all other matters that seemed of personal import.

"Did you invite Glenn to dinner," I asked her as we made our way down the hall and out to the more public areas of the manor.

"As always," was Charlotte's dry answer. "I wouldn't hold your breath, Madame...his mood was fouler than usual, if anything. I think he barely heard me."

I frowned despite myself. "I do wish he wouldn't be so withdrawn. I had high hopes—he was in a fairly fine mood this morning, or so I thought."

"Indeed; but that was this morning. It seems quite likely that Master's being home has given him a bad turn, don't you think?"

Of course, I could see the cause as clearly as she; but I couldn't help the spell of annoyance that shadowed my mood no matter how excited I was to see my husband and my mate. "Charlotte, it's been more than a *year*. How long does he plan to live in that little apartment, taking his meals apart from us, sleeping apart from us, living apart from us as though these things were not provided to him entirely out of Malin and Eleison's generosity?" With a dark glance away from the window we passed—and the unhealthy garden it revealed beyond—I thought aloud, "Perhaps we should refuse him meals alone. If he's to act like a child, shouldn't we treat him as one?"

"Then he'll go on hunger-strike, I think, Thecla," Charlotte advised me, speaking directly to my soul by use of my name. "He's a principled man; you know that as well as I. And I know you could hardly sleep to think you were denying food to Rosina's father."

At my sigh and shake of my head, I endured a flush of shame. "No—of course, you're right. Sometimes I wonder who it is who thinks these thoughts—I never used to have such uncompromising visions of reality."

"I thought you told me you were a loner when you were living in your little room in Lescaut, Thecla....most loners are who they are just because they are uncompromising, don't you suppose?" Chastened by this, I said nothing, and Charlotte regarded me from the corner of her eye before going on, "Though, perhaps you are right. Change is a natural part of life, but I've seen you change from a girl to a true woman in not yet three full years; and I've seen that woman change, too."

Hesitating at the top of the grand staircase so I was obliged to fall upon my heel and hang back with her, Charlotte parted her mouth to let the tip of her tongue dart across her lower lip. When she turned to face me, I witnessed a change in her expression: a kind of bracing mask she adopted when advising Malin of something as likely to irritate him as to inform him.

"Have you considered, perhaps, that this footman of yours has a great deal of influence over you and your manner of thought?"

Narrowly, I held back laughter or even a smile. For knowing all the household's business, Charlotte did not and could not possibly know the depths of my intimate connection to Dinon. She did not even know his true nature. No one in the household did, for if it became clear that we had a dharmine among the staff, and that this dharmine had constant access to myself and even my husband, such a choice bit of gossip would have been impossible to control. Even the Saalastian newspapers would have refrained from their usual habit of delicate self-censorship—and God only knew what ugly things would be printed far away in Valquist, and the capital cities of other territories unfriendly to our territory master.

"Has Dinon given you any reason to mistrust him," I inquired to Charlotte delicately, choosing what I felt was the most natural and believable tack. "Have you heard anything? Has anyone said anything to put you off?"

"The other servants are unnerved by him, Madame, I will admit to that—"

"And you?"

With a slight snort and a twitch of her mouth that she simply couldn't help, Charlotte looked at me quite dubiously. "After near to thirty years of service to your husband," said our beloved housekeeper, "the Devil himself couldn't have the least hope of upsetting my constitution, Thecla. You can be assured of that."

While I laughed and raised the scarlet froth of my skirts an inch or two to make my way down the stairs, Charlotte bent to catch the train and ease my burden. "However," she went on as we resumed our way to the dining hall, "I have taken my own note of Dinon's queer ways. We were just speaking of loners, but *he* is as much a hermit in a house full of people as I have ever noted. He never seems to eat or drink with us; and though he circulates with the rest of the staff on holidays, he seems quite remote even for a man of his household status." While I made a mental note to correct this negligence of Dinon's and command him to keep up a semblance of normal social life, Charlotte confessed, "I personally don't mind it, and would rather have an employee I need not correct as often as I do the others...but it is a little *odd*, Madame, how perfect he can seem to be. Doesn't he strike you as—unnatural, somehow?"

"This whole life of mine is still unnatural to me, Charlotte," I said with a gesture to the train she lowered back to the ground at the bottom of the staircase. "I'm afraid that no level of fastidiousness or formality shown by the household staff could strike me as particularly strange."

"Well, if you are not bothered by his service, I will let the matter drop...but I only bring him up because your temperament has appeared to alter since he came into your service, and it would seem to me that if you find yourself in expression of foreign thoughts, they may be arising from whatever words this footman of yours is setting in your ear."

There was no denying she was right—Dinon had a great deal of influence over my thought and behavior. Yet, because she was right, I was doubly dedicated to correcting her in the matter. "You misattribute the cause of my transformation, Charlotte," I said while we approached the great cherry wood doors of the formal dining hall.

"Would you say so?"

"I would. Don't forget—Dinon became my footman only

after I was already a mother...and a killer." The acrid ghost of gun smoke haunted my sinuses to remember the chaos of Glenn's house: the siren of the shutters, the blood splattering across my gown, the veteran of the Expansion falling dead at my feet. How frequently I found myself reflecting on he who had survived Malin's war only to fall by the hand of Malin's half-trained wife. That reflection showed in my face, and Charlotte, knowing better than to speak on this subject of which she had no personal experience, observed my grim expression until I turned away and summarized, "Perhaps the source of these foreign thoughts is more domestic than I realized."

"Perhaps," Charlotte pretended to agree, even if her tone was one of a woman unpersuaded. Then, without another word while turning away from me, she got the door and pulled it wide to announce my entrance.

"Madame Farrow," she called into the room, then adding to me with a nod as my husband and mate stood from their places, "please enjoy supper, Thecla...I will see to it that Glenn is served in the usual fashion."

HOW GOOD IT WAS TO SIT between Malin and Eleison after what seemed to be so many lonely meals! How good, and how natural. For all the world, I could have sworn I had been the one away from home: and at long last, after a thankless journey, I had returned to where my soul belonged. For the first time in three weeks, I truly saw the courtiers who laughed and chatted merrily at the table along with us; I tasted the food, and actually enjoyed the lightening effect of each progressively inebriating sip of wine. Eleison seemed the same, eating with great gusto and reclining in the back of his chair with his wine in one hand and his left arm draped around my shoulders as he chatted companionably with Aleister and his sister, our two favorite guests by far.

But as Eleison did an increasingly natural job of taking on his role of master of the property, Malin, it seemed, increasingly had eyes only for me.

How quiet he was during that supper back! I supposed him tired, owing to the effect travel had upon men of his age and the simple exertion of our reunion, which had worn me out quite a bit myself. Now, however, I look back on those days, and I see his contemplative turns inward so differently.

Seeing how little he had joined the conversation, and how his gaze had either been fixed on me or drifting off into some middle-distant point along the display of the table, I set down my fork to wipe my hand and slide it over his. My husband animated at once, drawn from his thoughts and turning back to face me with a tender smile he gave none but me.

"You seem exhausted," I told him sympathetically. "Perhaps we should retire early tonight? Just you and me—I've noticed you sleep better that way."

"Thecla..." His eyes crinkling at the edges, the faded scar contorting with the softness of his gaze, Malin raised my hand to his mouth and said when his lips were once again free, "You worry over me too much, my darling...I'm a bit tired, you're right. But you know me..." Releasing my hand to pick up his fork and knife again, he cut into his cooling portion of quail and said with a dry chuckle, "If I'm not thinking of you, or Eleison, or you and Eleison, then it's only because I'm preoccupied by some business of Gudrune's."

"Dare I ask how your trip to Azstoria went, then?" It truly was a matter of daring—though my husband could be very forthcoming about his work, wanting as he did to teach me to steward our territory as competently as he, (if such a thing were possible!), there were certain times when he wanted to flee from the burdens of his duties and hide himself in pleasure. There were times he wished to speak of nothing less than he wished to speak of Gudrune's business; but there were other times when he was so pleased with political or social developments that he simply could not withhold even a passing thought on such matters.

Tonight seemed closer to the latter. Making a noise of pleasure while chewing his bite, he raised his napkin to his lips to wipe his mouth before saying, "It was excellent, darling, thank you for asking. In fact, that's what's preoccupying me so tonight...it's all a matter of very good timing, you see—"

Lowering his voice just slightly—as if he had any need to, given how merrily the courtiers laughed and chatted amid their drinking—Malin worked his knife and fork while remaining focused on me. "Horizon Energy's new research facility will be opening in Saalast two weeks from now, so I'll be heading up north for the dedication and a little speech."

My face falling along with my shoulders, I begged, "Oh please, darling, let me come with you."

Though he hesitated, owing to the great deal of violent murmurings which had been routinely quelled since the disbanding of the Hunter's Guild—and knowing I normally detested the long, dull, and uncomfortable trip to Saalast from the Karris estate, or vice versa—Malin saw my face and reached over to squeeze and stroke my hand again. "I would love to have you by my side for it," he said encouragingly, soothing me with the knowledge that I would not lose him again so soon after having received him back into my company. Allocating his attention and hands to his cutlery again, Malin continued, "At any rate, where was I—ah, the propitious timing, yes. You see, aside from dealing with a bit of general housekeeping, that trip to Azstoria was meant to confirm something very exciting: something I'm just thrilled about."

His dark eyes glittering like polished obsidian, my husband leaned in to explain, "Our efforts at the digs have at last yielded fruit—one of our archaeological teams has uncovered a great deal of usable materials, a certain missing ingredient that will benefit Horizon's research with the Rift tremendously."

Keen with interest, excited by his excitement although I was still rather hazy on the details, I murmured, "Uranium?"

Surprised to hear the word out of my mouth, Malin flicked an inquiring glance to Eleison. "Parvati," Eleison explained helpfully, having had his attention drawn to the conversation around the time it was decided I would be heading north for the speech with them. My mate, who had been in the room with me during a frankly patronizing final lecture by the continent's Overseer, no doubt recalled the argument as well as I, and didn't hesitate to elaborate, "Right before Thecla walked out, the Overseer brought it up."

"Ah," said Malin, almost adequately disguising his withering displeasure for mere mention of the woman, let alone that difficult time in our lives. "I must hand it to Parvati...she doesn't hold anything back, does she. Anyway—yes, darling, though don't say that too loud in mixed company, if you please."

Cheeks burning with the embarrassment, I stuttered, "Goodness, I'm sorry, I—"

"That's all right," said Malin with a laugh. Patting my hand, then fondly caressing my warmed face, Malin gazed into me with eye-twinkling pleasure for a few long seconds before murmuring, "Such a smart woman," and letting his hand drop to his wine glass.

"I wouldn't be so sure of that," I replied with a laugh, now far hotter around my cheeks than the embarrassment had made me. "I feel very foolish these days, especially when the conversation turns to politics."

"That's a hallmark of intelligence, darling…only an idiot has full confidence in these matters. At any rate, the news will come out when I make the announcement in Horizon's dedication—I just want to control the information's release until then, that's all."

I nodded in understanding, my excitement rising again as I observed, "This means you'll really be able to make progress on your research project—oh, darling, you're right, it's wonderful timing. I'm very happy for you." Glowing with joy to imagine how he must have felt after decades of dreaming he could somehow harvest the Rift to provide an unlimited source of clean energy for Gudrune—and perhaps even the world—I found myself adding, "I'm so proud to be your consort. It's wonderful that you're being rewarded after so many years of refusing to give up on this dream of yours."

Looking genuinely gratified, Malin lowered his eyes with a soft smile and gazed into his wine. "Thank you, darling. It does feel like a great relief to stand on the precipice of this development."

He seemed poised to say more—his lips began to twitch with some unformed word, at least, before they froze. The most curiously dark expression transfigured his features. All at once, his thoughts were far away again, off with the same kind of mourning that altered him whenever he thought long on his age.

"I just hope it's not too late for me to enjoy the fruits," he said, raising his chin to knock back the remainder of his wine.

Unable to help my frown, I sat forward to invite him on a walk through the gardens to speak—or at least ease—his mind; but I was prevented from even beginning, for the doors at the end of the dining hall opened and, held in the arms of her nursemaid Nellie, my daughter was brought into the room. Little Rosina uttered a happy squeal of delight before Charlotte even had a chance to announce her.

At once, heedless of the courtiers who were half gladdened and half annoyed by the presence of the child, Malin dropped all his worries and perked with paternal joy. "Aha! There's our little rose—"

"My Rosina," I was myself saying happily, pushing my seat back from the table to receive her while Eleison freed me from his arm. "Thank you, Nellie, I'll take her from here, have a good break." With a smile of gratitude exchanged between us, Rosina's nurse passed her into my arms. My heart filled with delight just to hold the girl. How truly adorable Rosina was! And more so every day, or so she seemed in light of the increasing love of my heart. "My pretty baby," I said with great joy, pinching her chubby pink cheek and sweeping her dark curls back from her brilliant blue eyes, "oh, little Rosina, have you had a fun day?"

"Yeah," answered the cherub, shyly regarding the busy room with her hand against her mouth. Though I was about to move it away, she lowered it herself to smile giddily as she recognized Eleison to my right. "Uncle Ellie," she said, melting Eleison's heart with her adorable love for him.

"Hey," he said, "you remember me!" With a laugh and a pat of her head as I remonstrated him for thinking she would forget, he spread his hands and said, "Well, hell, I don't know! Three weeks—that's practically a lifetime when you're eighteen months old. Right?"

As he turned his attention conversationally to the baby, she laughed to be consulted for her opinion, the kind of twinkling little laugh that simply slayed my heart and filled my soul—and did the same, I knew, to Malin, who watched her with happiness to enjoy the life brought by her presence. Noting this, himself, Eleison leaned in and drew her attention to my husband with a tap on her shoulder and a point at the head of the table. "Hey," asked Eleison, "who's that? Who is that?"

Following his gesture, Rosina turned in my arms to beam. "Papa," she enthused, wiggling against the embrace she suddenly regarded as a prison. "Down," she fussed, her chubby hands reaching forward for freedom.

As reluctant as I was to put her down, it was worth relinquishing her to see the way she, carefully watching the floor, stepped around the table and then flung herself gladly against Malin's waist. He tutted with affection at the precious creature nestling beneath his arm to gaze with shy hope up into his face. "Up, peeze," she pleaded, her naively accented 'please' tacked on as a little mumble that was becoming instinctive—if only so she might avoid hearing it from me when she failed to say it. As with most children that age, Rosina's vocabulary was still somewhat limited, no more than twelve or fifteen words at that time; but everything she couldn't say with her speech she said with her face and filial glee as her Papa immediately swept her upon his knee to kiss her head and pet her curls.

"A little treasure," Malin remarked, exuding the same joy she did. "Ah—Eleison, look how big she's gotten in three weeks. And did you see the way she walked just now—"

"Before you know it, she'll be rolling her eyes and telling us we're boring her to death." Eleison smiled at the scene before refilling his wine glass.

Perhaps that would be Rosina's turn toward Eleison and even to me in the decades to come—but I somehow doubted she would ever develop such an attitude toward her Papa. Though Malin was not her biological sire, the two had taken such a shine to one another I was sometimes glad that Glenn refused my dinner invitations.

As deeply as he detested Malin, it would have made Rosina's true father very jealous to see with his own two eyes the role her papa held in her heart. "Did you miss us," Malin asked fondly, yielding a big smile and an eager nod from behind her once more shyly lifted hand. "You did? Poor little flower! Well, Papa and Uncle missed you, too, and certainly missed your mama very much. Were you a good girl while we were gone? Yes? You've been good?" More rapid nodding of her adorable head sent her curls springing around eyes that widened with recognition as Malin said, "Well, then I don't think Mama will complain if I give you a present...let's see..."

With a few playful pats along his person as though he had misplaced or forgotten where it was, Malin at last reached into his suitcoat and said, "Aha, here it is—"

"Rosina pressie," declared Rosina, her eyes aglow in delight.

"That's right, a present for Rosina—are you ready? Ta-da—"

Malin's hidden hand reappeared, and I smiled to see what sat in the well of his palm. Little Rosina was a child of many odd fancies, I was finding, and at her present age—perhaps owing to her small size—she was absolutely fascinated by bugs. Insects of all kinds fixed her interest with great awe: so it was with an amazed gasp that her tiny eyes focused on the amber stone whose semi-translucent center had formed the eternal resting place of a long-bodied dragonfly. "Bug," she declared with fascination bordering on reverence. "Rosina bug?"

"Yes, angel, it's your bug...I hope you don't mind," he added to me while the girl took the stone carefully into her pudgy hands, turning it over with great intrigue. "I wanted to bring her a little something from Azstoria."

"Of course I don't mind," I said with smiling delight, reaching over to stroke Malin's hand and hold it a few seconds as Eleison said with an aggrieved sigh, "Just try finding one of those big enough that she can't swallow it, but small enough that she can hold it...Malin was so stuck on the idea, we must have spent a week looking around for the right one."

"It was worth it, though," said Malin with a fond smile, basking in her enjoyment of the bug as a great hound basks in the Sunday morning sunshine, taking from it peace and comfort. Smiling a little myself, I reached over and touched Rosina's wrist, barely noticing as Malin's hand slipped into his jacket again.

"What do we say when someone gives us something nice, Rosina?" Her attention torn reluctantly from the wonder of her bug, Rosina looked at me with curious eyes, waiting for me to repeat myself or clarify. I reminded her, "'Thank you?' Can you thank Papa?"

Looking a little shy again, the girl grinned and, all dimples, let the fossilized insect drop into her lap as she instead clung to Malin's waist in a tight hug. Eleison chuckled softly and I cooed despite myself, while Malin, one hand stuck in his coat, patted the back of her head with his free palm.

"Such a sweet girl. You're welcome, angel. I'm sure your little bug loves you as much as you already love it, eh? We can put it somewhere nice and Aunt Nellie can show it to you whenever you feel like looking at it...you'll have to give it a name..."

As the girl released her hold on him to resume admiring the dragonfly, Malin at last extricated his hand from his jacket and set a small wooden box before me. I looked up at him imploringly, no doubt an adult emulation of Rosina's anticipation but a moment earlier. "That's for you." Malin gestured with a little nod, his eyes flashing between the box and my face. "Just a little something."

Moved, I opened the box and gasped with pleasure at the twinkling citrine stone within the petals of a diamond flower, the setting of a gold ring that glowed in the light of the dining room. "Oh, Malin," I said with a gasp of pleasure, gazing up at him with amazement. "Thank you, sweetheart—oh, my beloved—"

Half-forgetting the ring that had inspired it, I rose to bend over him and kiss him, then slid my arms around his neck so as to nuzzle my cheek against the top of his head. "You're so sweet to think of me—oh, Malin, my darling. I love you. Thank you."

"You're welcome, Thecla. You're so welcome." His face turned against the side of my throat, where he took a great breath that had a kind of tremor to it: and I felt the sorrow wash through him again, a tide whose return seemed inevitable that night. Yet, when I drew away to look at him, he assumed his warm, gentle smile as he reached out to pick up the box. "Here I was worried you might think it a little garish...you're a woman of good taste, I trust it more than my own."

"No, Malin, I love it. It's beautiful—" As he removed the ring from the box, I instinctively extended my hand. Malin looked upon me tenderly, sliding the ring along my third finger until it fit snugly against my wedding band. Pleased with the fit, he bent his head to kiss my knuckles, then studied the effect of my hand for a few long seconds before squeezing my fingers.

"Next time I go to Azstoria," he said, releasing me to let me kneel beside him and Rosina, "I think you'll almost certainly be able to come with me...and we can tour it a bit, as we couldn't last time."

Practically all I remembered of Azstoria was the tower overlooking the game reserve where Malin had kept me in the form of a ventil, waiting for me to return to myself: and that place, manicured and kept immaculate, was nothing like the rest of the territory, which was known to be beautiful but wild desert. "I would so love to see it with you," I told him, smiling softly. "Our train went through it"—I glanced slyly over at Eleison, my eyes crinkling with the smile we shared—"but we saw precious little of it."

Chuckling a bit, Malin said, "I imagine not," and patted Rosina on the head again. "All right, angel...I'll let Mama take you to say good-night to your daddy now...but Papa loves you, darling—oh, he missed you."

"Love Papa," said the sprite happily, receiving a kiss atop her head with a giddy noise of delight before allowing herself to be taken into my arms. "Love Unky."

"I love you, too, kiddo," said Eleison with a fond look. "Sleep tight, now, see you tomorrow..."

With a kiss upon Malin's head and another upon Eleison's, I smiled and shifted my embrace of the girl to open my slightly freer hand to her. "May Mama hold your bug until we're in Dada's room?" Looking at me with the utmost reluctance, the girl frowned and held the bug to her heart but was open to reason as I said, "Just to keep it safe—you can have it back very soon, I promise. Then you can look at your pretty bug all you like. All right?"

Her mouth screwed up, but her plaintive eyes passed from Eleison's smiling face to Malin's, and she was cowed by her desire to look like a polite little lady in front of her most impressive relatives. Still (for this temporary juncture) at an age of relatively willing compromise, she released the amber into my hand and leaned her head against my bosom while assessing the room at large. "Night," she said, impressing a few of the more charmed courtiers—Kalypso included—with her advanced vocabulary. As they cooed, I smiled, and together Rosina and I stole from the dining hall with Malin's gifts glittering in and upon my hand.

HOW GOOD HE WAS to us—to her. They had no genetic link in common, but they did have love: and that earnest paternal love with which Malin had embraced my daughter made me all the more certain that he would prove a good and worthy father to any natural heir I might provide him. How I truly longed to give him that! It was the only gift by which I could reward his profound fidelity. He had seen so many of my faults—my selfishness, my disloyalty, my streaks of cruelty, great and small—and still, he loved me in a way so true that I knew it did not matter to him whose children I bore. We were truly one flesh, my husband and I: and whatever sprung from my flesh was, in his opinion, as good as any child of his own...but how I longed to give him more!

Not everyone could appreciate the territory master's generous heart, however. Perhaps I was a little foolish to expect anything different from Glenn at that time; but, naive and hopeful and dreaming of a peaceful life without conflict between any of my lovers, I nightly made the journey to Glenn's chambers with hope in my heart that tonight would be the night I found his spirit had finally changed. Tonight would be the night he would show warmth at mention of Malin, rather than recoiling from it; tonight, ah, this would be the night that he would apologize for missing dinner and swear to me he would attend the next one!

How very wrong I was...especially that night.

With Rosina's eyes fixed upon her bug, I nodded at Dinon. He stood ready beside Glenn's apartment door, knowing my intent and waiting there to let me in. "Master Stone has had his supper already," Dinon assured me, rapping once upon the door before pushing it open. "Don't be surprised to find him in the mood for conversation."

It is truly a pity how naively I interpreted Dinon's warnings back in those days. I mistook his words for something positive and therefore went smiling into Glenn's domain, looking expectantly around and indeed finding him in a pleasant enough mien at the outset. Already in the midst of setting down his book, he came over to greet the child and me, his smile widening as Rosina extended her chubby hands and squealed, "Dada! Dada, up—"

"There's my sweetheart," he said, gladness in his eyes as I slid her into his arms and felt my smile widen when she giggled at his beard. "I missed you, sweetie. You look like you're happy!"

"Dada," said the girl, patting his cheek and then waving that same hand at me. "Bug, peeze?"

"No, that's Mama."

"She means this," I corrected with a laugh, showing him the fossil and putting it into her hands. "Careful, careful now, sweetheart..."

"Thank," was her somehow hilariously prim little response. Proudly showing this treasure to her father, she reiterated, "Bug!" and took to staring at it with a look of absolute enchantment. For a few seconds, Glenn looked intrigued with her; then, understanding, he flicked a glance at me once the child had been satisfied by his affectation of amazement.

"Is that, uh, Azstorian amber?"

"Just a little souvenir from Malin," I said, smiling sweetly as I could, hoping my resolute will to be normal and speak of normal things would prevent unnecessary conflict that night.

"Uh-huh," said Glenn, his eyes flicking over me head to toe and landing upon the citrine ring. "And that?"

"This, too," I said, self-consciously covering my ring with my free hand as though, like with the child, I could hide an object from Glenn's sight and make him forget all about it. As I could feel my smile starting to fade, I forced it wide again and bent to playfully kiss and nuzzle Rosina's dimpled cheek. "He just wanted to bring us something nice from his trip, didn't he, darling?"

"Papa bug," said the girl in innocent pride, confirming the provenance to the inevitable detriment of the conversation. While jealousy hardened Glenn's visage at the child's use of a paternal title to refer to his self-declared nemesis, Rosina went on softly babbling to the dragonfly as though telling it some secret in an untranslatable tongue.

"How nice," was Glenn's withering response as he set Rosina down upon a cushion of the couch to let her play with the bug. Directly, he addressed me. "You must be relieved."

Said by anyone else, the words would have been perfectly agreeable and elicited a happy response. By Glenn in that tone, however—a little withering, a little derisive—I couldn't help but roll my eyes.

"Goodness, Glenn, I wish you would at least try to be less jealous—next time I'll be sure to tell my husband to bring *you* a toy. It might save your temperament."

"It would save my temperament," he said softly, his golden eyes searching deeply into mine, "if you would choose me over him, even once."

Arms folding, I told him tersely, "And how am I supposed to do that when you never come out of your blasted apartment?"

"You could try knocking," he said, jerking his chin in the direction of the door. "Send me a note. Just walk in—it's not like you don't have a key."

So he wanted to have a proper fight, it seemed. While it wasn't every day Glenn let his frustration show, it had happened enough over the past year that I knew the warning signs—and, embarrassingly, so did Rosina, who raised her eyes from the amber and studied us with fascination. Seeing her so focused, I affixed a false smile and said in a voice of cheerful disappointment, "Poor Dada is tired tonight! And aren't you tired, too, my little rose? Come now, let Daddy rest—"

"I want to talk to you," he told me, eliciting a shush and a dagger look I couldn't help.

"We'll talk," I said, whisking Rosina back to the exit with me. "Once Rosina doesn't have to sit around for it...ah!"

The door opened without need for so much as a call, and I found on the other side my slave of perfect timing proving worth more than his weight in gold—by the strange sway he had over matters of synchronicity, an understated but undeniably obvious talent of his, Dinon had managed to waylay Nellie and seduce her (for that was the only proper word, given her shy smile) into conversation. Rosina's nurse therefore stood, surprised to see me appear with her charge but, I was always glad to note, never displeased no matter what she was in the middle of.

"What fine timing," I said, flicking a glance at Dinon before smiling to place the child in Nellie's arms. "Would you see to it that my little sweetheart gets to bed a bit early tonight? I think we're all quite tired from the excitement of Malin's return—good night, princess!" Bending to plant a smooch on her cheek, I smiled at her with true, deep fondness and told her, "Sweet dreams! Mama will see you tomorrow, yes, and maybe we can play a game in the garden..."

While Nellie whisked the baby off and Dinon lowered his smiling eyes in deference to my nod of approval, I stepped back into Glenn's apartment and shut the door somewhat heavily.

"Now," I said, steeling myself against the man I turned to face, "I hardly think—"

And I didn't think. Couldn't think, anyway, when Glenn caught me by the waist and jerked me hard against his chest. As I lost my footing and had to rely on his support to remain upright, his free hand tangled in my hair and craned my head back to keep my eyes locked on his.

"I know you're used to being worshiped by every man with a working prick," said Glenn, his words a low thunder as he tightened his grip on my hair, "but if you expect me to come crawling to you, hoping for the scraps of your free time—"

"What I expect, Glenn, is a little more *gratitude* for the man who's sheltered you from the blasted Hunter's Guild for a year and a half."

Lip lightly curling, the disgraced hunter asked, "And you want me to be grateful for the alteration, too?"

"It saved your life, you fool—of course, you should be grateful. You should feel lucky to even be alive!"

"Sorry I can't bring myself to kiss his ass the way your mate does." Before I could even begin to tear into him for this needless insult to Eleison, Glenn went on harshly, "Maybe I'd feel luckier if the method to save my life hadn't been an experimental procedure that made me dependent on your love for the rest of eternity."

Gritting my teeth, eyes blazing with frustration, I reached up to take hold of Glenn's broad wrist. What was so frustrating was I truly did understand the tragedy of his situation. After more than thirty years of humanity, of being able to live somewhat quietly in spite of his extreme vocational success—after being able to live in total independence, the likes of which I could only dream—Glenn was now bonded to me by our third-tier mating bond. The child we'd had together connected us deeply; and although the connection was not as naturally powerful as the one between Eleison and me, my bond with Glenn was still deep and primeval. Without me around, he would be dependent on the synthetic drug, Stabilify, that allowed altered individuals to maintain control of their senses throughout regular Rift Events—an increasing problem in a world where Rift Events were growing more common all the time, and were forecasted to continue increasing in length and severity.

"I'm sorry to hear you feel love with me for the rest of your life is a curse," I told him while yanking his hand away from me and staring darkly into his eyes. His expression tightening, Glenn studied the wrist I gripped.

"You know damn well it's not life with you that bothers me, Thecla," he said tersely. "It's life with Malin—with your husband."

The word curled from his lip in a soft snarl as he emphasized, "That's what I don't want. What I would never consent to."

By now my face must have been quite red, because it certainly felt aflame. Even after all I had learned of Malin and his bad habits of deception—or perhaps because of all I had learned—I was more loyal to him than ever, and hastened to his defense at the lightest insult. This particular insult, so far as I was concerned, was the furthest thing from light—and, frankly, an indictment on Glenn's character, rather than Malin's.

"My *husband*," I told him, attempting to tamp down my temper and instead sounding quite cold, "didn't just save your life with alteration, Glenn. He viewed you—still views you—with compassion. Look around you, you imbecile!" Though I could see the hurt and anger in his face, I felt my hurt and anger were greater and said with a wave of my hand, "He has given you everything you could possibly want. He's given you a *home*, he provides you meals, he offers you protection from the blasted Hunter's Guild which has every legal right to see you killed if you ever dare step foot outside Gudrune again. He's given you *me*, Glenn!" My tone softening, as I had caught myself raising my voice again, I took a deep breath and drew back from him to look into his face. "I wish you could see that," I told him softly.

"I wish I could feel that," he said in half-agreement. "And you're right. I won't sit here and pretend like Malin has never done anything for me personally. But—doesn't it seem to you like he's, I don't know, trying to make up for something when he's so overly generous?"

"He's precisely the right amount of generous for a man of his wealth and power," I admonished Glenn. "And if that generosity arises from some sense of larger guilt, more so the better. Most people go their entire lives without ever admitting to themselves they've done something worth repenting over."

His unpleasant laugh deepened my anger so immensely I had to grip my dress as he said, "If Malin were honest about his need to repent, he wouldn't be lording it up as territory master of Gudrune. He'd be—I don't know, a religious hermit somewhere, living alone in the dark, eating the scraps of men with more honest hearts."

"Men like you, I suppose you mean, Glenn?"

Beneath my defiant stare, Glenn ground his teeth. I waited him to claim he was the kind of pure, honest man he evidently held superior to Malin, eager to rebuke him on the point. Glenn had lied and omitted just as much to me as had all the other people in my life. He had betrayed my trust, inviting his guild members to try and woo me to their cause. From the start of our sexual relationship, he had nursed in his heart all the ideals of an assassin—and had even tried to embody that role in the Azstorian game preserve, before my presence softened his heart and Ba'al-Dinon kept him from staining his hands with my husband's blood.

Yet, seeing the frustration in his face as I stood before him, my heart moved me to look on Glenn with more compassion. After all: while it was no reason to perpetually reject Malin's efforts to extend him olive branch on olive branch, it was a fact that Glenn's father, like so many men across the continent, lost his life in Malin's war against the Overseer. The Expansion, as it was called, had claimed many, and orphaned countless children, and so it was easy for me, who had lost my own father in my teenage years, to understand why Glenn struggled on a personal level to accept what the territory master was giving him.

But to so continually deny its worth! To push it all away with such ingratitude and sulk, day on day, behind the shut door of an apartment that only seemed to have any light when Rosina—whose very presence in Glenn's life was another generous allotment of my husband, whatever genetics may have preferred—was about!

I was wounded when Glenn pretended his willful refusal to accept me and my family was a natural consequence of Malin denying Glenn the life he felt he deserved. There was more we both wished to say: more useless grievances to air, neither of one us being in a position to willingly change our minds no matter what evidence was presented.

But, before Glenn could rejoin me for my perhaps somewhat petty remark, that all-too ubiquitous chime echoed from the RMS panel on the front wall.

"Rift Event Imminent," the smooth electric voice declared while we shared a look of new frustration. "Twenty minutes advised."

"Maybe that explains why we're both so on-edge," muttered Glenn, averting his eyes, his cheeks tight beneath his beard with the realization.

"I doubt that's the only reason," I said, unable to check my fuming temper before, hearing how unpleasant I sounded, I moderated my tone and found diplomacy enough to agree, "but yes, perhaps you're right. You know, Glenn—you really should come out running with Eleison and me sometime."

Beginning to turn from him, I insisted, "Whatever grudge you hold against my husband need not extend to Eleison...and since you are both my mates, both benefiting from my love, one might argue that you and Eleison are more evenly matched than are Eleison and Malin. You really should give him a chance...you might even like each other."

"Thecla—"

My hand had landed on the doorknob, my wounded heart as eager to escape the conversation as my body was eager to experience the liberty of the Rift. Though reluctant to face him again, I turned at Glenn's soft voice.

Those large, powerful hands of his cupped my face with all the gentleness of a collector holding a butterfly.

Before I could react, he bent his head to kiss me, his mouth capturing mine without hesitation.

That was a quality of Glenn's that made our contentious natures so exceptionally difficult to bear. He was such a sensitive man: sensitive, and unhesitating in his love despite how outraged we made one another. I felt it all in the kiss he pressed against my slowly parting lips. The tenderness, the hope, the love—the plea that I keep him in my heart no matter our difficulties. It was all there in the stroke of his tongue, the work of his lips. In the gentle trailing of his thumb over my cheekbone, sweeping to the outer edge of my eye when at last he lifted his head from mine.

"I'm sorry," he murmured to me, a plea of repentance that meant too many things at once. "Just—please, Thecla. I don't want to spend my life as third best."

Sighing, my lower lip disappearing between my teeth to let me nibble away my annoyance, I murmured, "It isn't like that. It doesn't have to be like that, Glenn. All you need do is let yourself be a part of our family. Part of Rosina's family."

His eyes searched mine, almost pained to reflect on the point that so long as he was shutting himself out of Malin's life, he was shutting himself out of more complete access to Rosina. "Be safe," was all he said, releasing me and stepping away instead of giving voice to his difficult thoughts.

Unable to help but look at this handsome, noble soul with longing, I slipped from his apartments and went seeking the master of the house.

7

HOW INCREDIBLE IT WAS to reflect on the ways we had all changed since my arrival at the Karris house! Glenn was far from the only one among us who had experienced a metamorphosis: even my own changes, I felt, sometimes paled in comparison to the change exhibited by my sweet, once so regularly solemn Eleison. Where once he had been brooding, and his humor had always had a tinge of bleak irony that betrayed his internal tendency toward despair, his liberation from his debt to Malin had brought about a true transformation of his soul—to say nothing of his love for me, which brightened his brilliant crimson eyes when my hurrying down the stairs drew his attention from his conversation with his brother and those staff members responsible for patrolling the ground during Rift activity.

"Now, darling," I said, lightly chastising him as I strolled into the group to take his arm, "trust poor Kyrie to take the responsibility you've awarded him—can't you let yourself enjoy the privilege of your new station and allow your staff to fulfill their duties in peace?"

Looking abashed in only the most light-hearted of ways, Eleison laughed and shared a glance with his younger brother. Meanwhile I, regardless of present company, stood upon my toes to apply a kiss to my mate's cheek. "Listen to Thecla," pleaded Kyrie, his humorous tone of exaggerated exhaustion betraying a very real desire to divest himself of his brother's micromanagement. "I've got it covered, Eleison, I promise. Come on—all the time I spent protecting the horses in the stables, don't you think—"

"I know," said Eleison, waving his free hand as I tugged him rather forcefully out of the meeting. "I know, I know…I just can't help myself. And anyway, if it's my property, I'd ought to know what's going on."

"Take it from me," I told him with a mirthful laugh, "and from Malin…it's better to know nothing at all until something is going wrong. The household is like a lovely clock…we should only take note of it when one of its gears cease turning. Thank you for looking after us, Kyrie, dear," I said, rewarding the boy with a smile that made him faintly blush. "I'm sure with you managing the staff we could hardly hope to be safer."

I have made an error of the pen just now—I ought to have written 'young man' or some such, rather than 'boy'. Yet, I think I'd ought to leave the typo, since it reflects an undeniable reality of Kyrie's life. Though he was perhaps my age, give or take a few years, poor Kyrie was delicate and fresh-faced enough to appear perhaps fifteen years his brother's junior, or more. The frightful truth was that Kyrie had nearly lost his life to the blood poisoning of a dharmine: one that had taken the form of their deceased mother, no less. Given that Eleison had been unaltered at the time, his overcoming of the Rift monster had been a kind of miracle, and a testament to his natural calling as a monster hunter not unlike Glenn; but unlike Glenn, who submitted his talents to the treacherous Guild that granted him fame and wealth in exchange for a part of his soul, Eleison had offered his skills to the territory master, having no other means by which he could possibly afford to cure his younger brother's quickly worsening condition. Seeing Eleison's talents, Malin had gladly traded investment in the brothers' alteration in exchange for Eleison's indentured servitude. Kyrie, too, had been expected to serve the territory master's country property, and had done so faithfully until Malin liberated them as a gift to reward Eleison's love.

This was all I wanted for Glenn, I reflected as Eleison and I, arm-in-arm, hurried out the front doors of the great house to the expansive front yard with its wide-mouthed gravel sea narrowing to a path back to the highway. By embracing love and feeling that love fully—by giving himself to Malin as he had never given himself to a man—Eleison had been released from his servitude and given true freedom. Love had permitted Eleison to change his life: and love could change Glenn's life, too, without even requiring so great a depth of open-mindedness as it had from Eleison.

How healed my mate was in mind and soul! How nobly and easily he smiled up at the slowly intensifying purple hue of the sky before turning to me with a flirtatious smile and an eager flick of his eyes down my gown. "How about we find someplace a little more private, baby...I don't want the whole household getting an eyeful."

"No amount of Stabilify in the world would keep your borro from losing its mind over that," I agreed with a giggle, allowing him to whisk me to the far side of the garage where the carriages, our own and those of the visiting courtiers, were parked in anticipation of infrequent seasonal use. "Though I admit...I do love it when you're jealous, Eleison."

As a delicious shudder of pleasure rolled through me at the thought, Eleison smirked and glanced away. "I never would have guessed."

"Now, it isn't as though I make you jealous on *purpose*. I only mean to say—it's a fringe benefit, as it were."

"'Fringe benefit,'" repeated Eleison with a husky laugh, pushing me around the corner with a shake of his head. "You sure do talk like Malin these days."

"As if you don't," I teased, reaching back to struggle for the laces of my dress. "Why, given as many years as you've had with him, it's frankly a miracle you don't sound identic—"

My flow of words and movement were both interrupted by Eleison's possessive hands, one of which caught my waist. The other cradled my jaw, raising my face to his and forcing open my mouth with a commanding squeeze. As I gasped, he devoured my lips and played with my tongue, his own sliding past my teeth to take command of its territory. Moaning, I melted against his chest and ran my fingers along the buttons of his shirt, only remembering to undress him as his hands found the laces of my bodice. Drinking in every breath from my lungs, sucking down my love as if he could never have enough of it, Eleison softly growled against my lips and sent my heart fluttering wildly in my breast.

"I missed you so fucking much," he told me, a rush of pleasure blooming in my cheeks and down the column of my spine. "Oh,

Thecla, baby, I don't know how I ever lived without you...even before the alteration..."

The mere contemplation made his hands work more rapidly—and more roughly. While he jerked open my dress, some set of threads audibly tore. I couldn't help but reflect on the number of Charlotte's lectures Eleison had been spared since the arrival of my mystical servant to our household, and even this vague passage of Dinon through my mind made me aware of his presence. I swore I could feel his keen observation of the pleasure coursing through me as my mate's strong jaw lowered its trail of fierce kisses down my cheek and along the slope of my throat.

"Eleison," I moaned, "oh, my darling, sweet Adonis, I missed you—ah, too much—"

I had him but half out of his shirt before he was lowering to his knees before me, pushing me back against the wall of the garage while tugging away the layers of fabric that concealed my body from his hungry love. "We had one Rift Event when we were in Azstoria," he murmured, shrugging off his jacket and doing rapidly away with his shirt before tending to the garters of my stockings. Eyes lifting to me as he undressed me, he asked, "Did you have one here?"

"Yes," I gasped as he pressed a few hot kisses down the exposed flesh of my thigh, "yes, one—no, wait, two, a smaller one—"

"And you still didn't fuck anyone? Poor Thecla...that must have been torture."

I shuddered to find myself all too quickly naked, every inch of my flesh bared to his eager witness. "It was miserable," I whimpered, reflecting on the heat into which Rift Events plunged my body even before the animal within me, a second-generation ventil that took after my dead mother's beast, at last emerged. As Eleison clicked his tongue in sympathy and let his kisses blaze a trail toward the cleft between my thighs, I found myself already panting in anticipation, going on, "Oh, Eleison, it was like I had a fever, one gripping my whole body—a desperate pressure, a need I couldn't solve on my own no matter how I tried."

"But you did try," he asked with a dirty, somewhat boyish grin as he raised my leg and draped it over his shoulder to let him better see me. At once so distracted he couldn't even continue teasing me, his pupils suddenly expansive within the burning magma of his irises, Eleison inhaled sharply and said with a low vibrato of lust, "Oh, Thecla, sweetheart, are you still turned on from earlier?"

"No!" I gasped, my brow furrowing with the sharp pleasure that overwhelmed me at his tender kiss upon Ecstasy's very source. "No, oh, Eleison, this is just for you, my jealous lover—ah! My mate—"

Inspired, his tongue set to avid work at once, thumb raising to spread me open and make my every slightest centimeter of flesh more accessible to his love. I moaned his name in quick-growing desperation, my hand fitting to the back of his head to press him more tightly against my wanton core. My other hand pressed to the wall of the garage behind me, desperate for some stability, finding none but that which was provided by my beloved.

Perhaps it was only the effect of our mating bond, but I always had the sense that Eleison was occupied in tasting me as much as giving me pleasure whenever he buried his face between my legs. It certainly seemed he loved exploring me with tongue and lips as much as with his cock, but there was something else about the way he applied his tongue: the long, slow, thoughtful strokes, the wicked tickling of its dexterous tip along the leaking channel that yearned to be filled and made me scream with joy—when these were paired with the intense red eyes that raised to my face to absorb my reaction, I not infrequently felt the animal in him, the borro in him, commanding his heart to its predatory ways. Especially when his teeth scraped tantalizingly along the aching mound of my clitoris, which sent a lightning bolt of pleasure streaking up into my frontal lobe.

"Eleison," I cried, squirming as his finger raised to penetrate me while his tongue found this new point of focus, "oh, darling, you're teasing me—"

"You're always teasing me, Thecla," he murmured against me, pressing soft kisses between wet laps of his expert tongue. Now watching his own fingers disappearing into me and sliding slowly back out, his eyes hooded with deep lust, he went on, "Every time you walk by me, when you look at me, when you smile at me... you're always teasing me, baby. Even when you don't mean to."

Groaning, I bantered back, "Can't a woman exist without you disgraceful men thinking your filthy thoughts?"

"Not you, Thecla...no, you can't. Every time we're in the same room, I'm fucking you in my soul, baby...and even when we're rooms away, territories apart. You were all I could think about during the Rift Event in Azstoria...thinking about you stretching your pussy with that dildo Malin gave you made my dick so hard I had no choice but let the borro go hunting."

While I groaned and shuddered, Eleison withdrew his fingers. He slipped out from under my thigh to rise to his feet, his great hand keeping my knee bent until I could wrap it around his waist. As the atmosphere around us enriched to the unearthly velvet tone of the descending Rift that made our bodies pulse with the wild energy of animal desperation, he pushed his trousers down to make me gasp with the sight of him. "Oh, magnificent," I moaned, reaching down to stroke that proud column of male glory he pressed against the delta of my thighs. While he exhaled my name, looking down at my hand and then up into my eyes, I shuddered to whisper, "I felt so awful and empty without you to take me during the Events here, oh, darling—I need your cock in me when the weather turns bad, I need you to pin me down and bury yourself to the hilt in me until not even the ventil I become can manage to walk—"

"That can be arranged," he growled, his teeth baring, then parting to emit a groan as I guided the tip of his girth against the well-prepared entrance of my body. "Oh, Thecla, Thecla, sweetie—fuck—"

Before I could even play-chastise him for his obscenity, Eleison yielded to his animal nature and stabbed himself into me so roughly I swear I went blind for a few delicious seconds of supreme euphoria. "Oh," I cried, my brow furrowing as I gripped his shoulders and arched against him, "oh, Eleison, yes, please— fuck, fuck me—"

One hand catching my face to force my mouth open for another, deeper kiss to match the thrusting of his cock, my savage mate pinned me tightly to the wall of the garage and split me open with that sword of passion. My voice caught in my throat, the pleasure almost shocking. He was so thick and—particularly in that moment—so exceptionally hard that he had the effect of leaving me too speechless to even participate in erotic banter. Especially with his gaze as piercing as his cock, his desire for me as palpable as mine for him—absorbing every least flutter of my love-flushed face, I felt so completely exposed to him that there was no need for words. I knew just what he meant when he said without the least trace of irony that his soul was perpetually laying claim to mine. I knew that for certain; knew that more and more each time our passion was actualized into this bodily union that was mere confirmation of the tightly entangled intimacy of spirit which bound us to one another for life.

"You're gorgeous," he murmured between kisses, his breath catching as he filled my ears the way he filled my eyes and body and soul. "Thecla, oh, baby, you're perfect, you feel so fucking good—you feel how your body was made just for mine?"

"Yes," I gasped, quivering in his arms, my pleasure sweetening as he ducked his head to kiss and nip the sensitive flesh of my breasts. "Yes, oh, Eleison, oh, the way you fill me, ah—"

A hard streak of pleasure brought on by the hammer of his prick into that yielding spot of internal ecstasy made me lose what short train of thought I had begun. While my body fluttered around his, he raised a hand to roughly pinch my nipple and grin into my face with a hint of sadistic pleasure.

"I love fucking you," he said with a dark chuckle. "You're so smart, Thecla, wise beyond your years—and then you get a cock in you and you turn into a brainless little bimbo for me, ah, all you want is to get fucked, huh, baby—"

"Yes," I gasped, my toes curling, my thighs tensing as I pressed myself more completely to him. With every hard slam into me, every split of his powerful cock into my sensitive core, a great wave gathered: and its intensity only grew as he teased me so meanly, picking on me like a bullying older boy making sport of the innocent girl I had been back in Lescaut. Shuddering, clutching him more closely, I sucked another sharp kiss from him and whimpered, "Eleison, yes, please, fuck my brains out, oh, yes, fuck me stupid and senseless so I can't think of anything but how I want to ride perfect cock—oh, Eleison, Eleison—"

"Fuck," he said with a laugh, his prick twitching all the harder inside me, "ah, baby, you're so fucking hot it makes me insane, you're such a cute little slut, ah, hell...you want to know a secret, baby?"

While I peered at him with hazy curiosity, he poured his love into our next kiss, then drew roughly back while his hips bore so heavily against mine I could feel our shared explosion was clearly imminent.

"I love that you're a dirty, cock-thirsty slut," he told me, the words a growl. "Even if I want to strangle the men who look at you, oh, baby...imagining you riding some fuckboy's dick just makes me want to remind you what a real cock is like."

"Eleison," I gasped, "oh, Eleison—oh, my darling, oh, don't worry—next time Malin cums in me without you around to watch, I'll be sure to tell you all about it."

Amid a snarl of animal pleasure, Eleison forced another savage kiss of his heavy tongue into my nearly screaming mouth— nearly screaming, because my words had increased the vigor of his strokes to a point of no return, the rapid pumping of his thick shaft impossible to disobey. At the command of his mighty sex, my own clenched in a sudden rush of mind-numbing pleasure, and the fluttering manipulations of my channel around him— combined with the furrow of my brow, the desperation of my eyes, the open mouth that shouted his name when he drew back from our kiss—brought him to his own quick, quite brutal end. Snarling my name, then choking it out a second time, he yielded to the call of passion and, in twitching little bursts of pleasure that seemed endless as they enhanced my own, released inside me.

While my taut womb was rocked with elongated waves of the powerful climax, I wrapped my arms around Eleison and sang his name like the perfect prayer that it was, each rapid kiss of his lips along my neck adding a few more bolts to the storm that rocked my nerves.

Then, like a flood ebbing away as abruptly as it came, the height of pleasure drained into an afterglow as rich as the violet light of the Rift-filtered sunset. Careful, so as not to hurt me, Eleison negotiated his way out of my body, his mouth once again laying tender claim to mine. The low growl of pleasure that rumbled from his breast took on a new, more urgent note, like that of a happy pet purring with pleasure for its long-absent mistress. Still kissing me, he drew me down into the soft grass with him, nuzzling against me, the purple of the atmosphere around him thickening to a dense glow of Rift radiation.

Twenty seconds later, the black, almost canine head of the borro rested sweetly upon my heart, its red eyes fixed plaintively on my face as I likewise succumbed to the pressure of my own yearning beast.

OF ALL THE MANY CHANGES I had undergone since Malin plucked me from Lescaut, perhaps the most incredible transformation was in my perspective on Rift Events. I still perceived them as potentially deadly instances of unnatural weather, for that was what they were, and there was no avoiding it, nor any wisdom in forgetting it; but they were no longer entirely evil to me, either. In fact, as my hooves clattered rapidly upon the earth, hastening after speedy Eleison's head start, the feeling of pure, innocent freedom I enjoyed was one I hadn't felt since the death of my poor father.

It was the awakening of the ventil that brought such liberty to me. Before its emergence, my sensitivity to the Rift—really, I suspect now, only a physical symptom of the ventil's strain to overtake me—had made every event a period of nauseous misery, when migraines would incapacitate me so thoroughly I could hardly stand to leave my boudoir let alone open a window and look upon the violet sky. Now, as Eleison and I galloped together through the forest around the Karris estate, my ventil's eyes were drawn perpetually up to the magnificent indigo expanse. The expanded twilight of summertime was even more wonderful when painted with the hues of the Rift, the pink light along the horizon fading up into the brilliant dark purple of night between the similarly radiant trees.

The whole world had changed since Malin had taken me into his life—and my place within it had shifted completely. All that had once been so hateful to me was now a side of life as worthy of revelry as had been the circus that captured my imagination as a girl. The joy each Rift Event now brought me equaled, if not outweighed, the dread with which they once filled my heart; and, since the ventil's development within and without me, Eleison seemed the same. Like a joyful puppy, my beloved's externalized Rift beast bounded through the woods ahead. His tails wagged, eagerly thrashing whenever he spun about and pranced backward a few feet to brag over his speed. It was always difficult to discern if borros were more feline or more canine, but in Eleison's joyful mood, my lover certainly exhibited far more traits of the latter. After letting me get close, he would dart off again, rushing through the trees and challenging me to catch up with a few teasing yelps.

It wasn't fair, really—had we been sprinting through, say, the open pastures where Kyrie's horses grazed and played until called upon to work, I would surely have overtaken him. Aside from the lengths of my ventil's legs and the aptitude its hooves had shown for terrain of all kinds, there was the simple fact that ventils had been forced to develop as capital runners if they wished to keep their lives in a universe where borros also existed—to say nothing of many other natural predators which populated the Rift's universe of reverse entropy. It may even have been that there were creatures about which we did not know, which the Rift, for whatever reason, did not manifest on Earth—who was to say what dangers lurked in that parallel dimension, that opposing space from which our beasts were derived? Ventils, therefore, were built for escape and survival, and for defense, as well: but that very rack of antlers which raised proudly from her head forced my manifested beast to slow her pace, to duck and weave through trees between which Eleison effortlessly slipped. I—we—snorted with jealousy every time that braggart would circle around a set of trees, tap me on the ankle, then go dashing off again with a yelp that was for all the world like a human's laugh; but I could hardly bear a grudge against Eleison's playful moods. After having been forced to spend so many Rift Events deeply serious, defending the Karris property and risking his own life by exposing himself to the Rift without a mate, the very least he deserved was to enjoy his time as a borro as he never had.

Besides: he was still fiercely protective of me, even when we were animals whose consciousnesses were only held in place owing to our proximity to one another. Had he wandered off and spent too much time by himself, he might have fancied himself a true borro and whiled away the whole Rift Event chasing down animals with real intent to kill. Instead, we skipped gaily through the rocks and trees, making our merry way to a particular destination that had been a happy discovery of ours but a few months before.

When the clearing opened ahead of us, I pressed myself into greater speed and made one final sprint. Still, he beat me, skidding from such a velocity that he actually rolled before springing upright to face me with a few glad barks and a playful wiggling of his three tails in the air. Huffing, bringing my front hooves down in the soft grass that grew around the lovely glass lake whose waters shimmered with the effects of Rift radiation, I shook my head and had my attention drawn by a flower that fell from my left antler. While its petals drifted to the ground, Eleison sat back on his haunches with a great, mirthful yawn that ended in a whine of amusement.

A little amused, myself, I decided to remind him of the one thing I could do that he could not: I became myself again, even while still under the veil of the Rift.

That was one of the so-called rewards of being second generation altered. My ability to transform myself was not bound to the weather, but simply to my will—preferably, my undistracted will. With a little focus, I could turn my ventil's stream of consciousness inward upon itself, its attention inverting from the animal concerns of the external environment and instead to the depths of an internal life that did not belong to it, as such. By contemplating this internal life that was so different from its external experience, the ventil would remember it was a human, and then remember it was Thecla, and then, there I would be, standing on human feet, capable of raising my hands before my eyes—then resting them upon my hips while Eleison's ears pinned back in annoyance.

"Ah," I teased him, "I see, you brat—so long as it's you who's the more talented one, you're satisfied. But the moment I demonstrate some skill in excess of yours, you pout!"

Ears and lips twitching in some sign of barely repressed amusement, the beast streaked his eyes over my naked body and wagged his tail with a little 'boof' of approval on his muzzle. Rolling my eyes, I strode to the waters of the lake while admonishing with a blush, "Don't be *lewd*, Eleison, for Heaven's sake...here I thought you were satisfied before we left."

His black-furred lips peeling back from his gums to flash a grin of his fangs, Eleison wiggled his ears as he normally would have his human eyebrows. "I will never be satisfied," he seemed to say, even as a speechless beast. Hiding my amusement with a few of Malin's tuts on my lips, I strolled over to tap him across the muzzle before continuing on to the waters of the lake in our private little clearing.

"So crass...well, just wait until the next Extreme Rift Event, when you'll be as much a human as a beast. You can take me however you like then, you brute...ah—"

A great sigh heaved from me to set foot in the warm waters that shimmered before us. That was the magic of this lovely lake: having been warmed by the sun all day, in the early hours of the evening it was of such a perfect, comforting temperature that one could not hesitate to spring right in and enjoy the liquid embrace. I hurried in, my muscles unbinding, my soul at absolute ease as I paddled into the deeper end of the waters to float around awhile.

This was our custom, a peaceful tradition we had come to enjoy, and which we were overjoyed to reinitiate so soon after his return home from his trip with Malin. While Eleison watched over me, as lulled by the sight of me as I was by the sight of a beautiful painting, or a bouquet of flowers, or the tranq features of one of my beloveds sleeping in my arms, I would float and swim and dive into the crystalline waves that lapped so gently across my body they seemed as waters from a dream. His head upon his paws, his red eyes drinking me in with purest love, Eleison's borro would take his turn to indulge in my nearness. Occasionally, he swam with me, paddling happily through the water and splashing me with his tails in a mockery of accident; but far more often, my transfigured darling would simply rest along the lake and listen for sign of danger while I enjoyed a peaceful evening away from the constant business in which I managed to engage myself while I was at home in the manor.

Oh, I may have criticized Eleison for sticking his nose into Kyrie's responsibilities...but the truth was I was becoming just as bad. It was owed, I had discerned, to a need to feel my existence was worthwhile—or worth more, anyway, than the existences of the courtiers who seemed to contribute nothing to the world but complaints about the weather and frankly appalling political slander they liked to call idle gossip. As a result, there were some days where I would stay busy from sun-up to sun-down, shadowing Malin at meetings to better understand his responsibilities, then practicing fighting with Eleison, then going for a horseback ride with Charlotte before spending a bit of time reading, letter-writing, even sometimes—just to fill a void in time—indulging in my own cooking. Then it would be time to see Rosina, before or after supper; and then was the visit to Glenn; and somewhere in there, Malin or Eleison or both at once would lay hold on me, and Dinon would bathe me, and Charlotte would talk to me, and my time would be requested for the amusement of the courtiers like Aleister and Kalypso—until, at last, I would collapse into heavy slumber, ready to spring out of bed and do it all again the following morning.

And in all of that—amid all those busy activities—my weaving was nowhere to be found.

The thought descended upon me with a gloomy twinge of

guilt. When would this period of awful negligence end? What was it that was holding me back from the only work I truly valued? The dharmine's passive aggressive consolation returned to me—*"You know your husband would love you if you never wove a tapestry again, Madame"*—and soured my mood. My swimming gliding to a stop, I floated on my back awhile, staring up at the clear violet sky that glittered with Rift-recolored stars. All the time, I was plagued with nagging frustration and cold panic to think I may have truly woven my last tapestry. Surely, it couldn't be.

Yet—somehow, I could hardly imagine myself working on a new one.

Unable to help my frown, I swam back to the shallows and waded from the water to drop into the grass at Eleison's side. He turned his head toward me as I draped myself upon him and buried my face in the fur of his back, wagging his tails with a combination of pleasure and concern.

"I miss weaving," I told him pitifully, feeling like a little child whose toy had been taken away. As his ears drooped in sympathy, I sat up and pushed my wet hair from my face. "Oh, Eleison— what's in the way of my work? I just don't understand it. It's like I've lost the taste for it somehow...but how? Why?"

My darling whined, his hefty head resting in my lap with his vibrant crimson eyes raising toward mine. Sighing, I stroked his head between his ears and gazed into the trees around us.

"See how cowardly I am about this? I can't even speak on this subject when you're able to reply...it's like something in me doesn't want to weave anymore, but I can't imagine why—and even that's nothing I would be able to admit to anyone but you."

Huffing slightly, soothed by my nearness as much as he was annoyed by his inability to reply, Eleison shut his eyes beneath the stroking of my hand. I would have always thought borro-fur to be terrifically coarse, but when he was relaxed in my arms like this, he was plush as a velvet pillow. It was a reflection of his inner nature, truly. Left to his own devices, Eleison was serious and deadly—the skillful monster slayer who saved Glenn's life at the Torea festival, then again by shooting down the dharmine at the game preserve and giving Malin time to place it under his influence.

But, soothed by me, Eleison opened his heart in a way he never could have otherwise. A sense of security descended upon him, making him surely more casual and easy-going than he had been since before Kyrie's illness.

Ah—yet how quickly that sense of ease could be shattered by his protective instincts!

The twitching of his ears was the first indication I had of anything amiss, several seconds before the footfall snapped a branch several yards from the tree line. Alerted head raising from my lap, Eleison lumbered to all four paws and let his ears pin flat. He scented the air, his nose turning back and forth before, satisfied he had the direction correct, he lowered his head beneath his arching back and, putting himself between me and the trees, released a low, dark growl.

The rustle of foliage reached my human ears seconds later. Tensing, pushing myself upright, I opened my mind to the control of the ventil as the dark shape of a man made itself clear through the woods.

Yet, before I could slip into the safety of my animal's skin, I recognized the face that emerged in the clearing, and I was so paralyzed I barely even thought of covering myself.

His was a face I had only seen one night in my life, and not for very long; yet, it was a night I had replayed endlessly, and a face I evoked more often than I would have preferred. The dark hair of his slightly unkempt moustache; the stringy limbs and somewhat wild eyes.

Everything about the man I had killed, had shot that fatal night in Glenn's Valquist home, was the same, save for one telling detail: he had two arms, with no trace of his amputation remaining.

While Eleison released an unnatural snarl and snapped his jaws in warning, my blood ran cold with comprehension that was delayed but a second. I had killed this man, I was certain: yet he stood before me here in Gudrune.

All three of us made moves at once, as though conducted by an invisible maestro charged with the workings of our bodies. While the dharmine, the undead rift beast that had come for vengeance on the one who took its earthly life, shot forward at unnatural speed, Eleison launched himself straight at the throat of the man-shaped demon. I, meanwhile, darted back, my arm folded over my breast, and attempted to call the ventil out of my heart once again.

The panic of the moment prevented it, or at least delayed it. While the beast had first emerged unconsciously, at a great height of stress, since it had made itself a natural part of my life I had found the change required some will; some measure of focus. It were as though the creature required the consent of my heart, and I could not narrow my attention enough amid the chaos to fully grant that openness to it.

I was therefore helpless while Eleison, snarling with rage, his great paws thrashing through the air to rake across the dead man's travel-worn clothes, defended me with his very life. As the heinously tainted blood of the demon oozed down its dusty shirt, it stumbled back a number of steps and lowered its defiled gaze down to the injury. After wondering at itself for a moment, it raised its eyes, and smiled.

Hateful fangs shone bright in its mouth, which configured into an animal hiss of its own as it threw itself upon Eleison with renewed vigor. While I cried out, the dharmine used unholy strength to wrestle my beloved to his back upon the ground, ignoring the brutal claws that Eleison used to tear at the demon's flesh. Only in retrospect did I realize that the borro was wise never to use his mouth, having been well-enough acquainted with blood sickness in his lifetime to know that any ingestion of a dharmine's blood was bound to bring it on. As intelligent as this strategy was, it handicapped my mate and made the fight a great deal more difficult than it needed be.

And, as the demon's gaping mouth and vile fangs lowered toward Eleison's furred neck while he struggled against the knee in his chest, it began to seem a futile effort.

Mind reeling, unable to relax myself into unity with the ventil, I looked around for a weapon and found little more than tree branches—and although I had heard legends that a dharmine could be killed by a stake to the heart as much as by beheading or by fire, these were certainly far from sharpened implements designed for second deaths.

Instead, palms clammy, I reached out to my own dharmine, which was—so it seemed—far less an animal than the feral one with his jaws closing in on my mate.

"Dinon," I cried, "come to me—help us, oh, don't let him die—"

Foliage rustled wildly, the undergrowth of the clearing's edge once again alive. My heart leapt with amazement: with relief. I spun, expecting my servant.

And instead, in a flash of sandy fur, with his own black claws extended like hooks, a luptich I had seen but twice pounced out of the trees and sank those claws so deeply into the back of the dharmine that I swore I caught a graphic glimpse of shining pink bone. With a howl, the demon whirled around and made a blind grab for its new opponent.

Eleison was up in an instant, raging, mouth foaming with the fury of his snarls. While the golden-eyed luptich deftly avoided the grip of the dharmine, the dark borro raised one mighty paw and smashed the back of the demon's head. With a hateful howl that made me cringe and cover my ears, the dead man—my dead victim!—stumbled back, tripping over a stone and careening dizzily down.

The beasts worked quickly, in an unspoken harmony that once again seemed choreographed. While the luptich pinned the dharmine down, the borro raked a great paw across the creature's throat and opened a gash so wide I, nauseous, squeezed shut my eyes and covered my face.

Sh, Madame, soothed the voice of Dinon, curling around my mind like a serpent coiling around a sun-warmed rock. *Be not afraid. This Rift-slave would have done far worse to you.*

I knew that—but I still could not help ascribing blame for this to myself, and could not stand to put a vision to the awful sounds of tearing flesh and popping tendons. The wailing of the demon, which had reduced to an uncanny wheeze with the opening of its throat, soon ceased altogether: the forest was blanketed in an eerie silence and something rolled across the grass, like a stone propelled by the momentum of a child's toss.

Peering just above my fingers to avoid seeing the headless body that now tainted our pleasant little oasis, I watched Eleison's Rift beast straighten up and turn to regard its savior.

Glenn's luptich, with a leonine rumble, returned his stare for a few long seconds, then glanced at me.

Without another sound, the interloping beast dashed back into the trees and was gone.

THE HORROR OF WHAT we had endured was too great for me, and Eleison knew it without the least need of language. Lowering himself before me, my mate's borro encouraged me to mount his back, and I clung to the creature's body with my face buried in thick black fur as he bore me through the trees back to the Karris house.

A kind of delirious disbelief overwhelmed me as we made our way back home. Until that hour, Dinon had been the only dharmine upon which I had ever set eye—outside, anyway, of the strange dream I had while on my honeymoon with Malin. But that, I was sure, had only ever been some symbol provoked by the rumors of my husband's reputation. In waking life, dharmines were exceedingly rare. Not even the one which took the life of my father had made itself known to me; and, so far as Dinon went, I was increasingly unconvinced that he was a simple dharmine in any sense the word was usually meant, even if he thrived on blood and flesh and sex as those lesser demons did. There was far more to him than the animation of a corpse.

But had there not also been more to that dead veteran, the resurrected man I'd shot with my own hand well over a year before? Had there not been a light, true knowledge in his eyes? In movement and drives, he was animal, perhaps; a Rift beast the same as any other.

Yet the awful doppelgänger of a man buried in Valquist had known, consciously or not, to find me in Gudrune. If it was indeed the dharmine rumored to be lurking in the area, it had been wise enough to pose as a traveler to gain distance and keep itself sated and strong on the road.

It—he—had been coming to kill me with the murderous intentions of a knowingly vengeful man. A human being.

And the ideas that lay behind that thought made me sicker than had the sounds of his beheading at the digging claws of Eleison.

It was one thing to kill a man and be quietly haunted by it—to shut one's eyes and, even if only occasionally, experience the drifting of his shocked face across one's contemplation. But the thought that such a man might know, in a fully aware way, that I had been the one to kill him—to snuff the life that had been in him since his time at his mother's breast! Now that was true horror to me: a true shame.

There was a greater shame, though. The shame that I had, weak as a kitten, been unable to do anything to assist Eleison in his time of need. He had been able and ready to defend me: yet, when he was pinned and in grave danger, I had not even been able to submit to the animal which yearned so frequently to emerge from its human host. Mere yearning was not enough. Action was required, and I had been unable to take that action just as I had for so many months been unable to weave.

By the time we reached the property and I felt Eleison's borro heave a low sigh of relief to recognize the thinning trees, my own frustration had increased to a humiliated peak. Why was I like this? How was it that, in a world full of competent, strong people, I seemed wholly dependent upon all those around me? Why was it that, in a great emergency, I was lucky if I could contribute the least act that might serve my loved ones as they served me? I ought to have been doubly gifted, competent twice over—I was not just second-generation altered, but Riftborn, too. For that matter, so was my child.

Yet would she, like me, grow up to seem powerless? Would she reach near her thirties and still have no sign of those uncanny abilities for which Riftborn were known? The fortune-teller, who had once shown me Eleison; Vivian, that ugly-hearted woman who could enslave altered individuals to her will as if they had been converted to service of the Rift by years of destabilized exposure to its radiation; Malin, who held instinctive sway over Rift beasts as dangerous as Dinon. There seemed no discernable pattern to the powers of the Riftborn, and no way to guess how or when such gifts would manifest, if ever. It was worse, far worse, than waiting for the beast within my heart to awaken. At least once I learned I was altered I could prepare myself somewhat for the eventual transformation, inasmuch as anyone could ever be prepared.

But how could I prepare myself for the emergence of whatever charism the Rift had awarded me on my birth? Moreover—how could I wait patiently for it when I felt so impotent otherwise?

"I'm sorry, darling," I said as Eleison, discreetly bearing me back to the garage out of sight of the patrolling officers of our estate, lowered himself to the ground to allow me to dismount. Home again, my clothes and his piled where we left them, I felt the shock at last ebb away to leave me overwrought with tears. While the borro's tall ears twitched in a combination of confusion of sympathy, I threw my arms around his neck and, weeping, kissed him. "Oh, thank you. Thank you for saving me again and again, but I— I wish you didn't have to, oh, Eleison—"

I sobbed, utterly wretched in that moment, the emotion of having escaped with my life and his intermingling with my feeling of uselessness. Amid a soft whine, he turned to nuzzle his great head against the side of my face, his wet nose nudging my cheek and into my hair. As his tails wagged consolingly, I took a great breath and swallowed my grief.

"If you could speak right now," I told him, sitting up to wipe my face before turning to put on what of my clothes I could don without assistance, "I suppose you would remind me of that time with that hideous little doctor and that evil Vivian woman, and how my nearness helped you recover from her mesmerism—"

"Boof," responded Eleison agreeably, his lips pulling back from his teeth as though to humorously indicate that was exactly what he would say.

"But can't you see how little that is? Can't you feel how much more I owe you? And Malin, too—how could I ever begin to protect him if we were in danger again? Oh, don't look at me like that—" I swear, the beast had managed to cock his brow as if half-amused. "You can hardly say I really had anything to do with saving Malin that time. If it weren't for Dinon following me to the warehouse—*carrying* me there, no less!—I never could have done anything. Eleison, oh, my darling—"

Jaw tensed, I let my hands drop from their contortion to the back of my bodice and stared uselessly down at my own half-open gown.

"I can't even *dress* myself these days," I told him with dark annoyance. "I'm just so frustrated—don't you see you deserve someone as capable of caring for you as you are of caring for her? Can't you see how much better I'd ought to be?"

When no animal bark responded, I turned and peered through the violet dark to find the borro staring up at me with absolute tenderness.

"You're already perfect to me," I felt Eleison say in my heart, the words communicated through the beast so clearly I couldn't help but look away with a new wave of tears.

"I wish I could see myself the way you see me, Eleison," I told him, feeling and sounding tired. As I stooped to stroke his face, his tails wagged, and I smiled despite myself. "Perhaps, once I'm more used to this business of being altered, I'll have an easier time transforming at will. The Overseer seemed perfectly capable of it, after all, since she's had decades of practice..."

The frustration and urgency of the moment creeping upon me again, I gnawed lightly on my lower lip. "At least we won't have to tell Malin about this until tomorrow, late as it is...maybe you'd better let me talk to him, darling—I don't want him winding you up so neither of you let me leave the blasted house again... don't look so intrigued by that thought." As the borro made a noise like a laugh, I smirked. "I suppose you'll patrol the grounds like old times, since you can hardly help yourself..."

Eleison's snort of confirmation made me shake my head in amusement. "Well," I told him, "just be careful...and if you run into Glenn, now or at the end of the Rift Event..." My lip tucking between my teeth, I said softly, "Express our—my gratitude to him, please, darling."

With a light bark of agreement and a lick of my hand, Eleison turned tails and galloped off to search out his brother.

The manor was dimmed for the night as I entered it through its one unshuttered entrance, all the windows and doors except this one side exit through the kitchens covered to weather the Event. Glad to find nobody around within its halls, all the staff who had been trained to fight or hunt out on the grounds while the household stole what sleep they were capable of, I held my skirts up to climb the stairs and made my exhausted way toward the master apartment, though it was not my destination. Rather, I was intent on the suite that had once been mine—had once been filled with flowers and haunted by hawkish Malin, who lurked upon the other side of a conjoining bookshelf's hidden door and ached with longing for me until neither could resist the other.

Now, with the transference of the estate's ownership to Eleison, that suite was Malin's; and, much to my surprise, the door's bottom gap glowed softly with a still-lit lamp. A remonstration already on my lips for my husband's unusually late hours, I extended a hand toward the door handle, then froze midway to hear his voice, soft and unintelligible, from within.

My ears strained. Holding my breath, I leaned toward the door and turned my ear toward it. It was not that I mistrusted my husband, or that I was particularly prone to eavesdropping—but it was very strange for him to be up at midnight, let alone up at midnight talking to anyone.

Let alone to be up at midnight talking to Dinon, whose soft, placid response was equally unclear to even my close listening.

My heart sank. So, Dinon was already telling Malin about the incident in the woods? That would explain why he wasn't lurking around the garage, ready to dress me and accompany me back to the house. Well...I supposed that would make it somewhat easier to speak to Malin about the issue; and, knowing Dinon's talent for diplomacy, perhaps he had been able to smooth the incident out a bit for Malin's mind.

With a deep breath, prepared for a lecture, I knocked upon the door and heard Dinon say at a slightly louder volume, "That would be her, Master."

"Oh—come in." Malin's call sounded pleasantly surprised. As I turned the knob and let myself into the suite, my husband already strode toward me, his dressing gown swirling about his feet with the fast pace of his movements. "Darling," he said, his tone softer now, his glad eyes streaking over my disheveled dress, "I wasn't expecting you back at all tonight. Is anything the matter?"

Even as I smiled, I flicked a brief glance toward Dinon's knowing scrutiny; then, focused completely upon my husband, I poured myself into his arms and offered him my mouth. "It was fine," I lied, immediately ashamed of my dishonesty and telling myself I would reveal the truth tomorrow, after my husband had been given a chance to sleep a bit. "Fine, just—Eleison seemed to want to patrol the grounds. What of you, though?"

My hand raised to fit along the side of his face. At the contact, Malin's eyes closed and his lips parted in relief. "You're never up so late," I observed, reflecting on his rigorous schedule. "Are you all right?"

"Now that you're here, Thecla, I'm better than all right...you are dismissed, Dinon."

Bowing at the waist, that feline smile still in place upon his delicate lips, Dinon said with lowered eyes, "I will see you tomorrow morning, Madame."

Then, slipping past us and engaging in the charade of using the door like a normal person, Dinon left me alone with my husband.

"Now," I told Malin at once, as his hands slid up my arms and, reaching my shoulders, did not hesitate to push away my loose gown and all that lay beneath, "darling, why are you up? Please don't say it's because of me."

"No," he said, perhaps a little quickly, sweeping his dark eyes over my revealed flesh as he worked to reveal more. "No," Malin repeated, now taking his time to undress me. "I know Eleison will keep you safe, whatever happens...Thecla, oh...I can never tell you enough how beautiful you are."

Drawing me close to his chest, Malin bent his head to kiss his way along my throat. I moaned gently and tilted back my head to give him access, my hands running through his short hair and tickling over his scalp.

"You won't distract me, you wicked old rogue," I told him between the sighs his kisses inspired. "What has you so alarmed you would be conferring with the dharmine at well past midnight?"

"Mm...just feeling my age without you in my bed. Ah, Thecla..." As his hand raised to gently cup my breast, his thumb toying over my hardening nipple to make us both sigh low with desire, Malin raised his head enough to nibble my earlobe. "Make me a young man again, my bride...hold me in your arms awhile."

Though once I would have been annoyed by his omission, my heart ached to see again that same heaviness that had been on his mind at dinner. Owing to that and my own decision to omit some truth of the night, I caressed his brow, then told him, "Come on, Malin...let me hold you awhile."

I snuffed the lights around us, then in the new darkness stripped my husband's robe from his shoulders and found him nude beneath. His body was always so warm, so powerful despite his age; yet, that night, there was a curious kind of needfulness about him. The vulnerability of a boy seeking comfort, as though I were the one thirty years his senior and not the other way around. Frowning, I stroked my fingers along his back and let him rest in the silence of my body, hoping he might doze off and find thorough sleep when left alone with the contents of his thoughts.

Instead, he said, "You are so young, Thecla, that I can only pray the answer is 'no'...but I know you so well by now that I suspect the truth is the opposite. Have you thought much about what happens after death?"

"Such a dour mood, my husband." My hand folded over his head as I bent to kiss his brow. "Yes," I confessed, having been brooding over related matters myself that very night. "Yes, I have thought of it often. After Rigel died, it preoccupied me."

"The loss of a father will do that...the loss of any parent. What do you think about it, darling?"

Laughing softly, I said, "Surely you've had more time to think on it than I have, my beloved."

"Yet we are each as likely to come up with the proper answer, considering neither of us has experienced it."

Suitably rebuffed, I stared at the ceiling. "I suppose that's true. Well...while I can hardly know anything at all..." My eyes narrowed. "I've always had the impression that death is—an illusion, in some ways."

"Now that's interesting."

"Well, I don't know. When my father was teaching me about God, that was what he said, more or less. I was very young, so I may have misunderstood him. But—I remember when he was still alive, he described to me several times the concept of eternity; and I wondered quite a lot over how anything could be eternal, until I took up weaving." With a sting of longing for my absent artform, I glanced down at Malin to meet, through the dark, the assessing eyes he had raised to me. "Tapestries make me think of spacetime; you can tell an entire story upon one, you know, representing countless different locations and countless different times on one great textile."

"They do call spacetime a fabric, don't they," Malin mused while I went on.

"Yes, that's quite right. So it seems to me that, if one could pull one's mind entirely back, back, away from all space and time, and perhaps experience the way something like the Holy Spirit my father described sees that eternity, all of space and time would fit into a single unit. A single tapestry. The way early space explorers were able to view Earth as the perfect globe it is, perhaps our traveling souls will in death behold the completed tapestry of linear time in which we have heretofore participated. So we are already in eternity, by that measure, although it seems we are subject to time; really, what we know as time is, I suppose, an imaginary byproduct of eternity. A way of unfolding and unpacking it and consciously comprehending it when we are within it. Perhaps a book would be an even clearer metaphor...when we read, each page is already part of a finished volume no matter how uncertain the action seems, and each second of time is, in the same way, part of eternity. So, if that's true—"

I hesitated, never having given clear voice to this thought before: but Malin was gazing at me in such fascination that I knew he would not reject the thought out-of-hand, as so many—even Eleison or Glenn—might.

"If it's true that we're already in eternity," I summarized with a shrug, "then there really can't be such a thing as death, can there? At least, not internally. Externally, it may seem to be... but the threads woven through the characters of my tapestries often continue great lengths through the work. And, metaphors aside—" Somewhat shyly, I smiled. "I have always thought— perhaps somewhat illogically—that I cannot remember my birth, or any definite start to my life at all; I cannot remember non-existence. Therefore, in my illogic, it seems to me illogical, in a way I cannot really explain, that non-existence is a state that even exists. The human experience, even that which seems present, is dependent on memory; in fact, I sometimes wonder if I am not something else, some other being entirely, remembering Thecla, rather than Thecla in the present experiencing her own life."

Dinon's eyes flashed through the center of my mind and sent a strange chill rolling along my cheeks. Meanwhile, Malin lowered his gaze with a look of intense contemplation. "That is a fascinating thought," he said after a few seconds of letting it settle on him. "Is that the soul, do you suppose, Thecla?"

With a laugh I couldn't help, I spread my free hand from the bosom where it lay and confessed helplessly, "I suspect I know even less about the concept of the soul than I do about eternity. Is it the true me? Or is my soul perhaps the threads making me up? Is it, yes, that remembering entity who is remembering me?"

"Perhaps the Lord is the one remembering," Malin posited.

"Perhaps," I agreed. "That is all that makes sense, ultimately. It makes more sense than the idea that I am remembering myself."

Quieted by these heavy contemplations, Malin rested his head upon my heart again, but he did not close his eyes. Fingers curling into his gray hair, I softly begged, "What is it that has you ruminating on such profound thoughts, my love?" I hesitated for a second before I dared to venture, "Is it the effort to conceive?"

"Perhaps," Malin allowed, his eyes sliding shut. "I won't pretend that it isn't on my mind, at any rate."

I tilted his head back up so he opened his eyes and looked into my face. "I know it will happen, Malin," I told him, meaning every word. "I feel it in my heart more clearly than I feel anything, anything in this world: I will have your child. Don't you feel it, too?"

Stirred, he murmured, "Yes," in a tone so hushed I would hardly have detected the word if not for the movement of his lips.

"Then I know it's true." Bolstered, smiling no matter the solemn subjects we discussed, I bent my head to press my mouth to his. Malin sighed into our kiss, his lips opening, his tongue meeting mine as he allowed me to take command and penetrate his mouth the way he so often claimed mine. After letting him feel my undying hunger for him, I drew back to whisper gently, "We'll just have to keep trying. Perhaps, if you feel very pressured, we might let science help us—there are fertility doctors in Saalast, certainly."

"Oh, many." He added with a chuckle as he raised a hand to stroke my hair, "I'm glad your experience with Dr. Gall didn't sully your view of modern medicine."

Nose wrinkling, I said, "Perhaps it would have, if he had any resemblance to an actual doctor..." As Malin laughed a little harder, his truly good humor returning to leave his mouth in a soft, wonderfully handsome smile even once his laughter faded, I brushed my nose over his. "But regardless—with or without help, however it will happen...I know, Malin." Pouring my love into his eyes, I let him feel the intensity of my words. "As I know the sky is blue when the Rift fades away, and as I know you are master of Gudrune, and as I know I am your wife now and forever— so I also know, my love, that I will bear your child. Yes—Malin Farrow's firstborn child will be delivered from this womb."

I caught his hand and pressed it to the bare flesh of my abdomen, the word and the contact making him inhale with a growing expression of male appetite. "You'll see soon," I swore to him. "We both will."

With a playful arch to his brow, Malin slid his hand from mine to caress a little lower. "Have you been inquiring with your pet, Thecla? I thought you opposed to its prophecies."

"I am." The brush of his fingertips produced a gasp from the bottoms of my lungs. "But neither do I need its prophecies to know with certainty what my heart—perhaps my soul—tells me every time you hold me in your arms."

Moved as much as aroused, my husband pushed himself up to clamp his skillful mouth upon mine. When his ministrations had combined with his powerful kiss to elicit my low moan, he drew away enough to tell me, that diabolical libertine's light twinkling in his dark gaze, "Well, angel, I must confess...you certainly make the effort its own reward."

10

THAT NIGHT, WHEN MALIN and I collapsed into deep slumber in one another's arms, I dreamed of the Black Loom for the first time in months—perhaps in a year, or more.

How long it had been—yet, how natural it was to me (or to my dream-self, at least) when I set eyes upon the familiar object only faintly distinguished from the void of space around it! The fuligin threads were exactly as I remembered them, still at the precise point in which I had left the textile whose template sat in the back of my mind even as I seated myself upon the little bench. Most wonderfully, in spite of how neglected my terrestrial loom had been, as soon as my hands touched the shuttle, my brain sparked awake in the familiar way for which I had so deeply pined. Without the slightest external impetus, I flew to work, the brocaded fabric of the ultra-black cloth manifesting beneath this collaboration of my body and the smoothly operating device.

What was I crafting? Even in the dream, I wondered. I knew the dark textile seemed familiar somehow, as though I had seen it with my own two waking eyes, and perhaps even more than once. Yet I could not seem to put a name or place to it. A curtain, perhaps, somewhere in Malin's Saalast home? Or a blanket being picnicked upon at the Torea Festival where first I set eyes on Glenn?

No—neither of those were right. Still: whatever it was, the weaving of this object seemed necessary. As vital as if I were weaving the fabric of spacetime Malin and I had been discussing before—

Before I fell asleep.

My head jerked upright from the loom and it suddenly occurred to me so distinctly I said it out loud, laughing as I did: "Why, I'm dreaming!"

It was not the first time I had caught myself dreaming, though it was the first time such a realization did not at once thrust me straight out of the dream and into a new one. Indeed, it were as though the Black Loom was too real to permit it: as though it had its own center of gravity, its own tangibility, no matter how real it was or wasn't when I would eventually awaken in my bed.

Therefore, excited to be so self-aware and supported by this anchor, I peered up and around the space, my heart racing. I could do anything, if this really were a dream. I could fly—I could make myself a queen. I could—

I could make love to Malin, I thought with a coy expression, having looked up and discovered him in the strange, reflectionless mirror before me.

As soon as my attention was pulled out of myself, the dream mesmerized me again. I forgot all about my dreaming. Instead, under my husband's spell, I perked to see him on the other side of the strange looking glass where I recalled seeing Glenn some time before. Neither I nor the Loom appeared, yet I maintained the stubborn sense that this vast plane was a reflective surface. Perhaps it was a window, I contemplated as my eyes met my husband's. I rose from my seat to ask him about it, suddenly worried he was trapped upon its other side.

As I took a few steps, he smiled. Something about that smile frightened me. It was not an unattractive smile by any means—far from it. Yet there was something about his expression, perhaps the mirthful humor in his eyes: it made me realize that this man in the mirror, this Malin, was at once my husband...and not my husband. What could explain that impression? What metaphor could I draw to make sense of it? It seemed for all the world as though I beheld an actor embodying the character of my husband. That the spirit was there, but the true reality of his being was somehow flawed—corrupted, like an RMS message broken up by electrical interference from the Rift.

Tongue darting across my lips, I frowned and began to ask, "Who are you?"

Before the question could fully form, its third word still clinging to my lips, a heavy hand dropped upon my shoulder.

I turned—and there, behind me, unscarred, his usually dark eyes shining like quicksilver, stood my true husband.

And no matter how handsome and sophisticated—somehow youthful!—he appeared in that instant, I was overwhelmed by fear of him.

With a jolt so sharp I was amazed I did not awaken Malin as he slept beside me, I stirred in bed and found myself, after a few heart-racing seconds, awake in the suite where we'd fallen asleep. With a long, slow breath, I looked down at my husband's sleeping face—his shut eyes, his parted lips, his facial scar—and soothed myself.

Just a queer dream. Brought on by the dharmine, perhaps: it must have stirred in my subconscious some memories of the dream from the honeymoon, whose motifs repeated themselves for my stress-plagued mind.

Yet, the dream had brought more than stress. I was now left with very real longing. How I wished I had been actually weaving! How I wished that the textile at which I'd been so hard at work was available for my hands to touch, for my eyes to see. Already, my sense of it faded so completely that I knew I had no hope of recalling where I had seen it before: only that I was now more certain than ever that I had, in fact, seen it in its completed form.

There was nothing to be done about it, of course. The stuff of dreams were the stuff of dreams and little more. Yet—there were those dreams that gave us the strength to do what we could not on our own. And that dream, which had filled me with longing for my weaving, had been given to me for a distinct purpose.

Sitting up completely, I bent to kiss Malin's ear. Now he did stir, just slightly, as a man who clearly desired more sleep. "I'm going to weave," I told my husband, who made a pleased hum and turned his face more fully into the pillow.

"Now that's nice," he said, adding, "have fun, my little artist...see you at breakfast?"

"If I can tear myself away," I said, fetching a robe to make my way to my weaving room before the taste for work left my mouth.

In the privacy of my workroom, where the lights made me cringe at the dust which had settled over my work in progress, I used a handkerchief to wipe away all signs of negligence while reviewing the tapestry to the point where I had left it. How many such works had I completed by that point in time? Six, perhaps? The one sitting half-finished in the loom was the 7th, then—yes, seven tapestries, all of them woven for Malin's pleasure, all of them depicting pivotal scenes in our favorite play of treachery and murder. I created them not in chronological order but whatever order inspiration commanded me to, and at the time, I had suspected I lost interest in this one because there was nothing especially inspirational about it—at least, not to me. It dealt with a scene near the end of the play, when the scheming lady of the house endured the development of her guilty conscience into the habit of sleepwalking, wherein she would repeat key details of her scheming with her murderous husband and would fancy herself incapable of washing the dead king's blood from her stained hands.

In my tapestries, the genders of these characters had been reversed for reasons of style and personal interpretation; and I could not work the tapestry without contemplating the dreadful fate of the character depicted. The insidious spouse of our title character was soon to die—either of madness or suicide, depending on the director's interpretation.

It was too ugly to think about. That was the reason I did not want overmuch to proceed: the story no longer appealed to me. No reason else.

Yet...was there not some queer thematic link between the flow of my life and the completions of these various tapestries? Perhaps it only seemed as such since I often allowed my life to inspire the subject matter and themes; yet, as I sat at my loom and stared down the figure desperately washing his hands beneath the oversight of the dharmine-inspired witch, I could not help my sense of faint anxiety.

Pure superstition. Pure projection, only. More excuses being made to avoid the hard work of starting where I had left off, which always seemed so much more forbidding than starting a brand-new piece.

And so, as I pushed through the resistance and my loom creaked into motion, lurching back and forth with the working of my feet, I felt more myself than I had in months. The warm feeling the dream of the Black Loom inspired in my mind and heart now filled my soul, and my hands fell into work so quickly that, by the end of the first hour, it seemed as though I had never taken any break at all.

"Isn't that better, Madame?"

Who could tell how long Dinon had been watching me work? I had the sense that, the entire time, he had been standing behind me in perfect silence, his eyes fixed upon some portion of my mind it gave him pleasure to observe. "It *will* feel better," I corrected, continuing my work, "once this piece is done and I can begin another at my leisure."

"There is so much more to it than that, Madame." My servant's skillful hands gathered my hair back from my face, his fingers combing through the strands and grazing down the back of my neck. "Can't you see? All your needs are met by God through your weaving. Even when you were a girl weaving textiles for others...they kept you afloat. They brought you to your husband when the world wished to hide you from him."

I did often wonder what might have happened to me if the Parsons' textile factory had not been bought by some highfalutin investor eager to modernize and rectify the system by which Mrs. Parson had handled her taxes. Would Malin ever have discovered I hadn't run away as he'd been told? Would I have simply gone on to live a bland life as a peasant girl in Lescaut, barely scraping by until I found a man I could deign to wed? And what of Malin then—what would his life have resembled? The idea of Malin's life without me made me even sadder than the idea of my life without him—without Eleison, without Glenn. Even without Dinon.

"You flatter me, Madame."

"You're an eavesdropping hound," I reprimanded him lightly, resolutely not looking over as, with a chuckle, he opened the shutter to of the window to my left to reveal a dawn free of the Rift's violet pollution. "Speaking of eavesdropping"—I paused my work to fix him with my gaze—"just what was my husband discussing with you last night?"

"I must respect Master's privacy as I respect yours, Madame," said Dinon very lightly. "What he asks me to keep in confidence, I must honor."

"Is a woman not one flesh with her husband?"

"Two hearts beating as one, it's true; but when a third heart beats between them, I cannot risk revealing what I know for fear that one might stop."

Who knew what the devil he was talking about? My mind fluttered through a few possibilities—Eleison? A child who had been conceived but not yet discovered?—and Dinon smiled on, enjoying every second of my speculation. "Stop that," I told him harshly, turning in my seat to face him completely. "How tiresome you are, Dinon! You refuse to speak clearly on any matter, while at the same time helping yourself to my thoughts like a vineyard's manager helping himself to his master's grapes. You're a dreadful servant; a terrible slave."

His affect changed in an instant, as I had never seen it change before; brow furrowing, lips parting, Dinon genuflected before me, begging, "Pray, Madame, insult me in any way other than that. Let me be your mongrel, your wretch—but, when you call me your slave, call me only your good slave."

Scoffing in disgust, I glanced askance to hide my pleasure at his kneeling. "You fear my husband, and that's why the issue is of import to you; were it not for that, you would thrill to be called a disobedient, shameful excuse for property."

With a truly sad little moan, as though I stabbed him in the heart with each word, Dinon made me jump by clutching the leg that extended from the folds of my robe to cross over the other. "You mistake me, Madame," he said softly, his tone more earnest than I had heard it since the night he found me tormented by my headache in the Rift. His eyes raising to my face, then lowering to the slipper he worked free of my foot, Dinon said reverently, "It is my love for you that makes me crave to be obedient to you: to be a good slave to you. Perhaps I took some small advantage of you before Malin bound me formally to your service in this linear stretch of time...but"—he bent, the silver braid of his hair slipping down his shoulder like a glittering waterfall as he lowered toward my exposed foot—"now, remembering better and better all the time your beauty, your power, your wonder...now, Madame, I am embarrassed by myself."

His cool lips, soft and gentle, pressed against the top of my foot. I exhaled, watching him while he murmured against my flesh, "But that is the way of things—the nature of time, and our roles within it. When I come to find you, Madame, I forget everything but my longing for you." Carefully rotating my ankle, he bent lower to apply his mouth to the arch of my foot, and now I could not help but sigh. "I do not forget you—I can never forget you, not ever. Nor would I want to. You are all I think about, Thecla—Madame."

His eyes fell shut as if the simple act of debasing himself by nuzzling my foot was more pleasure than he could bear. "Yet," he went on, each graze of his lip along my sensitive flesh another surprising circuit of pleasure that ran to my groin and on to the center of my soul, "I do always forget the original nature of our relationship, since, by the moment of my entry into time, we have come so far...so far, Madame, oh—" With a shudder of intense pleasure, his eyes opened. He dared raise them to meet mine.

"I can't wait. Oh, Madame...no, I can never wait."

Overcome by a shudder of my own, I studied Dinon for a few long seconds before raising my foot to grind my instep along his softly groaning face. Pushing my toes against his mouth and forcing him to suck them much as I fellated my lovers, I let him see the dark pleasure in my face while telling him, "If you mean to imply that I'll let you into my bed someday, Dinon, perhaps that was the weakness of some old iteration—some far more foolish version of me. But I assure you, such a thing will never happen here."

"Oh, Madame." Twisting his face just slightly to speak, letting my foot remain against his cheek, Dinon slid his hand from my ankle and caressed my calf. He then took the liberty of exposing my thigh by pushing his fingertips up a few inches further, nudging aside the fabric of my robe. "Madame...you say that every time. And every time, the inevitability is my sweetest ecstasy."

My foot naturally slid from his face and came to rest upon his shoulder, my knee bent while his eyes unapologetically fixed on the apex of my revealed thigh. While I let him look, I asked myself if I really wanted to know—but I could not resist my own curiosity, which was why I so frequently commanded him to silence his prophetic tongue before he could tantalize me into an error.

An error such as the one I made when I asked before I could stop myself, "How many times is 'every time,' Dinon?"

"More times than even I could ever hope to count," he whispered, a chill rolling through me as his gaze raised toward mine again. While I inhaled softly, he looked into my face with his own transfigured by the expression of a dreamer: the soft, wonderous love of one who was quite literally entranced by the vision before them. "'Forever' means the future and the past…'forever' means *forever*, Madame. And I love you forever, and ever, and ever."

It were as though his words had provoked in me a flu: and these chills increased as he gazed up at me with his hand still poised upon the underside of my thigh, his fingertip within millimeters of my aching sex.

"You haven't fed me properly for days," he reminded me, looking into my very soul, his desires in excess of even Malin's libertine cravings.

Nostrils lightly flaring in a combination of amusement and annoyance, I flicked a glance at the door, then coaxed him with a finger. "Come give Madame a kiss, then," I bade Dinon, reaching down to cup his chin in my hand and draw him closer to my mouth. "I suppose, as slaves go—even when you are not obedient— you are still quite a desirable slave. And that is something to be commended."

From the center of his diaphragm sounded the great motor of an uncanny purr; an expression of the true pleasure my patronizing adulation provided him, perhaps made more so by its condescension. "Thank you, Madame," Dinon murmured, his lips brushing mine with sensual contemplation. "Let me be a loyal slave to you for all my days, O Beauty, O Radiance…let me indulge in that exquisite mind you share with me, ah—forever…"

I shuddered, my mouth opening to allow the slide of his tongue into my mouth, his nearness as he pressed to my body so intense I soon succumbed to my own heat. Lifting my hands to the dharmine's face, I yielded more thoroughly than sense ought to have permitted: after a few seconds, the experimental brushing of our lips had opened fully to the deeper explorations of his tongue, the impudent slave stealing into his mistress's mouth and plundering the pleasure on which he thrived.

There was no denying it...the kisses of the dharmine were pleasure itself. If I had any reason to doubt its frightful use of the word 'forever', that doubt would have been most consistently abated by its kiss. The demon knew which pleasures were sweetest to me, as the slave of forty years knows better than his own master how to prepare breakfast and bath and bed linens to suit his lord's needs. In such fashion, Dinon stroked my tongue with his, marking himself my equal—perhaps even, audaciously, my superior—with the way his bold mouth lit my body aflame. "Madame," he murmured into my mouth, breathing deep from my lungs as though intoxicated by some drug's sweet smoke. "Ah—Madame, your body aches, won't you let your slave give you some comfort..."

While one hand remained beneath my thigh, a narrow gap of flesh the only barrier between his fingertip and the heat of a raging furnace, his other hand slid into my robe to caress along my breast. Reason overshadowed by the unruly demon and the pleasure he brought, I lost myself in his kiss; in his hand.

"You're too bold, Dinon," I moaned while his kisses migrated to my ear, where I felt the barest scrape of an experimental pressure. A sharp fang had glided from his gums and now craved my flesh as any dharmine would. "Yes, slave, too bold to touch your mistress thus, oh—"

"Then I swear not to touch you," he murmured, withdrawing his hand but slowly, "until it be your command that I do."

"You truly will have to wait forever before I make such a mistake."

My body throbbed even without the intercession of his hand. Once, in the privacy of this very workroom, he had come upon me, incorporeal, and had subjected my flesh to all manner of ecstatic caresses without hands, let alone the need to slide them under my clothes. Now, he did not even need to overwhelm me with the fancy of some phantom touch. Instead, simply holding my thigh and kissing my neck, the dharmine flooded me from top to bottom with such an intense bliss that I gasped. His fingers tightened against my thigh, squeezing me while, as though one of my lovers took me that very instant, my body clenched and the fire in my aching womb increased in its hot fervor.

"Dinon—blast it, how do you perform these feats—"

"As you yourself just thought, my mistress, oh, Madame...I know your body." He leaned back, his vibrant silver eyes— glittering newly with his glutton's feast of my erotic enjoyment— flickered along my open robe and to my splayed thighs. One heel digging into the floor, the other into his back, I gripped my seat and found my body responded like that of a woman possessed. Every muscle in my legs and abdomen felt like a coiling spring; and, like a spring of an altogether different sort, the cleft between my thighs freely flowed.

This was a dangerous game. The deeper my pleasure, the more intense my ache; and the more intense my ache, the more I always found myself willing to eschew prudence and say anything, do anything, promise anything to ease that ache with the powerful relief of a man's cock. That had been partly why things happened as they had with Glenn, who had been too much a gentleman to take advantage of my drunken improprieties during my first night staying in his home. He had more than made up for that gentlemanly nature before long; but I had little doubt that, had my own infernal lust not laid the groundwork, our attraction may not have escalated into the passion that still roiled between us—and more greatly for its repression.

Now, that same flagrant craving for gratification turned me into the slut Malin loved me to be. Even as I panted beneath the fluttering, tensing heat evoked by the dharmine's will, I resolved to resist the temptation to command my slave to fill me with the prick I could tell had tensed in his trousers.

And this scorn only made the dharmine smile all the more cruelly.

"You are so willful, Madame," he said. As he spoke, I gasped, for I swore for all the world I had just been fully penetrated by the weapon I could see was secured away. Moaning, I leaned back from the demon, having to keep my eyes fixed upon him just to order things out in my mind—to confirm to myself that his body had not truly penetrated mine.

But what did it matter? When I felt the thrusting of a cock within me—even saw, as I had seen his eyes, flashes of his hard fucking into me through some powerful imaginal lens—it didn't seem relevant that his anatomy remained imprisoned and mine remained empty. The complete tangibility of the visions which increasingly filled my head was such that I had might as well have thrown off my robe and begged him for every inch.

"It's no use, Madame," Dinon murmured, his forehead resting against mine while his smiling silver eyes drank in every second of my pleasure. "Your defenses crumble even now. How sweet your resistance is to me! Sweeter still, knowing the inevitability of your yielding heart...and your desperation when the night at last comes."

Shuddering with each thrust Dinon imagined making into my body—for that was what I took it to be when I reflected on it later, the product of the demon's imagination working within my own—I gripped my seat with one hand and pulled at my hair with the other. "Oh," I gasped, "damn you, you violate me with your appetites, Dinon—even without touching me, you disgrace me, you use me—"

"Oh yes, Madame." His eyes gleamed bright with shared ecstasy as, by will alone, he sent another surge of pleasure rushing through my core, sent another vision of his deep penetration into the heart of me. "Yes, I use your body—use your soul. And what a gift to me it is...its pleasure, your pleasure, is finer than any terrestrial wine—oh—Madame—"

Lips parted in wonder to behold the climax that tore through me with the sudden peak of tension in my muscles, Dinon smiled, then shut his eyes and sighed with a pleasure of his own. "Yes," he murmured, his fingers stroking along the flesh of my thigh, "yes, Madame, that's it—"

"Release me, demon," I commanded him, squirming with the ecstatic fluttering and tremoring of my legs, my core. "Release me, oh—get away from me, damn you, slave."

"A happy slave," agreed Dinon, lowering my limb and stealing an extra stroke along my flesh before rising to his feet. "Thank you, Madame...there is no feast in the world like your ecstasy."

While I shuddered and ground my teeth, telling him even as the pleasure ebbed away, "Impudent swine," Dinon shuddered with some pleasure of his own.

"Your most hateful curses are like the sweetest songs," he went on, somehow more enraptured than ever as he bowed lightly at the waist. "Have an excellent day of work, Madame; may your tapestry be as exquisite as you."

Without fanfare or further sign, Dinon vanished; still panting, I glowered not at the space where he had been, but at my own longing for him when I beheld that space. Longing—for a beast, for a slave! For a true monster, like the very one Eleison and Glenn had slain the night prior to protect me.

At once awash with unpleasant, unwelcome thoughts, I grit my teeth and turned back to my work.

NOTHING COULD MAKE THE DAYS fly by the way my weaving could! When Dinon left me to my work and the rest of my staff, hearing the familiar loom, knew better than to disrupt me, I spent hours in total focus before the gathering threads. In the same way, the threads of time were gathered, and hours became days: long days. Even Malin and Eleison, knowing how sterile my workroom had been for the past months, seemed content to leave me be until the coming of night, when suppertime at last called me from my work and gave me an excuse to see my family.

Yet there was an uneasiness to this work that still remained, unshakable. Still, at night, when I eased into Malin's arms or felt him smile upon Eleison and me as we kissed and murmured beside him at the table, something seemed to occupy my husband—to keep him at a kind of spiritual distance from those he best loved.

He was there in body—certainly in body, every night and often in the morning before I slipped off to my weaving—but his mind was leagues away, and I tried to tell myself it was only a preoccupation with whatever next steps would be required to hasten Horizon's energy project.

Only Eleison seemed to share my concern well enough to remark on it. As we strolled through the garden, (which was, it seemed, healthier every day since the elimination of the feral dharmine), my mate glanced around to ensure us out of hearing range of anyone else—nosy courtiers especially. "Has Malin seemed a little 'off' to you lately?"

With an instant sigh of exasperation, I shared his glance about us before nodding. "Yes," I said, my voice low. "He's been acting so strangely—I haven't even dared bring up that incident during the last Event."

Though his mouth tightened, a reflexive criticism justly forming on the back of his tongue, Eleison simply clicked his tongue and flicked his eyes in the direction of the hedge maze. "Well...maybe it's better that we don't bring it up for now. It was just another dead Rift beast, when you get right down to it...if we bothered him about every rodi we killed, he'd be too annoyed to be so pensive."

"It wasn't *really* just another Rift beast, though." I worked my tongue nervously along my bottom row of teeth. While Eleison arched his brow at me, I said softly, "That man I killed—the veteran at Glenn's house. It was his dharmine."

Eyebrows lifting and mouth slightly opened at the thought, Eleison reflected, "That's where I've seen his face before. I couldn't place it...he was one of the hunters who went into Glenn's house while I was doing surveillance on it that night."

"Exactly. I'm sure it's just some vengeful instinct that drove it to search for me, but—the idea of a man dying in Valquist only for his revenant to seek me in Gudrune, all the way across the continent—" I shuddered, pressing closer to Eleison. "There's something so especially ghastly about it."

"Is that what chased you back into your workroom? I'm happy to hear you weaving again...but I do miss you while you're occupied all day."

As Eleison steered us into the maze, his intent telegraphed by the hand that slid into the small of my back, I smiled over at him. "Well, you'll be glad to know it's only a few days more before this part of the project is finished...but I'd like to start the next tapestry just as soon as we're in Saalast. I don't want to lose any more momentum than I must."

"You're so driven, baby. If I were you, I don't know how I'd resist lying around with the courtiers, doing nothing all day."

"I used to think that, too, when I was in my little room in Lescaut and reading books about women living romantic, courtly lives...but while the body longs for indolence, the mind craves occupation. It's all the same sitting at the loom for hours, anyway."

"I wouldn't be so sure about that." Now his hand slid up along my bicep, making me shiver with the pleasure of his contact on my flesh as we continued through the private corridors of the hedges. "Seems to me like your arms and legs work all day. It must be at least a little tiring...maybe you should lie back and let me do the hard work today."

While I giggled at my incorrigible lover, turning to throw my arms around his neck and feast upon his mouth, he folded me in his embrace and murmured, "Maybe, since Malin's been feeling so bad, you and he and I should all—"

The thought remained unfinished, the rustling of fabric and a footfall some ways around a corner dismissing us from passion into a hush of mirthful annoyance. At least, I was mirthful about it, tittering slightly in spite of Eleison's irritated look—and it took the greatest self-control for him to soothe that irritation when around the corner stepped Glenn, his marked book in his hand and his expression visibly relieved when he did not immediately behold Eleison's passion for me on full display.

"Glenn," said Eleison with a jerk of his head.

"Sorry to interrupt," Glenn relayed, nodding back while gesturing over his shoulder with the little leatherbound volume. "I heard you two coming from the center and thought you might want it to yourselves."

"You're always welcome to spend time with us, Glenn," I emphasized, adding by way of apology, "if anything, we're the ones interrupting you by acting like a couple of schoolchildren— Oh—"

Eleison had released me and strode forward to meet Glenn, sending my heart racing in my chest. At once, my mind flooded with immaculate flashbacks of the Extreme Rift Event in Valquist, when Eleison, half a beast and half a man owing to the extraordinary nature of the weather, had burst into Glenn's house and wreaked havoc. To my knowledge, they had maintained a sort of cold war ever since: a silence of grudging respect but fairly mutual dislike.

Now, however, my tension released. Eleison extended his hand in offering to Glenn, who took it after but a heartbeat of uncertainty. "Thanks for your help last week," Eleison said, firmly shaking Glenn's hand with a sincere look. "I could have died without you there—died, or worse."

"I had to help Thecla," said Glenn, adding, "and anyway— between the Torea Festival and that time in Azstoria, I was down two."

Masterfully choosing not to correct Glenn and add the time at his house in Valquist, when Eleison easily could have killed him and insisted on taking me out of the house, my mate released his grip and slid his hands casually into the pockets of his trousers. "We were just discussing the incident, actually," Eleison explained as I came to his side. "That was one of your pals, wasn't it?"

With a nod of assent, Glenn flicked a glance at me and then confessed to us both, "I try not to be a superstitious man... but it's hard to avoid taking a dharmine's appearance as a bad omen. Especially when it was somebody I knew. Did it speak to you?"

We shook our heads. "No, but they don't often speak when they're fresh. Not more than a few words at a time, unless they've had a lot to eat."

"You think it was fresh from the Rift?"

"Within a few weeks of emergence," Eleison assessed, his hand rubbing his jaw in contemplation. "Always hard to say, but...it's a good bet that if it hadn't been fresh, we would have had a lot more trouble killing it without injury to ourselves."

Glenn thought on the matter a few seconds more, then let his golden eyes glitter my way before he turned his attention back to Eleison. "Say," he began, "uh—"

Even as Glenn was unable to fully form the words, Eleison seemed to take his meaning. Chuckling a little, lowering his eyes slightly, he said, "Sure," then glanced at me. "Thecla, baby... you want to talk to Glenn a few minutes? Why don't you take a walk—I don't remember the last time I saw you two together."

My heart swelling with love for Eleison's growing compassion, this new generosity into which he shaped his soul, I smiled at Glenn before leaning up to kiss my mate's cheek. "See you at supper?"

"Always. Glenn." After receiving my kiss, Eleison shook Glenn's hand again and returned the way we'd come. As he rounded the corner and disappeared, Glenn exhaled in slow relief and said, "He's more...I don't want to use the word 'civil', but—"

"Then don't." I put my hand on his heart to stay his tongue. Almost flinching with the affection, Glenn raised his free hand and pressed it over mine, his thumb moving along my knuckles as I said on, "Rest assured, Eleison is a man before he's a beast...but he's my beloved before he's either of those things. And so are you, and so is Malin...I know in my heart you three will find a way to get along someday."

With a slight flare of his nostrils, Glenn raised my hand to his mouth. Then, lowering it to walk with me through the hedge maze with our fingers interlinked in a familiar, almost innocent way that pleased me, Glenn began, "Speaking of Malin—I heard a few servants saying he'll be leaving again soon."

"Unfortunately, yes...he's got a speech of some kind, some bit of political business to celebrate Horizon Energy's new research center in Saalast." I tried not to let my cringe become visible when I reflected on what I had just said; Glenn mistrusted Malin generally, but had a special paranoia concerning my husband's interest in utilizing the Rift for energy production. Yet, to my relief, Glenn seemed to simply listen without judgment.

"How long is he going to be gone?"

"Oh, I don't know...one week, two—I can't imagine we'll spend a long time in the city. Malin prefers—"

"Wait—" With a little scoff of displeasure, Glenn stopped us both in the middle of the pathway and turned to face me properly. "*You're* going with him?"

"Of course! Oh, Glenn—he's *just* come home. Surely you

understand I can't let him whisk off to some other engagement without insisting I come along."

"But—do you think that's really a good idea?"

Beneath the pressure of Glenn's assessing gaze, I occasionally felt I was once again beneath the anticipatory displeasure of my father. At the very least, Glenn and Rigel had a similar way of looking hard into my face, the line between their expectation and their disapproval equally fine. "Why wouldn't it be," I asked with a laugh. "Goodness, it's only a week, two weeks—a few days in the grand scheme, and then we'll be back."

"This isn't a Sunday trip to church, Thecla. You're talking about going to Saalast when it's the worst it's been in years—and it was never a very safe city in the first place."

"Tosh," I said with a wave of my hand, "I've always felt perfectly safe." Even as I said it, I realized this was something of an unintentional lie. There I was, back on the first night Eleison took me, my pulse pounding as I made my way through the dark streets of the city while increasingly aware of its undeniable criminal element. In spite of this, I had to stick to my point. I insisted, "Dinon will be with me, and of course Eleison will watch over Malin and me—there's no danger to be had."

"Look—" As he stepped toward me, his tongue darting across his lower lip in his reluctance to speak, I found myself longing to kiss him; to be kissed by him. Knowing the impulse inappropriate in the moment, I pushed it away, yet could not help the fancy as Glenn said in a soft tone with his head lowered over mine, "I know you're an optimist, Thecla, but I need you to be realistic. You heard the Hunter's Guild members in Valquist—and that was just a small sampling of their general sentiment. They hate you." While I blanched a little, Glenn said, "And your husband, of course—but even if they blame me for what happened in Valquist, even if it's my head they've got a price on, they're also smart enough to put together your involvement in the whole incident. They know you were there that night and weren't there after the Event was over. They also know that, after you came out of hiding, the Hunter's Guild was forced to dissolve in Gudrune...but that doesn't mean there aren't still hunters here in the territory."

"Any man who tried to hurt me would be signing his own death warrant," I assured Glenn, who sighed haggardly.

"If you won't think of yourself," Glenn insisted, "then think of Rosina. Think what a target she—you both—present if you go up there. If somebody kidnapped her, or—"

"Actually"—I stopped him, my hand slipping into his again and making his jaw clench into silence—"I was thinking perhaps I might leave Rosina here with you."

"Thecla—"

"It's only a short time, as I said—and you're right. I may not be worried about myself, but I'm not sure Saalast is anyplace for a little child—not to mention the long journey up, the threat of Rift weather on the way that whole day, oh, I don't know. It's a logistical nightmare."

Having let my eyes drift from his, I rectified my attention and found Glenn peering intensely into my face. "Besides—perhaps, with Malin and Eleison and I all out of the house, you might be inclined to come out and visit her a bit more freely! It would be nice for both of you to have a little break, don't you think?"

Though I spoke the truth, there was a deeper intent hidden in my bosom—namely, that if Glenn got sufficiently used to freely spending time with Rosina, he might not be willing to relinquish the practice on our return to the country house. It was a gambit, and, I reasoned, as likely to fail as it was to work; but if it did work, and he did acclimate to spending the better part of his days with Rosina instead of evenings only, perhaps we might return to a Glenn who had higher spirits; who left his room more often; who responded to Malin not with dread and jealousy and mistrust, but with simple gratitude.

"I—yes," Glenn admitted after a few seconds, deciding this was something he couldn't or shouldn't lie about. "Yes, of course, it sounds nice to have a chance to spend time with Rosina. It would be nicer if you were there, too, though."

"Glenn..." Smiling despite myself, I studied his hand and gently rubbed my fingers over the tattoo sleeve ending at his wrist. "I *was* here. I've been here, without Malin or Eleison, for three weeks. And...you've avoided me as though I were one of them. So, I just thought—perhaps if we had a while apart...absence would make our hearts grow fonder."

How sad he looked! Sad, and as if in the throes of some realization. Brow furrowing, Glenn murmured my name, then slipped his hand from mine to cradle my cheek. "I love you so much, Thecla," he murmured. "You don't even understand how much."

"Then I wish—no, I won't say that. I'll only say that I hope you'll stop treating me like I'm little more than an extension of the man you want to avoid...that you'll stop wanting to avoid him."

I could see it in the depths of Glenn's eyes—in the soul that burned brilliantly through them, heroic and kind and too compassionate for the world into which he had been born. Even now, all these months later, Glenn still wanted what he had when we first met. He wanted to save me—perhaps not even from Malin so much as from something he found within me.

"I'm sorry," he murmured, his eyes darting down to my lips and then back up. Hand raising to smooth an errant lock of dark hair back into place along my brow, Glenn then let his grip fit to the back of my neck. I exhaled, obeying the pressure that urged me toward him. After a step, I was pressed to his chest, and I sank my head, with complete trust, into the support of his hand.

"You don't need to apologize," I whispered, offering my mouth to his love. "Not ever, Glenn—not for struggling to change. But you must change, my love: your heart must change, and your mind. You and Eleison have so much in common." Laughing lightly, I gazed into Glenn's now heavy-lidded eyes as he bent to let his lips graze my nose, my cheek, the corners of my mouth. Pleasure rising in my loins, I parted my lips between murmured words. "You're both stubborn," I told him, his curling fingers against the nape of my neck sending soft ecstasy through my sensitive frame. "You each decided long ago that you're the only sane man in all the world. The difference is that Eleison is the sane man who humors us pitiful lunatics...you're the sane man who longs to cure us. To convert us, so you won't be the only sane one left anymore."

With a slight, almost abashed laugh, as though I had caught him at something, Glenn leaned his forehead against mine and gazed intently into my eyes. "Maybe that's true...but, if it is, there's only one lunatic I'm hoping to convert."

As his lips fully covered mine, I moaned into the hollow of his mouth. Malin's kisses were commanding, and Eleison's hungry: but Glenn's kisses were truly romantic, slow and persistent movements of lip and tongue designed to steadily draw love from me so he could drink it down. He opened my mouth like a poppy blossoming open for the sunlight in spring: there was passion there, and longing without question; but there was also a plea. A sense that, no matter how deeply his soul longed to penetrate mine, it was still mine that was meant to be in control. I was a woman in some ancient fairy tale whenever I was in Glenn's arms: a character in a painting, as Charlotte had once called me. A lady with a knight who, even after all the ways she had corrupted and sullied herself with wicked deeds, still saw her as worth rescuing from the snares of her own selfish mistakes.

Yet—what mistakes had I made? None in my own eyes, certainly. He was the one who was so piteously mistaken: the one who could not see the simple truth. Whatever his reputation and history, my husband was a man worthy of my life. A man who had saved me and elevated me. A man without whom I may never have met Glenn—without whom our daughter would not exist.

"Please swear to me," said Glenn, searching my face with great intensity as our kiss parted, "that you'll be careful in Saalast."

"I promise," I murmured, a circuit of sweet pleasure flowing gently through my body with each stroke of Glenn's thumb along the side of my neck. "I swear it. Why, darling...you know better than anyone that not even the country here is safe. Please, next time you go running, don't do so alone. Ask Eleison's brother, Kyrie, to come with you—or stay on the property, at the very least."

"I usually do...I just—" Glancing away as he released his tender hold on me, Glenn confessed, "I guess I felt a little restlessness, Malin having just come home."

"I understand, darling. But since Eleison won't be there in emergencies—just please, be safe."

"With Rosina to take care of," said Glenn, offering me his arm to lead me through the rest of the maze, "I have to be."

12

WHEN I LOOK BACK on this time, it is so obvious that Malin knew everything. With perfect clarity, he was aware of what was about to happen to him, and to us. I say that now, not just having since heard it from his lips, but having had time in the course of these memoirs to investigate his manner and movements...or how my mind represents them in retrospect.

It is impossible to recount this narrative without knowing where the future destined us both; without seeing or perhaps even imagining a thousand little signposts are now so painfully obvious. I fear I look like quite a fool, quite naive, when moving through the narrative in this fashion. Why didn't I shake my husband from his brooding and demand, on no uncertain terms, that he tell me why death weighed so heavily on his mind? Why didn't I take it more seriously and raise more concerns with him during the period of preparation before and after our trip to Saalast? Why didn't I see some definitive warning in the tears that shined in his eyes when, a mere two days before we left for the city, I managed to finish the tapestry and present it to him in pride that collapsed to shock for the emotion such a gift had never stirred in him before?

Ultimately, all I can do is point to my history with Malin and his secrets—and with my then still burdensome preoccupation over being a pleasing and cooperative wife to my powerful husband. Over the course of our relationship, I had been privy to the opening of more than one secret, and with the most recent, Malin had sworn to me that there was only one more he kept. He had sworn, likewise, that it was *his* secret, pertaining to him, and a deeply personal one.

Yet does not the death of a husband concern the wife perhaps more than it concerns even the dead man?

I almost left Dinon behind to look after Glenn, though at the last second, I decided to bring the demon along for his own good. Glenn, I reasoned, could be policed effectively enough by his responsibility toward Rosina, and by the eyes of the staff. On the other hand, Dinon would need to sustain himself somehow, and without my pleasure to feast upon, I feared he might turn his appetites to the blood and flesh of the household. Therefore, I commanded him with us, and it was he who held the door as, having kissed Rosina and embraced Glenn, I entered the carriage with a merry wave. "We'll be back soon, and with some gifts— perhaps another bug, if you're a good girl for Daddy!"

"Bug," called Rosina, "bug, Mama!"

As I exchanged a smile with Eleison, already in the carriage beside me, I turned in expectation of continuing the smile to Malin—but my husband delayed just outside the carriage door, one hand upon the opening, the other braced upon the knee that had been frozen mid-step into the car. He had turned back—looking, I thought, at Rosina and Glenn. But as he tore his eyes away, I realized he had been drinking in the facade of the country house where first we met in this strange world of space and time.

"I've always loved this house," said Malin, sliding into the car with us. He took the seat to my right so I was pressed closely between both husband and mate, my heart safe with love's blanket of sheer contentment. While Dinon shut the door and climbed up into the driver's seat without the slightest rock of the carriage beneath his skillful movements, Malin continued peering out the window and speaking as though lost in a dream. "I'm glad it's yours now, Eleison...it suits you, somehow."

Exchanging a knowing glance with me—knowing, at least, that he and I had previously discussed Malin's odd turn—Eleison reached across my lap to lay his hand on Malin's. While the master of Gudrune turned to face us, Eleison said, "You can have it back, you know...I still think of it as yours, to tell the truth."

Malin laughed softly, squeezing Eleison's hand, then raising it to his mouth to kiss it as gallantly as he would have mine. As the carriage lurched into motion, my husband released my mate and told him, "I wouldn't take it back if you had the pen in my hand and the deed before me. It's yours, Eleison— you deserve it, you need it. Erase all thoughts of my holdings from your mind...at least, as they pertain to this property. How would you feel if Thecla said that to you about one of your gifts, old boy?"

"I don't really give Thecla gifts," Eleison mused, half-realizing it as he settled back to drape his arm around my shoulders. "Maybe I should."

"Goodness gracious, absolutely *not*." Laughing, I stroked Eleison's knee and said, "You'll turn it into some perverse competition, whether or not you mean to...every second I enjoy with each of you, together or individually, is the greatest gift I could possibly imagine."

"That's why you're my wife, Thecla," said Malin with sincere approval, his knuckles grazing down my cheek while I smiled over at him. "That's how I feel, too."

Yes, that was surely so; just as it was so that I was, among other reasons, Eleison's mate—because Malin's very tender statement imbued in me the impulse to shower him with gifts. But what? Oh, it drove me mad to come up with something I could give him aside from the tapestries, my body, someday a child. Malin's treasuries overflowed with wealth, his closets with fineries, his caskets with cufflinks and tiepins galore. He had endless baubles with which to subtly (or less subtly) adorn himself...yet I not infrequently found myself wishing I could present him with something beautiful, something unique, as he so often presented to me. Even as we made the trip to the city, an all-day affair that left us all drained by the time Saalast stood proudly in the distance, the citrine ring from Azstoria glittered upon my hand, and the jewel box Charlotte packed contained the ruby necklace presented on our wedding day. Malin's custom of saturating his surroundings with lofty aesthetics made him a singularly difficult man to shop for, or to surprise.

It didn't help that his interests seemed so narrow. Aside from reading the works of ancient poets and storytellers, and taking me to the theater whenever we were in the city, Malin's primary hobby was his hedonistic pursuit of my arms and sometimes Eleison's. Otherwise, he was at work, for Gudrune was not only a fulltime position: it was a lifetime one, a truly round-the-clock effort of maintenance; and even when he was not occupied by meetings, phone calls, letter-writing and speech-drafting, he was prone to ruminating on the next steps of any given goal. I was quite surprised, for instance, when we exited the carriage at the Saalast house and were greeted right away by a face that was half-familiar to me, owing mostly to the crooked glasses and slightly messy hair. The young man sprang up off the bench half a block from our house and called, "Master Farrow," drawing the somewhat sharp attention of Eleison and our security man, Ignatius.

Malin, however, clearly having expected this, removed his hat with a gesture of his free hand. "Arthur, good evening. Come along, let's have that chat...I trust you two can get settled in," he asked on, glancing over at Eleison and me.

"A meeting already?" Pouting, I smoothed Malin's lapel before raising my eyes to his with a pleading expression. "I thought we might have an hour for supper, at least."

"Oh, Thecla—"

Inhaling against the temptation his fondness for me inspired, Malin raised my hand to his mouth and toyed with the ring around my finger. "Why not just enjoy dinner with Eleison tonight," my husband said gently, "and I promise, I'll take you out on the town in a night or so. Drinks, dancing—if my poor body has recovered from this blasted carriage ride—maybe a trip to the opera. Won't that be nice? Ah—I hate to see you frown. Please, smile. I promise, tomorrow."

"Very well," I said, standing on my toes to kiss his cheek. "Tomorrow. Just—don't work your endless hours tonight,

Husband." He had been staying up dreadfully late, on and off, since I found him speaking with the dharmine: I sensed the threat of this becoming a pattern in Saalast, where there were more people to bother him and more responsibilities pressing imminently upon his mind. "I can do nothing without you."

In his gentle smile were the hallmarks of pain, but before I could spend more than a second growing concerned, Malin squeezed my hand and turned away to greet Arthur. Up close, I could place him at last: a researcher from the Horizon Clean Energy team, who had been in the meeting I listened to while Malin awarded them a grant. No doubt, the very grant that built the center. "Arthur," said Malin, gesturing between the weedy but pleasantly smiling man and me, "this is my wife, Thecla, my appointed heir and future Matrix of Gudrune—once the Overseer has approved her position and I'm out of the picture, anyway. Make friends with her now...you may need her later."

"Hopefully not," laughed Arthur, bowing a little over my hand, then adding with an awkward sputter, "uh, of course, I just mean—"

"I know what you mean," I said, laughing. "It's quite all right...I feel much the same."

A little relieved, the man offered his full name—"A real pleasure to meet you, Madame Farrow. Arthur Tanning"—before turning his attention back to my husband. "I'll try not to take up too much of your time, Master; I know you must be tired, but I just thought—"

"Arthur," said Malin, his hand fitting to the back of the young man's shoulder as, with his other hand, he gestured into the house, "if anything, I'm at risk of taking up *your* time. This project is among the most important tasks of my life, and I want to give you whatever is required to see it run without a hitch. Let's talk in my office, please. Follow me—"

That quickly, Malin disappeared into the house with the researcher, and I, exhausted by the ride as much as by my husband's incredible resources of energy, turned to offer Eleison a smile. "Well—shall we go out to eat tonight?"

It was a grand time, I'm quite sure; but how curiously little I recall of that week! How greatly the trauma eclipses all other aspects of memory, which already risked blurring into the other times we had arrived at Saalast and set about our city business. I remember feeling very secure with Eleison as my escort and Ba'al-Dinon accompanying us as footman; and I remember the light glances Dinon cast upon me whenever I contemplated, with a soft thrill, first meeting him in the city streets. I remember Eleison itching to tear away my clothes and make love to me with such savagery that I could barely flee the elevator before his hands were on my body.

And I remember waiting long for Malin—amazed to think he had withstood the hours of transit to Saalast and had stayed up so long to work—until I began to doze. Catching myself falling fully asleep against Eleison's body, I stirred and sat up in the dark of the room, then groped around on the nightstand for my pocket watch. Past midnight again, I realized. Frowning, I threw Eleison's shirt around my body and made my way through the townhouse to discover a light burned in Malin's study. The handle was unlocked, and though I listened at the door, I heard no sign of conversation as I had when he spoke with Dinon.

When I opened the door, I discovered why all this was true, at least to superficial extent: my husband had worked himself to sleep at his desk, his head tipped back and his mouth open as, no doubt having meant to close his eyes only a moment, he dreamed soundly upright in the hard back of his wooden chair.

Oh, Malin! Lip worrying between my teeth, I made my way across the floor and, gently, softly, one hand tickling across his cheek, kissed the edges of his mouth, and his slumbering eyes, and the hawkish beak of his handsome nose; until at last, with a few more tender kisses of his brow, he produced a snore of surprise like the tearing of fabric, worked his jaw in his stir, and hummed in the deep exhaustion of disorienting sleep. "Time is it," he asked, the sentence half-formed, a bit bossy in a way that struck me as quite adorable.

"It's time for bed, darling," I told him, "past midnight."

"Oh...already, blast—I fell asleep— Ah—"

Grimacing a little to feel the ache in his neck, Malin slowly raised his head and rubbed his own shoulder. I intercepted the motion, pushing away his hand and digging my thumbs and fingers into the nape of his neck while he groaned in relief.

"Thecla...I don't know how I ever lived without you..."

"I don't know how you ever slept without me, either, if working like this is your usual custom. Don't tell me you've been on honeymoon all this time and only now you're revealing your true working habits."

With a dry chuckle, Malin allowed me to push back his unbuttoned shirt collar and reveal the A-line beneath. While I kneaded his flesh more thoroughly, he rubbed the corners of his eyes and said, "If anything, I was a regular layabout before I met you...a bit more like our dear friend Aleister, if you want to know the truth...but...there's so much to do...I feel rushed by this project...it's so vital, I want it well underway...no, I want it done..."

"Why this urgency, darling?" As my fingers worked now at the base of his skull, his shoulders rolled and his arms stretched. "I know it's important to you, of course—it's important to all Gudrune. But, surely, if Horizon gets what they need from you only next week, or two weeks from now, it won't make that great a difference in the long run."

"The worsening weather is more than enough reason to feel the urgency of the assignment...and God knows the kind of pushback I'm going to receive from Parvati when she realizes how far the project has come."

"Then need you make a speech at all? Can't you hide it from her awhile longer?"

With a chuckle, Malin reached up to pat my hand. I caught his palm and, lightly tugging, drew him to his feet to kiss him. He spoke as I led him to the sofa beneath the curtained window overlooking the Saalast street. "Aside from interlopers like Ambassador Platt and anyone else at risk of selling information... oh"—he sighed heavily as I drew him into my arms—"no, it's not the right choice. Not now. Hiding the energy research makes it look like we're doing something wrong—makes it look like Parvati was right to mistrust my intentions with this project. If we're straightforward about it, show all our cards from the very start, I have no doubt she'll continue giving us a difficult time; but she'll also have a more difficult time proving we're doing anything wrong."

With only the slightest hesitation, as I did not want Malin to doubt my trust in him, I pressed, "Are we doing anything wrong?"

"By supporting Horizon? No, angel." Relieved to rest his head upon my bosom, Malin shut his eyes again and said, "Horizon's research into the Rift is the second-most important thing I've ever done. I stand by it completely...I won't let Parvati interfere with it."

My principled husband! "And the first most important thing," I asked as his breathing deepened with almost immediate retreat back into sleep.

"Marrying you, of course," he murmured, already up to his neck in the sea of dreams. "Maybe Horizon's third most important...caring for Eleison, that's second..."

"Fourth," I whispered to him, "after we've had our child."

The edges of his lip twitched; in a smile or a frown, I could not quite say.

"I love you, Thecla," Malin murmured, nestling against my heart and falling, completely now, asleep.

The next morning, I awoke to his kisses on my throat and his hand pushing back the fabric of Eleison's shirt around my waist; when my husband found me awake, his dark eyes brightened with pleasure and his mouth claimed mine. Wordless, his flurry of kisses lowered, cruising down along the swell of my revealed breasts and down the slope of my stomach. As he pushed wide my legs and knelt between them, I whimpered in light protest.

"Oh, darling, you'll ache your poor knees on the floor—after the trip and your long night, please, let's—"

"I can't wait a second," my husband told me, the delicious sternness of his tone enriching the heat his manipulations of my sleeping body had already provoked. "You look so soft and yielding in sleep, angel...ah, your body is divine...Thecla..."

His kisses over the cleft of my pleasure made me choke back an immediate gasp, which momentarily rolled into a lewd moan. While the back of my hand pressed to my mouth, I savored the sight of Malin's eager work between my legs. I had the impression that Eleison loved applying his mouth to my sex because he loved me, and my pleasure gave him pleasure; but Malin, I could tell, simply loved the human body, and while he especially loved my body, there was no doubt that his skills in eliciting pleasure were practiced over a great many years before I found my way into his arms. He kissed and lapped and nibbled as though tasting me, his intimate acquaintance with my every nerve as natural as an artist's understanding of the brush; as his tongue eagerly worked that most sensitive little gem, I groaned and stroked his hair.

"And to think," I teased, "you call me a slut...you're no innocent virgin, you dirty old man. Oh, how many lucky girls were your partners in practice before me...how many boys before Eleison at last gave you the privilege of enjoying his prick..."

"More than I could guess," Malin admitted, lips still softly brushing my clit with every word even as his finger probed, then sheathed itself within me. "One for every day of the week sometimes, I admit...well. One, at least."

"You wretch," I moaned. "How lucky for them you don't know their names! Lucky for them you're an incorrigible rake—otherwise, I'd have as many heads to decorate the gates of this townhouse, the spires of the country manor—"

With a shudder and a groan of his own dark pleasure, my husband worked his fingers in and out of me. "I'm sure I could remember one or two names, if my cruel Madame Farrow would demand it...but who could compare? Whose beauty, whose wit, whose sensual embrace could match yours well enough for even a name to remain in my mind when surpassed by that one I most adore? 'Thecla,' 'Thecla'...oh, Thecla—"

Shuddering with pleasure, Malin slid his hand from me and, after a few seconds of his belt's rattle, was upon me, then within me. That first shock and deep stretch of his penetration was never any less intense, and I gasped his name, my fingers biting into the backs of his shoulders. "Oh, you ghastly lecher—oh"—I shuddered and roiled with pleasure beneath him, arching my hips to offer my depths to his increasingly rough plunges into my taut, aching core—"a lucky thing all your experience has taught you a thing or two about women, oh—! Were it not for your education, you would just be an old man, three decades my senior, thirty years—Master of Gudrune, taking advantage of a poor peasant girl, making her slave to your passions—your own step-daughter, oh, wicked! Whatever the legal status, mere technicality, Malin, oh—Daddy—"

"Thecla—darling, dearest—my life and my bride—"

Though he hardly spared any tender sentiment when making love to me before Eleison, Malin's sensual longings and romantic recitations tripled in intensity when he and I were alone. His fingers tangling in my hair, his mouth swallowing up my tongue, my breath, my very soul, Malin pushed himself nearly violently into my inner chamber while each deep thrust made me pulse from head to toe with pleasure. I groaned, my foot bracing against the floor and the other draping across the back of the sofa to completely open my body for his pleasure.

"Were you not such a delicious lover," I moaned, gasping for air as he drew back a bit, "oh, I would whip you senseless, Malin—I would flay the flesh from your bones, you belong on the rack broken and bloodied for my pleasure—"

"And what pleasure it would be," he said, his eyes searching mine, his teeth bared, "to suffer for you, my Thecla, my darling—

ah, my sweet, you may be of a peasant's background, but of the two of us, I'm the slave—yes, a slave to this body, this mind—Thecla—"

His hand gripped my thigh, holding me down as he drove into me with ferocity such I nearly screamed. Toes curling, breath panting, I looked into his eyes and glanced away only to watch the thick shaft of his skillful cock splitting me completely in twain. As my legs tightened, my body arching, he watched me with equal amazement, his every word a breathless growl.

"Such a good girl," Malin said, "yes, oh, darling...I love the way you take it, I always have...sweet Madame Farrow, you deserve to have your adorable cunt filled every second you're awake...take all the lovers you like, ah, supplement wherever you need, my darling, yes—Eleison, the hunter, even that dharmine...just don't forget your poor old husband, angel, don't forget about me—"

"Malin," I cried, the climax rising in me with his next kiss's thirsty plunge along the length of my tongue ,"Malin, oh—take me first and last and between! Oh, my love, my husband—all my lovers are your lovers, for my body is your body—my love is your love—my cunt is yours, yours to fuck, yours to use, oh, yes—yours to bring you pleasure!"

While my body clamped around his, my legs twitching and kicking to tighten around his hips, Malin's throat produced a strangled little noise of half-shocked ecstasy. Drowning himself in the vision of the orgasm rippling through my face, he kissed me, his cock hardening with every heavy slam until he, too, released his tension and spilled the glory of pleasure within me.

By the time I finished catching my breath, I swore he regarded me with a glisten of tears at the edges of his eyes: at the time, I could not be sure.

Now, of course, I understand.

Over the next five days, it seemed that if he was not working, he was pursuing me and feasting upon my body like a starving man sating himself on the only fig tree for miles around in a terrible, merciless desert. The urgency was due to the nearness of my menstrual cycle, I assumed—he wanted to take all the chances he could, and I was glad to oblige him, particularly since its delay of more than a week began to lift my hopes.

And between these many instances of pleasure was nothing but his work. Meetings, endless meetings, with Platt (whom I also recognized from that meeting that yielded Horizons' grant), with Arthur, with countless others whose names I did not know. Hours spent writing a speech; and then a long meeting, featuring myself and Eleison, in which a motorcade was planned before Malin's address. "I want an open top carriage," insisted Malin, drawing a slight click of Ignatius's tongue as our security man braced himself against the notion.

"I really wouldn't advise that, sir. Between the usual crowds and the kinds of extremist activity we've been seeing relating to the dissolution of the Hunter's Guild—"

"I won't sit in a covered car like some prince in his chariot too good to be seen by the people. Besides"—with a faint smile, Malin patted Eleison on the shoulder—"our cavalier will be riding with us. If anyone so much as hurls a tomato, I have no doubt Eleison will make them regret it."

"It's a little more serious than rotten fruit, sir," said Ignatius wisely, his tone polite but firm. "The amount of violence in Saalast has tripled since the dissolution of the Hunter's Guild, and there's a great deal of public unrest. If—"

"I'm sure," said Malin, his tone far sterner to have been met with argument, "that the citizens of Gudrune need to see their territory master is unruffled by the dangers of Saalast more than they need to see him as untouchable. That's the point of this speech, Ignatius. It's something to turn the city's—the territory's—attention toward the future and from the old ways of doing things. We need a new relationship with the Rift. I—hm, I'd ought to write that down." From his breast pocket, Malin withdrew a little red notebook into which he jotted his thoughts relating to work, especially as of late. My darling was always alert, always poised for an idea to come through and solve whatever problem currently occupied him.

A good thing one of us felt that way. For all my efforts to shadow Malin and learn the nuances of his duties to Gudrune, I must confess...I have always found politics exceedingly dull. As my husband tells me, I have an artist's mind, and it is not a mind to be constrained by petty terrestrial issues such as whom to install in what position, or how to appease this particular sector of the citizenry. Not to say these matters are not of great import: they are, of course. But my soul is emotional, my imagination creative, and, I am embarrassed to admit, I have always been prone to flights of fancy in those instances when I am confronted by a topic that does not hold my interest.

So it was that, as we planned the motorcade—as Ignatius and Eleison reviewed all the paths we would be taking across town, a journey that would begin at a particularly famous park and end at Horizon's new facility on the northern edge of town—my attention drifted like that of a student trapped in a tedious lecture. The evening before, Malin had brought me out to dinner and taken me to a quite interesting play about a torturer who journeys to restore the light of a dying sun over his world; it was an intriguing story, fanciful and surreal, and it occurred to me after that there were many things in this world to which I never might have turned my eye if not for Malin. It was thanks to him that I had experienced so many fantastic stories since coming into his life—why, it was thanks to him that I had taken up the task of producing these tapestries, the next in which series I had begun drafting.

My Malin! He gave me so many treasures, tangible and not. Could I come up with one single gesture, one item he could keep on his person and enjoy as a memento of my love?

Something wrong, Madame?

Dinon stood in the hallway outside the meeting, good footman that he was, though I had no doubt he was perfectly capable of absorbing every last detail of the conversation by way of my consciousness. Similarly, he knew my thoughts, and I was tempted to remonstrate him for playing dumb about them...but he was being polite, I supposed, by not presuming to speak on them without permission.

Pre-occupied, I found myself thinking, the words flowing in above and around my already split attention. *Gift for Malin? Can't seem to come up with anything. Nothing ostentatious; charming.*

Why not let me do the thinking for you, Madame? Ask me what you need, and I'll help you acquire it.

Pulled from the conversation completely enough to form more conversant thoughts, I glanced sidelong at the door and completely lost track of the motorcade planning. *All right*, I thought after a few seconds. *I'll tell you what—if you're a good boy and help me come up with a fine little gift for your master, I'll give you a special reward like the good slave you are. You can feast on me for hours...I might even let you have a little of my blood, if it's a very nice gift and he likes it sufficiently.*

An image leapt into my mind, an unhesitating thrust so sudden that I did not understand for upwards of twenty seconds that Dinon was putting it into my head. Indeed, it was so indistinguishable from my own thoughts that even once I realized it was some creation of his, I still was not entirely sure I was not simply imagining it. The image was of a lapel pin, a beautiful set of sapphire gems set in black metal to resemble the shimmering wings of a blue morpho butterfly. Well I could already see Malin wearing it, holding and kissing me with tender pleasure in his gratitude for it—and only then did I sit up a little and ask Dinon, *Are you showing me this?*

It's in a little shop, a jeweler not ten blocks north of here. Shall I go purchase it for you?

Oh, yes, do. My purse is—

"Is that all right with you, darling?"

"Mm?" Head raising from the mesmerism of my conversation with Dinon, I glanced over at Malin and, with a shy smile, pretended to have been listening. "Oh, yes—it's your motorcade of course. I don't want to interfere with the planning."

"It's *our* motorcade, Thecla," he corrected me gently. "Just as it's our money. Real horses will be more expensive, but I think they'll be worth it for reasons of aesthetic and messaging. Don't you agree?"

Oh, horses. Something mild, incidental; something to make me feel included in the planning. A little touched that he was trying to lure me back into the conversation in any way, I smiled and agreed without thinking, "Yes, of course. The autos are so ubiquitous...real horses will stand out."

By the time the meeting was over, after another dull and elongated hour, I discovered a small silver and blue box upon the vanity of my boudoir. Exactly as I had pictured it, the splendid lapel pin sat nestled in black velvet. I smiled at it and slipped it into my purse, eager to give it to Malin on the day of the motorcade. Perhaps, I decided, I would save it to present to him directly before the speech—something to immortalize the moment and increase his confidence, as though he needed such a thing.

And that was that. Days turned to nights; nights back into day. One, two, three, four. Malin kept busy: exceedingly busy. I was not busy, and diverted myself with my husband's love in the morning and Eleison's love at night. I called Rosina on the pocket watch once a day, and wrote to my sister, Sable, at our home in Lescaut. Mercilessly, I tormented Dinon, knowing he loved my teasing and enjoying it myself rather more than I would have cared to admit.

And then: the day came.

I turned over in bed and, to my great surprise, found Malin sitting up already, his dark eyes fixed somewhere into space. Seeing me turn over in search of his arms, he lowered his hand to stroke the tendrils of my hair back from my sleep-softened face.

"It's going to be a long day, Thecla," he told me, unsmiling with what I assumed was simple insomnia. "I hope you're ready."

Even had I known then all things I know now, I never could have been ready.

Not ever.

T

HE DAY BEGAN AS CLEAR and cloudless as the sapphires of the lapel pin whose box I checked in my clutch purse with a smile of pleased anticipation. How I cringe and gnash my teeth with agony to think of the meaningless fancies that seemed to me of such great import! I was like a maiden miming the part of an adult. My concerns where a child's concerns: the joys and fears and hopes of a little girl were what lay in my soul on the morning of the motorcade. Would my darling husband like his gift? Actually care of it at all? Or would he just humor me and put the little butterfly away after tonight, never to wear it again? Would I feel like a fool?

Oh, yes...I would certainly feel like a fool.

"There will be a Rift Event today," Dinon observed, pinning the last of my curls in careful place and stepping back to admire his handiwork.

Like the ignorant creature I was, I scoffed; almost laughed, even knowing the increasingly limitless expanse of his understanding. "Perhaps your mind is centered on some other day of this week, and your strange perception of time mistakes it for today. I just checked the weather report...it's a 5% chance."

"5% is a far cry from 0%, Madame...even if it doesn't seem to be the case. Why, even 1% is a far cry from 0% when it comes right down to it. Wouldn't you say?"

"I suppose," I told him, unable to disguise the pettish impatience from my voice. I felt as though, by his observance of the coming Rift Event, he had willed it into being. "Then I'll humor you. It won't be another blasted Extreme one, will it?"

"No," Dinon allotted. "A freak incident. Mild, but worthy of note. It may be worth delaying the motorcade."

My tongue darting across my dry lips, I contemplated Dinon and frowned. If we delayed the motorcade due to my urging, and nothing happened in the end, I would look silly and be less likely to be believed in more important advisements in the future; but, if we went ahead, and the event truly was mild, perhaps we could divert the motorcade and seek shelter someplace. A restaurant, or a hotel lobby.

"It's not really my decision to make," I said. "But I do appreciate the warning...that's the kind of prophecy I suppose I don't particularly mind. You'll be in the carriage behind ours?"

"Yes, Madame." Politely and patiently, knowing that I had not been listening at all during the planning since my role was essentially to sit in the car with Malin and smile at waving children, Dinon explained the format of the motorcade again. Of the four carriages, ours would be third; the first carriage in the motorcade would contain Ambassador Platt and his small entourage. The second, in a show of solidarity with Malin, would contain the Saalastian police chief and a few officers, with more officers walking along the motorcade. Then would come our open carriage, the third in line, with Ignatius driving, Eleison in the driver's seat beside him, and Malin and I seated where the crowd could see us. "The final carriage," Dinon went on to explain, "is where I'll be, with a few members of Ignatius's team. Should you wish to return home early, when the motorcade is over, I will be happy to transport you back in it."

"I'm quite sure I can find the patience to tolerate Malin's speech, Dinon, thank you." Overcome with a pulse of suggestive excitement despite myself, I smiled and slid up from my vanity seat. "I'll be giving him his pin tonight...you remember what I said. If he likes it, perhaps I'll give you your treat once he's in bed."

With uncharacteristic thinness, the dharmine smiled. "We'll see, Madame," he said, bowing at the waist as I took up my handbag and made my way to meet Malin. "Enjoy your time with Master before the proceedings."

By now, knowing my slave's use of language as well as I do, I have come to interpret his words very differently. Namely, I have learned that when I suggest a plan and Dinon responds with some variety of the words, "We'll see," he is really telegraphing a warning—telling me not to allow my hopes to rise too high. As with so much else, though, at the time it was all just another piece of a puzzle I did not realize to be gathering itself. Feeling pleased— in fact, quite optimistic that when this day would be over, my exhausted husband would recover his mood and be capable of turning his attention more thoroughly to the matter of our heir—I let myself into our bedroom with a pleased smile already stuck on my silly face.

And that smile disappeared when I found Malin in the armchair in the corner of the room, his face in his hands, his body slumped forward in his seat.

It had never truly struck me before how much older my husband was—what that age meant. He was more experienced, yes, and more confident in so many things in the world. He was a fearsome politician with a devastating, frightful reputation, and at the snap of a finger, he could command any human being in Gudrune to leap at his least command.

Yet—he was also so aged. So tired. In the twilight of his life, he could still maintain the superficial characteristics of all those things that made him a threat to the Overseer and the devastating enemy of the Hunters. Excited by his passion for me, he could love me like a man twenty years his junior, and amaze me with a sharp mind and regal wit. His zeal for life was infectious.

But beneath all that, when no one was looking and I was not around—he was just a man. A tired man. An old man: one whose powers were leaving him day on day. Malin was near sixty; in ten years, as he was fond of pointing out, he would begin a process of transition into states of increasing helplessness. The burden of care would shift from him to me, and it would be my responsibility to look after him as he now looked after me.

And in that second—as, hearing me, he rocketed upright in his seat and interrupted his quiet prayers with a brush of his thumb and forefinger briskly over his eyes—I wanted nothing more than to step immediately into that role of caring for him. I wanted to grow: to be ready to truly serve him and support him as he deserved.

"Thecla," he said with a laugh that betrayed his tears, "come in."

"Malin...oh, darling...please—"

Setting down my purse, I hurried to his side and knelt at his feet. His nostrils flared and his lips strained as, taking one hand, I let him caress my face with the other.

"Won't you talk to me," I whispered, looking into his taut visage. "Rest assured, I trust you—I know there are those things you would like to tell me that you cannot, as you yourself have said. But...my angel, my love—can't you unburden your heart to me a little? Of all the scant things I can do for you, isn't offering my soul as a receptacle of your woes chief among my duties as your wife?"

"I was so preoccupied with prayer I didn't hear you coming," he said with a raw chuckle, ignoring my concerns and instead surprising me with the confirmation that he had truly been praying. "Don't mind me—don't trouble yourself with an old man's woes."

"They're not an old man's woes. They're my husband's woes." Frowning, my thumb worrying in the well of his palm, I looked up into his face and insisted, "There's nothing in this world you cannot tell me."

"I know, Thecla. I know—and I will. I swear, I will. Maybe— maybe even after tonight." Distant though his eyes were, they softened with something like hope. Just a little, he smiled, although it was no more his true smile than Dinon's had been. "Yes—you know, darling...soon the day will come when I may speak freely to you. Speak of anything, anytime; and how happy that will make me."

With a flick of my eyes toward the door, I asked in a somewhat sharpish tone, "Does this concern that blasted dharmine?"

Surprise—understanding. The emotions transfigured his face, one after another, in the course of quick seconds: too quick for me to make an interpretation of their appearances.

"What? What—oh—Dinon."

Laughing slightly, Malin kissed my hand, then rose with a hefty sigh for the transition to standing. "No, my pet, it has nothing at all to do with him...though I will confess, he has been an unexpected bulwark these past two weeks. You'd ought to commend him for me when you get a chance. He keeps his distance, and cannot change what he is any more than I can change what I am...but, despite that, there is a core of something in him, I think. Something almost good...even if he is beyond goodness, or even evil."

Before I could roll my eyes and speculate that perhaps the beast had managed to sink his tendrils into Malin's mind as or more deeply than he had done so in mine, Malin drew me to my feet and into his arms. "Just like you," he told me, smiling, his words a little teasing as his eyes flickered over my face. "You can be a downright brat, Thecla...my spoiled little wife...but within you glows a light as radiant as the rising sun. It shines from you like gold and bathes me in serenity whenever you walk into my chambers. Every time you demean yourself with my presence, ah...I am more grateful than I could ever express with a thousand properties, a legion of slaves, a safehouse of jewels...a vineyard of the finest wines." As his thumb traced down my brow, Malin bent to kiss my mouth, then straightened up and looked into my eyes.

In that second, his dark gaze was so soft, so warmed with love, that it seemed he looked into the very essence of my soul. I felt he had more to say—more he craved to say, at any rate.

But, rather than expressing it, he offered me his elbow and said, "Come now, Wife...let's get this over with."

Oh, my poor darling! My husband, my love. How I've fretted over writing this; how I've dragged my feet these past few days, the dread event closing in upon my happier memories until, as inescapable as the gravity of a black hole, it is upon me once again. My only solace is the knowledge that, no matter how immediate it all feels when the pen is in my hand, it is in my past that this dreadful day is now forever consigned: has always been consigned, in a sense I cannot explain. But now, I must describe it. I can delay it no further. The more I tarry, the more painful the expository process will become.

Let us begin.

As mentioned, the day was beautiful. The sky, even over sometimes smoggy Saalast, was brilliantly blue. Eleison smiled warmly at both of us. He wished Malin luck in his speech and then, praising my dress, kissed me on the cheek. Our cavalier held the door for us to enter the carriage, where Malin permitted me to hold and stroke his hand in my lap.

For the drive to the park, it was decided the carriage top had ought to go up. Malin sat with his speech in his free hand, his eyes scanning dryly over it for the first few minutes of the drive before, in the manner of one no longer reading the book over which their eye traveled, he folded the papers crisply up and extended them to me.

"Put these in your handbag, would you," he urged me with a tender tone, apparently grateful for my help in getting the blasted things away from him. "I doubt I'll need them at this point...if I change my mind, I'll know where I can find them."

Without hesitation, I stowed them in my purse. Then, while the carriage rocked around us, Malin slid his arm around my shoulders and folded himself, his great body, down over me to swallow up my mouth in a sudden and insatiable torrent of passion. Under the cover of the carriage, I moaned and gave my lips and tongue and teeth to him utterly—though, I confess, exposure to the crowd's eye would only have added to my pleasure in doing so. He made me collapse, my husband, my sweet Malin. Far more than the pleasure his kiss provided me, it was the palpable intensity of his consuming love that raced my heart and made me sink against his chest.

"Oh, Malin," I sighed, caressing his scar with my free hand while the other bunched somewhat the crisp ironing of his suitcoat. "Husband, my love, my adored Master Farrow—when we're through here and you're relieved of your duties for the night, rest assured, I and perhaps even Eleison will spare nothing to ease your tension and celebrate the completion of the day."

"What a pretty thought," Malin said, his voice soft against my lips even as his expression hardened with an aggravated sigh for that very same cavalier who rang through on the RMS watch. While I giggled, Malin picked up the call with a terse, "What the devil is it, Eleison?"

"Sorry if I'm interrupting, Malin," said Eleison, only just barely resisting slipping into an old role and calling him 'sir', "but the hair on the back of my neck is standing up. Literally. My watch just updated with a new Rift advisory."

My diaphragm tightened, though I could not explain why. Even when Eleison went on to emphasize, "It's suddenly 90%; we're looking at a freak event," I felt I hardly had cause to be so frightened. Particularly not as Malin clicked his tongue in soft displeasure, then thought it through.

"Not Extreme, though?"

"No," Eleison allotted. "Very mild. Probably won't last longer than twenty minutes; my borro might not even be able to come out in it."

"Well," said my husband, "that isn't so bad. I think the crowd can handle that...and the police lining the motorcade's route can deal with a stray rodi or two."

"It could always produce something bigger."

Eleison's concern elicited from Malin a scoff of the old arrogance that had become to me something of a comfort, for it was a sign of my husband's true heart bucking up from beneath the waves of his recent distress.

"Oh, a rodi, a harpros, even a ventil...a damned giganturn. It's all the same. I want this motorcade to run as scheduled; we don't want to look weak, especially not in front of a twenty minute little micro-event."

Eleison chuckled, saying, "All right...I don't want to step on your big day, after all."

The call ended, and Malin navigated across the screen of the watch with the edge of his thumb to confirm the new weather report. With another, softer sound of derision, he snapped the device shut and peered out the window with the case's metal edge pressed to the corner of his mouth.

"If only it were a harpros," he said, half to himself. "I'd coach it to land on my arm...add to the effect of my mystique. You know, Thecla"—glancing back at me, his eyes sweeping across my face and, in reflex, down to my decolletage for a quick second— "I had the most beautiful hunting harpros when I was a young man. Aristophanes; gorgeous creature."

Smiling, I stroked his free hand and told him, "I saw a picture of it in some silly biography about you I happened to read while at Glenn's house. Though, I confess, I was not nearly so taken with the Rift falcon as I was with his handsome keeper."

His smile returned, crooked, somewhat pleased despite

himself. Drawing me close to his side, Malin nuzzled his cheek against the temple of my forehead and said, "I loved that bird. A capital hunter...and loyal even without my need to influence him. Just like you, Thecla. Loyal, and beautiful, and vicious when required."

"I'm not so sure that third is the compliment you intended," I said with a laugh, eliciting a soft chuckle.

"Why? Because you think you should be soft and feminine all the time? Or—are you embarrassed about that business with the dharmine in the woods? I heard the men worked together to save you."

Blanching, I turned to look into my husband's eyes and stuttered out, "You—you knew about it?"

"Oh, Ba'al-Dinon told me all about it, but assured me it was under control. I trust him...and you."

"Why on earth didn't you bring it up?"

"You sound almost angry that I didn't put you over my knee with a lecture about going too far from home..." Chuckling, his hand sliding up and down the curve of my shoulder, Malin admitted, "I thought about bringing it up...but God knows, Thecla...as much as I've kept from you during our short period of matrimony, the very least I can do is let you pick and choose what you tell me about yourself...about your mind, your life. About you."

I inhaled against a swell of unaccountable emotion: a state for which I blamed the upcoming Rift event, no matter how small. Yet that same emotion filled me with longing until it spilled over. I could no longer contain my thoughts and, while Malin turned his distracted attention back to the window, I caught his face and drew him back for another impassioned kiss. While his lips parted in a soft, almost submissive sigh that permitted me entrance into his mouth, if only I should choose to breach the entry, I drew back a millimeter enough to look into his eyes.

"I want to be totally open with one another," I whispered, my thumb petting his high cheekbone. "I don't want to keep secrets from you, Malin. Please...when the last of what you keep from me is revealed, oh, Husband...let's learn how to be fully honest with one another."

His mouth strained: not in any displeasure, but in the simple swell of emotion that had risen also in him upon finding my body an insufficient vessel. "My angel," he said softly. "I promise. One day, each of us will know all there is to know about the other: no secrets, not one, will remain between us. Just do your best to be patient...I know it's very hard."

It was hard: almost as impossibly hard as it was to be patient with the motorcade's planned start. Ignatius and Eleison did, upon reaching the park, manage to talk Malin into delaying by thirty minutes to see if the Event might come and pass. Instead, the weather held tightly on; and with the top down, I became more aware of the sensation Eleison had described. The familiar tingling of sensual energy trailed down my spine and built in the center of my torso, waiting to develop into something substantial enough to emerge from me in the form of that animal who was content enough to come when called upon during calm climates, but who craved and begged and sometimes demanded to see its release when the weather turned foul.

Yet the sky remained blue, not indigo; and by the passage of the half hour, Malin was visibly impatient, his hard face daring anyone, even Eleison, to approach him with a further delay. So, the top of our carriage down, we drove onwards, exiting the park and following along the barricaded motorcade route which had been prepared to empty the streets of other vehicles while allowing ample space for the eager crowds.

And the crowds were most assuredly eager. It is funny to me even all these years later that, whatever my husband's fearsome reputation both in and out of Gudrune, and however hated he was by those whom he had humiliated in war, the admiration he commanded from our own citizens bordered on out and out love. The fear was certainly there, of course—when he and I walked down the street or took dinner in a restaurant that was more populated than our preference, the individuals there paled and hastened to mind their business. But, insulated by the anonymity of the crowd, that fear could manifest as what it really was: respect, less easily overwhelmed when not in the direct presence of his splendor.

And so it was that, as we turned a block and were greeted with a veritable sea of people whose murmurings and late coming additions had been increasingly apparent to me since the park, I was astonished into a smile of surprise. You may find pictures of that smile in many history books, I think; fewer images of the kiss Malin doled out to me after his initial, far more reserved smile and gallant wave to the crowd.

Yet these are only ever present in such records to add to the emotional impact of the horror.

The motorcade was intended to be substantial, twenty-four blocks of the city of Saalast. With his right hand firmly holding mine, Malin used his left to wave at those we passed, and I mirrored him. Just as every man who made fleeting eye contact with their territory master in such a circumstance was sure to feel bolstered and blessed, each mother I favored with a sympathetic smile and approving wave at her children seemed to glow with honor and return my smile at double-breadth; and every little girl who saw I looked upon her burst with excitement, sometimes turning to tug on her mother's or nursemaid's skirts to swear I had smiled at her; and every little boy blushed and gawked, sometimes hiding himself a little behind his parents as though my fondness was far too much for him to take; and all the husbands, and single men, and officers over whom my gaze quickly passed seemed to have their eyes fixed upon me with covetous longing that increased my pride as Malin's bride: his and his alone to take and dispense for his pleasure.

I reminisce on this not to stoke my ego, but to reflect on why it was that, when the blue of the sky dimmed to purple so quickly that it was at least a full minute before the pocket watches of the crowd jingled with an expansive wave of RMS alarms, so many witnesses chose to stay. They, like us, weighed the risk and the opportunity: and, like us, they deemed the opportunity in excess of all that concerned them. I heard words like "mild," "passing," "quick one" amid the babble of the crowd as we passed along; and though some who had not yet seen us dispersed down alleys and back up avenues with skulking disappointment I could detect from even ten blocks away, far more remained.

Halfway through the motorcade, the first incident drew my attention. "Hey," shouted one of the officers we had just passed, diverting a pair walking along with our carriage into falling back. A few people in the crowd gasped. I turned to follow the sound, as did Eleison, but we were already almost around the corner and so, though we could detect some rippling of observers and some movement of police, there was no way to see precisely what it was that had happened.

"There's your harpros, Eleison," said Malin with a wry chuckle. "Statistically speaking, in weather like this, I doubt we'll encounter any more along our route...you can relax."

"With this many people," admitted Eleison, "it's a little hard."

"All the more reason we're safe. Given a crowd like this, even a giganturn would think twice before wandering in. You need to relax, old boy. Ah—blast."

Malin's pocket watch rang with another busy chime. He flipped it open with agitation, then answered it only as he saw it was the chief of Saalast's police. "Is now the time," Malin asked into the watch, at roughly the same second I noted the route ahead had been thinned not just of spectators, but also of officers. Where, along our previous blocks, there had been at least one man every ten or so feet, ahead their arrangement was far wider. A response to the Rift Event, I assumed without thinking more on it; though there may have been but a few beasts about to be released upon the city, even the smallest Rift Event merited some patrolling to ensure no infestation of unnatural animals could take root.

"S—a—fin—"

And even the smallest Rift Event could cause interference with electronics, if one was unlucky, which it seemed we were. With a roll of his eyes as the pocket watch stuttered the chief's message, Malin said in irritation, "I can't hear you; can you speak up?"

As he turned at the waist to look back from his seat in the autocarriage ahead of us, the police chief shouted into his watch again.

"Sh—ta—ca—"

"Why not let's save this for when we're parked at Horizon,"

said Malin, cutting him off with a brisk snapping shut of his watch. Wearing a look of profound annoyance, the chief balked at his own watch, then shoved it into the hands of one of his officers while, to my amazement, he dismounted from his moving carriage and took a few great strides toward us down the left side of the parade route.

And, much like our organic horses, my attention was so caught by this unusual decision that I did not see the man squeezing out of the crowd on the right side of the motorcade.

We were all subject to the misdirection, purely accidental, on the part of the chief; but the horses were by far the most unwitting assistants in the foul deed unfolding, for, as the tense fellow in the gray coat sprinted between the barriers with more than six yards between himself and the nearest police officer, their captured attention made them vulnerable to fright. Catching his motion from the corner of their eyes, they protested it with a dual neighing and, on the part of one, a half-rear that brought our carriage to a halt. Now, we followed the attention of the horses.

And before I could even understand what was happening—before I could even register the man was not a police officer, or one of the motorcade, but instead a stranger who bore the Hunter's Guild seal tattooed upon the back of his hand—the gun was being raised toward me.

Eleison shouted; someone in the crowd screamed. With a great crack, louder than a thunderclap in my ears, something punched into my abdomen so hard I wheezed even before the pain. "Thecla," cried Malin as his rough hands caught me, pulled me back, pushed me down amid the shouts, the chaos, the flurry of male panic that alarmed me so much more intensely than even my own fear—Malin's body pushing before mine—the second crack, the third (Eleison's gun), screams from the spectators, so many screams, my husband's weight as he fell back in my arms with a sharp, staggered gasp: all of it nothing, nothing compared to the hot splatter of his blood that flowed in ribbons from his side and over my hand, over my own wound, the way his voice, rasping my name ("Thecla—") flowed over my ears and my heart.

Another shot ended the rasp.

My husband slumped back, dead in my arms not three seconds after his stunned eyes fixed upon mine and revealed, to my great sorrow, nothing.

14

THE PAIN OF THAT MOMENT was greater than what any bullet could have caused me. I scarcely realized I had been shot, for I was so consumed by the incomprehensible experience of looking down into my husband's dead face, his mouth slack with his final breath and his brow's great distress easing as with the kiss of sleep.

For a few seconds, I daresay my expression mirrored his: mouth agape, eyes hazy, flesh draining of all color. Only after the initial seconds of shock had calculated through my mind (Dream? No. Misunderstanding? No. Delusion? No, no—reality—) did I managed to gasp his name, to say it: to scream it. Like the bullet wound in my body, I was not even aware of my own screaming, nor of the tears that gushed down my cheeks. I clutched him, touching his face, staunching the fount of blood that sprang from his throat, then crying out anew to find my gown soaked through with the blood from his side. No—from my own blood, too.

Someone shouted "He's getting away" while Eleison, having landed a shot in the assassin's shoulder to succeed in repelling him, dropped his pistol in the scramble to assess Malin's condition, and mine. "Oh, Christ," said Eleison, his face wracked with grief as his eyes fled from wound to wound on Malin's body, then finally landed on mine. "Fuck, ah, shit—Thecla—"

But I was preoccupied. Eleison slid his hand between my husband's body and mine to put pressure on my wound; yet, hearing only the urgency of chasing down the perpetrator, and perhaps knowing it was the most reliable way to save its own life and mine, the ventil was already half-free of my body. While the antlers burst from my skull, members of the crowd who had lingered to watch the unfolding chaos gasped in astonishment: and by the time Ignatius had control of the horses well enough to drive the carriage forward at top speed, I was free of the vehicle— free of my clothes—and landing upon the asphalt of the Saalast street with four hooves beneath me.

It amazes me how clear were my thoughts of pursuit even with the animal in charge: my soul was like an arrow loosed from the archer's bow, and the momentum of vengeance carried me, galloping, down the path that frightened spectators hastened to clear. For a few long seconds, I couldn't seem to discern how it was I knew the path the killer had taken: then I detected with full consciousness the coppery scent of blood, the ventil's nose sensitive and poised to detect such things in the name of evading threats. Now, it drove into those threats, raging down the alley while Eleison shouted my name.

The delay in my response had allowed the assassin head-start enough to clear the alley's exit by the time I entered. Leaping over a garbage can that had been upended by the bastard, I sprinted so quickly one of the ventil's antlers clipped a metal fire escape and made our heads ring with the shock. By the time we emerged, the passersby—some of whom, I am sure, had been early escapees from the chaos of the motorcade—mostly stood staring lamely in the wake of the man who let his coat fall from his shoulders to lighten his load. The white sleeve of his shirt had been soaked through with blood, unmistakable and almost black with the fluid's density. Once, twice, he looked over his shoulder, but I caught no more than a quick glimpse of his face as, each time, he took stock of my increasing proximity and righted his gaze to push onward. Pedestrians, meanwhile, stumbled from my path, mistaking me for a wild animal that had been agitated into violence by the unlucky fool I pursued.

And I was a wild animal. Without doubt, I was insane. I could not accept that there was nothing I could do. I could not accept when, at the end of the second block, a silver autocarriage screeched to a halt and the door flung open for the killer. Without hesitation, he dove into the shadowed interior of the car; the driver didn't wait for the door to shut before urging the horses into action again, and the mechanical creatures, more reliable than fleshly ones, galloped off along the road while I changed course. Heart sinking with the inevitability of his escape, I pushed myself, even the ventil's muscles burning—

And from around the apartment building at the end of the block stepped Dinon, whose black cloak swirled around his feet, his footman's guise forgotten.

"Madame," he said, his hands raised to reveal his white palms while the ventil snorted and raged to have been cut off, "it doesn't matter."

How could he say such a thing? I would have had more than a few choice words for my slave in that instant of his interference: as it was, the ventil lowered herself to threaten him with the spear tips of her antlers. When that did not frighten him off, she paced and reared and paced some more, a clear warning that if he— or anyone—should dare to come near, even his dharmine's self-healing powers would fail to surmount the violence he would endure.

No one in that moment could have eased me, the wildness and fury of my heart: no one but Eleison, whose footfalls drew my sharp attention until, fully feeling the clarifying energy of his presence, all threatening display came to a panting halt.

"Baby," he said, his voice straining to portray calmness, his red eyes gleaming with a battle against tears, "baby, I know. I know, Thecla. But, right now—"

"Right now," said Ba'al-Dinon, helpfully inserting his calm assessment before Eleison could yield to his own emotions, "you are the Matrix of Gudrune, in the form of an animal, in the streets of Saalast with assassins about; and, unless I am mistaken, you will not heal so easily from a bullet wound as a ventil transforming back to a woman. Indeed, you're lucky you're still freshly acquainted enough with the animal that she's healed you at all."

He was right. Of course, he was right. The ventil's overcoming of my body meant that the wound had knit itself shut and perhaps even extruded the bullet, this latter matter being a question for doctors. But if, in this animal form, another killer emerged and fired another round, there would be nothing simple in the healing process. Just as Eleison's borro, gravely wounded by the fight in the factory during our first year together, had required the intercession of my love to experience any modicum of healing, so would I require his if the ventil was wounded...and, depending on where I was hypothetically shot, it was possible not even that could heal me before death took me in his arms.

Oh! Death! Death! How I longed for death—for if I could not have vengeance, I craved Malin. With an awful shock of horror as Eleison closed in to place a gentle hand upon the ventil's nose, I realized Malin could no longer comfort me. Never—not ever. That his consciousness—his soul—had departed his body; my husband's body.

I was Matrix of Gudrune, and a widow.

"Eleison," I wept, trembling, naked in the streets of Saalast without even realizing his touch had summoned me back from the body of the deer, "oh, Eleison—"

"I know," Eleison gasped, his own tears brimming over. "Thecla, oh, sweetheart—oh, Jesus—"

While I sobbed, Eleison released a strangled gasp and snatched me to his chest. Something soft as spider's gossamer was lain upon my shoulders, enfolding me in warmth and dignity that meant less than nothing in that awful moment. Only when Dinon's hand pressed to my shoulder through the fabric did I recognize it was his cloak; I looked back to find him restored to his footman's guise, his wild silver hair once more neatly braided, his footman's uniform missing its suitcoat but otherwise impeccable.

"I don't know why you're standing here, Dinon," I spat at him, gnashing my teeth through my wretched tears. "You fool, you should be chasing down that carriage—"

"And reveal to all of Saalast that its mistress employs a dharmine, while being herself an altered woman?"

Only about to point out that his change of costume was surely worth as much revelation, I noticed the block around us was half-empty: that officers, themselves occupied with that task charged to them, busily pushed back the nosy crowd and cleared the street with such prejudice that not a single eye could have remained upon us. In a city overflowing with people, we were alone.

We were alone, and my husband was dead, and I was not.

"I shouldn't have changed," I gasped, turning to hide my face against Eleison's heart. "Oh, God—I should have stayed with Malin, I should have died there with him—"

"It would have taken you hours to die from a wound in the stomach like that," Eleison informed me gruffly, his hands tightening and his demeanor hardening at my unapologetically selfish longing to follow my husband. "And what the fuck would I have done, huh, Thecla? If you had died—Christ—"

His hand tightening in my hair as, somewhere on the edges of my awareness, another carriage—this one, ours—hastened to the scene, Eleison kissed the top of my head and whispered, "I'm so glad you're alive. Oh, Thecla—"

"How can you say that to me? How can you be glad for anything now? Malin is dead—oh, God, my husband is dead—"

"Sh." Stroking my back, Dinon gestured toward the carriage that had halted at the block's end. "We need to get you both to the hospital, Madame."

Hope stirred like a bird caged in my chest. "There's a chance he might live?"

For once unsmiling, his beautiful expression instead painted with deep solemnity, Dinon informed me, "The coroner is there," before adding, "Dr. Singer will be on her way to meet us there momentarily."

Dr. Singer—our household doctor's name rose over me with a sharp pinch of soul-pain, all her advice in the art of engendering children forever amounting to nothing. My heart sank all the deeper into the black muck of despair.

Yes—that was it, wasn't it? No child. There would be no child now. No more chances. No more love. No more, no more—nothing, forever. An entire lifetime without Malin. All plans interrupted. All dreams shattered.

"You ride in the front," Eleison urged me. Then, hesitating to give my cloak-wrapped nudity new consideration, he cursed and looked briskly around. "Wait, no—Thecla—"

I had slipped away from him and made my way toward the carriage door, unhesitating—nearly running, in fact, as if intent on throwing myself into my living husband's arms. Indeed, some small part of me all but swore that would be the case: that I would throw open the carriage and, like the actor in some obscene practical joke, Malin would wrap me in his arms and let me weep for relief instead of sorrow.

Instead, as I jerked open the door, all the blood that had pooled upon the floor poured down over my bare feet. I cringed away but a second before, with a wretched hitch of my breath, I stood looking in.

"Thecla," Eleison urged me, at my right hand with his fingers deftly slipping round my elbow, "come away, let's—"

"I will ride with my husband." I forced my eyes to fix upon Malin's body, slumped back against the seat. Mounting the step into the car while Eleison made a noise of disapproval, I had my attention diverted by the green glint of the handbag floating in the blood. The inevitability of his speech renewed itself, as if I already held it in my hand.

Perhaps our shared dreams had died—but I would not let Malin's dreams die with him.

"Sit in the front," I commanded Eleison smoothly, my voice still given a ragged edge despite the ease with which I ordered my lover about, "and instruct Ignatius he is to bring us straightaway to Horizon. We have a speech to give."

'We'. The royal we, or Malin and I? His phantom, placing words in my mouth. Eleison looked at me, incredulous, and insisted, "You can't think that's a good idea."

"He doesn't—he didn't—doesn't want us to look weak." I was unable to acknowledge through the tense of my speech that my husband's life now lay in the past. "I won't fail him—Horizon is too important, and the strength of Gudrune— Now it will be in question, won't it?"

Yes. In serious question. With its infamous master dead and its power handed off to some inexperienced young woman from the country, whose inheritance had not even been confirmed by the continent's Overseer—

"Dinon," I commanded, stepping into the pooling blood of my husband to kneel beside his limp body, "come in with me and dress me on the way."

"Yes, Madame," the obedient creature said, obedient still after Malin's death by his own choice or by the simple strength of Malin's original command. Eleison watched with his teeth bared, his red eyes flashing with grief and fury—but, seeing me wrap my arms around my husband's body, he realized I would hear no more of it and wisely shut the door without protracted argument.

Then, alone but for my servant, I stared grimly into my husband's faded eyes and expected a torrent of tears.

And I did cry: I gasped, my mouth trembling as I caressed his cheek and closed his eyes before the rigor of death could make the task horrifically impossible. I kissed the scar down the side of his face and pressed his head to my breast, and soon his hair was as wet with tears as with blood.

Yet it was not the wailing, the terrible typhoons of grief and sorrow, that would wrack me through the rest of that vile summer. The shock was still such that even as the tears poured down, my mind turned again and again to practical matters: to finishing the day, the motorcade.

The speech.

With only the greatest reluctance, I eased my husband's head back against the seat, then snatched up the patent leather of the green handbag now stained with vivid red gore. Sniffing sharply, wiping my wrist beneath my eyes, I told Dinon, "When you dress me, slave, leave my husband's blood where it is upon me."

"As you wish, Madame," said Dinon, looking on while I fished the pages of the speech from my purse. "Your husband is proud of you."

"Don't soothe me," I remonstrated him, frowning at the blood that had leaked into the bag and oozed along the left edge of the papers. Dropping the handbag back where I found it to separate the pages, I scanned my husband's final speech in search of key points to adjust for the new realities of the day—

And I discovered it was never a speech in the first place.

My darling Thecla, it began, arresting my attention as soon as my eye worked its way to the top line, *if I have let you read this letter, it means that I am dead.*

My mouth opened. Mute, unable to even look up as, around me, the purple Rift radiation of Dinon's magic enfolded me to make a gown, I fell back against the same seat where my husband's body reclined, and read the letter to the end.

15

MY DARLING *Thecla,*

If I have let you read this letter, it means that I am dead. It is said no man knows the day or the time, and it is true that I still know nothing of these matters at all. Yet, upon reviewing the array of evidence before me, I have concluded that the odds of my death coming to me today rest uncomfortably beyond the usual daily odds of an old man's demise—and remember, my darling, to console yourself with the fact that I am—was—an old man.

You must be quite astonished, perhaps enraged, and you have every right to be. After all the secrets I have kept from you, this is perhaps still among the most egregiously cruel: and I have felt cruel for hiding it. Indeed, I feel unconscionably cruel to think of what you have witnessed by the time you read these words. I would not blame you for feeling betrayed, knowing your husband had some advanced premonition of his own death but did not confide it in you.

Yet, how could I? You are a well-read woman. You know as well as I that the stories of ancient times indicate it is not the pursuit or avoidance of prophecy that dooms a man, but the simple hearing of that prophecy at all. How could I avoid what has been commissioned without bringing about some far greater, far more horrible punishment for the both of us? How could I risk you, your precious life—and perhaps, if we are blessed, a precious life growing inside you—when accepting the reality of my fate might release the tension and give you some protection?

You know as well as I do that the political path ahead of you is a difficult one, fraught with resistance and danger. You have not yet been ratified as my successor by the Overseer, and so, while you are interim Matrix and de facto custodian of the territory, you will need to fight like a hellcat to maintain the position. And, tempting as it must feel at this very moment to simply abdicate and pass the power to someone you feel better suited, I can promise you, Thecla: there is none better suited to lead Gudrune than you, my wife.

My wife! I speak of such abhorrently practical matters in this letter, don't I? It is to my shame that I can find no other place to turn, for when I think of the pain this will cause your sensitive soul, I am so immensely grieved that I am tempted to relinquish my powers, myself. Perhaps there is a world where I tell you all this beforehand and, abdicating Gudrune's control, you and I and Eleison flee the continent entire for a peaceful life elsewhere in this wide world...but, as strange as it may seem to suggest it at the moment, that would actually be a far more hopeless and empty world than this one. And, besides: what would your poor Rosina do for a mother?

So, I have accepted it, as much as any man can accept

knowledge of his fate. I have accepted for years now that my death would be inevitable and violent; but I only began to despair that notion upon meeting you, my precious jewel—my life—my bride. Since experiencing your meritless love, which is so deep and absolute no man could deserve it, (let alone one such as I!), I have come to love life as I never have in all my decades of living. Indeed, you make me realize that, all this time, I have been dead; and it is only by your love that I have ever had a prayer of feeling truly alive.

Prayer—yes, prayer. Pray for me, Thecla! Pray for me always, if you do nothing else to remember my name in this life. Pray for your husband, so that your soul—the sweet and holy vineyard planted upon the dark dungeon of my heart—might pour just a bit of its light into whatever dark, bleak place a man such as I should find himself after his death. Let your love light my way, now and forever, as it has in these too few but deeply important years at the end of my life.

I love you, Thecla, my precious one, my treasure. Thank you for making the end of my life such a joy.

Your Husband Eternally,
Malin Farrow

Now I did weep, madly, frantically, somehow ashamed by the fathomless depths of what had obviously been a love in keeping with or even excess of what Malin took care to show to me every day we were together—and now would show no more. Subsequent pages were likewise related to his letter's contents, consisting of important contacts, private instructions to me about his unfinished administrative matters, and a suggested to-do list of items for me to newly initiate in wrapping up his death. What a strange and almost amusingly organized man my husband was! 'Contact Charlotte' sat at the top of the list, a heading beneath which was listed 'Plan: Funeral, Media Broadcast, Wake', among other choice lines. There was more—calling a meeting of the Gudrune territory's governors to garner their support, visiting Azstoria as soon as could be managed to quell any hopes of renewed independence, any number of other political dealings he thought would benefit me—but I could hardly read them at the time.

Awed, I lowered the letter into my now-adorned lap, the indigo tulle of my green-accented gown already absorbing my husband's blood enough to leave it blackish crimson up to my knees. "Did you tell him something of this, Dinon," I asked, addressing my servant but unable to tear my gaze from Malin's discordantly peaceful face.

"He knew long before I met either of you in this life of yours, Madame."

I did not sense any lie in his words, and anyway had no reason to doubt them. Given my experience with the Riftborn fortune teller who once came through Lescaut and delivered dreams of Eleison in advance of my meeting him by roughly ten years, there was no shortage of places Malin could obtain such grim intelligence. It hardly seemed worth reflecting on the matter at the time; I merely nodded, drinking in his face, knowing all the portraits and photographs and videos in the world could never amount to the handsome features of my husband when he was present before me.

These handsome features, buried beneath the earth for the rest of human time!

New tears came to my eyes. I thrust the papers in Dinon's

direction. "Hold on to these," I commanded him, relieved that the carriage rolled to a stop as I spoke. "I will need them later, even if I'm not sure I could bear to read them again with my own eyes. Will you fix my hair before I face them?"

What an oddly meek request, considering my customary tone of address for Dinon! Yet, in that instant, I felt so helpless with uncertainty—still so much a child who had now lost father and husband alike—that I could not even posture at unkindness. With a soft edge to his otherwise unflappable expression, Dinon said, "I already have, Madame." His gaze followed my hand to the dark curls that had been, by his will alone, arranged into a high chignon and adorned with a black tiara whose edges swept around each side of my head into peaks like wicked horns.

"Very good," I said, softly. "Very good."

With a lingering study that pained me more by the second, I pressed a kiss to Malin's drooping mouth. His lips, limp beneath mine as they never were in even the deepest of slumbers, already seemed to be growing cold. Drawing back, my breath hitching in my throat, I told his still body, "I love you," in a way that felt useless and empty: wasted.

Not wanting to waste my love for Malin on his dead doppelgänger, I turned away and exited the carriage for our speech.

PART II

16

WHO COULD REMEMBER what I said before the people of Gudrune on that awful day, when my heart died along with my poor husband? It is recorded in enough volumes concerning his life and mine; and you, reader, know the themes of its contents better than anyone who attended the Horizon center's opening that day. No speech could ever have gotten across the pain of my loss as you understand it; no onlooker could hear in my words my true dedication to protecting my husband's legacy. I had done almost no public speaking at all since my time in Valquist, and I do remember feeling a vague hint of surprise for my own strength of voice and confidence of expression—yet even that surprise was felt as a dead nerve feels. Distantly, vaguely, as through a thick barrier of sackcloth.

Those who were assembled remained utterly silent. Photographs were taken because I insisted it. And when it was over, Eleison and Dinon helped me from the stage to take my husband and me to the hospital. Only there was I separated from him: while he saw the coroner, I met with Dr. Singer and Charlotte, both of whom had been evidently crying to lesser or greater degrees. Charlotte, being Charlotte, stuffed her emotions down into some sealed vault in the bottom of her soul while Dr. Singer examined my nude body. She ordered imaging that was initiated with a speed I doubt the average person experiences from even the finest hospitals of Saalast; and after another speedy hour of processing, in which Eleison sat by my side and grim-faced Charlotte paced back and forth from urgent phone call to urgent phone call, Singer returned with a look of profound distress.

"The bullet seems to have been expelled when you transformed during the motorcade, Madame," said Dr. Singer, her hands folded over a file she held before her stomach as she addressed me from beside my hospital bed. "I assumed as such, since you've been able to walk under your own power since. However..."

I was so taken aback by her next words that I asked her to repeat herself, even as Eleison inhaled like he himself had been shot.

"I said," Dr. Singer repeated, "the ultrasound indicated you're about six weeks pregnant, and—I'm concerned, Madame, that the bullet's penetration into your abdomen may have caused irreversible damage to the fetus. At least, the trauma to your body may cause the loss of the pregnancy, and I am not confident your transformation resolved it—we need to keep you on bedrest for the next six weeks."

"I can't be on bedrest for six weeks," I hissed. "I'm Matrix of Gudrune. My husband left so much work for me to do, I—are you sure? Are you absolutely sure?"

"About the pregnancy? Yes, I am. About the bullet?" Dr. Singer spread her hands while my hand pressed to the spot in my abdomen that had been earlier wet with blood. "Without even an entry wound, it's impossible for me to be sure exactly where and how you were shot, and to predict what the effect will be. However—on close analysis of the ultrasound, it looks like the placenta may have separated from the uterine wall, and—"

"Oh, God— Don't. Stop. I don't want to hear it." My feet digging into the mattress against the new wave of premature grief, I thrust up my hand and said with a pained gasp, "It's too horrible, Doctor. Stop, stop—I can't."

"I'm sorry," said Dr. Singer softly, her expression drawn and her eyes lightly misted with tears that were no comparison for my own gathering storm. With her gaze flicking briefly to my abdomen, then back to my face, she assured me in as professional a tone as she could muster, "If you want to improve the odds of a positive outcome, it's important you remain at rest for long as possible. I understand you have a lot to do, but—consider delegation. The territory will understand if you refuse to make any public appearances for a time."

"And the Overseer will take full advantage of my absence." With a deep gasp that did nothing to dispel my tears but did, at least, keep their surging at bay for now, I gestured Dr. Singer to the door. "You may go, Doctor, thank you. I—I mean that," I added as she stepped back from my bed. "Thank you."

Lowering her head in a deferent nod, Dr. Singer turned away and hastened from the room to shut the door silently behind her.

Now, alone with Eleison for the first time all day, let alone since the trauma, I turned to face him—and the moment we locked eyes, I could not bear the sight of his sorrow. His pained expression deepened my agony, and my agony sharpened his sorrow, and soon we were a feedback loop of grief and weeping. "It's okay," Eleison said uselessly, climbing into the bed to wrap me in his arms and rock me against his chest, his own tears belying the tender doubts of his supportive words. "It's okay, Thecla, oh, I know, but it's okay—we're here together, baby. I've got you."

"And when will this awful world take *you* from me, too? Oh, God—oh, Malin." My hand flying at first over my eyes, I then twisted my face away from my palm and buried it in Eleison's tear-soaked shirt. "Eleison, oh, Eleison, don't leave me—"

"I won't, baby. I won't. I promise. Not even death could take me from you."

How often Malin used to express such heartfelt sentiments of eternal love to me! How gravely he meant them, or seemed to at the time. Yet grave they were, indeed. His own awaited him; and it was not three days of useless bedrest before the child followed, a bloody mess and awful female pain clutching at my insides until the fetus and all that accompanied it had passed fully from me.

How cruel, how sick, that the ventil could save me, but that her transformation did nothing to help the child! I wept without ceasing that first day, intermittently cursing God and praying out long, pathetic apologies—to Him, to Malin, to the heir whose carriage I had not been strong enough to maintain. Yet now, looking back with a more rational eye across all that had to happen, I know there was none at fault but that same assassin who took my husband's life: that same assassin whose pursuit I commissioned to no avail.

"I'm sure he was one of that damned guild," I remember telling Eleison and the others in the meeting I held on the subject two days before Malin's funeral. "You mean to say not one former Hunter has come into a Saalastian hospital with a bullet in his shoulder in the past two weeks?"

"An extremist operative like that probably got his surgery done in-house," Eleison explained to me while, in a physical affectation inherited from Malin (oh—*late* Malin!) I leaned back in my seat and rubbed my face from my brow to my mouth. He worried his scar when performing such a motion of self-stimulating thought; I, with no scar to worry but the one on my soul, simply worked the tension from my face and covered my lips as if to contain the complexity of my cogitation.

"Then we must have some old registry, mustn't we?" My hand dropped as I looked around the table, from Eleison to the security men to the very chief of police who had been trying to warn us at the time of the trauma (and therefore provided key misdirection permitting the approach of the assassin) that a prior attempt had been prevented during the slight commotion before the motorcade took a corner. "The Hunter's Guild surely had to keep Gudrune informed of its licensed members if it was to stay on good terms with us."

With a slight scoff, Chief Arlington leaned forward in his seat and folded his hands upon the highly polished wood of the very table where Malin had awarded Horizon their grant. "With all due respect, Madame—"

"Matrix," Eleison and I corrected in unison, leading to a slight wiggle of Arlington's moustache.

"With all due respect, *Matrix*," he revised, meeting my eyes, "are you suggesting we go through the entire list of registered hunters in Gudrune, including the innocent ones that serve our territories during Rift Events even now, and investigate them one by one?"

Aware of a strange impudence I knew I would encounter again and again but had not yet learned to adequately identify as misogyny, I stared flatly back into Arlington's face and told him, "Isn't that what my husband would expect of you?"

Nostrils flaring, Arlington dropped his eyes. I lowered mine in a calculatedly demure display of satisfaction and, collecting the documents that had been arrayed before me throughout the course of the meeting, tapped them all straight as I spoke. "It seems to me that such an investigation is something you'd ought to be focused on regardless of the territory master's—regardless of their most recent act of defiance. Has crime in Saalast not increased substantially since the Hunters dissolved in Gudrune?"

"That's—"

"I would choose your defense with care," I told him, amazed at my own ability to speak this way to a man I hardly knew; but in truth it was because I hardly knew him...and because a petty part of me ascribed some unjust share of the blame to the distraction he clumsily provided. "If you would claim that the former members of the Hunter's Guild remain necessary to maintain some semblance of law and order during Rift Events, that begs the question if your fraternity is of any value at all. Does anyone here have a better suggestion than using the old registry for a systematic investigation?"

The table was silent. Arlington made one last stab at avoiding work, suggesting, "You may be looking at retaliation from the Guild—within or without Gudrune."

"From without," I said coldly, "I would welcome an invitation to turn my attentions to something that could occupy my mind.

From within, there is no Hunter's Guild, Chief Arlington; and you would do well to remember that. I'll expect you at the same time next week with a briefing on your progress."

"Matrix," he said, rising with the whole of the table when I pushed myself up from my seat. I could see it in his mottled face, his beady eyes: whether because of my age or my sex, Arlington did not relish taking my orders.

And I hardly relished giving them.

When all had been seen from the room by Eleison, and I remained to stare through the window whose red velvet curtain I pushed aside, Charlotte appeared at my elbow—a custom of silent movement that, I suspect, had kept me so relatively unphased by Dinon's literal ability to do so. "It's three hours past lunchtime," Charlotte said, her eyes sweeping me from the black collar that rose high about my throat to the very hem of the somber dress falling in empire waist to the joints of my ankles. "So you will be taking supper late, then?"

"No," I said, feeling hardly connected to my body now that the meeting was over. My eyes following a little blue bird that hopped upon the terrace of the neighboring house, I thought to clarify after a few seconds of delay, "I'd rather have it over with at the usual time so I can get some rest, if it's all the same to you."

"You mean you intend on skipping lunch again? Thecla—" Her tone quite tart, Charlotte at last drew my attention. I almost smiled at her stern expression. For the past week and a half, everyone, even Eleison, treated me as though I were made of spun sugar—ready to shatter or dissolve upon the least rough handling. Dinon aside, within our human household, only Charlotte had seemed capable of maintaining some meaningful percentage of her old demeanor.

"You *must* eat," she insisted. "Even if I need strap you to a chair and funnel broth down your throat, I'll see to it you take lunch."

"Malin skipped his meals all the time."

"Malin wasn't hoping to starve himself to death," she told me with a look so knowing that I could not hold it. Instead found myself focused on a floral broach upon her bosom. "And besides," she added in a somewhat more compassionate tone, raising an elegant hand to fix a disarrayed strand of my hair before patting her own in reflex, "your husband often took his meals while at work, even if he had to eat in front of a meeting of people to do it."

With an indelicate snort, I peeked through the window again to find, frowning, my bird had flown away. I let the drapes fall closed again and told her, "I'm sure that Arlington fellow would have detested me all the more for that...you know, perhaps it wouldn't be so unwise to serve lunch at the next security briefing."

Her expression eased out of her defensive posture just a bit. "I'll make a note of it."

Just then, a hint of motion in the doorway drew our attention. Dinon stood there, hands folded behind him, his enchanting eyes fixed upon me with that strange, permanent look of devotion.

"I'm sorry for the interruption, Matrix," he told me, bowing slightly at the waist, "but the party from Karris has arrived."

My heart raced. Oh, yes! Thank God. Unable to suppress my gasp, I darted past Charlotte, then hesitated the second required to say, "Yes, you really had better fix lunch, please, and stew some fruits for Rosina— Dinon, take me to them."

Dinon nodded, his smile faint upon his exquisite lips. I hurried past him, my mind eagerly anticipating the group I would find waiting in the checkered foyer: Glenn, handsome and kind, now relieved by death of his hatred for Malin and able to focus on our love; and poor, sweet Rosina, who, my heart broke to reflect, might very well grow up and not even remember her Papa and how he loved her.

Oh! How would I explain this to her? It was difficult enough getting a child to comprehend death anytime; but at not yet two years old, still a baby, really, what would I say to her? How could I communicate to a child with a fifteen-word vocabulary that Papa was on a trip from which he would never return?

My eyes smarted with tears as that thought occurred to me. I could not take it: I focused my ears on the distance of the house, on the hustle and bustle of attendants coming in and out, my aching heart ready to be healed by the sound of my daughter's merry babbling.

I was not halfway there before, that heart sinking and my smile fading, I realized something must have been wrong. It was only the banal chatter of adults I heard; exclamations of grown-up relief and the desire, in a very disappointingly familiar voice, for bed and a bath and "A drink, for God's sake—that Podunk little inn, *dry!* I've never heard of a thing like it. How exactly is one meant to pass the time in such a locale without— Thecla!"

I turned the corner, and my sunken heart dropped fully past my feet to tumble down into the darkness of the earth. That same dungeon that held my husband's soul now held me. Vaguely watching the activities of the footmen who bore their bags, there in the foyer stood Aleister, and his sister, and no one else I could see.

"Oh, dear." Considering my face, Aleister wore a more serious expression as he crossed to collect me in his arms. "I'm so sorry for your loss. Poor Thecla! You look as pale as a ghost."

The pain in his face was real; indeed, I later reflected that I had never seen Aleister outside his preferred color pallet of pastel blues and radiant lilacs, or the occasional distinguished gray—yet here he was in a suit so black I was put to mind of the mortician handling my husband's body, and my throat tightened to see how truly solemn the dim fabric made the duke appear. Upon kissing my cheek, Aleister looked at me with a pair of assessing eyes that searched my whole face for some hint of my condition. "How are you keeping?"

"Exactly as one expects," I said, forcing my lips into a tense, fleeting little contortion that nearly resembled a smile. It dropped quickly, though, as Kalypso approached to likewise kiss me and pet my arm through the velvet sleeve of my mourning gown. I looked between the two of them, their faces so similar, each set a distillation of the other, each given a rounded and almost childlike softness for all their years of easy living and perpetual indulgence. They knew nothing of pain, Duke Montagne and his sister: I felt toward them a sting of resentment that only grew as I asked, "Where are my daughter and her father? Is their carriage lagging behind?"

With a brisk, shared look as that exchanged between two teammates amid a pre-agreed plan of attack—or defense—Kalypso folded her hands demurely before her and said, "Perhaps we'd ought to sit and have a bit of tea! You look bushed, Thecla, dear."

"Forget the tea," Aleister insisted, sliding his hand around my elbow to lead me toward the nearest parlor. "After that trip, I need something hard—and it looks like you do, too—"

"No, damn you." Taking advantage of the shock that loosened his hand, I stepped back to regard them with an expression I fear must have bordered on frantic hysteria. The siblings certainly looked at me with a curious anxiety. "No, I will not sit; nor take any liquor. I will hear what's going on—where is my child, Aleister?"

With a hefty sigh through lightly bared teeth, Aleister glanced askance. "I do always seem to be the bearer of bad news around these parts, don't I? Thecla—"

"That sullen boyfriend of yours ran off," blurted inelegant Kalypso, "and he took the baby with him."

The blood drained from my face. A thousand questions flew through my mind and, after looking between them, I whipped my head back toward Dinon. "Is this some—sick joke?"

"They are correct, Matrix."

My eyes batting wildly—not yet against tears, but instead in a total failure to comprehend the incompetence involved—I sputtered out at last, "But—the nurse—"

"Oh, Nellie is absolutely sick." Waving his hand, Aleister said, "I assure you, you've never seen a woman so contrite—but if you ask me, Thecla, you should give her a bit of pity. She loves that girl like her own daughter, but what could she do when Glenn seemed so trustworthy?"

"I think he's been playing a long game, as they say," Kalypso speculated in a tone of almost excited gossip she thought to dampen only when she saw my bleak expression of rage. "I mean—he's been playing at being such a morose loner all this time. What better way to lower everyone's guard?"

"I certainly didn't expect anything like this out of the old boy," Aleister said, having an easier time delivering this information with the tact required. "But I do wonder if Kalypso has a point. He's had the mindset of a captive of all this time, or at least has portrayed himself as having that...is it any wonder he took his first offered opportunity of escape?"

Still nearly awed by the information—too much so to feel any emotion other than betrayal and incredulity, as though I had been skillfully robbed of a jewel box, or the entire treasure-house of Gudrune, rather than my little daughter—I managed after a few seconds of processing, "I—*when* was this?"

"The evening after Uncle—after that blasted motorcade." Evidently no more able to acknowledge Malin's death than I, Aleister slid a hand over his hair like a cat grooming its feelings away. "Took the girl for a walk during their evening visit and stole a horse. He apparently had so many clothes missing that some of us—myself, mostly—suspect there must have been a cache of supplies he was storing up somewhere in the woods. At the very least, it would have looked exceedingly suspicious if he had walked out with the baby in one arm and a suitcase in the other."

Feeling almost dizzy, now I did sit slowly down in the in-built bench positioned in a little alcove of the foyer. "During Rift Events," I knew at once, recalling the unexpected presence of the luptich during Eleison's fight with the wild dharmine. "Oh—damn that Hunter, damn him— They're all the same."

Now I understood. His sudden interest in leaving his room had been related to reconnaissance; and it would have made perfect sense for him to find some safe place in the woods to leave his clothes when he transformed. A simple way to construct a cache of supplies for himself in a manner that would elicit little or no attention. And as for the horse—who knew. With Kyrie no longer seeing to their keeping, it would have been easy enough to take advantage of the new, more naive groom. Even to bribe him.

"Dinon," I said, my throat dry, "tell Eleison he must speak

to Kyrie. Have the groomsman at the Karris estate investigated and fired."

"Yes, Matrix, right away. And the nurse?"

"I—I don't know—" My head throbbed as it hadn't since the emergence of the ventil; I felt her aching to come out, begging to let her take control so we could both be free. Oh, yes! To drop it all, all of Gudrune—the funeral planning, all the endless loss. To simply live as an animal idling in the woods! What a luridly tempting conceit.

What a bitter disappointment it would be to kind, patient Eleison, who seemed increasingly to be my last reason to live.

"Has the household been looking for them, Aleister?"

"Well—yes, but he got quite a head start on us, and who knows just where he's hiding? He's a survivalist. Didn't he follow you through the wilderness when you were frolicking about as that blasted ventil?"

"I was hardly *frolicking*. I was—"

Running from Malin. Wasting months of what had been precious time I would never get back.

My hand pressed over my eyes, which shut beneath the cool shield of my flesh. "I should have been called immediately."

Though I could not see him, I could hear in Aleister's voice that his custom of wry amusement was nowhere to be found. "It didn't seem right, darling."

"None of it's fucking right," I screamed, my hand dropping from my abruptly heated face.

Seeing their shock and realizing I should have felt humiliated for my loss of comportment, then remembering times Malin lost his temper and exhibited not the least hint of visible shame, I rose swiftly to my feet and refused to dismiss my admittedly unbecoming reaction. "None of this is right, damn it," I said again, tears in my eyes. "My husband is dead, and the police chief speaks to me like I'm a store clerk hoping they'll investigate a shoplifter; my daughter has been stolen by her father; the child I should have borne for Malin was aborted by that same bullet that left me too stupid and helpless to keep him from dying for me!"

For obvious reasons, the miscarriage had not been made public knowledge. Aleister looked as if I had struck him, saying softly, "Oh, darling," while Kalypso quietly gasped.

"Nothing about this is right," I went on, my voice quivering even as I managed to constrain its volume to something somewhat more reasonable, "or normal, or *just*. I should have been called immediately so I might put half of Gudrune—"

Malin, pursuing my parents for seven years. Did you have the same fit in the same hallway, my darling?

"—half of Gudrune on the blasted search while we still had a prayer of catching him."

Panting for breath, now aware of something wet upon my cheek, I wiped a brisk hand across my tears while turning to add to Dinon, "Keep Nellie on the payroll for now and see to it we add more men to the search."

"Yes, Matrix," Dinon said, bowing at the waist and turning to go make the call elsewhere, where he might not be bothered. "Welcome to Saalast, Duke; my Lady."

So preoccupied by the awful news, this final nail in the coffin of my soul, I did not even remonstrate him for his lightly amused tone. I only told Aleister with an effort at more dignified comportment, "Yes, welcome. You must forgive me. I hardly sleep—I'm not myself."

"I dare not blame you," Aleister said, making no move

to pat or console me as he generally would in a more normal circumstance.

"I trust you two have already been assigned to your rooms? Very good. Then—I will see you at supper tomorrow, or some such. Please do not expect me tonight. Thank you for coming to attend Malin's funeral service."

As I turned away, intent on escaping up the stairs, Kalypso said in a somewhat nervous tone, "Actually, Thecla—"

I paused, one hand on the banister, and fixed her with a stare such that she shrank a little beneath it.

"—we came to look after you," she concluded in a smaller voice, adding an equally small but pretty little smile that had the slightest hint of hope about its edges.

Lowering my eyes from hers, ashamed of being so harsh with them, I drew my gown higher to mount the staircase. "That's very kind," I said as I made my way upstairs, "but don't be surprised if I don't have much time to spend mourning with both of you. There's just so much to do...I'm Matrix of Gudrune now—depending on whom you ask."

I could not make myself go up to Malin's penthouse—to my penthouse. Not to where the smell of him was blotted by the sickly sweet aroma of conciliatory flowers. Oh, those flowers! They served as a cruel reminder of how my husband had inundated me with such beauty when we were courting: when he thought he had some competitor for my love amid the staff. Eleison certainly had loved me, of course. But there had not been then, nor was there ever, any competition between the two of them. Not so far as my heart was concerned. Their loves were different as night and day; as vastly separated in their domains as were the Grecian idols of Apollo and Dionysus.

Or perhaps, I thought with bitter sorrow as I let myself into Eleison's Saalastian suite, as Apollo and Hades.

Weakness overcame me. I slumped upon the edge of Eleison's empty bed and managed to slide off my shoes before falling back upon linens that soothed me with the scent of my mate. Near the second I did, thoughts of my other, albeit more tenuously conjoined mate arose in my heart, and it was hardly another second before my face contorted with a new torrent of tears.

I'm not certain I wept like that even upon the miscarriage. That unhappy event, coming so soon after Malin's assassination and a consequence of the same, had been a great trauma—but it was also the end of a condition I had not known myself to be in. I had not had time to raise my hopes for the pregnancy before they were dashed (thank God!).

But now, my only consolation outside of Eleison's love had been snatched from me. My child had been taken. Glenn might as well have hand-carved a dagger to stab in my heart. Like the snowflake that leads to the violent cascading of an avalanche down a once silent mountainside, this loss was the burden that fully overwhelmed me. I sobbed: messy, awful weeping as I had not experienced since the death of my father, whose unjust death floated back to me now to renew my mourning for he who had been dead nearly twelve years. Frustrated, unable to find any comfort in my tears with my hair drawn tight atop my head, I sat up and tore out pin on pin while letting my lap grow wet with the salt of my grief; and, when at last my hair had fallen free, I contorted to undress myself, tearing open the fabric at my frustration and shoving it all away from me as if it had committed some grievous offense. Naked and helpless as the day I was born—the day my mother died, now there was a tragedy for which I had never truly wept!—I slid beneath the sheets of Eleison's cool bed and sobbed until my mind and body felt purged, with nothing remaining of the infection of heartbreak.

By the time Eleison let himself into the room and paused in the doorway to find me lying there, listlessly facing the wall, I scarcely felt anything at all.

Silent as a borro in the night, he shut the door behind him and made his way to sit upon the bed beside me. "Hey," he whispered only then, one wonderful, warm hand pressing to my brow and pushing back my hair. "You got something you want to talk about, baby?"

How grateful I was that Eleison didn't ask questions like 'Are you all right' or 'Why don't you eat something', or any of the other nonsense things I heard in the evil period following the motorcade. "Has Dinon spoken to you yet," I asked my mate as he tucked my hair behind my ear, then turned to remove his jacket and shoes.

"The dharmine," asked Eleison with a tone of slight derision. "No...about what?"

"Glenn's taken Rosina off," I said, applauding myself for my ability to express this thought without a new set of wailing, body-wracking sobs. Feeling Eleison pause in his shock before he could slide under the covers whose edge he had lifted, I went on. "Took her away in the night, it would seem, after Malin was shot. Nobody wanted to tell me because it 'didn't seem right' so soon after my husband's death, or so Aleister explained."

"What the hell? Are you kidding me?"

"Wouldn't it be nice? What a funny joke...oh, I would be too glad to be upset. To walk into a room and realize it's all been a dream, because yes, there they are...Malin and Glenn and Rosina...

and me, still with Malin's child, and everything comfortable and safe again." The emotion threatened me, my lips trembling until I shut my eyes and took a deep, quivering breath. "But all I have is reality."

"No wonder Kyrie's been dodging my calls," said Eleison, a growl in his voice. "I thought he was just busy writing letters and answering questions about Malin. I didn't realize—that fucking Hunter." The animal growl of Eleison's diaphragm deepened hatefully as I turned upon my back to watch him. The focus of his scarlet gaze drawn to my face, Eleison demanded, "Are they searching? Do you need me to go down there?"

"No," I begged hoarsely, extending an arm to slide my hand along his. "No, please, Eleison—stay with me. I need you here. They're looking, and I've told Dinon to hire more members for the search party. I hope you'll forgive me...I presumed to order your brother about on this matter, though it's your estate that he runs."

Watching my hand come to rest over his, Eleison shook his head. "You're Matrix of Gudrune, Thecla. You can order any man in this territory to do whatever you want, and if he wasn't inclined to obey you before, he'd have no choice but do it now." Raising my hand to his mouth to kiss my knuckles, Eleison muttered, "And if they don't listen to you, just let me talk to them."

"Eleison, darling...I'm just so glad I have you."

Exhaling in a huff against my knuckles, my mate released my hand to bend over me and catch my mouth in his. I moaned softly, my eyes falling closed so I could submit to the relief of his love. His tongue stroked longingly across mine, my heart racing, my loins stirring with need—

But, as his kiss intensified and his hand slid down beneath the sheets to caress my breast, I acutely felt the absence of my husband. Before I could stop myself, I wept again.

"I'm sorry!" I gasped for air while, with a soft noise of consolation, Eleison ceased his lover's petting to draw me into his arms as a friend. Hushing me tenderly, he rocked me against his chest, one hand fitting to my arm and the other stroking my hair. All the while, I stuttered between deep sobs, "I want to—I want to, Eleison, I just—"

"I understand, baby," he whispered, kissing my head, breathing me in, nuzzling against me to comfort me and show me his love in ways other than sex. "Thecla, sweetie, it's okay...there's no rush."

"I feel rushed," I confessed. "We haven't made love since Malin died, and I worry—you're so handsome. If I don't give myself into your hands, you might grow bored of me—you could so easily find someone else—"

With a scoff of amazement, Eleison asked, "Have you slept? Is your mind sound right now, baby? I've never heard you talk this way."

"I've never *felt* this way," I admitted, grateful for the handkerchief he retrieved to tenderly mop my face. Raising my eyes to his, I said miserably, "I never could have imagined Glenn would do something like that. And Malin—oh, God, Eleison. I know it's not his fault...but I feel abandoned."

"You're not the only one," he said, his words dark even with their empathetic effort to make me feel less alone. "I keep thinking about it over and over. I've spent years by his side...and when it counted most, I—"

Falling into grim silence, Eleison focused on wiping away my tears. I raised my eyes to see him, sniffling a little, stroking his chest. "Please, you mustn't blame yourself. You aren't his footman anymore. We shouldn't have been relying on you as part of the security team, oh, I don't know what he was thinking—"

"Yeah," grunted Eleison, "I don't know, either."

His handsome jaw tightened, those intriguing eyes once more distant as he lowered the handkerchief. After a few long seconds of pondering, my lover glanced down at me and said in the cautious tone of one negotiating an uncleared minefield, "You know, Thecla—I keep playing the last few weeks over and over in my head. Trying to make sense of things, I guess. And...maybe it's wishful thinking, like I'm trying to gain some control over it all, but—doesn't it seem to you like he knew something was about to happen?"

Malin's letter, bloodstained and wrinkled, sat upon the desk that had once been his and that I still could not stand to truly think of as mine.

"Yes," I whispered without elaboration. "Sometimes I do get that impression."

Not knowing what to say when I did not dismiss his idea as irrational, Eleison bunched his handkerchief into a ball in his fist, then turned away to toss it upon his nightstand. He twisted back to me, his great hand fitting to my cheek to hold me for his striking stare.

"There's nobody else, Thecla," he told me, his words as serious as his look into the depths of my very being. "There never has been—there never could be. I love my brother, and I'm grateful Malin promoted me and awarded me the Karris house, but—really, Thecla, when it comes to this world, you're all I have. All I truly have left to protect. I love you, baby. And—I'm ashamed to say that I hesitated to die for Malin."

Looking at me seriously through this confession, Eleison told me with equal honesty, "But I would never, not for a second, hesitate to die for you."

My eyes shimmering, my throat tight, I fit my hands to his face and drew him down into my kiss. So respectful, my darling! He didn't let it deepen until he felt the probing of my tongue along his; then he did kiss me, deep and hard, pushing me gently back into the pillows with one hand tangling into my hair. With the other, he shoved back the bedding to slide, still clothed, into the sheets with me. His arms folding around me in a comfort that could never be replicated, Eleison drew my naked body close against his covered one and kissed me until my exhaustion and his love succeeded in putting me to sleep.

INSOMNIACAL AS I HAD BEEN, I slept away the rest of the day in Eleison's arms; and Charlotte, looking in on us to find us both heavily carried into dreams, left us to our rest and cancelled whatever appointments I had. I assumed as such, at any rate, given that I awoke to find the hour half past nine and the curtains of the room pulled shut. Obviously suffering from the ramifications of sleep loss, himself, Eleison turned over with a grumble as I kissed his cheek and slipped up from his arms. Then, tiptoeing my way to my abandoned clothes, I drew the white shift over my head and made my beleaguered way to the elevator.

My reflection stared back at me, my dark hair hanging loose around my shoulders and my eyes dimmed from my crying—or from my loss.

What was I supposed to do? Was I to spend the entire rest of my life fearing my own assassination while flying from meeting to meeting, with Malin's absence forever on the tip of my tongue like a half-forgotten word struggling to make its way back into my mind? I avoided eye contact with my own reflection, the ruins of my mourning dress from that day hanging from my hand like the knapsack of a weary schoolgirl.

Would I find Rosina before she was that schoolgirl? I prayed Glenn would have the decency to send her to school if things got so bad, rather than raising her like a wild animal as the daughter of an isolated woodsman. But, I reflected, Glenn had made a dangerous decision by fleeing me. As Eleison was before we met, Glenn would be dependent entirely upon the drug Stabilify to maintain his sanity through Rift events. Our mating bond may have been one that was only brought about because of Rosina's existence, rather than some powerful inborn union of souls as with Eleison—but it was still enough to keep Glenn from spending money and time acquiring prescriptions of the chemical stabilizer that allowed altered individuals to maintain their long-term humanity.

That meant, wherever Glenn was, he would have to stay someplace with reliable access to the drug; and, given altered individuals were welcome in precious few territories in this or any other continent, he was most likely to maintain that access while in Gudrune.

So there was a chance. As I stalked past the tapestries lining the entryway to the penthouse apartment, my eyes turned away from the work for which I longed, I consoled myself with the notion that if he was in Gudrune, I could find him and Rosina. I could get my daughter back.

But what of her father?

My heart ached to think of him. The gentleness in him, the sorrow in him. The lies in him, so much like the lies that were in Malin. Kalypso, I thought, was on to something. I didn't want to believe it, but I could not drop her suggestion that Glenn's cowed demeanor and brooding isolation had been, at least in part, an act. He had resisted his urges to escape, forbearing them until the ideal moment and, until then, acting as meek and fatalistic as a lamb in its pen. And I had believed him.

But had all else been a charade? Had his desire for me from the start, all the way back to Valquist, been a lie to lure me in? I remembered showing him my body while he barely resisted my drunken pleas in the living room of his house; oh, how gentle and vulnerable he'd been when, recovering from Eleison's attack, he'd let me make love to him! How he'd looked at me—how he'd spoken then, and continued to speak, of his concern for me and my corruption at the hands of the Master of Gudrune.

Small wonder he thought now the ideal time to flee! With me the new Matrix, he surely thought the transformation of my morals was now irrevocable. And taking Rosina with him had been a natural consequence of—

Oh, damn him. What was I saying? How weak I felt in my own mind! Disgusting. Glenn Stone had kidnapped our—my—little girl, and here I was, my bleeding heart attempting to rationalize and excuse the behavior. Struggling, despite its own pain, to find some hint of redemption in his actions! Well...that would be for him to justify when at last I had my hands on him. When Glenn was dragged before me, bound and gagged, I would give him an opportunity to tell me why he thought it heroic to take advantage of a widow's grief and pain to also remove from her life both himself and her daughter.

Exhausted anew, I dumped my ruined gown into a hamper located in what had once been my boudoir—now just another room in a penthouse I didn't want to be mine. Dropping the lid shut for Dinon to worry about the next day, I emerged and made my aching way through the long hall to the office, passing the gauntlet of flowers I cursed myself for allowing the staff to accept and arrange on my behalf. Tomorrow, I decided, I would have all these useless displays thrown away—no, burned.

Especially the display of yellow roses and pink chrysanthemums that had been delivered the very day I returned from the hospital, and had since been wilting. With a sigh of heavy reluctance, I eyed them in their position beside the office door. Charlotte's doing, no doubt: wisely (and even justifiably) placed so I could not work in solitude without being forced to reflect on what was surely among my foremost responsibilities as Matrix.

Reaching into the vase, I withdrew the card I had been unable to make myself throw away no matter how I longed to.

Thecla—

Words can't express how sorry I am. There's no love lost between myself and your husband, but that doesn't mean you deserve to have lived through an event so horrific. Since you're meant to be interim custodian of Gudrune, we should have a conversation soon...but know that I'm here if you ever need a listening ear and a little advice.

Much Love,

Overseer Parvati Richterich

Disgusted at the way Parvati seamlessly integrated work into condolence—and annoyed by her decision to refer to me as 'interim custodian of Gudrune' rather than 'Matrix'—I let the note fall limply from my hand. As I blew a few locks of hair from my face, I stepped into the office and slid into the desk.

Malin's bloodied to-do list sat before me, each line perfectly straight across the page.

My love! Everything about you is perfect. And to call you 'humble' during your human life would certainly be wrong. Yet you never rubbed your intellect or your power in my face. You let me see it all, yes, and so many more of your other fine qualities—but that was only ever to inspire me. To show me the greater limits of human achievement and uplift my soul toward yours. For yours may have felt like a dungeon, but when I looked on you, Malin Farrow, I saw only the brightest of suns. A sky full of stars could not outnumber the qualities I admired in you: I cherished you more deeply than I once looked up to my own father, the only other truly great loss in my life.

Would you have wanted me to dwell self-indulgently in my own pain? Would you want me to look at the list of steps to take in my noble position and crumble beneath the pressure, no matter what other burdens lay upon my shoulders? For, I reminded myself as I withdrew a pen and selected austere letterhead from my husband's desk, there was nothing I could do at that very moment to find Rosina and Glenn. It did not seem as though I could snap my fingers and—

Pausing, wiggling the pen, I opened my mouth but realized there was no need. Dinon's shadow fell across the desk, cast by the lamp that glowed beside the door of the still-shut office.

"You know I would present them to you if I could, my beloved mistress," said my servant solemnly, his eyes fixed so intensely upon the back of my neck that I felt his gaze before I turned to face him.

"And you can't because—why, exactly? Because you like to keep me dangling by a thread for your own amusement?"

Unruffled by my accusation, he showed his fang-edged teeth in a smile that was so gorgeous it took me all too far from mourning and into deep desire. As I averted my eyes, the nearly omniscient dharmine suggested, "No, Matrix; not at all."

"Then why?"

"Because you could never enjoy his love if you forced him to return to you."

Jaw tightening, I uncapped the pen and addressed a letter to Platt. "Who's to say I even care for the love of a man who seems to think I'm a villain, as he fancied my husband?"

"I know what you want," Dinon said, his finely polished shoes beating a soft, slow path along the carpet as he stalked toward me through Malin's office. "And I know what you need, Matrix...I don't need to tell you that any more than I need to tell you Master Stone is an extremely willful man. If you do not allow him even a taste of freedom and instead impinge upon that free will by sending me to whisk him and the girl back here, he will never forgive you. He will never trust you well enough to open his heart to you."

"You mean if I let him run roughshod over me, he'll see fit to forgive me when I finally do discover where he's taken her? How truly noble of him."

"I mean," corrected Dinon patiently, tracing a thumb down the nape of my neck while I forced back a shudder of lust, "if you show him you respect his craving for liberty more than you care about being respected as Matrix of Gudrune, he will see you as far more than Malin Farrow's wife."

"You mean widow," I corrected darkly, unable to focus on

the letter with my slave fondling my throat amid obvious fantasies of what he could do if given the opportunity. While he chuckled at my thought, a low and sensual mirth that further aroused my passion, I turned in my seat to meet the dharmine's eye.

Before I could speak, an explosion of laughter carried through the window from the rooftop above.

Laughter. Fun. Imagine that. How could anyone take any joy in life with Malin Farrow less than forty-eight hours from his internment in the family mausoleum? Part of me was insulted—but the rest of me was jealous, overfull of longing for any respite. For the slightest break from my constant, wearisome thoughts.

"I want you to write some letters on my behalf," I said, thrusting the pen into Dinon's hand no matter how unnecessary the action surely was. Rising to stare up into his face—and blushing a bit to be reminded that he towered over me more greatly than any of my lovers, my head hardly level with his shoulder when we stood before one another—I gestured to the desk and said, "You may start with the one to Platt, then address the other governors and statesmen associated with Gudrune as you see fit. We will not be holding the wake immediately, but putting it out for some weeks so it may be well-attended."

"Very good, Matrix. The other territory masters?"

"Certainly: invite them, as well. I would not anticipate their appearance, of course...but I suppose it would look diplomatic."

"And what of Overseer Parvati?"

Scoffing despite all obligation, I said, "Her presence would only dishonor the dead man who hated her. No, I'll not have it. Send her a card thanking her for the flowers and leave it at that."

"As you wish, Matrix. Ah, Thecla—"

Heading already to the door, I turned back to him with an

arched brow of derision for his use of my name. To my amazement, his cheeks were faintly colored, as though this demon were some longing country boy with a fancy for a girl at church.

"You look so gorgeous when you've been weeping...how I love it when you cry."

With another shudder—as much of pleasure as of disgust, I was horrified to note in myself—I hurried from the room and practically slammed the door behind me.

Something had grown in me since Malin's death, and it was not just my grief or the new seriousness that had possessed me. By some quirk of my lonely soul, or some perversion of biology I had not known to afflict vulnerable widows in the absence of their husbands, I suddenly found myself more intrigued by the dharmine. Oh, yes, I had found him very attractive before, and certainly had felt the lure of his erotic enticements—I even enjoyed his talents in that regard while we were alone in Valquist.

But now, without my husband to keep me on my best behavior and only poor Eleison around to manage my needs, the dharmine's presence electrified me. Alone with Dinon, I could no longer clearly perceive the consequences of yielding to his advances. No matter how many times I looked at his elegant fangs and reminded myself that a single penetration during the carnal act could lead to blood-poisoning, I was simply unable to shake myself free of the lust he inspired. I even caught myself wondering if he might not provide me with a novel distraction to help me get through the days and nights without my darling Malin.

And that, perhaps, was why I was so drawn to the diversions offered by Aleister and his younger sister.

When wrapped in a thin robe with my hair drawn back by a ribbon, I made my way to the rooftop garden where I found them chatting and laughing like a pair of sailors in a tavern. Sweet-smelling smoke of some kind blew on the night breeze, their glasses clinking and rattling with ice amid their conversation. Only my approaching footfall interrupted them, Aleister glancing up from his sister and, seeing me, straightening in his seat with an instantly more serious affectation.

"Thecla," he said, lowering his glass and then, with a glance to the cigarette in his hand, hastily tapping it out in the nearby flowerpot the miscreants had displaced for use as their ashtray. "I'm sorry, darling, are we keeping you up? We can go elsewhere. I'm sure the last thing you want—"

"It's fine," I said, raising my hand to stay his haste and urge him back into his seat. As he relaxed, so did Kalypso, who smiled somewhat more guiltily than the often clueless socialite had seemed capable of before that week. "I don't mean to interrupt your fun," I went on, glancing toward the door from the penthouse, "but I—I just heard you both having a good time and I found myself wondering when I'd last had a good time of my own."

"Well," said Aleister with great cheer, "you're in luck. Look at what Kalypso and I brought up from the bar." With a wave of one of Malin's favorite scotch bottles, Aleister finished his glass of the foul stuff for which I had no fondness, then gleefully unscrewed the cap. "Let me pour you a finger or two. Sit down, reminisce about your husband with us! You'll feel better, I promise."

"Oh," I said, raising a hand as he extended the glass toward me, "no, thank you, I've never liked the taste."

"Well you're not meant to *taste* it, Auntie." Aleister wiggled the glass to rattle the ice in its pool of rancid brown bourbon. "You're meant to swallow it...it's a little like sem—"

"*Aleister*," remonstrated Kalypso, kicking her brother beneath the table while he howled with laughter, "*really*, must you always be so obscene! There's wine, too, Thecla, dear...I can't stand that stuff, either."

As Kalypso made a face, Aleister continued attempting to draw me to the glass. "Come on, now. Just a sip for fun. This vintage was Malin's favorite, as I recall."

"It was," I said, staring down at the glass with a look of longing for my absent husband. Oh...how awful the liquor tasted in my mouth, but how sweet it was when its phantom clung upon his lips or cooled his avid tongue!

Pained, I snatched the glass from Aleister and forced myself to imbibe its contents in one regrettable mouthful. As it burned on its way down to leave me choking and coughing, Aleister cheered me on and clapped his hands with pride. "Very good, Thecla, well done! That was quite a feat...I think the first time Uncle shared his more expensive bourbon with me, I ended up with my head over the toilet bowl not more than a few minutes later."

"We'll see how it goes." I coughed, passing the glass back to Aleister before dragging over a wrought-iron chair from another one of the garden tables. "Let's have the wine instead, Kalypso, please."

Smiling, Kalypso filled her own glass quite full, nearly to the top—then, before I could protest, handed me the remainder of the bottle. "There," she said gaily while Aleister giggled and topped himself off, "that will settle your nerves rather pleasantly. Oh, Thecla, dear, you look exhausted!"

"I am." I sniffed the contents of the bottle and then, after deciding I was in quite indelicate company, simply sipped from the neck. As the wine washed over my palate and, I was somewhat displeased to reflect, dismissed the taste of my husband's liquor, I settled back into the seat and told Montagne and his sister, "I'm miserable. So busy I feel I haven't even had time to even accept Malin's—dead." Grimly, I raised the bottle to my lips again. "And then that awful news you brought today...you both really must forgive me for—"

"Oh, Auntie, *please*." Patting my hand, then squeezing it with real fraternal affection, Aleister said, "You have nothing to apologize for. Besides! If you think that amounted to even a quarter of the intensity of Malin's tantrums, rest assured, he must have been keeping his worst tendencies well hidden from you. That time I told him Parvati wanted to see you, I really thought he was going to leap across the table and strangle me!"

Aleister laughed so freely that I couldn't help but laugh along with him, though now what had been an uncomfortable glimpse into Malin's temper amounted to another agonizing memory of the man I had loved. "My goodness, but he was cross...I admit, I was a bit worried for you, myself."

"Master Farrow always seemed quite polite to me," said Kalypso, swirling her glass on its way to her lips. "Then again, I was half a stranger."

"And my sister, besides," Aleister added with a knowing nod. "It was in his interest to be polite to you if he wanted to keep— *mentoring* me back in the day."

With a wry smirk, I found myself not reflecting on my husband's hedonistic past but instead on my own, far quieter one. Longing for my own sister stirred in my lonely heart. How was Sable? I needed write to her. Perhaps tomorrow—

I could write every word you yourself would desire to, my dharmine slave advised me in the back of my mind. *Exactly as you would write it.*

Then do, I ordered him as I said to Aleister, "I often felt that Malin took one of two highly divergent positions with strangers or work acquaintances. Polite and charming—"

"Or a totalitarian psychopath ready to snap at any moment," reminisced Aleister, staring fondly into the distance. "Mm, yes. I always did love that about him."

"You two really are quite strange," Kalypso said at my agreeable sigh. "Weren't you ever worried about that, Thecla? My goodness, he's such a frightening man in reputation alone. Were he my husband, I'd have fretted day and night waiting for his evil mood to turn on me."

"But it was never like that." I stared at the row of manicured flowers arranged upon the break wall behind the siblings' heads, too many intimate memories flying through my mind to look at my conversational partners. "Not even for a second. Malin always made me feel so special, so—sacred."

Yes—that was what made me inclined toward Dinon's amorous coaxing now that my husband was gone. For Eleison was the archetypal wild lover, it was certain, and made me feel very much a gorgeous, borderline irresistible lady worth any man's affection—but Malin and Dinon both had a way of treating me as though I were a very goddess of sex, unparalleled in this world or any other. With the only exception being our shared cavalier, my husband had been willing to sacrifice at the altar of my love his entire way of Epicurean life; and I had the sense that Dinon would have piled at my feet the head of every hunter in Saalast if only I made love to him and promised him more.

Oh, Matrix, sighed my slave into my mind's ear, *oh, Thecla, to feel your body on mine, I would deliver every active hunter on the continent. Please...*

"Stay out," I said, catching myself when my friends glanced queerly at my change in tone. With an embarrassed clear of my throat, then the sudden fear it would be all too easy to depict me as mad and displace me from my already perilous position upon Gudrune's throne, I covered myself. "Stay out of conversation with Parvati," I clumsily amended as if having changed my train of thought, looking at Aleister, "please, darling. I know you're close, but—"

"I wouldn't say we were ever 'close', but you have nothing to worry about...I've barely said two words to the woman since you yourself were in Valquist."

"Oh, yes," agreed Kalypso with a wave of her free hand. "Everyone's been asking at all the parties where Aleister's hiding... and it's finally such that he's convinced me to summer here instead of Valquist. I must admit, I'm really quite surprised to find myself enjoying Gudrune so much! Eleison's estate is lovely."

"That was all decorated to Malin's taste," I said with a distant sigh. "Or his family's, at least...I wish I had thought to ask how long it had been with the Farrows."

And so much else! There were so many things—opinions, historical events, preferences in clothes and food—that I had passively absorbed but never specifically inquired into, and now never could. While my heart ached, I imbibed a great swig of wine and wiped the purple stain from my lips with the back of my hand. "What was that funny-smelling cigarette you were smoking when I came out here, by the by," I asked, nodding at the flower pot. "It didn't smell like tobacco."

"You innocent little ingenue," Aleister teased, laughing along with his sister at my question. "You mean you don't recognize the smell of mithrae?"

My eyebrows raised. I knew what mithrae was—a specific kind of Rift flower, a blue bud of the sort that grew upon my ventil's antlers, and notoriously difficult to displace when it managed to sow its seeds in terrestrial soil. I also knew that it was reputed to have all number of strange, sometimes even alarming cognitive effects when dried and smoked. But, Aleister was quite right—being innocent, some might say naive, before I left Lescaut, I was not at all acquainted with its incense-like scent.

"I had no idea you smoked such stuff, Aleister," I said as he fished the cigarette out of the flowerpot, then patted himself for his matches. "Here I thought it was supposed to be frightful."

"Silly girl—if that were the case, why would anybody use it? Perhaps it makes some people who have nefarious hearts experience what they deserve, but for the rest of us—aha"—sticking the cigarette in the corner of his mouth, he withdrew a matchbook and snapped out a match he swept familiarly along the back of the pack—"it's just a grand time. Mild, too, unless one intends to sit there smoking a whole cigarette of it by themselves... then you might want to brace yourself for some curious effects. Here!"

After drawing in a mouthful of smoke, Aleister removed the cigarette from his lips and offered it over to me. "Go on—I know you know how to *smoke*, at least, if only by observation. I can always tell Malin's had his way with you both when I see Eleison shirtless and out for a cigarette on the balcony of that Karris house."

As I sputtered and coughed in embarrassment as much as at the burning of the smoke in my unaccustomed lungs, I passed the cigarette to Kalypso and was forced to admit in the privacy of my own head that the taste really was quite delicious—especially when combined with the next swallow of wine. "And how do you know Malin has anything to do with that? It's Eleison's house, after all—his master apartment."

"Then he'd be smoking in the bedroom, wouldn't he?" With a grin for his deductive reasoning, Aleister tapped his temple. "Simple logic, Thecla, darling."

Despite myself, I laughed—and it wasn't long before the barrier of my mourning no longer stood between me and that laughter. Between the three of us, the cigarette was quickly smoked to a tiny nub; and about halfway through its length, I began to marvel at its effects. I felt lightheaded in a way that seemed so sweet and clean compared to the drunkenness of alcohol. I had heard from some parties that mithrae flowers, before they induced frightful visions, uplifted the mood and even brought about quite lovely dreams: I did not know about the dreams, but I could say with certainty that, for a blissful thirty minutes, I was no longer quite so actively stabbed through the heart by thoughts of Malin's demise. Somehow, I could step outside of myself and receive some small objectivity: remind myself for the first time that, yes, he had died, and I was now burdened with heavy responsibility, but he had not left me with that alone. He had passed on to me all those properties which were in his name; wealth and investments beyond any reasonable measure; beautiful artwork and splendid furniture, and bevvies of servants at every property to look after them.

And, I thought to myself as Aleister and Kalypso chatted about something inconsequential, he left me with friends. The tapestry of my life was so much richer for having loved Malin, even if having also lost him; and his soul deserved my grief, but I swore I could feel him, from some strange afterlife, longing for my joy.

It was at this thought that I consciously noticed, to my great amazement, what I had been thinking for some minutes to be an effect of the city against the night. Some electric light on in some window, sending stripes across my friends—not vivid, mind, but faint and thin. As passing as a floater in the corner of one's vision, or a mote of dust dancing across a column of sunshine.

Then, as I took comfort from the joy I knew Malin wished me to experience, I found myself struck by the effect of these stripes—these lines, really—upon Aleister's suit. They swept down, shimmering slightly when I focused my attention on them, looking like violet strands of Rift energy that stood, along with silver crosshatching, in relief from the environment around.

And that was when, in my mithrae haze, I recognized what these hallucinatory impressions were:

Threads.

A bit amazed—and suddenly persuaded by the power of the drug to increase, sometimes erroneously and fancifully, the logical connections made by the human brain—I laughed, my head tipping back. So we *were* in a tapestry of some sort! It made perfect sense. I marveled at this reality and, extending my hand to examine it front and back, barely half-heard as Aleister repeated my name three or four times. Only on the fourth repetition did he succeed in getting my attention, at which point I met his eyes to find them shining with hints of that uncanny radiance around the smiling edges.

"Something funny, darling," he asked while finishing the cigarette.

"No, no...only..." With a conspiratorial whisper, I leaned in to tell my friends, "I think I like this stuff a fair bit better than wine!"

GIVEN THE CIRCUMSTANCES OF Malin's death, I personally found the general insistence on a procession to be in exceedingly poor taste. I did not want a big production, with cameras filming and public displays of mourning from the citizens of Saalast; but it was, like so much else I was forced to occasion, the 'done thing', and since the wake was to be delayed a few weeks to allow the various invited politicians to make the pilgrimages and leave their territories in worthy hands, Gudrune needed closure.

So, with choreographed military members and what was not just the entire citizenry of Saalast but a great many from the countryside, I followed my husband from the mortuary to the church, then from the church to the grave. We went on foot, Eleison and I, walking arm in arm behind the auto-carriage whose mechanical horse had been fit with a fuligin skin that made it seem some awful hole in space: a pit in reality, leading my husband away.

I tried not to weep. I tried to look very strong. In addition to Arlington's police, a large number of mercenaries had been hired to maintain civil obedience and discourage follow-ups of the previous attempt on my life. In truth, I welcomed such an episode...pined for it every step we took on that long, long walk, my feet miserably aching and my gown stifling, and the netting of my veil pressing to my sweat-dotted brow. As miserable as I was, that misery paled in comparison to the suffering of my husband. I only wished to ease that suffering by finding him in the depths of Sheol—of whatever pit into which his soul had been cast. For how could I believe in Heaven when Heaven was what I found in his arms, with his love and Eleison's love doled out upon me in equal measure?

The service was long; the sun was setting by the time the procession arrived at the mausoleum. Before his interment, I asked to see him one last time and immediately regretted it. Even with all the most advanced techniques of mortuary science, this corpse was not my husband. It was as hollow as a cicada shell; and, as the bullet hole in his throat could not be otherwise disguised or sealed, his suit collar had been pulled up too high. Makeup had been applied to hide the greenish cast of death, and when I touched his face, my glove came away with waxy orange cosmetic staining it. I stared dumbly at the substance, then looked up from my hand for my eyes to land not on Malin's sepulcher, but my own.

It *would* be my own someday, I realized with a funny chill of finality. Oh, how impossible death had once seemed to I who was so young! How distant it had been from me, even having lost my own father. I had certainly pondered on it, as I revealed to Malin in our intimacy that night not long before his demise; but it was so abstract. Death was something that happened to other people—not to me.

Yet there, that empty sepulcher beside the one into which my husband's shut casket was slid by Eleison, Dinon, Aleister and myself: that slab of marble would someday bear the words 'Thecla Farrow', and some numbers that would always seem too small a spread for my liking.

And, perhaps, the appellation 'Matrix of Gudrune.'

That latter addition would depend entirely on the scrupulous judgment of the overseer, who wrote to me once again a few days after the funeral. I happened to be reclining in the game room, nursing a bottle of wine sweetened with a splash of mithrae tincture while watching a round of table tennis between Aleister and one of the courtiers who had come up for the funeral. Perceiving this scene—and the five other courtiers who, in this group and that one, half-watched while chatting among themselves—Charlotte masterfully distilled her disapproval into an arched brow.

"Do you suppose these...charming guests will be staying until the wake?"

"They can spend the whole rest of the season with us, for all I care." I poured the rest of the bottle into my glass and raised it to my mouth, flicking a glance of derision at the familiar, pink-accented envelope in Charlotte's hand. "Is that from Parvati? Have you read it yet?"

"I have."

"Is it state business?"

"Well—no, but yes. She's asking about the funeral and requesting you call her. Did you invite her to the wake?"

I laughed and looked about myself for the bowl of cherries and chocolates I'd been picking at as idle substitute for the meals Charlotte had learned she could truly not pressure me to eat without force, or Eleison's influence. "Heavens, no," I told her, smirking dryly at the dumb laughter from the courtiers who had heard my bleak mirth and assumed I'd made some joke. While a muscle at the edge of Charlotte's mouth twitched dangerously, I nipped a cherry from its stem and told her, "I won't have that insufferable woman coming to any event in my husband's honor. God only knows the insidious, ugly little things she'd say about him."

"That may be so," said Charlotte with growing tension in her voice. "But she is still the Overseer of the continent, and you will have to rely on her grace if you're to be formalized as Matrix of Gudrune."

Malin's death had reduced me to an embarrassing state of inadequacy. It were as though my father's death had required so much immediate responsibility that I'd had no choice but act as an adult; and now, as an adult, my husband's death had left me with too much responsibility—so much that I had buckled and regressed, and now could not do more for Gudrune than hound its chief of police for movement on the investigation of its master's assassin.

Accordingly, I shrugged like a sullen teenager, avoiding Charlotte's eyes altogether while I masticated the bitter little cherry and chased it down with wine. "So I'll call her soon. Here"—I passed my watch over to Charlotte without looking—"put her number in my watch, will you? There's a lamb— Oh, Aleister! That was smashing."

"Aha," shouted the duke, slapping his paddle down on the edge of the table which had just hosted a wild escalation of their prolonged volley. Pacing with pride from one side of the table to the other, Aleister flexed his arms and said, "I am the god of table tennis. There's no one in the continent who's better than me—"

Charlotte took a step to stand directly before me, wryly passing both watch and note into my hand. "There; I've added her watch ID number. But—Thecla, if you do want to maintain your husband's affairs—"

"Charlotte," I begged, "all I've thought about for more than two weeks are my husband's affairs. I'm tired. May I please be allowed to have a little fun this afternoon? Rest assured, I'll take care of everything in due time...but I'm—I'm just not feeling myself yet. All right?"

The truth was that this was more than a little fun in an afternoon. This was another day in a chain of days where I had accomplished nothing but the construction of a violent hangover that, through Aleister's technique of early imbibing, was typically under control again by about noon. The nasty consequences of drinking were the reason I had begun to lean more toward mithrae as an intoxicant—and I was not really indulging for fun, either.

Mithrae's cognitive effects were, so far as I had seen, quite gentle and kind. While alcohol in too great a quantity would leave me brooding until I wept and had to put myself to bed not too far from a bathroom, mithrae flowers were conciliatory when they were used in smoke or tincture. The more I ingested, the calmer and more accepting I became. While sobriety was painful, forcing my consciousness to constantly reconcile with the reality of Malin's absence wherever I looked and whatever I did, the heady state of mithrae consumption slowly eased my suffering with each puff or sip until, to my relief, I was once again able to experience joy, inspiration—even pleasure. With the mithrae, I was able to look outside of myself; to look at the world around. And even if

I could not perform my duties, I was at the very least able to live without constant suffering.

After Charlotte had given up and left me to my devices, I skimmed the letter, then hesitated. How difficult it was to focus! My mind was distractable, and the mithrae made it wish to turn to matters of artistic inspiration—to pursue my latest tapestry, rather than any work or even the lightest reading. I had to really focus on reading that short note; and the more I focused, the more I was distracted by the details before me. Namely, the threads.

They appeared every time I imbibed more than a puff or two of mithrae, shimmering across reality to a lesser or greater extent. No doubt, they were beautiful, the warp shining in little Rift-violet patches here and there across my field of vision, especially on those objects upon which I concentrated; while the weft flowed like silver across, shimmering against its vertical counterpart with somewhat less intensity but no less beauty. Indeed, while the so-called warp threads I observed seemed the same stuff as Rift radiation, the weft was the silver found in the eyes of those corrupted by that radiation: the eyes of Eleison when he had been briefly enslaved; the eyes of Ba'al-Dinon, gleaming in perpetual pleasure.

The silver eyes that had so frightened me in the dream of my honeymoon, when, owing to so many vile rumors, my husband had appeared to me as a dharmine trapped in the basement of his own house.

Oh, if only! I had no love for feral dharmines like the one that had attacked me in the woods, of course; but if my husband had been a dharmine as was so commonly speculated, how readily he would have survived being shot! How grateful I would have been... how comforted, how relieved. The mere idea was too wonderful to bear and managed to make me sad even with the variety of substances flowing through my blood. Frowning, I set aside my glass to be cleaned up later, then, rising to my feet, stumbled slightly and laughed.

"Careful, Thecla dear," said Aleister, waving his paddle at me. "If you fall and crack your precious skull while we sit and watch, that mate of yours will execute us all personally, I have no doubt."

The courtiers laughed and so did I, although I found myself blushing at Aleister's casual reference to Eleison as my mate in front of mixed company. It was unavoidable public knowledge that I was altered now; after my transformation into a ventil before the crowd, the news had spread quickly, and while my office had not confirmed it, my condition was now something of an open secret. Only the micro-Event that had been occurred at the time kept the full truth from the public—it camouflaged my nature as a valuable second-generation specimen, and hid that my missing Rosina, who was allegedly still enjoying a peaceful country life, was an even rarer third-generation—but the truth remained evident for anyone with ears, and it was one of many little things along with my youth, sex, and obscure background that would make my political life truly hellish when I could no longer avoid it. Even in Gudrune, altered individuals faced a great deal of prejudice; and though their registry system was not as stringent as those for Riftborn individuals, the state (or the corporations that reported to it, at any rate) still maintained a general awareness of altered and their movements in and out of Gudrune. Altered individuals were therefore still individuals who were 'other than' a wholly terrestrial human being, and this engendered natural prejudice.

This was one of the reasons I was so very surprised to make my way downstairs to the foyer, intent on finding Charlotte to at last get a little food in me, only to discover Dinon speaking to a somehow familiar man.

Now...where had I seen this fellow before? I squinted as I descended the stairs and the pair emerged in view, the shining hints of hallucinatory threads making it all the harder to place his identity. But I knew the moustache that was trimmed to neat perfect; knew the ingratiating white smile and the hard but polite features that reminded one, along with the definition of his short haircut, of a military officer or policeman. Was he someone I had met at the funeral? One of Malin's friends, perhaps?

Ah! No— At the bottom of the stairs, when both men turned to smile, I recognized him even as Dinon gestured. "Here's the Matrix now. Matrix, I'm sure you remember Master Winston Garland, of the former Hunter's Guild?"

My teeth flashing with a quick smile that soon simplified to a slight upturn at the edges of my mouth, I offered my hand. "Winston—how interesting I should meet you in person now. What brings you to my house?"

"Matrix," he said with great deference, extending the hand that did not hold his hat to take and shake mine in a manner that was, much to my surprise, immediately more respectful than any gesture received from Arlington or the politicians I had met. "Truly, it's a pleasure to make your acquaintance—I'm just sorry it's on the tail of such a great tragedy for you and the nation. How are you?"

"Slowly adjusting to reality," I said as he released me. He'd had the good taste to dress in mourning colors, his suit and tie equally black and his somehow too-toothy smile turned down a few degrees from the one he'd flashed across the crowd at the Torea festival. "I imagine most widows have a difficult enough time without a sudden promotion to Matrix of Gudrune."

"Mm." His smile dropping entirely with a sympathetic shake of his head—obviously affected, but still a conscientious display of which none of the courtiers, for instance, were capable—Winston said, "I can't even begin to guess what you must be going through. It's made me reluctant to come and for your time, I admit, but—well, I suppose you must be very busy at all hours no matter what tragedies you're facing."

"Constantly busy, indeed." Somewhere in the back of my drug-addled mind, an idea began to form from the mists of creativity. "But," I said with a gesture down the hall, "you happened to catch me about to have lunch. Care to join me for a bite to eat and a little wine, Winston?"

"Ah!" The weft threads hinted at the edges of his features contorted with his new smile, which was quite genuinely pleased. "I'd be honored, if it's not too much trouble."

"No trouble at all. Dinon, would you speak to Charlotte about fixing something?"

"With pleasure, Matrix." While my servant made himself scarce—to literally disappear, I was sure, as soon as he rounded the first corner—I said, "Let's enjoy the tearoom, shall we? It's so stuffy and formal in the dining room."

And it reminded me far too much of eating with my husband.

While Winston followed me through the house and made appreciative noises, I ached with awful pain for my departed love. Oh, Malin! Malin, Malin. There were times I would sit and stare into space and let his name roll through my head like a crashing wave, often until Eleison or Charlotte interrupted me. Dinon never did; not in those moments.

The tearoom was charming, baroque in its design and full of the visual busy-ness that Malin seemed to most enjoy. Winston's eyes swept around it with interest, if not with pleasure, then settled upon me in a lingering way to which I had grown accustomed. Interested only in business, pretending not to notice, I poured the wine Dinon momentarily brought us and said, "So what may I do for you, Winston? I admit I have quite a few interests demanding my attention at the moment, and I'm still sorting out my husband's affairs, so if the matter pertains to some issue between the two of you, I hope you'll forgive me for being somewhat uninformed."

"No forgiveness necessary," said Winston, raising his glass to his lips without giving it the appreciation I felt it deserved. Even in my most drunken state, I still sniffed at the wine and let myself sit with the anticipation of it before imbibing from the glass. "It does, in fact, pertain to some old business with your husband; but I have some new concerns, too."

Setting the glass down while resting back in his seat, Winston turned the stem between thumb and forefinger and said with an air of concern, "It would seem Police Chief Arlington and his men—along with the police of other cities across Gudrune—are…how can I put this delicately…they're convinced that my inactive chapter of the guild has had something to do with Master Farrow's murder."

"Because I told them so."

Eyebrows raising with interest, Winston said, "Really? Now why is that?"

"Because I saw with my own two eyes the assassin's tattoo," I said, tapping the back of my right hand. "Your guild's symbol—a crest with a rapier and rifle crossing one another."

Moustache wiggling over his lip, Winston said, "Hm!" and sipped his wine. "You're very sure," he pressed when he had lowered his glass and swallowed. "I only ask because, well, in a moment of crisis—"

"I'm positive it was the symbol of the Hunter's Guild," I told him firmly, disinterested in even the lamest effort to persuade me that my memory could not be believed. "As difficult as it must be for you to accept, one or more of your former guild members was involved in the conspiracy to assassinate my husband. In fact—"

Glancing up amid a nod as a staff member arrived with plates whose contents were obscured by silver cloches, I looked back at Winston in humorless intensity.

"There was one suspect apprehended moments before the actual crime was committed; this man—I cannot recall his name—is a confirmed member of the Guild. A former member, anyway."

"Wow," said Winston for the food the servant revealed before bowing at the waist and whisking the cloches away. After realizing his attention had been captured by the duck breast with its orange glaze—or perhaps having gotten across that he perceived the food as being more real and important to him than my claims about rogue hunters—Winston spread his napkin over his lap and plucked up his fork. "Well, if it really is the case that these are members of my guild conspiring to assassinate your husband, all I can say is how sorry I am that I don't have the power I used to. Now I feel like I could have put a stop to it before things got bad... if the Guild hadn't been banned from operating in the territory, that is."

While Winston sawed off a bite of duck and stuck it in his mouth with a noise of theatrical enjoyment, I felt my face tighten in disgust. Unable to touch my food no matter how delicious it was, I stared him down. "You mean to imply that my husband orchestrated his own demise by dissolving the Guild that was already known to have a distinct interest in assassinating him?"

"What? No." With a laugh as easy as his lie, Winston washed his mouthful of food down in a swig of wine and said after clearing his throat, "I mean just what I said, Matrix. If the Guild still operated, I could have done something."

His eyes lowering to his plate again, knife and fork hard at work, he shrugged his shoulders and let his eyebrows express his dubious opinion. "Besides—those assassination schemes you're referring to, those were in Valquist, weren't they? I think your husband mentioned that to me when he informed me of his decision to end our operations within the territory."

"It is all the same Guild, is it not, Winston?"

"Oh, well sure—but individual chapters have their own community and territory interests. I can't control what goes on in a place like Valquist any more than you can."

"No," I reflected after a few seconds, "perhaps not—but you could easily influence mobile members to carry information and seed opinions between territories."

Brow furrowing, Winston glanced from his plate. "Uh, how do you mean?"

"Take, for instance, Glenn Stone." I gestured with my free hand off into the room, indicating someplace far away—wherever my traitorous lover was hiding with my only living child. "He resides in Valquist, yet I saw you borrowed him for the Torea Festival in Gudrune about two years ago—surely you recall that."

"Oh, yes." Agreeing with a nod, Winston tilted his head before averting his eyes to his food again. "Yes, well, of course we request popular hunters from other regions to come work with us. But, now, in all fairness—Glenn *clearly* wasn't related to the assassination attempt, if any hunter was. Why, the way I recall it, he killed eight, maybe nine members of the Valquist chapter and booked it out of town! Doesn't seem very aligned with our values, if you ask me."

"But Malin's death is."

"Well—" With a sharp, quick laugh that had no humor to it, Winston finished the duck he had downright wolfed down and sat back in his seat again. He was already wiping his mouth just as I was able to subject myself to my second bite. "Look, Matrix—I won't sit here and pretend your husband had a perfect relationship with the Guild, or with me personally. But you know what *is* in the Guild's interests? Stability. Normalcy. It's what we're all about! Preserving the status quo so the good people of the continent can live their lives in peace and security, without having to cringe in fear every time the sky goes a little purple. This was delicious, by the way," he added, tapping the edge of his empty plate. "I don't know how you manage to stay so trim, eating like this every day."

His casual banter got on my nerves, but there was something paradoxically honest about his false, almost salesman-like persona. He *was* here to sell to me; he didn't want to or need to hide that. Giving up on my food and instead nursing my wine, I folded my free arm across my diaphragm and regarded him with cool but real interest. "Winston, did you come here to ask me to drop my investigation into your former guild members, or did you really come here to ask me to restore the Guild's operations?"

With another flash of that bright smile that, among his other traits, made it obvious why he ran Gudrune's chapter and played liaison for its private and political interests, Winston raised his own glass. "Why—both, if possible. Look at it this way—"

With his wine now gone, he gestured with his empty hands. "If the Guild is restored to power, it would be a simple thing for us to perform our own internal investigation. If there are guilty parties within our ranks, we'll find them easier than even Arlington and his men could. I may even be able to produce other conspirators for you—people who have been working behind-the-scenes, if it's the case this really is a conspiracy and not just a bad actor or two who got lucky."

There was, in fact, something intriguing about this idea. The man we had in custody was not talking and quite willing to die to protect what he knew, or so I had heard it told to me; and I had little doubt that the deed had been commissioned by more than just the captured suspect and the escaped shooter. The carriage that had picked the killer up was evidence of that.

"And if the Guild is restored, and the conspiracy's silence is maintained, I will have undone my husband's work and gotten nowhere."

At my observation, Winston raised his eyebrows. "But surely you can see that the incentive to maintain silence would disappear if the Guild were restored. Members withholding information could be stripped of their licenses; and if these are in fact misguided members acting on what they believe to be the good of the organization, those who know them won't risk their relationship with the reinstated Guild just to protect a couple of murderers. Do you see?"

I did see; but I also saw that, much as I was being manipulated into the restoral of an organization that had always detested my husband, I would also be signing off on the death of my child's father. Glenn still had a price on his head, which was what had inspired me to entertain Winston's company in the first place.

"I'm not convinced." I glanced at the back of the bottle in a reflection of Winston's earlier technique of inattention. Pretending I scanned the label for my own interest, I set it back down while suggesting, "After all, it seems to me that the matter of finding the killer should be obvious and easy. Look for the hunters who have been shot in the shoulder within the past few weeks, then interrogate them."

"If you can find them."

"I'm quite sure Arlington's investigators aren't *that* incompetent...but perhaps, if you added in a little contingency for my own personal interest, I might see my way to allowing your organization to resume probationary operations within Gudrune's borders."

His posture relaxing such that I hadn't even realized him to be so tense until that moment, Winston leaned forward in his seat with a look of now very serious interest. "That contingency being?"

"Glenn Stone." I tipped the bottle to refill my glass, then generously allotted my guest a little more. Raising my drink for a sip, I looked into Winston's face. "I want you to drop the price on his head...and, when and if your organization finds him, you're to bring him to me, instead."

His lips contorting along with those animated eyebrows of his, Winston drummed the fingers of his empty hand upon the surface of the small table between us. "You think he's somewhere in Gudrune?"

"I think that, if he is, I would like to speak with him personally—him, and anyone he is with at the time of his capture."

Winston's eyes narrowed so slightly that, if I had not been keenly attentive to his every facial tic, I might have missed it. "May I inquire as to this interest in Glenn?"

"No," I told him simply, "you may not."

A little laugh showed me his teeth again: those unnaturally crisp, straight, white bones beneath his facial hair. "You know,

Matrix, I wasn't sure what to expect when I came here...but I think I like you." After stroking thumb and forefinger along his moustache and sweeping his fingers over his fresh-shaven jaw, he opened that same hand in a shrug that, for the first time since our meeting, closed his eyes for more than the space of a blink. "I'll have to talk to my contacts in the Valquist chapter, but I suspect we can find our way to a mutually satisfying arrangement. Although, I do admit, Glenn is a famous man for a reason. He's a superb hunter, and an excellent survivalist—and patient. Even knowing he might be in the territory, he could be very difficult to locate."

"Then I suppose," I said with as charming a smile as I could muster, girlish and twinkling though it failed utterly to reach my eyes, "you may wish to gather some friends of your disbanded organization and hire them freelance to begin the search now."

Lowering his eyes with a chuckle and something of a nod, Winston agreed, "You know, Matrix...it sounds like I just might." After he had drained his glass with astonishing speed, Winston set it down and dropped his napkin upon his emptied plate. "Well"— he stood—"I won't take any more of your time today. But may I call upon you again in a few weeks to see how you're feeling about the matter, assuming I haven't heard from you by then?"

"Certainly." I extended my right hand while making no move to rise and see him out. As he took it for a parting shake, I suggested, "Why don't you come to Malin's wake? I'll be very busy at that event, as you may imagine, but I also have no doubt everyone I speak with will have this or that piece of business for me. It may be the perfect time for us to follow up."

"I will do just that," said the hunter, smiling, his focused green eyes barely crinkled around the edges as, much to my displeasure, he bent to kiss my knuckles before relinquishing my hand. "Matrix...it was a pleasure."

"My footman will see you out—Dinon."

"Here I am, Matrix."

He stepped into the room so abruptly that Winston, spring-loaded from years of constant vigilance for Rift beasts and all else, startled just slightly. Disguising my amusement with the glass I raised to my lips, I said, "Show Winston back to the door...and give him the information on Malin's wake. Good day, Winston...I have no doubt we will have much to discuss when next we see one another."

19

HOW UNKNOWINGLY PROPHETIC, my words to Winston! At my current rate of procrastination, speaking to me face-to-face at Malin's wake would be the *only* way for my fellow politicians to initiate the least action on my part.

The wretched truth was that, as miserable with work-related anxiety as I could be, I responded by eschewing all thought of my duties and instead pretended they did not exist. Nothing could hold my attention or persuade me to focus on anything more than a meaningless conversation with the increasingly chaotic pack of courtiers who—by Aleister's invitation, or Kalypso's, combining with my own frequently inebriated consent—used the Saalast house as a waystation: a base of operations and amusement from which they could enjoy the city without emptying their pockets for boarding fees, thereby having more money to spend on amusements and intoxicants.

When I look back on this time, my face burns with humiliation to reflect on the squandered money—and the uses to which I subjected myself. Though I had been extremely self-motivated with Malin around to take stock of my lifestyle, and Eleison to serve as a constant example of hard work, without the former I could find no motivation for any purpose more extensive than pretending to listen at a meeting; and with the latter acting in my stead all across Saalast, including in the task of investigating Malin's assassination and putting constant pressure on the useless police force, I was a horse given entirely too much free rein.

The hours I kept! Oh, they were awful. Encouraged by Aleister, (I should not blame him, but there is no doubt that the Duke Montagne is as conducive to a healthy lifestyle as fuel is to stopping a fire), I kept hours so late I often did not awaken until nearly noon the next day; and even when Eleison was there, his efforts to get me away to the bedchambers for some early rest were routinely refuted. "How can you go to bed so *early*," I recall protesting once while he found me playing darts with Aleister and a few others in the midst of a particularly raucous party—a game Eleison himself once taught me to play during the first period of our solitude, when our love was still so illicit and Malin, still oblivious to it.

"We used to go to bed early all the time," Eleison pointed out, his mouth warm near my ear and his breath inciting goosebumps I resisted for all the fun I felt I was having with my alleged friends.

"Yes, dear, well—that was when we were getting up at four in the morning to breakfast with Malin, wasn't it? I skip it these days. Blast!" Drunk and distracted, I had sunk the dart into the plaster below the board, leaving my audience to howl with laughter and push me aside for the next player's turn. "Anyway," I said, stroking Eleison's chest, "come now, darling! Why don't you let your hair down and join the party awhile? You've been working endlessly."

"Because there's endless work," Eleison said, adding with an expectant look, "and I could use some help."

"Why didn't you say so? Let's hire you some servants of your own—you can delegate a few things, now that will free you up for more amusement."

"No, Thecla, I—"

With a sidelong glance and an absent scoff to reflect with deep displeasure on his inability to reach me in present company, Eleison shook his head.

"You know what? Never mind. We'll talk later...for now, I'm going to bed."

Drunk, fancying myself more carefree than I had been in weeks, I smiled idiotically and blew him a kiss while he turned from me. "I'll be there in a few hours, I promise! Not as late as last night."

"You mean this morning," he corrected somewhat humorlessly as he squeezed his way between two groups of oblivious courtiers, half of whom I was not sure I had yet met. "See you later, baby... maybe I'll stay up and get a little extra work done."

My poor darling! I look back now and see what deep denial I had thrust myself into: a poor defense mechanism that was a pitiful substitute for actual confrontation of what I had lost and how it had impacted me. It was not that I couldn't see how he wanted me, and certainly not that I didn't want him; but being with Eleison implied a level of emotional vulnerability for which

I felt I was not ready. It was so much easier to cocoon myself in drink and drug; to play silly games; to gossip with people I barely knew and who didn't really care about me. Why—as difficult as the idea of weaving had been after my emergence into motherhood, it seemed downright impossible now. If something that was once so natural to me was now as foreign as a beast from the Rift, how could I be expected to engage in administrative work for the territory of Gudrune?

A sorrow swept across me as Eleison left me to the courtiers. The guilt was immediate evidence that I knew I was in the wrong, but I had no desire to confront myself. "Roll me a cigarette, Aleister," I said, catching him by the shoulder and leaning up to half-shout into his ear above the quartet who provided background to the decadent party. "I'm in an awful mood tonight."

"Poor Auntie! I don't blame you...that wake is closer every day. Here, take mine—I think I might turn in fairly soon. I'm bushed!"

Pouting to find even Aleister was showing more responsibility, I let him relight the cigarette he'd produced from behind his ear, then accepted it from him with a knitting brow. "I thought this party was your idea—and I'm supposed to run it by myself?"

"It *is* your house," said Aleister with a grin and a pinch of my cheek. "You'll have to figure out how to manage these courtiers sooner or later. Might as well push you into the pool and let you figure out how to swim on your own!"

While I scowled, Aleister laughed, kissed my cheek, then turned back to his game to wrap things up. Feeling a bit put-out, I declined to join the next round and took advantage of my station to vacate a conveniently situated chaise from which I could watch while ruminating over the cigarette. As the two smiling nobles went giggling off to find someplace else to kiss, I was stung by jealousy.

How unbelievably free these people seemed! They had not a care in the world: neither for the judgments of others, nor for the responsibilities of their stations. Once, a month ago, I had been just as free, but had neither realized it nor appreciated it. I'd filled my time with work I wanted to do, work I enjoyed—yet near the end, I had even ceased to enjoy it. What I wouldn't give to return to the old times, the old ways! How sweet it would have been to rise early, my husband still asleep, and seat myself at my loom for eight glorious hours of the craft I adored!

It was not long before my attention was pulled entirely from the scene at-hand. Intoxicated by the cigarette I imbibed alone, my imagination took on a more vivid quality than sobriety often allowed. I could almost feel my loom beneath my hands; could almost hear the clattering of its mechanism, the wave-like rocking of its frame as a boat upon the ocean. Indeed, the violet and silver strands, more powerfully visible to my eyes than ever before, seemed to compile into an objective image before me: an object shining from relief against the endless, unabsorbed background of the noise and movement of the party. I sat up, my heart racing, gladdening with all the naturalness of a dream.

And, as in a dream, the Black Loom invited me to it.

Eager to behold its artistry with my waking eyes, I lost all interest in the cigarette, which I put aside in an ashtray without tearing my eyes from the obsidian device. It was not so much that it seemed natural the loom should appear before me in this place; rather, it was quite the inverse. My senses confused, I suddenly grew convinced that the occupants of Aleister's fete were crowding my workroom. I longed for them to leave me undisturbed; but I had the sense that I was in danger of losing my train of thought and ceasing work for the day altogether, and I would then be quite embarrassed when Malin came to kiss my neck and take me off to supper to find I had completed nothing of interest for the day. He wouldn't mind, I knew; he viewed my tapestries as my pleasures and not as my duties. But all the same, he was such a productive man I could not help but put myself under pressure to in some way keep pace with him.

So, plucking up the shuttle with one hand, I set my feet upon the pedals and resumed my work at once.

What a beautiful textile I wove! It was difficult to make out its nuances in dreams, but with the violet and silver shimmering across its detailing, I could make out hints of the rich pattern woven almost secretly into the hyper-darkness of the fuligin fabric. It reminded me of a rose garden, with clusters of swirling flowers with sharp little leaves: impossible to discern unless one was exceedingly close, or capable of touching the fabric, or blessed by these helpful luminaries as was I. Amazing that I did not even know what it was I produced—yet, as though the template lay at my left, I proceeded as naturally as I did in all my dreams!

In the periphery of my awareness, I heard someone say something that may have been to me, or pertaining to me. Some person laughed. If I had not been focused on my task I would have been very annoyed and surely would have said something to expel these revelers from my workroom, but I was so intensely plunged into the flow—so much a servant of the loom—that I could not distract my attention from it long enough for the least cross word. As smooth and silent as ever I had heard a device of its size, the loom quietly rocked while my hands fulfilled their bone-deep longing to be at the work for which I was meant.

The textile drew my eye to it, as attractive as a black hole to the debris of stars in space. Once again, I found myself pondering where I had seen this object, for I was more certain than ever I had beheld it with my own two eyes. But, as last time, I simply could not place where; and anyway, I could not make the least sense of this thought. As a great, giddy babbling rose up around me, I reflected that, if I had indeed seen this fabric before in my life, then how could it be I was only just weaving it? How could I create what already existed—and, moreover, to what end?

I paused in my work and, much too tempted, reached out to caress the developing fabric with my fingertips. I hoped to inspire some sense-memory that might identify my work to me.

Someone caught my wrist in a cold but gentle grip, the familiar voice of Dinon quickly revealing the owner's identity. "Matrix," he said, snapping my attention away from the loom and to his tranquil face, "I think it may be time for you to take to bed, if you'll forgive the presumption."

Baffled, brow furrowing, I looked from him to the loom—

Or where the loom ought to have been.

Able to make no more sense of its sudden absence than I was of the laughing courtiers who had assembled to jeer at my inebriated workings upon a loom that did not exist—or that, at any rate, they could not see—I frowned all the deeper and asked Dinon, "Why, where did you put it?"

Without missing a beat, my mysterious slave answered, "I've had your loom brought to your chambers, Matrix; shall I take you to it?"

"Oh," I said, relieved to hear it was not gone, "yes, please— I'd much rather work there than here. Why on earth did you permit these idiots to crowd into my workroom, Dinon?"

"Who could help but wish to witness such a master of their craft? Or mistress...careful—"

I had rushed up from my seat too quickly and, head light and body off-balance, I swayed back down with a little exclamation of surprise. "I'm so dizzy—I must have been at work for hours."

The courtiers laughed on, and I am quite sure the whole lot of them are lucky I had no notion of their names and retained no memories of their faces. Nevertheless, they ceased laughing—or, in most cases, at least tempered their amusement—when Dinon bent to slip his arms around my waist.

"Hold on to my neck, Matrix...since you are in no state to walk, I'll gladly carry you anywhere."

While quite a few of the women looked on with visible jealousy, I did as my servant advised and folded my hands around his neck. As he drew me to his chest, our faces were so achingly close that my lips tingled with longing for a kiss.

"You really are offensively attractive," I told him as, the crowd parting about him, Dinon bore me through the room and into the halls of the house. Dinon chuckled and lowered his eyes.

"Shall I endeavor to make myself appear uglier to you?"

"I won't have it! Goodness, no. Although—hm..."

It was difficult to focus through the high visibility of the threads out of which my slave was woven. While he stepped smoothly past the couple now blocking half the hall with their impatient rutting, Dinon looked at me expectantly. "Yes, Matrix?"

"Is this *really* how you look, Dinon," I inquired, recalling the occasion where he had so easily placed Eleison's face over his own.

With a newly chilling edge, the dharmine's smile widened. The doors of the elevator into which he whisked me opened without his need to touch a button.

"It is how I look to you, Matrix," he said innocently. "How you find me most beautiful."

"But it's not really how you look?"

"How I look is how you see me," said my slave, adjusting his grip on me as the doors closed. Those silver eyes flashing upon my face in pleasure now that we were alone and he could stare at me as unabashedly as he liked, Dinon asked on without answering the question, "Is it not sufficient to know my preference is to appear before you thus?"

I felt like berating him just then—felt like commanding him to answer me with some modicum of logic or honesty—yet, in a second, the atmosphere had changed. It was as though I experienced the pressure of another planet: a new gravity that took hold of me behind the elevator doors, alone with Dinon. Newly aware of how effortlessly he held me, my body yearned. The desire to be taken throbbed not just in my sex, but in my feet, my hands—my heart.

Without speaking, Dinon lowered his head to place upon my mouth a kiss so sensually intense I could not help but moan. His tongue slithered in against mine, then further on, further, its unnatural length thrilling me as he penetrated my throat to remind me of where else that dexterous tongue had been within my body. Groaning to be opened by him in even this way, my entire face a flood of heat that rushed down my neck and breasts, I left my mouth open without protest for his explorations. Only when the elevator doors opened did his tongue retract; yet, while the dharmine bore me over the threshold, I was lunging upon him again, my hands sinking into the luscious silver-white locks of his long hair while my moaning mouth found his. He yielded at once, refusing me nothing, allowing me full ownership of his deadly mouth—even, or especially, as the fangs for which dharmine were so well-known came sliding out.

Under normal conditions, such a sensation as the sharp edge of the demon's fang would have made me recoil with terror, no matter what intrigue they kindled in my loins; yet, having lost any trace of good judgment with my inebriation, I simply groaned and let my tongue stroke along his, pleading for more.

Ba'al-Dinon was not a creature of morals; he did not stop to insist, as Glenn had, that I wait to give my body to him until I was fresh-minded and fully sane. Indeed, he couldn't wait long enough to bring us to a bed. Propping me against the table in the foyer of the penthouse, with my back to the dying flowers and the tapestries I had woven for Malin, Dinon rapidly loosed the laces of my bodice and bent his head run his tongue along the swells of my freed breasts. My legs sagged apart as I groaned, his caresses sliding up my skirts and along my limbs to stroke along my inner thighs.

My poor Matrix, his voice purred in my head even as his mouth was occupied with teasing a nipple, *my poor beloved— how sad to see you in such a state that you cannot soberly submit to Love!*

"To pleasure, you mean," I stubbornly corrected before his fingers silenced me into a sharp gasp. The wily digits had slipped beneath the fabric of my underwear and took great liberty in their explorations: as his cool fingertips stroked and petted my clitoris to make me whimper, his kisses blazed a path back up along my throat.

"What pleasure could be greater than Love's embrace," Dinon asked, his coaxing along the soft petals of my sex quickly evoking a flood from the river of my soul. "And what Love could be greater than yours, Matrix? Ah—Thecla—"

The Rift beast gasped against my throat, his tongue lashing out along my pulse while those bold fingers pushed into my inner chamber. I moaned, clutching the backs of his head and shoulder, pressing the demon's kisses to mine and only finding the brush of his fangs made my core strain around him. As his long fingers, a tease compared to what I craved, pumped steadily into me, I raised my eyes ceilingward for the excitement building within.

Would it be so bad if I let the dharmine fuck me? It was still a matter of scientific question as to whether the emissions of such beings *really* possessed the ill effect of their fangs. Why, I'd been able to kiss him a great many times and not wind up poisoned by his saliva, so surely sex could be made safe, if it was not safe already. Say I did not let him ejaculate within me—say I gagged his mouth and rode his prick so as to have complete control of all those aspects of his being that were most dangerous to me. Would it not then be an activity of risk, but no guarantee when it came to blood-poisoning? Besides—the idea of Dinon, restrained, gagged and blindfolded—helpless—

"Oh," he moaned at the thought, a third finger stretching me open a little wider as his mouth raised to mine, "oh, Matrix, yes, please, I would so gladly be your fucktoy, the vulnerable instrument of your pleasure....perhaps even Eleison could warm himself to me, ah, his prick is so beautiful in your mind, so gorgeous when I feel it buried in your aching cunt—"

With a tremor of ecstasy to realize for the first time there was nothing stopping the dharmine from experiencing my sexual encounters as completely as I did, I drank up a few long kisses from his mouth and murmured with a soft gasp, "It is ecstasy itself, oh, so thick and hard, slave—a weapon of pleasure such that even you might struggle to endure the bliss of it."

"Oh," sighed the demon, his fingers sliding from me so he could press between my legs the sheathed outline of his own mercilessly hard sword, "but fain would I put forth the effort, if it would please the wicked mistress of my heart and soul and—"

The hammer of a gun clicked back. I gasped, leaping nearly out of my skin to discover Eleison—as though evoked from mist by the utterance of his name—had made his silent way into the penthouse foyer and now pressed his pistol to the dharmine's temple.

"Some mistress," Eleison growled, his crimson eyes blazing with disgust that curled his lip. "Most slaves aren't quite so friendly with their owners...especially when those owners have been drinking since noon. Get the hell out of here."

"Eleison," I begged, catching his hand and earning such a sharp look I cringed again, aware of a coming remonstration. "He didn't take advantage of me," I protested a bit more meekly.

Dinon, with an expression that seemed to indicate this was all part of the pleasure, stepped back to encourage Eleison to lower his gun.

"Just because you think you want it doesn't mean he didn't take advantage," Eleison said, keeping the weapon pointed on the demon. "You'll thank me tomorrow, Thecla. Get the fuck out of here, dog."

"Yes, Master Eleison," said Dinon with a short bow, his eyes turning from the interloper to fix me with such a look I swore I felt an altogether new, deeper stab of pleasure between my legs. "Eleison is right, Matrix...I was taking advantage of you. But"—a chuckle rolled deep from the demon's throat even as he faded into the shadows of the foyer and was gone—"we both know that is something you enjoy...good night, Matrix."

278

When the demon's form had faded completely to our eyes, Eleison holstered his gun under his arm and turned to me with his expression tight in frustration. "You're lucky I heard the elevator going up to your room—I thought we'd have a chance to talk, but looks like we need to have another conversation altogether. What the hell is wrong with you, Thecla?"

Blanching darkly, I sputtered out, "Well—you said it yourself. I'm hardly sober, darling—"

"Oh, don't act like you're not always looking at that thing like you want it to fuck you. I hate that you let it serve you in the bath—that it gets to dress you."

My frown deepening, I slid down from the table to stand against Eleison. To my relief, his arms still slid around my waist no matter how annoyed he was—even if one hand rose to catch mine while I petted his chest, saying as I did, "Ba'al-Dinon will serve you, too, if I command him—I'll give him to you as a present, if he bothers you so much."

"The last thing I want is some fucking dharmine following me around." The borro-growl low in his chest, Eleison squeezed my hand, then drew it to his mouth to press his warm lips into the well of my palm. "I wish Malin had let me shoot it through the heart when I had the chance."

Something in me—perhaps Dinon himself—whispered not even that would be enough to kill this particular dharmine... but I dared not suggest to Eleison that the demon with whom we dealt was beyond even the average specimen from the Rift. "I would hardly call him tame," I confessed instead, "but his loyalty feels unfeigned to me—he is devoted to me...although I don't understand why."

"And that doesn't bother you?"

Biting my lip, I confessed, "It confuses me, yes—but no more than your love confuses me, or Malin's love confused me."

Nostrils flaring, Eleison released my hand to caress his big palm up and down my waist. "What's confusing about it, Thecla?"

"Because! Because—in my soul, in my heart, I'm just some little country girl."

"But don't you understand that's exactly why we love you? I think that's what Glenn—what he loves about you, too." Eleison hesitated only a fraction of a second before deciding that, having brought the forbidden topic up, he was better off finishing his thought than leaving the sentiment unspoken. While I lowered my eyes and leaned my cheek against his heart, Eleison kissed the top of my head, his lips nuzzling me as he absorbed the scent of my hair. "There's something about you that's very...I don't know— incorruptible. No matter what you've seen or done, I look into your eyes, Thecla, and I see something so pure...and I don't want some fucking dharmine to take that from you, or to hurt you."

Returning to the subject of his greatest concern, Eleison gently pushed me back to look into my eyes. "Do the words 'blood-poisoning' mean anything to you?"

My temper flared at his sarcastic tone. "A fine thing to say so smugly to a woman whose father died of it. Anyway, what the devil does it matter? I'm altered, aren't I? Isn't alteration what saved your brother's life?"

"Yeah, baby—the *procedure* saved his life. It's a one-shot situation, and even that isn't a sure thing. We're not talking about pushing out a bullet." With a flick of his eyes down at my waist, then back up to my face, he said, "We were very lucky Kyrie's Rift beast was able to cure his host. In a lot of people, the procedure cures disease and resets genetic markers associated with things like aging or hereditary conditions—but once the Rift beast's DNA is integrated with the human host's, healing for anything other than physical ailments like cuts or superficial wounds fades out over time. Think of it like trauma—the first time, it's such a shock that everything changes. But each time the body is re-traumatized by the transformation into a Rift beast, it's more used to it, and the effects are lessened."

I ground my teeth a little. "Well, even so—I wasn't going to let Dinon have his *way* with me, Eleison. It was just a—what's funny?" He had scoffed himself into incredulous chuckling, as if I had said something amazing, and I blushed in fury to insist, "I really mean it!"

"I know you think you mean it...which is why it's a good thing that I got here. Get real, Thecla. You know how desperate you get when you're turned on."

Even as pleasure swept from my cheek to my womb, I attempted a displeased huff. "What a thing to say to the woman you love! You really suppose I can't indulge in a bit of petting and draw then a firm boundary?"

Eleison's eyes sparked like flames of passion. Before I could react, his hand raised to catch my neck, high up against my jaw. While his thumb fit along my chin and I gasped, he craned my head aside to lower his mouth to my ear.

"I think you *think* you can draw a firm boundary," he growled, his breath hot on the sensitive ridge, his lips brushing along with his teeth as he spoke. "But *I* know you better. I know you start out with the best of intentions...but all it takes are a few choice words, a strong hand, a kiss—"

He twisted my face back, his mouth slamming upon mine with such hungry force I buckled beneath him. Relentless, tongue swirling about mine, he pushed me back into that same table where the dharmine had just had me perched. I groaned, clinging to him, pressing every inch of my body to his and yearning to feel his flesh.

Parting from me before I was ready, Eleison gazed down into my face with hooded eyes.

"—and suddenly you're a wanton little slut," he told me, shivers rolling down my spine at the delicious truth, "who'd do anything for a cock in every hole."

How frustratingly right he was! Especially when he proved his point by speaking to me and handling me this rough way. I nearly lost all sense and gave into my urge to end the conversation by begging him to come to bed with me. Instead, panting a little, I licked my lips and inclined my chin.

"And you're any better, Eleison? I seem to recall our first kisses weren't exactly hampered by good sense."

"I didn't make any claims about being temperate," he said with a low chuckle. "Which, if anything, qualifies me as an authority on keeping you under control. I won't stand here and pretend like one look down your dress doesn't make my cock ache to see the rest of you"—those intense crimson eyes flashed down my disordered bust, his pupils large with desire for the rosy edge of a half-exposed nipple—"but you'll notice, baby, I'm not pinning you down to fuck the hell out of you right now, am I?"

Unable to resist any longer, I bit my lip. "Perhaps, if you did, we both might feel a bit better."

How his stare enflamed me! One look from Eleison was worth all the caresses of any lesser man; I always felt naked beneath his eyes, completely exposed to the power of the imagination where he undressed me and fucked me at will. "You're still drunk," he told me while I whimpered.

"It's different with you, though, darling...you're my mate. You know I want you...drunk, sober...sleeping..."

The growl of his Rift beast sustaining in his chest, Eleison looked me up and down and released a slow exhalation of frustrated desire.

Then, to my delight, he snatched up my wrist.

"Come with me, you spoiled brat."

With a little moan, I hurried after Eleison and tried not to look too eager. The idea of a proper punishment from my mate sparked my loins—but, to my surprise, when he threw me down on the bed, he opened the drawer of the nightstand instead of removing his belt.

"What are you doing," I begged, pouting, protesting, ready to plead with him for his cock if that was what it would take for him to give himself to me tonight.

Without giving me the chance to, he tossed the Rift ivory dildo from Malin upon the bed.

"Show me how much you want it, baby," said Eleison gruffly, catching my face in his great hand to place another, rougher kiss on my mouth. After leaning away with one more flick of his eyes toward the artificial phallus, he unstrapped his holster from his shoulders and set his gun upon the table beside the chair where he sat to watch. "Maybe if you do a good job convincing me, I'll give you every inch of what you really need."

Moaning in delight and humiliation, I insisted, "You're as wicked as Malin, oh, my cruel mate—as wicked, and as interested in watching me engage in all number of entertainments for your pleasure."

His smirk a little dry, a little pained at mention of our dead beloved, Eleison spread his hands. "What can I say? Malin persuaded me there are some things worth opening my mind to...watching you take a dick is one of them. Especially if it's not attached to some son of a bitch I want to kill for touching you."

How complicated, the mind of a man as possessive as Eleison's! I shuddered with pleasure for it, for his conflicting cravings to see me in ecstasy yet to have me all to himself. While, from his breast pocket, he removed a tobacco cigarette and a lighter, I sat up in bed to look into his eyes from across the room. As I reached up to free my hair before completing the dharmine's unfinished task of stripping me bare, I told my mate in a husky tone, "Why kill my lovers when you could demonstrate which man between you has the real power?"

"You didn't seem to like it much when I put Glenn in his place."

"Oh, Eleison, darling...don't you think there are ways other than violence?" His eyes swept over my body as I pushed my gown down, exposing my legs and the still slightly crooked lace panties left wet by the dharmine. Letting my legs fall wider to enjoy his admiration through the lacy window, I silently thanked Dinon's eager hands and the work he had done to loosen my clothes, for it allowed me to rid myself entirely of my bodice as I went on. "Rest assured, not every man would be willing to admit the pleasure of taking your cock...but that would just add to the sweetness of his humiliation for you. Tell me you wouldn't enjoy using our pretty dharmine to punish him for his brash attempt to defile his mistress's body."

"Is that what you were discussing with it when I caught you..."

Biting my lip to wiggle out of my underwear and be exposed before my lover, I savored the predatory pressure of my mate's gaze upon every inch of my body. My hand closed around the ivory phallus even as my eyes remained fixed upon his. "I confess, my sweet, the idea struck my fancy as being too delicious to leave unspoken...you're such a powerful man...oh..."

The tip of the hard toy fit snugly within the cleft of my sex, nestling comfortably against my clitoris once I had drawn it along my stomach to lure Eleison's eye down with the motion. While I teased myself with it, letting him hear how I whimpered with immediate need, I went on, "I love to see you in control...I love it when you control me, Eleison..."

"Be careful what you wish for, baby...that's how bad girls get locked in a room and fucked until they're good girls again."

Shuddering at the thought, amazed to find how wet I was simply with Eleison's commanding presence, I let the dildo's tip trail down to the slit that wept with love for my darling's proximity. "But can't you see that's what I need," I said with a pout, gasping to push the tip of the toy into myself with Eleison's eyes so intense upon me. While he watched, his red irises aglow like the tip of his cigarette as he sat transfixed by my self-penetration, I begged on. "Perhaps you're right, oh, Eleison, darling"—the deeper I worked it, the more intensely full my cunt, and still it was no match for my beloved's longed-for prick—"oh, yes, my sweet, I need you to put me in my place— my mate, I need you to claim me, to mark me...I need to know I'm your territory, Eleison..."

Smoke billowing from his nose, he sat forward in his seat while asking, "Don't you already know that, baby?"

"No, no! I need to be reminded every day, oh—"

Whining to be met with the flared base of the ivory cock against my vulva, I drew it out and worked it in again, tipping it up to drive its insistent head against the shockingly pleasurable spot that Eleison never struggled to overwhelm. That toy, on the other hand, just couldn't satisfy me—not by my own hand. Arching my hips, my pleasure most increased by linking eyes with Eleison and knowing he watched me fuck myself, I said in a pleading moan, "I need your cum in me, Eleison—I need to be kept wet and ready to be used by you every second of every day, like the good little slut I am...oh! You're right, I'm a slut, your dirty whore—"

I swore his hand tightened as though my words made the struggle to stay in his seat almost too intense to tolerate. Even as he gasped, it was through a smile that made him look savagely desirous. The toy worked slickly in and out of me, yet it kept me on the border of insanity, driving my ecstasy higher and pulsing pleasure through me all the time—but never coming close to satisfying me in the way for which I was meant.

"I need your cock, Eleison," I whimpered wretchedly, displaying myself to him with legs that opened all the wider and my back arched as my body longed for his mouth upon my breasts. "I need to feel you fucking me in two, oh, this little toy is so useless! I need the heat of you, the smell of you, your big body atop mine—"

He stubbed his cigarette out on the end table while I gasped, too inebriated on wine and sex and mithrae to care about anything but the way he launched from his seat and covered the distance between us in five long strides. Then, as he bent to kiss me, his hand pushed mine away. Taking the base of the dildo in his palm, Eleison looked me in the eye.

"It's not useless when I use it on you," he observed as, in a few long, fluid strokes, he worked the toy in and out of me in a way and at an angle that very nearly replicated the ecstatic pressure of his cock. "Seems to do a pretty good job, in fact."

Rendered mute for a few gasping seconds by the pleasurable shock, I glanced down to watch my lover's hand work the toy in and out of me, then raised my eyes and furrowed brow toward him as his mouth consumed mine once again. Groaning against his tongue, suckling on it as I pawed at the protrusion in his trousers, I worked my hips up to meet his hand at every full, smooth downstroke he used to pound the toy into me. I did all I could to express how desperately I wanted him, but Eleison, stubborn, leaned back to watch my face through those heavy bedroom eyes.

"That sure does feel good, doesn't it, baby? It must...ah, fuck, you're such a horny bitch for me...you love putting on a show for your mate, don't you, honey..."

Gasping, may face and throat red with the same lust that hardened my nipples and made my pussy flow around the toy, I nodded. "Yes, oh, Eleison, yes—I need you to look at me, look at me all day, oh, think about nothing but me, my love—spend all day fondling and fucking me in your mind's eye until you can't help but come pin me to the bed and take me for hours!"

"Trust me," he said, that dangerous growl in the base of his throat while his hand rapidly hammered the toy in and out of my tensing cunt, "I do, baby...not a day goes by that I don't spend hours imagining how good it's going to feel when I get my dick inside you again."

Brow furrowing while he bent to kiss my throat, the lewd laps of his tongue further increasing my need for him, I clutched at his back. "Then let me have it, oh, please, oh, darling—you can't take advantage of me, you least of all people ever could! Oh—"

With a groan as he raised his head to look me in the eye and gauge my seriousness, I nuzzled against his nose and whispered, "Let your innocent little country girl ride you, Eleison, darling. Let me sit in your lap and feel you inside me until you explode. Then you'll know for certain you're taking no advantage...though oh, how I wish you would!"

Shuddering, Eleison looked hard into my eyes for a few long seconds; then, capitulating, he bore his teeth and muttered, "Fuck."

The dildo disappeared from me; he tossed it away to the foot of the bed while his mouth clamped down on mine. I very nearly laughed in victory, and may even have if his kisses hadn't been so delicious. Moaning, submitting my mouth to his total control, I hurriedly worked open the buttons of his shirt as he pushed away his trousers. Together, we had him undressed in a trice. Our kisses never ceasing, he fit one hand around my thigh and pressed the other to my face, by this means drawing me upright as he leaned back against the headboard of the bed. Only as, trembling with desire, I spared no time in impaling myself upon his length, did our kiss separate—and then only so we could share a moan of soul-deep pleasure. How incredible it was that I could accommodate him! The way he stretched me full made me scream with primal ecstasy. He truly made me feel like an animal, Eleison, and as he groaned to fully experience how wet and willing I was with every inch of him I took, he certainly had the look of a beast about his glowing eyes and bared white teeth.

"Oh yeah, baby," he murmured, one hand on my hip and the other supporting my neck as I worked myself up and down upon him, "that really is what you need, isn't it...ah, Thecla, my mate is so hot—"

"Eleison, Eleison—" Leaning back a little to increase the pressure of his heavy prick within me, I kept one hand upon his shoulder and let it balance me while I worked myself upon him. Whatever tension the dildo had begun in me was nothing compared to the absolute submission of my body when filled by Eleison's. Every muscle not related to pleasure relaxed so every ounce of concentration I had could be focused on the sensations of the downright sacred cock with which I hammered myself again and again. My brow furrowed as I cried, "Oh, darling, yes, Eleison, yes, I need your big prick to make me feel owned—darling, oh, darling, my only master now—"

Growling with the aggression of overwhelming love, Eleison used his hand to keep me in place while, leaning forward to press his mouth to mine, he pistoned his hips to work himself high and hard into my aching body. Gasping, almost paralyzed by the pleasure, I cried his name and held tightly onto him.

He could resist now no more than he could before. In seconds, he had flipped me down upon my back and filled my mouth with kisses the way he filled my sex with his hot male longing. "Look at what you make me do, Thecla," he said, mouth erupting with admonishments while he stabbed that wonderful cock into my drenched, swollen cunt. "Look, look—I tried to be good, I tried to protect you from yourself...and now—"

"And now you're the one taking advantage of me," I teased, throwing him a false pout that I swear made his prick throb more deliciously. Trying not to smile, I moaned like a helpless farmer's wife waylaid by some handsome, brutal bandit in the middle of the wilderness, a moan of pleasure and agony. "Oh, Eleison, what a wicked man, I'm helpless and you would use me like this—"

"Like you deserve," he growled, bruising my mouth with more kisses, his scrotum slapping against my sensitive flesh with every rough pound into the depths of my body. "That's right, baby...I'm just giving you what you deserve...and what you deserve is to get fucked all the time. You need your pussy filled by somebody who knows what to do with it...you need to be reminded what a horny, crazy slut you are for dick—"

"Yes," I gasped, on the cusp of orgasm, my brow furrowing at the wildness of his fucking while he bore down, pinning me against the mattress with the sheer glory of his strength, "yes, please, oh, let me be a slut for you, Eleison—I'll be a good girl in public, I swear, only let me be your hot little harlot and satisfy you as only a desperate whore can! Oh, yes, use me every way, every day and night—awaken me in the morning with your perfect cock and put me back to sleep with it—"

"Thecla..." He groaned, stiffening within me, his jaw tight as he tried to resist. "You turn me on so fucking much, baby—"

"Eleison!" A height of emotion I hadn't realized was coming surged up in me with the nearing of my orgasm. Clutching his face to mine with both hands, I drank countless kisses from his lips— then, without thinking, tilted my head away from his, twisting to my left with my mouth open to receive a kiss from—

Empty space.

The emotion erupted in an explosion of ecstasy that was triggered by intense memories of Malin's mouth: of his watchful eyes and smiling wonder to see Eleison's handling of me. But that memory, unfulfilled by reality, combined with the orgasm so that even as I was awash in bliss, I found myself bursting into tears.

"Oh," Eleison said now, gentle, slowing his strokes and seeming to know without my least word just what had so wounded me.

"I miss him so much." I wept senselessly as Eleison drew me to his heart. "Oh—oh, Eleison—I'm so sad, oh, Eleison, darling—"

He hushed me, a gentle noise not made to suppress my sorrow but simply console me as his hand stroked through my hair. "I know, baby, oh, Thecla, I know. I miss him, too—"

He tried to draw out of me, but I arched up after him and begged, "No, please—"

Though he appeared reluctant, clearly unwilling to upset me further or use me when he worried I didn't consent, I clutched at his hips. "Please, don't stop—just—hold me, Eleison, my love. Oh, Eleison—please, hold me."

An hour later, after our fierce fucking had completely dissolved into the tender consolation of lovemaking, Eleison slept peacefully in the darkness at my side. I watched him for a time, sitting upright in bed, amazing sobered after my crying jag. He dreamed to my right, the statuesque muscles of his beautiful back exposed by the waist-high sheets: pure alabaster in the dark of the room.

And to my left slept no one.

Throat tightening, I slid my hand back and forth over Malin's pillow, almost fancying I could feel his hair—could touch his sleeping head and wonder after his dreams.

Oh, my husband! What dreamed you now? In that sleep of death, were you a happy man? That was all I wanted for you. If I could not have you with me, then I prayed you could be happy without me—that God had shown mercy to your sinful heart and let you rest in some Elysian paradise, instead of the Hell I know you felt you deserved.

Sleep further from my mind than was my husband's life, I slipped out of bed and fetched my robe to pad to the penthouse office. The flowers had all been thrown away, though the letter with which Charlotte had presented me a few days prior sat accusingly upon the stack of mail growing on the desk. My choices were to tend to it, to read Malin's letter to me for the thousandth time, or to brood over the sealed gift box—stained with his blood just like the letter—within which sat the butterfly ornament cruel Dinon would have been better advising me I would not need. Accordingly, I picked up the stack of letters and sorted through them, eyes glazing at the thought of replying to any of the political nonsense in my current emotional state. Even Horizon, to which I felt I owed the greatest responsibility for my husband's sake, would not benefit from my overtired and high-strung heart. I put this, too, aside, and was in fact about to abandon the letter entirely when I noticed the return address of the next letter in the stack.

Village of Lescaut,

Miller's Crossing #3

Southern Region, Gudrune Territory

Excitement sparked in me—and intrigue. Lescaut! And my sister's handwriting—but not the address where I had left her and my stepmother when last I saw them in person. Curious, I cut the envelope and hastened to open the letter, the first I had read from her in what I realized must have been months.

Dearest Thecla (or shall I write 'Matrix'?),

How I have struggled with how to start this letter! Especially given how kind you were to take the time to write me last week. I dare not ask how you are doing, for, owing to all you have shared about how happy your husband has made you, I am sure whatever inheritance you received is but the coldest comfort. You must be enduring many strange days, and I have nothing but the deepest sympathy for you, my dear sister, who are strong of mind but soft of heart, at least so far as I have known you.

If grief has not altered your attentiveness, you may by now have noticed my address, and must be wondering why I write from the milling district. Amazingly, (I hope this does not upset you, given your circumstances), I am married! I'm sure you remember Lawrence, the third son of Joseph from Threshbrook Mill? Well, I'm sure I need not remind you we have always somewhat fancied one another, at least as friends if not as greater intimates. But life is quite mysterious, and the Maker has the queerest sense of humor! You know, we used to pick on one another all the time. I can't name how many times I slapped his hymnal out of his hands or tripped him while we were walking from market together, and who could guess how often he slipped frogs into my apron or hid my shoes when we and all our friends were playing by the creek. But now we are grown, at least enough to realize what it means when we would rather endure each other's pettiness than lose one another completely.

I have hesitated to share this happy news with you; but after your last letter, I talked it over with Mother, and with some discussion, we both agreed it would hurt you more if you felt I had kept this from you even for reasons of affection. So, I went ahead and wrote this note, but decided I would keep it short: if you would like to know more, please feel free to say so. I cannot blame you if you wish to be spared further evidence of our happiness; similarly, I will understand any delay in your response, as I have no doubt you are saddled with more duties than you have hours in a day. Just know my husband and I are both praying for you, and send our love to you. I hope that in this difficult time you find some semblance of happiness.

Your loving sister,
Sable (of Threshbrook Mill!)

The one-page note was, as usual, signed with a number of childishly appended hearts, which only added to the sense of delirium I endured while rereading the missive.

Sable! *Married*? My sister—*my* sister, whose childhood I watched unfold in staggered fashion with my own, all the stages I surpassed emerging belatedly in her. It followed that she was marrying age by now...but somehow still so incomprehensible I could not understand it. In my heart, she was always the age she had been when, at seventeen, my stepmother moved me out of the house and into the room over the bookbinder. I saw Sable with fair frequency after that, but there was a quite a far cry between seeing someone every day and seeing them once weekly. One's perception of them was not as readily synchronized to reality; and between this natural delay, and the subsequent total visual severance which occurred when Charlotte whisked me from Lescaut, I could not picture my Sable in a wedding dress—my Sable, making a husband of Lawrence Threshbrook!

My eyes filled with tears—not out of pain or jealousy, as Sable had sensitively worried I might experience, but only of strange melancholy for the passage of time. If Malin's death had made me aware of it in a truly concrete way, then Sable's marriage seemed not just to emphasize time but to hasten it.

Incredulous, I set the letter down and stared at the contents until the markings blurred into an unfocused block of black ink upon creme paper.

Before I stood, Dinon's shadow once more fell across the desk; he stood so near, bent so low, that his cool breath upon my nape sent goosebumps down my flesh.

"When shall I prepare your carriage, Matrix?"

"Tomorrow," I answered, unhesitating.

His smile widening, his gaze lowering deferentially, Dinon brushed my hair back from my cheek with the sweep of a finger I no longer felt inclined to deny him.

"'There would have been a time for such a word,'" he quoted, bringing to mind my longed-for tapestries as his finger raised from my cheek and faded with the rest of him. "I will see to it at once, Matrix; we can leave at first light and you may rest the whole way...but you had ought to sleep more now, before your mate awakens and wishes to avail himself of your love. Good night, my beauty, good night, my precious mistress...never hesitate to call me to your dreams...I trust your imagination."

FROM SAALAST, THE JOURNEY to Lescaut is two full days rocking in a carriage while the countryside progresses as a long seascape of rolling hills, mountains that have browned for the summertime, fabulous vineyards, and bustling farms. Eleison was hardly thrilled by my impulsive decision to visit my hometown, but, having insisted on accompanying me to ensure the dharmine didn't take any liberties, he made the most of it and broke up the time by reading, making stops for food from roadside inns, or sliding his arms around my waist to pet and kiss me whenever he became too fully conscious of my presence.

These affections did my heart most good. Against expectation, I felt nervous about visiting my hometown for the first time in nearly three years. Why? It was hardly as though I had left by choice—yet, that in and of itself made me feel somewhat guilty.

It seemed to me I ought to have longed for my old life more; that in taking so readily to my new existence in Malin's household, I had somehow betrayed my younger self and the town that had raised me. Existence there had been so simple, so slow and gentle, that I felt I must have been turning my back on something very wholesome to instead choose a life of decadence.

That could have been a consequence of my past few weeks of living, however. Dissevered from alcohol and mithrae while in that swaying carriage, I felt almost relieved; even Charlotte—who, due to Eleison's accompanying me, was left with the duty of managing the police chief—did not complain particularly. "I think that's a nice idea," she said, in fact. "The country air could do you some good. Why not stay a week or so? The wake isn't for nearly a fortnight, and you've sent all the invitations out. Oh—and you did remember to invite the Overseer, didn't you?"

Bless Charlotte and her tack. She was never ignorant, not of anything or anyone; yet she played to ignorance so well, her eyebrows raising in expectant innocence as she waited to hear my answer.

"I haven't even called her yet," was my response. "Goodness knows, I should probably get it over with just to purge it from my mind!"

And as I laughed, she had smiled thinly before saying, "Well—perhaps you'll have a chance to call her from the road. Two days—almost three, if you take it easy and stop along the way. That's plenty of time to get a bit of proverbial housekeeping done."

Of course, it was. And I was quite certain that Malin would have brought mountains of paperwork and letterhead along with him so as to spend the days on the road dashing off notes to drop in postboxes along the way, or making calls to chew out incompetent administrators, or even stopping off at the little towns so as to have a better sense of Gudrune's functioning in rural regions.

But—I simply could not. Aside from requiring a few days of convalescence to fully shed the ill effects of overindulgence, I could focus on nothing, could think of nothing. Sobriety was so much worse in the immediate aftermath of such substances that I couldn't even focus enough to read. I could only sit and think: about Malin, about Rosina, about Glenn. Wherever we stopped, I always cast a brisk eye about in hopes that, by some strange chance, I might find myself at the exact inn where my treacherous lover and missing daughter had settled for the night.

But, I was likewise sure I would enjoy nothing so convenient. Glenn was taking good care of Rosina, no doubt—but I also found it more likely he had taken her camping rather than exposing himself to the dangers of even the modicum of civilization represented by roadside establishments. I had little hope, therefore, that I would see her; but, even without some happy gift of divine grace, I still found the trip raised my spirits slightly. The countryside really was beautiful, and the weather remained fine, and it was pleasant to be alone with Eleison, with Ba'al-Dinon driving and seeing to the details of the trip.

And, as I began to recognize elements of the landscape, I even felt just a little excited.

"I wish my father were still alive," I found myself reflecting while we peered down the mountainside along which Dinon guided the auto-carriage. "I haven't had that thought in so long… but I think he truly would have loved you, Eleison."

My mate's lips pressed to my shoulder, a firm and tender pressure against the black silk of my mourning dress. "I can honestly say that I've never been more excited to meet a girlfriend's family," he told me with a chuckle that trickled to a halt. "'Girlfriend'... that makes us sound like teenagers."

"Well, you haven't exactly been the cavalier of many women before," I said with a light laugh. "It's the only comparison you can make...and it's probably the socially polite one to settle on in a village like Lescaut." I ran my lower lip nervously along the top row of my teeth as Eleison drew me closely to his chest, his mouth brushing the temple of my forehead and his hand stroking along my arm in casual affection that still managed to run my blood hot as magma. "I suppose everyone here knows I'm altered by now, if they didn't already—and some of them did know already, I think, but there's no way to guess just who. But...still, darling, it's a small town, and—"

"Don't worry," he said, patting the sunglasses in his breast pocket. "Nobody has to know but your family."

I nodded, ashamed of myself for this need to conceal the true nature of my profound love with Eleison from my old friends and neighbors; but, for some reason, this inspired a second question and a quick glance over at my beloved.

"Darling," I said, "what color do you find Ba'al-Dinon's eyes to be?"

"Uh...blue?" He laughed. "What kind of question is that?"

"Just wondering how you interpret them," I said, glancing at the silver braid visible through the window into the driver's seat. Silver as his eyes, which I could feel curled in a smile without his needing to face me.

"It is a little strange," Eleison allotted after a few seconds, "when I thought dharmine are all supposed to have silver eyes if they're not regularly drinking blood—but maybe that's just because he's tamer than the average demon of his species. Who knows what domestication has done to him...he's been out of the Rift a long time, after all."

Longer than any of us could guess, I was sure.

At the base of the mountain, the creek running wild between the trees that lined the road was the first true sign of Lescaut's nearness. We followed it for three hours, a period which was at once the shortest and longest portion of the trip. Sensing my excitement, Eleison drew me into his lap to kiss and pet me, hoping to apply my energy to positive purpose rather than letting it twist into anxiety. Every caress made me sigh, my body heightened into a greater sense of focus. I craved him deeply, but for that I longed to have a bed, a room, and a bath—and, at any rate, it wasn't long before the countryside gave way to the farmland of Lescaut.

How amazed I was to find my eyes filled with tears! Just as soon as I recognized the homesteads and ranches of those laborers who provided Lescaut with the greater part of her food, I sucked in a breath of longing. Perhaps I really would call the Overseer. Perhaps I would beg her to take my title from me and leave me enough of Malin's fortune so I might afford some land, and a home, and a quiet, simple life.

"Have you ever thought about living in the country," I asked Eleison, who had grown up in Karris, one of Gudrune's less bustling cities. He laughed a little at the idea and I was embarrassed at myself even before his answer.

"I don't know—I don't mind vacationing in it, but it seems kind of boring to live in a place like this a long time. No offense...I know you didn't choose to be born here, after all."

"None taken," I said, covering my tracks with a light laugh and a shake of my head. "It really is a fair bit dull...when I was a little girl, I was always longing for something more. Something exciting."

And now, as a woman, I wished for less: for someone who might come along and lift the yoke of increasingly unavoidable responsibility from shoulders I feared might have been too weak to bear it.

Before I expected it to, the carriage rolled to a stop. I frowned, about to lean forward to knock on the window and tell Dinon to carry on; but then, with a cold sort of recognition, I glanced out the window to my right and realized where we were. The farm of Threshbrook Mill had a lovely house that rose two simple but well-built stories, the centerpiece of a sprawling network of granaries, dyehouses, and the eponymous mill building that sat upon the creek and was in busy operation even at that very moment.

"Is this your sister's place," asked Eleison, his mouth contorting in appreciation. "She hasn't done too bad for herself, has she?"

"I was never any great friend of little Lawrence," I confessed as Dinon dismounted to get the door for us, "but if he really has grown up the least bit, she could certainly have picked a far worse husband insofar as security is concerned."

To tell the truth, I was more worried that she was happy. After all, I could have easily provided for her and my stepmother out of Malin's coffers, and had frequently sent them money from the allowance my husband generously allotted me until his death; but my stepmother had assured me amid my fretting that they were perfectly fine, and I did not want to patronize them by bribing them for love.

Now, on the way up to the door, I wondered if I ought to have stopped. Had Sable only married for this security? Had she felt the pressure, as I once had, of working day in and out to simply keep a roof over one's head? Had she truly cared for Lawrence, or had she sensed his fancy and passed herself into his hands to kill the sleepless hound of poverty baying at her door?

Eleison knocked for us, then stood aside while I fiddled nervously with the lace of my gloves. Head ducking, I quickly worked the right off, and had just slipped my thumb into the palm of the left when the door opened. I glanced up, my heart icy with the strange fear that this was the wrong house, or I had mistaken her letter, or that some other member of the household might come and deny me my sister—

And there stood Sable, her great eyes peering curiously around the door, then growing all the greater as she recognized me.

"*Thecla*," she gasped, flinging the door wide and gawking as if, through the narrow gap, she had not been able to fully absorb her impression of me.

I must admit—as she revealed the great swell of her pregnant belly, I gawked a fair bit, myself.

My mouth opened; my eyes blinked rapidly, and after a few such blinks I managed to contort my expression of shock into a smile of true joy to see my sister—while my heart gave a bitter little twist of envy, a shock of sorrow, as the miscarriage I had worked so hard to put out of my mind came rushing back to me.

"Sable," I breathed, taking her into my arms and swinging left to right for a few rotations of my waist when she hurried over the threshold to kiss me. "Oh, darling, Sable, congratulations—"

But even as I celebrated her, she consoled me, tears in her eyes. "I'm so sorry about your husband, Thecla—I wish I knew what to say."

Suddenly aware of my own tears, I maintained as much of a smile as I could and said, "Yes, well, well—"

What could *I* say? I may have been Matrix of Gudrune, even if for an interim—but my throat clenched tight to recognize in those seconds that my sister had everything, and I had nothing.

No—not nothing.

"Well, let me introduce my mate." I hastily wiped my tear from the corner of my eye before it could escape, then gestured with the same hand in one motion. With a look of happy surprise, having been so focused on me she hadn't even seen the man standing with us, she turned and perked.

"Oh, this is Eleison?"

"That's me. Nice to meet you, Sable." While Eleison took my sister's hand and shook it in a meeting of my worlds that was somehow surreal, I glanced over my shoulder. Ba'al-Dinon remained with the carriage, having returned to the driver's seat from which he watched with an expression of contentment. Did he feast upon my sister's pure joy? Upon my pain and sorrow, my bitter envy?

Every second I'm with you is a feast, Matrix, said my servant, turning to look elsewhere as he often did when speaking in the privacy of my soul. *Enjoy your visit; I'll be here.*

I turned back, focusing on the conversation again to find Eleison in the middle of praising the property before adding with a nod down at her stomach, "And congratulations."

"Thank you!" Her hand returned to her, Sable beamed with sheer ecstasy to pat her baby through the fabric of her dress, the taut flesh of her stomach. "I'm so excited. We both are—but, of course, Lawrence is awfully nervous. I keep telling him he'd ought not to be, since he has so much family here, and Mama will always be happy to help us, too, but—come in! Oh, my goodness—"

With a laugh of pride to look between us, Sable shook her head and turned to hold the door. "The Matrix of Gudrune in our house, won't everyone be talking about *this* for months..."

"I'm your sister before I'm anything of Gudrune's," I said, brushing past her belly as I stepped into the open living room.

"Of course! Yes, of course, but, well—goodness, Thecla, you can't imagine the way people talk about you around here. In a *good* way," she hastened to add, seeing my grim expression. "You were Consort of Gudrune, now you're Matrix—we're all so proud of you!"

"Only interim Matrix," I corrected her gently. "Whether I keep the position is up to the Overseer."

"Yes, yes, but I'm sure she would be very silly to displace you. I can't speak for the rest of Gudrune, but everyone in Lescaut is very excited to see what you'll do—it will be so nice to have a woman in charge. Please, come sit! Can I get you water? I was just in the middle of sweeping the kitchen, but—"

"Goodness, in your condition?" Annoyed at the Threshbrook family that quickly, I regarded my sister with an arched brow. "They should be waiting on you hand and foot."

"Not for want of their trying," she assured me with a wave of her hand, laughing. "I can't stand it! At any rate, I still have four months to go—how can I possibly sit around now, when I'll be sitting around so much yet?"

Five months, eh...I had thought as much. She certainly seemed a bit rotund to have waited for the wedding. Indeed, I had to wonder if her condition and the decision to marry weren't inextricably linked—far be it from me to judge her for that, of course, with Glenn to think about. As if reading my mind, Sable perked and hopefully asked, "Oh, yes, I've been so excited to see you, I nearly forgot! Did you bring your little daughter? I want to meet my niece!"

Ignoring the icy grip on my heart, I fixed my lips with a smile a la Charlotte and told her, "Poor Rosina is much too young and fussy for a two-day journey by carriage...I'm afraid her father had to take up the task of looking after her. But just as soon as I can, rest assured, I'll bring her to meet you."

"Oh, phoo! I suppose I understand, though...one's thinking really must change when one is made a mother. So much that seems simple now is going to be quite difficult in the very near future...even just getting a good night's sleep, I understand!"

But a few minutes in, and our happy visit felt more and more like a mistake. I was more embarrassed and guilty of myself than ever. How could I really look my sister in the face when, through no quality of my own other than my unknown heritage, I had been whisked out of this life and into a kind of luxury that made simpler forms of motherhood unrelatable? As Sable made her way into the kitchen to fetch cool water from the pitcher in the ice box, I glanced around the house with its hand-knitted blankets and dusty old photographs of someone else's family. An awful thought struck me—a thought that only reinforced a previous awful thought I'd endured.

"It's a pity Father isn't here to see you married," I told her, sliding into a seat which Eleison kindly pulled from the kitchen table for me. "Do you think of him much, Sable?"

"More lately than I used to..." With a slightly pained look she pushed away with a shake of her head, my sister set a cool glass before me, then looked flattered and pleased as Eleison got her seat for her, too. "Thank you, sir—anyway, to tell you the truth, Thecla..." She frowned, her lips pursing slightly. "It's

wrong to say I don't remember him. I do, I certainly do. But...
I was quite young when he died, wasn't I? So...when I think of
Papa, I suppose I think of him more like a very beautiful sunrise
that lingered at the start of my day and was gone...and heralded
a great storm."

"Well," I said, grateful to nurse a bit of Lescaut's fresh water
after our long hours in the carriage, "God willing, your storm
has passed you by. And Lawrence treats you well?"

"Oh, yes. We're very much in love!" Beaming prettily, my
sister glanced up before going on. Upstairs, a board had creaked.
"You'll be amazed to find what a hard worker he's turned into,
remembering the lazy boy he was—that'll be his mother, she
just happened to lie down for a rest a few minutes before you
arrived."

"Speaking of mothers," I said, always glad to see and
meet a relation of my sister's but less interested in making new
connections than I was in shoring up old ones, "is yours doing
well? I was hoping we might have a chance to take you into town
to see her."

"Oh, yes! She'd like that very much." With a hopeful
brightness about her eyes, a transfiguring light that made her whole
face shine, Sable asked, "You mean I get to ride in the carriage?"

I managed a little laugh, even though her excitement
reinforced the gulf between our lives. My God. In the short time
since my own first carriage ride with Charlotte, how completely
I had become a stranger to myself! I could not fathom it—could
not accept it with any degree of comfort to my soul.

The Threshbrook family was extremely kind. They insisted
we stay for luncheon, which Eleison and I could hardly refuse,
for we were quite famished after our long morning. I remembered

meeting Mrs. Threshbrook a handful of times—at least in the way one meets adults when one is a young girl—at the market or other such areas of common interest; and she was certainly eager to remind me of these instances, and to remind me that she had always treated me with kindness.

"And now you treat my sister with kindness," I told her in smiling imitation of Malin's manner of beneficently veiled warnings, "and that is a true testament to your character, since not every mother-in-law is quite so fond of her son's wife!"

The tone of her laughter indicated my warning had been received, and I felt assured that her compassion toward my sister would not cease once Sable no longer carried Lawrence's infant. We talked on, and had an opportunity to meet the men when they came in for something to sustain them through the rest of their busy workday, and I sensed that all would have gladly kept me on and even put us up for the night, were it necessary; but eventually, after three hours of cheerful conversation, Sable perceived my waning energy and tapped my arm.

"If you want to go into town to visit Mama, you should likely go now. She works in weaving like you used to, but now she has a late shift."

"Oh, is that so? Well, then yes—Dinah"—addressed to Mrs. Threshbrook—"I hope you won't mind if we borrow your daughter-in-law for the afternoon. We'll handle her with great care, rest assured, and send her back by evening."

"Of course! Go on, then, Sable. The forecast looks very mild, so have fun and don't worry. How nice it is to see your sister after all this time!"

Yes—very nice, for both of us. Given pause only by the sight of my driver, who smiled gallantly at her, blushing Sable hurried into the carriage with undisguised eagerness to simply peer out the window when the vehicle lurched into motion. "You're surrounded by such handsome men," she whispered into my ear with a furtive glance at Eleison. "Are they all so attractive in the cities?"

"Goodness, no," I assured her while Eleison smirked out the window and pretended not to hear us. "I frequently suspect that Eleison's good looks were as much Malin's motive for hiring him as any skill in dharmine-slaying."

"And that pretty driver of yours?"

"Mere luck," I responded, deciding there was no point in distinguishing good luck from bad given the current subject of our conversation. "Though as his service is also a gift from my husband, I think it's really more the case that Malin has immaculate taste in the good looks of all terrestrial beings."

Sable laughed a little, but we realized what I said at the same second, that present tense of 'has' settling uncomfortably between us and no doubt bouncing cruelly off Eleison's ears as well. With a gentle expression, Sable placed her hand upon mine. "I wish I had aught to say."

"There's nothing to be said, really," I confessed with a droll smile and a small, purely affected shrug of my shoulders. "I miss him terribly, but sooner or later I am going to have to accept my emotions—accept his death—and pick up his work where he left it off."

Her eyes alight with great interest, my sister searched my face in a way I found very strange. How odd to see a woman's shrewdness in my little sister! How odd to find my little sister a woman. I could not process it any more than I could process Malin's death.

"I think Mama and I were both very skeptical to hear you were marrying the territory master, with him so old and you

so young. But to see you now, and hear you speak of him—"
Redirecting her thoughts, she bit her lip and meekly said, "I
suppose I had simply better be grateful that Love put me in the
hands of a man my own age."

"Grateful," I told her, "but just as wary that Death could
come at a moment's notice. It's terrible to say, Sable, and I don't
mean to scare you...but, even knowing his age, I still find myself
shocked death was even possible for him. I pray you will never
endure the same shock. Certainly not for many, many decades of
happiness."

We talked on, the carriage rocking us, Eleison lowering his
head into a sincere doze as we rode the forty minutes into Lescaut
and its heart. How strangely like traveling through time this journey
was! I felt myself bounding back into the past like whatever multi-
dimensional explosion had made the Rift, my soul flying over
hill and dale to pick back up from that very day that Charlotte
brought me to meet Malin. Nearly everything was just as I had
left it, which made me sad: and every small change—a new door
for the Burrough family, a general store built on what was once an
empty lot, the sorrowful discovery that my stepmother had pulled
up the roses and replaced them with more practical vegetables—
made me only sadder, until I found it miserably difficult to smile
when we found my stepmother at the door. How happy it should
have been to see her—and how miserable that 'should have been'
made me feel.

This conversation was, in so many ways, a mirror of the one
in which I had just engaged, albeit more compact and more greatly
assisted. Sable was able to prompt me and speak for me as we sat
in the small parlor sipping tea; and, much to my relief, Eleison was
more animated after his little nap, and happy to answer for me in

those instances when, say, Rosina would come into the periphery of the conversation and require redirection back out. Indeed, I was most relieved when Eleison himself became the natural subject of interest for the women who wanted to know more about my mate, a man as good to me as any spouse and therefore worth their investigation. While he regaled them of his life, I was able to sit and absorb the familiar voices: the old house where I had grown and where my father had died and where once I had walked right in through that door to find an unfamiliar woman, a beautiful stranger, standing in this very room in tense conversation with my stepmother.

This old parlor room, where my sister and I so often caught the first melodies of the most exciting procession of the year.

As I noticed it that day beneath the lighthearted conversation with which Eleison supplied my family, I very nearly thought I was hallucinating. Only after a few seconds had passed and the distant percussion was joined by horns did I experience a chill of astonished recognition—an excitement bordering on fright that made me reach out and grab Sable's bicep. She interrupted herself to look at me urgently. Knowing better than to presume the ubiquity of my sensory experiences after the Black Loom episode, I asked softly, "Do you hear that?"

She frowned, listening; then, aglow with delight, her eyes grew round as her belly. "Oh," gasped Sable, clambering to her feet with greater speed than I would have thought it possible, "is it, can it really be—"

How quickly we were little girls again! The boring world of adult conversation forgotten altogether, we rushed to the door and threw it open to hurry to the short fence enclosing my stepmother's plot. In the houses up and down the street, other denizens of Lescaut joined us, children dashing to their fences and smiling adults standing in the doorways, their work and play all interrupted for the unfolding.

And Dinon, perched upon the driver's seat of the carriage he had insisted on parking in an alley two blocks from my stepmother's house, smiled softly in my direction while the carnival's merry procession paraded into view.

Behind me, Eleison had approached unheard. He slid a hand around my waist and drew me back to him, holding me while he smiled up the street. "You sure can pick a good time to travel," he said, laughing.

"I didn't even think about it," I somehow managed to respond, my body frozen with shock. Waves of chills ebbed through me from the center of my spine, rushing up my skull and down my legs, rolling through the tips of my fingers and back again into my brain. Somehow—somehow, it was like I *had* known. I had known I would be thrilled with the jubilant parade that came through once a year, always as summer edged toward autumn; I had known I would see the contortionists and acrobats; the fire-breathers who illuminated the suddenly crowded street as the carnival made its way through Lescaut and on to the far side of town, where they would have their booths established and ready for us by nightfall. I had known I would see the well-trained horses and the half-tame Rift beasts growling in their masters' cages.

And—though I had only ever seen him once before—there, in the thick of it all, in the vibrant river of motion and joy, I knew I would see *him,* too. While clowns juggled and the master of some game tarried to offer my pregnant sister a complimentary token for a rigged ring toss or whatever other playful scam she might enjoy, my eye swept across him and locked to his patient, almost businesslike stride just as it had the first time. Just like that first time, he stuck out to me amid the carnival for being so incongruous among their merry ranks.

And—just like that first time, those years ago, not long before my father died—the blind old fortune-teller turned his milky eyes toward me, and tipped his hat, and smiled as he walked on to the festival grounds.

EAR SABLE REQUIRED NO PERSUASION to extend her evening in town and indulge in the circus with me, but my stepmother could not take off work and so tearfully kissed me good-bye before setting off to her shift about an hour later. Waiting with excitement in her parlor, Sable and I reminisced until the sunlight faded and left the stars nakedly exposed. Her excitement was for the carnival as much as for our happy memories of it, and for my good timing to have given us a chance to relive those memories together. My excitement was for something else altogether: something I could not explain.

What was I hoping to get out of the fortune-teller? I wasn't sure. It seemed to me, after all, that my greatest joy rested in the past; and if Dinon would not tell me for my own good where Glenn and Rosina were, was it not the height of foolishness to inquire with this rogue fortune-teller, this Riftborn carnival worker whose interests had no reason to be aligned with mine? Dinon, at least, owed me loyalty, however forced or motivated by some strange bond he felt we shared.

Yet this old man, this alien whose very name was unknown to me, had no reason to serve me. Not even my station as Matrix of Gudrune could prove motivation for an itinerant like him to provide me with useful information.

So why did my heart race with excitement as we made our way through the carnival? Why did I view every amusement as a banal distraction between myself and the fortune-teller's booth? As Sable stopped off in the games to use her token and then my purse to throw balls at bottles and shoot cardboard replicas of Rift beasts, all of which Eleison accomplished with skill so sure that I could see the game masters growing alert with displeasure, I tried to look patient—but I could not stop my occasional fidgeting sigh. The old man had disappeared so quickly last time, after all; and though there was no Rift Event now, could he not choose to roll up his little tent and shut down for the night as quickly as the time before?

"I can take you, Matrix," Dinon said in my ear, his words vibrating through my body and exciting my flesh into goosebumps. Feeling my pleasure—and noting Eleison was occupied in winning my sister an adorable stuffed borro—Dinon let his lips graze the ridge of my ear, then brush a kiss just behind it. "He will not leave until he has seen you; but I can tell you're sick of waiting."

"The way you feast off pain, I would think my displeasure only excited you."

My words were very soft, but Eleison was primed for the sound of my voice, and Dinon had less than a second to lean away from me before my mate glanced over to see if I was speaking to him. Innocently standing at my side, Dinon smiled, and I smiled along with him.

"Eleison, darling, why don't you and Sable finish up your games here for a few minutes while I go see the fortune-teller?"

"I don't think we'll be much longer if you want us to come with you," Eleison offered, lowering his cork gun and inspiring some hope in the faces of the barkers around the games.

"I don't want to interrupt you! Besides—well, I'm more superstitious than I'd like to admit these days. If this fellow says something ominous, it's better that it should fall only upon my ears and no one else's."

I had expected Eleison to chuckle; but my love, paying great attention to everything I said and did, asked while raising the gun again, "Is this the same fortune-teller you saw when you were a kid?"

While Sable looked over at me curiously, I cleared my throat and maintained that light smile. "So it would seem—and I owe him a debt from back then. As bad luck as it sounds for more than one person to hear a prophecy, it must be worse luck to owe money to a fellow such as him."

"Probably not a great idea," Eleison agreed with a wry chuckle, revealing his own skepticism for the whole matter and easing somewhat my anxiety about refusing his company. "Have fun, baby...want to meet back here, or maybe by the exhibitions?"

Thirty seconds of discussion later, I was free and slipping into the crowd with Dinon guiding my arm, his navigation a simple thing when his height and general demeanor of refinement made the crowd hasten open for us even more quickly than for me alone. Lescaut, remote as it was, did not receive a great deal of detailed news from the rest of Gudrune, and suffered from poor RMS transmission that allowed through weather reports and calls but little in the way of news broadcasts. I had therefore not expected my presence to draw much attention—but I underestimated the power of gossip as a medium, especially when the subject of that gossip was the death of the territory master and his replacement by a peasant girl from their own isolated little town. I should not have been surprised when eyes that swept quickly past me returned to me in new shock and then often hurried to avert, as though looking too long might cause the beholder to turn to stone; others, as during that ill-fated motorcade, marveled openly, and it was perhaps that very association that made me so uncomfortable with even the vague attention of these former neighbors of mine. I smiled, and nodded, and was polite, but when the crowd thinned out toward the edges of the carnival, my diaphragm was so tense I could hardly breathe, and my shoulders so tight I had to concentrate to ease them back into a lower, more natural position.

"You don't much seem to care for your job, Miss," observed the familiar voice seconds before I could focus enough to see the fortune-teller and his tent not fifteen feet from us. "May I suggest joining up with a carnival like ours? The hours are difficult, but I suspect the stress level just can't be compared."

While Dinon released my arm with a half a bow, a set of motions I did not fully register with my attention so captured, I found myself saying only, "You," and then stumbling forward a few steps. The old man smiled at me, his teeth a lightning bolt of brilliant white against a dark mouth lined with years of private mirth at the futures he beheld in all who came to see him. Reaching back with a groping hand that needed only a swipe or two before he caught the flap of his tent, he raised his eyebrows at me.

"Would you like to have your fortune told, my dear?"

That little tent! I thought about it so often that, even having only seen it once, I recognized it as well as I recognized my own home; and when I stepped into it, the only difference was that it was even more cramped than I recalled it to be when I was a girl. The flap fell loose from his hand and closed behind me, buffeting back the raucous sounds of the carnival festivities: and, as I drew the chair back from the small table in the tent's center, I had to count the fingers I used to touch it to ensure I was fully awake and not in the half-memory of some persuasive dream.

"How much do I owe you for last time," I asked, certain he knew me as well as I knew him, my free hand searching my overgown for the small purse I'd brought.

"Nothing." He hobbled upon his cane to the table's other side and eased himself into the chair. "I won't accept payment twice for the same fortune told."

"You don't remember." It was difficult to preserve this observation from the disappointment I felt to find the man not as omniscient as I had expected. "This was over ten years ago, so I don't know why I would expect you to. But there was a Rift Event, and—"

"I remember it, Thecla," he told me, leaning his cane against the table's edge and scooting his seat forward. As his use of my name frightened me more than his initial appearance had—silly, considering how simple that information was to obtain—his smile widened just so. "You've already paid me," he insisted again. "In the future."

Just like that, my fright melted into magmatic annoyance.

"How irritating you fortune-tellers are!" While the old man laughed at my abruptly bad attitude, I lit into him with a voice

I struggled to keep measured. "My slave is as adept at reading the future as you are, or more—and he's always saying nonsense things like that without explanation."

"It's just the truth," the carnival worker said, spreading his hands in amiable dismissal of my annoyance. "Neither I nor your 'slave,' as you called him, have any control over the nature of causality, or chronology."

"You're a fine one to discuss causality when you are acutely aware of events which have not yet been caused."

"Do you need the powers of the Rift to look into the future and predict that when your mate throws a ball at a stack of bottles, they'll go toppling over?"

"We're discussing things rather more complicated than that," I assured him stiffly, earning a smaller, altogether more amused smile.

"Are we?"

Inhaling quite sharply, then leaning toward him in spite of myself, I stared into the man's milk-white eyes without understanding or caring for the precise mechanism of his sight. "Perhaps if my blasted power as a Riftborn would make itself manifest," I told him in a tone as taut as Charlotte's most controlled and therefore most peevish lectures, "I would know that for certain."

"If you're a Seer like me," said the fellow, gesturing to his empty eyes with one hand while the other remained flat on the table between us. "Which, of course, you are not."

"'Of course.'" I slumped back into my seat and folded my arms before my bosom as though to contain my huff. "You make it sound so very simple, but in fact I know next to nothing about what it means to be a Riftborn—less, even, than what I knew about being altered before the ventil came out of me."

"Now, you know a few things. I know you do. Haven't you met a Riftborn aside from me?"

"Yes," I said, "and I noticed no commonality between her powers and yours, except that perhaps one could make the argument both were psychical in some manner. And my husband, too—" Just bringing Malin up knocked the wind out of my sails. I glanced down to worry the brocading of my sleeve with thumb and forefinger as I told the fortune-teller, "Malin was also Riftborn, which is something I tell you merely because I suspect you already know. And his power, too, concerned the mind."

"So, you see? You know a little something of our shared nature. You're a Weaver, Thecla—it's your skill to bring it all together. To see both sides of the tapestry."

I snorted. "I've had enough of vague metaphors since my husband died, thank you, Mr.— what is your name?"

"You can call me Renard," answered the sly old man.

"Well, Renard; as you may no doubt tell from my tone, I'm quite tired in body and spirit. My mate and I have traveled for days, and since this morning I've done nothing but socialize and play the part of a charming socialite for the benefit of my friends and family. Indeed, since my husband's death I'd say I've done precious little else. I'm exhausted, do you understand?"

My throat tightened to feel how true the words were. Yes—I was *truly* exhausted, as in depleted. I was like an auto-carriage whose solar panels were no longer functioning and which seemed likely to wind up stranded in the middle of the wilderness. There was no path forward that I could see. Either I would be deposed by the Overseer and sent off to live in Eleison's country estate as the placid wife of an honorary aristocrat, or I would be formalized as the territory matrix and spend the rest of my days running hither and thither from meeting to meeting to the grave—or perhaps I would crack beneath my pressure and lose my mind so completely I would be committed. Indeed, in that instant, the peace of an asylum seemed as good to me as a convent to the desperate sinner! I could not fathom going back to Saalast and submitting myself to the work which had quite literally killed my husband: yet I needed do it. There was no one else *to* do it.

While I fought back tears of frustration, a self-control which had begun to elicit for the first time I noticed—but not the first time I felt—a chronic spasm in my right eyelid, I let the old man hear the desperation in my voice. "Please, Renard, oh, *help* me. If you can see the future, then surely you must be equipped to detect the path I cannot. How can I do this for the nation? How can I open my heart to the duties my husband left behind when I'm just, as you put it, a Weaver from Lescaut?"

"The Weaver is the most powerful woman in the world," Renard said softly, both his hands now flat before him as though the very environment whispered information. "Don't you know your fairy tales, Thecla? You're a smart woman now, just like you were a smart girl then. All over the world, in all the stories that are most important to the human race stretching back to the beginning of time, there are always two people. Always the woman who weaves." Renard's thumb raised from the table, his hand closing into a fist from which his index finger likewise extended.

"And always the man who returns from the dead."

It was all so quiet. So absolutely silent that I heard my own rising heartbeat slamming louder in my ears by the second. My mouth opened and shut.

Leaning forward, I asked in a desperate whisper, "What are you saying to me?"

"You know what I'm saying."

For the first time in weeks, the little bird of hope once more stirred in my soul.

If it's true that we're already in eternity, then there really can't be such a thing as death, can there?

I reached forward to snatch up Renard's hands, but he drew them back from me before I could touch him and siphon, as he had allowed last time we met, some of the vision which it seemed he experienced even now. "My husband," I stammered out, nearly unable to form a complete thought let alone a complete sentence, all the blood having drained from my face. "Oh, sir, Renard— please, where is he? Where is Malin that I might have him, hold him? Is he alive already? Tell me—I'll make you rich. You'll never have to tell a fortune for your wages ever again."

"If I speak more on this matter," said the old man, lowering his hands to rest in fists upon his knees while I gripped the edges of the table, "it won't be right—you won't do it."

"Do what? Do what—I'll do anything. Anything to have Malin back with me, here, on Earth!"

"Yes," agreed Renard, his tone hushed. "You certainly would."

By now a true insanity was rising over me. That desperation, I found, was worse than sorrow, because it was the desperation of that little bird dashing itself to death upon my ribcage.

"Renard," I begged, gulping down a breath at the tearful edge of my own voice, "I cannot leave this tent until you tell me something I can use. Not until you give me a sense of direction. Please, oh—what must I do to bring him here? How can I call him up out of the Earth?"

"That is the sort of secret that belongs to the dharmines you have met," Renard told me, his tone patient and distant—almost compassionate—even given my increasing sense of urgency. Now, so frustrated I nearly upended the table, I instead shook it with my eyes blazing in tears I was not sure he could see in the conventional sense of sight.

"Blast it, you mad old carnie, Ba'al-Dinon is *more* tight-lipped than you—and the only other dharmine I have met had his head torn off in front of me in the woods last month!"

"Are you sure about that?"

Now I really was about to knock the contemptible table over, so as to wrap my hands around the old man's throat and send him on to my husband in Hell ahead of me—

And that very evocation arose in me with the sharpness of revelation, as though I were a woman awakening from a vivid dream.

Or a nightmare.

Pray for your husband, so that your soul—the sweet and holy vineyard planted upon the dark dungeon of my heart—might pour just a bit of its light into whatever bleak place a man such as I should find himself after his death.

Now, I did spring upon the old man, and he let me: after planting a grandchild's kiss upon each one of his cheeks, I tore the citrine ring from my finger and pushed it into the palm of his hand.

"Sell that ring, let no one cheat you, and it will serve as payment for today since my payment for twelve years ago has already been seen to someday—oh, Renard—"

Squeezing his shoulders, then laughing, I told him, "I suppose this means I shall see you again and have another chance to thank you?"

"Yes, miss," he said, pocketing the ring with a pleased smile as I hurried back out the flap of the tent, "you certainly will."

WE ARRIVED AT the honeymoon villa with the first light of morning, Dinon having driven us all through the night despite Eleison's protests. I would not hear of it, would not be reasoned with, and could not give a reasonable explanation for my urgency. My hopes were too delicate, too fragile. Like the child that died in my womb, I dared not breathe a word of them lest their very speaking might cause them to utterly shatter.

"I'd like you to go on to Saalast, Eleison."

These were unhappy words for a man to hear upon awakening in his mate's arms in the early hours. With a noise that was half offense and half bafflement, Eleison sat up and demanded, "What the hell is that supposed to mean?"

"Exactly what I said. I need you to manage my affairs while I'm here: Charlotte can't possibly juggle the household and filling in for me at the same time. And, anyway, I get the feeling that

Chief Arlington takes orders from you better than he does from any woman. Poor Charlotte deserves more respect than he's going to give her, and she shouldn't be subjected to him."

"Thecla—"

"Please, Eleison." As I begged, I gazed deeply into his eyes to let him see my sleepless sincerity. "Don't argue with me on this. I know it's a long trip, but—"

"It's not that." Jaw setting, he caught my hand and asked, tempering his gruff tone as best he could, "What's going on? We were having a nice time with your sister, then suddenly it was like you couldn't get her back to her house fast enough. I thought we were going to stay the night someplace in Lescaut: instead we've been on the road all night, and you look like you haven't slept a second."

"I haven't," I confessed. "I can't."

"So," he repeated, "what's going on?"

How could I tell him? How could I say anything at all? I could not—dared not. As loathed as Dinon was in his eyes, I could not voice my speculations to my mate. This made me feel guilty and ashamed—but no more guilty or ashamed than I might have felt for keeping any of Malin's secrets from him.

So, I lied—but, as it would soon enough turn out, I did not lie completely.

"That Riftborn fortune-teller at the carnival," I said, weaving my fingers through Eleison's and gazing into his worried face. "He revealed to me something of my powers—my nature as a Riftborn. But I do not think I can make them manifest if I am in Saalast, where it's busy and I have so many responsibilities."

"Your responsibilities won't go away because you're not there," Eleison pointed out, his tone not unkind but still quite a bit befuddled with sleep. "And some of what needs doing is time-sensitive, or dependent on you—the wake, for instance."

"I know that. I know, but—"

My tongue darted across my dry lips. I glanced at the back of Dinon's head, the silver of his hair taking on the orange radiance of dawn.

"I think this is something that will benefit us very greatly if I can find a way to accomplish it," I told Eleison. "I can't say how—I daren't say how. But if I can see to this matter in privacy, my love, I think the future that has seemed so grim will brighten drastically."

Eleison's mouth tightened in displeasure. Now it was his turn to glance at Dinon through the carriage window. "And him?"

"I will need someone to attend to me while I am focused on this matter." While Eleison heaved the beleaguered sigh of an irritated parent, my name half-formed on his lips, I squeezed his hand and let my other leap upon his chest. "Please, Eleison, please—I won't imbibe a thing while I'm here, no matter how sweet the wine or how ample the opportunity. I have much else to do, and my mind must be clear. There will be no opportunity for my resolve to slip and submit to the will of my body. I promise, Eleison. Please—"

Letting him hear the need in my voice, I told him, "You can trust me."

Another sigh: this one longer, with evidence of reluctant yielding. He turned his eyes toward the landscape; to the rows of the vineyard through which the carriage swiftly trundled.

"Let me send Charlotte to you," he compromised. As I perked, he told me, "As soon as I've reached Saalast, I'll send her back here—"

"Yes, please, please do! Whatever will make you comfortable."

"—and, while I don't want to give you the impression I'm ordering you around, baby, I really want to impart the need for—"

"One week," I told him, altogether too eager to let him finish his thoughts as the villa, brilliant and glittering white in the sunrise, came into view at the crest of a rolling sea of grapevines. "One week, perhaps less, and I swear, my darling, I will be back in Saalast to be of service to our country, and to alleviate your burdens. Besides—"

I bit my lip. "I hate being firm with people I care about, and have no idea how to wrest control of the household back from Aleister."

With a roll of his eyes, Eleison surmised, "You want me to throw the courtiers out? With absolute pleasure. You should have led with that, baby." Allowing a bit of a smirk to show upon his roguish lips, Eleison assured me, "I would have volunteered to go home ahead of you and kick them all out onto the streets of Saalast."

Laughing more easily than I had in weeks, I patted Eleison's chest and could tell he noted the change in my tone by the way he looked at me. As if measuring some component of my person visible only to him. "No, darling, don't be too harsh." I added one last pat of his chest with a playful stage whisper, "But do be a *little* harsh...I'd say a few of them deserve it."

As the carriage rolled to a stop before the villa, I found myself more thrilled to be there than I'd even been upon the eve of my honeymoon—when, as now, I arrived without Malin at my side. Dismounting with me, flicking a warning glance at Dinon as he did, Eleison took me in his arms.

"You're absolutely sure you don't want me to stay with you? If only for your own safety?"

"I trust Malin's control of our servant extends well beyond the grave. And, anyway, darling—"

Folding my hands around his face, I gazed into those beautiful ruby eyes of my Eleison, my heart: the mate of my instincts, as my husband was the partner of my mind.

"It isn't that I don't want you with me. I do. I wish to make love with you round-the-clock: to be isolated someplace private with you and savor your arms all day, every day." As his nostrils flared and his gaze flickered down my bodice, then back up to my face, I shared with him an inviting smile. "But you've said yourself, my darling...there's just too much to be done. Soon, though, I swear it—when the dust has settled, my cavalier, you and I can retreat together to some private suite in Azstoria—perhaps back to that game preserve where I was held—and you can be a prisoner to my love there, my darling, or vice versa...I'll treat you like a prince to whom *I* am slave. For already my heart is a slave to yours, Eleison, darling. You have much too much power over me. Let me have this one little week, and I will make my body slave to yours four times as long."

His tongue darting across his lips, which peeled back from his teeth in a grimace of unbearable desire, he flicked his eyes away and barked a laugh in time with the flash of his smile. "God damn it," he muttered.

Quickly as he could draw his pistol was as quickly as Eleison fit his hand to the back of my neck and craned my head up for his mouth, which sank upon mine to elicit a low, long moan. While his tongue lashed, I yielded utterly, available for his use and pressed tight against his body with promises of all I could provide. When his head lifted away, it was only so he could gasp for air and gaze sternly into my flushed face.

"I'm going to hold you to that."

"Please do," I murmured, intoxicated by his love.

Smirking, Eleison planted another, gentler kiss upon my mouth. He glanced at Dinon, who opened the villa's unlocked front door. "Do you promise to call me if you need me?"

"I promise—but send Charlotte along, and you'll feel better knowing she's here. Don't worry." While his forehead pressed to mine, I swore to Eleison, "While Dinon is far from tame, I promise—I'll be safe."

With a sigh, Eleison planted one last kiss upon my brow and tore himself away. "Call me every day," he commanded while mounting the carriage.

My heart ached as much as eased to see him go, I blew him kiss on kiss and swore, "I'll see you in a week!"

And, as the auto-carriage bore him back along the rode whence we came, the mingled emotions of my heart gave way to one I never thought I would feel again: giddiness. An excitement better than anything the coming carnival had inspired. It was sweet as that joy I had felt on the night of my wedding, when, in this very villa, I waited for my bridegroom to appear and take me in his arms.

Yes, it was precisely as sweet—for it was the same feeling, and more. So much more.

At my command, Dinon had called ahead to the staff responsible for patrolling the vineyard and keeping its ground secure; they had liaisoned with the vineyard manager's family to open the house and prepare for my arrival, and while I pitied the poor people forced to work into the night to make ready for us, I was far too abuzz with excitement to feel much guilt. As I stepped into the somewhat quite dramatic house outfitted in what seemed the antithesis of Malin's usual aesthetic style—his classic baroque and rococo adherence giving way, in this place, to the hard lines and solid colors of brutalism—the memories of our honeymoon came flooding back to me. It was all so vivid I might have sworn that Malin was already with me.

And only Dinon's shutting of the door behind us could interrupt that.

At once, the air was thickly suffused with pleasurable anticipation: a tension I truly was set on resisting, as I had promised Eleison. "Shall I turn down your bed, Matrix," Ba'al-Dinon asked, his tone perfectly innocent. "You had ought to rest up after spending the whole night awake."

"I couldn't possibly shut my eyes for more than a few seconds, and even that seems a waste of my resources. Dinon—"

When I turned to face him, I found him looming not a few steps from me. I raised my chin to gaze up into his eyes, so strangely warm whenever those silver irises were fixed upon me.

"Would you tell me—am I mad?"

"No madder than any other terrestrial whose ambition exceeds their ability to act alone."

"That's not comforting."

"The truth is seldom comforting, Matrix."

He was right about that; but, as he had not told me I harbored false hopes, I nodded toward the bedroom. "Go on and see to the bed for me to collapse into later," I told him, "and prepare something for me to eat, if you would."

"Just after I get this door, Matrix," he said with mirth that only increased when I gave a little jump at the abrupt knock behind us. "I warned you," my slave sang, turning about to answer it.

Outside stood the fellow I took to be the vineyard's manager. He was a leathered, middle-aged man who whisked away his hat and smiled upon seeing me just past Dinon's shoulder. "Matrix," manager stuttered while some daughter of his peered around his shoulder with a basket in her hands, "what an honor this is."

Tired as I was of meeting people, I still managed to summon a small smile and curtsey for the fellow who had made himself non-existent during my last visit to the vineyard, and whom I prayed would continue in this fashion. "It is a pleasure, sir. Thank you for maintaining this property on behalf of my husband."

"Such as it is. Oh, uh—we won't take much of your time, but my wife thought it might make you feel welcome if we offered you a little gift. And my daughter, well—I hope you don't mind. She just wanted to meet you."

"Of course, I don't mind. Hello, princess." While the little girl nervously approached to thrust the basket of grapes and wine and cheeses into my hands, I smiled to witness her anxiety defuse just slightly. "Thank you very much for your gift, I was just telling my servant here how hungry I was."

"These are the nicest grapes in the vineyard," the girl, who could not have been more than seven, anxiously babbled while hurrying back to her father. "I wanted them," she confessed, "but Mama said I mustn't touch them because they're for a special lady."

I laughed lightly, telling her, "Well, lucky for you, there are no doubt plenty of grapes around here for you to enjoy."

Before her father could placate me with banal agreement, the girl, in childish honesty, shook her head. "Uh-uh," she told me. "They're sick."

Never in all my days had I been so excited to hear of blight.

"Oh really?" I tempered my interest into blasé curiosity for her father's sake. "Is that so? Malin never mentioned that to me when I was here last time."

With a guilty cringe, the keeper laughed in an awkward way. "We, ah, we've had a few problems here or there...to tell the truth, we produce about half the wine we should given our size, but your husband—well, he never really seemed to mind. At the very least, he never blamed me for it."

Ignoring the hopeful tone of the keeper, who surely felt he had good reason get in my good graces early in this relationship, I asked, "How long have you been having these problems, exactly?"

"Oh, near thirteen years—they come and go, and they're worse in some spots than others. Some areas grow beautifully. Never have managed to discern the problem." Awkwardly scratching the back of his head, then abruptly recalling why else he had come, the man said, "Oh, uh, that's right—you'll need this."

With a laugh, the vineyard keeper drew from his pocket a key I recognized as an identical twin to the one Malin had given me on the night of our honeymoon. "This oughta open every door in the house—your servant said you left yours up in Saalast."

"Is Saalast as frightening as they say," the girl asked, clearly dying to talk to me but unsure where to begin.

"I quite like Saalast," I told her, smiling as I slipped the key into a well-hidden pocket within the folds of my gown. "There's much to do—many fun and lovely things to enjoy, like theatre and the arts. And many lovely parks, although they pale compared to this nice countryside you have all around you. You must have an awful lot of fun romping in these fields—have you any playmates to enjoy them with?"

"Only Telemachus," answered the girl, eliciting an awkward laugh from her father.

"Imaginary friend," he explained to the immediate consternation of a child who had been forced to explain and re-explain this point many times.

"He is *not* imaginary. He's a nice boy! Even though he's older, he's not a bully like that mean Freddie and his rude sister whose mother came to harvest for us last year. Telemachus is always nice to me—he's a gentleman."

A strange thought tickled in the back of my head. "How old is your friend Telemachus, angel?"

Shrugging a little—peering at me sidelong, as if less than thrilled to be humored by yet another patronizing adult—the child answered, "I'm not sure. Twelve, I think, or maybe he's already a teenager. He's becoming quite tall, so that must be the case."

Well...perhaps it was indeed just some imaginal companion to ease the heart of a lonely girl. Smiling on, I said, "I see—well, you must be glad to play with someone, if you have no siblings of your own. But you know"—affecting a hefty sigh, I brandished the basket still in my hands—"there are quite a lot of grapes here. Would you two perhaps care to come in and break fast with me? I simply can't eat this all by myself...and my servant eats very little."

And, anyway...as tired as I was from the visit to Lescaut, and the journey, and my life entire since that hateful motorcade—a little touch of normalcy before I descended deep into madness sounded very sweet.

The keeper and his daughter were ultimately very charming, and when they left, as with Eleison's leaving, I found myself a touch melancholy. It was the fear of being left alone with my own thoughts, which I had so assiduously avoided since Malin's death that my inner monologue felt like the words of a stranger.

Moreover, I stood at a moment in time where my hopes were beyond fragile. Reality itself felt in a state of tension, pregnant with infinite possibilities which would, perhaps by the time the week was out, collapse into a single, concrete truth. Alone in the house save for my servant, I stood in the middle of the vast, open parlor with high ceilings and broad streams of sunlight, my weary eyes fixed to the key in my palm.

"Are you really sure you wouldn't care for some sleep, Matrix," Dinon pondered respectfully, having banished the scraps of breakfast with the wave of a hand and turned down the bed in much the same eerie ease. "It may help your thinking to rest awhile."

"I was a fool to consent to a deadline rather than to push out the wake," I said, my fingers closing over the little scrap of iron weighing cool and heavy in my palm. "But Eleison won't hear of an extension now, I'm quite sure. At the very least, he'll insist on being here with me while I do—whatever it is I am doing."

Given pause by my own failure to find the words, I peered up at my servant. "What *am* I doing, Dinon?"

"What God requires of you, Matrix."

Rolling the stem of the key through my fingers, I asked, "That's not the first time you've invoked the Lord to me, Dinon. Do you believe in God?"

"God is Love. I have no more need to believe in God than I have need to believe in the sky, or the clouds—or you, Thecla." While my given name upon his lips crawled through my flesh to provoke a shudder of longing, Dinon assured me, "No more than I have need to believe in Master Farrow."

"He *is* here," I said, unable to transmute the plea into the triumph I would have preferred. "Isn't he? The blight on the grapes—the dream I had. Is his dharmine about?"

"You know the answer to that already, Matrix."

Heart racing so quickly I tried to ease it by pressing my fist and the key to my chest, I inhaled a deep, quavering breath. "Yet he knows me," I murmured. "He spoke to me. That was no dream, Dinon—you were there. You led me down into the secret room of my husband's bloody chamber and showed him to me. Will you do it again? Will you show me how to gain entry to the labyrinth beneath this place?"

"You know I am sworn to never reveal Master's secrets to you, Matrix."

"So it *is* him then," I insisted, reflecting also on the dharmine killed in the woods before my very eyes. "This revenant is not just some shade that has stolen the body of my husband—it is him, isn't it?"

"There are many secrets the beings called dharmines hold close to their hearts," said my own Rift servant, whose nature was by the day growing more and more obscure to my understanding. "Even the most expert hunter of their kind could not yet reckon with the secrets of their being."

Feeling myself growing irritated, my nerves especially short after so little sleep, I thrust my fist down to my side. "Enough of your cryptic talk. Dust off my loom and ready my workroom here for me—I'll need something to do while I organize my thoughts."

"With pleasure, Matrix. Please do remember to take some time to rest...I think you need it."

As he disappeared, smiling into my slight sneer, I looked back down at the key in my hand: then, around the room. Unlit candles of colors as vivid as the abstract paintings upon the white walls sat here and there, adding accents in the stern living space. I snatched up the nearest, a wax column of vivid pink, and quickly enough found a book of matches with which to light it.

Then—driven, impatient—I retraced my steps from my honeymoon.

How long ago that sacred night seemed! How completely I had accepted that there were things about Malin I did not need to know to love him—facts that danced on the edge of my knowledge to further tantalize me, thrill me. I had not pondered over this strange basement chamber to which I descended in more than a year—certainly not since the birth of Rosina, whose very existence seemed to wipe away all final doubts I could have had about my husband and his undeniably checkered past.

The red door left hanging open behind me, the staircase darker every step, I wondered to myself whether what I had seen in this place had been evidence of a checkered past—or of a checkered future.

How was it that a man could be in two places—two states—at once? I had heard it said that dharmines often took the forms of living friends and neighbors to fool well-meaning humans into inviting them in during Rift Events. Therefore, it seemed plausible that Malin's dharmine existed in the same timeframe as the mortal, terrestrial man.

But I remembered well that dream—the love-cry in the demon's voice, the well of desire as he had said my name. As if he had not seen me in years, I remembered thinking at the time. The dharmine *knew* me, and not in the manner of a sinister ploy. He knew me as a lover knew me—as a husband knew his wife.

As Malin himself knew me.

The light flickered on beneath my groping hand, bulbs installed in the ceiling quickly illuminating the grim scene that had frozen my blood and made me frightened to contemplate the soul of the man I married. Now, I barely registered the implements of torture and dismemberment lining the walls; barely noticed the bloodstains upon the stone floor and the walls that had been painted red in an effort to disguise them. Instead, my attention first lingered on the table where Malin had so deliciously taken me when I revealed to him I had snooped in this private, profane space of his. I paused near it, my fingers playing along the cool metal of an open manacle, then the chilly table beneath. At the pressure of my touch, the entire table depressed with a slight click, but nothing changed in the room.

Then, eyes fixing upon the spot on the wall not ten feet from the table's head, I snuffed my candle and launched into my investigation.

Somewhere, some place, there had to be a way in. There had to be some mechanism by which the secret door into that dark labyrinth would open for me: it was only a matter of finding it. My husband had a great love of secret doors and hidden compartments, as an aesthetic choice as much as a choice of privacy or security or convenience. I remembered how, in this very house, I had watched his skillful hand glide along the bottom of the bed to free a camouflaged drawer from which he had obtained a few coils of rope to bind me. This secret entrance had to be discovered by similar means.

So, one quadrant at a time, one object at a time—eventually, one blasted stone at a time—I interrogated the room without mercy. First sliding my fingers along the underside of that table to feel for switches or buttons, then getting down on my knees to examine the mechanism allowing it to rock up or down at whatever angle the user preferred, I quickly investigated the tiles of the bloodstained floor. Conventions of nobility were the furthest thing from my mind: in my mourning dress and travel boots, I got down on my hands and knees and systematically fondled the edges of every brick. All to no avail. No happy button revealed itself at the pushing of my hands: and as I began inquiring with the cabinets, throwing open the doors and rifling through the whips, the hooks, the cruel blades and other implements of torture that might have thrilled or frightened me under less driven circumstances, my heart steadily sank into deeper and deeper doubt.

Perhaps I really was mad. Would it not be like Dinon to humor me in my madness? For his own amusement—or even the simple act of feasting on my hope and eventual disappointment—would he not gladly allow me to believe my own fallacious interpretation of Renard's abstract prophecy? Teeth gritted, I held fast to the so-called dream that increasingly had the texture of a waking memory—but the longer I searched, and the more desperately I bruised my fingers and ached my thumbs by pounding and pulling at every surface imaginable, the less that dream-memory seemed to mean anything. Yes, yes. I had dreamed of my husband as a dharmine. What of it? Such a rumor, that Malin was a secret Rift demon, had swirled for as long as I was alive, and had increased in its insistence in time. As that biographer, R. J. Lankin, had insisted in his book on Malin's life, the true secret was not that he was a dharmine, but that he was Riftborn. So had that dream not therefore been a simple manifestation of the anxieties relating to these rumors, and meaningless in the end?

By the close of my search, tears of frustration welled in my eyes. Drawers slammed under my hands and cursed every object I beheld. When at last, in the final cabinet I checked, I discovered no secret latches or buttons but only a few black, eyeless hoods of the sort used to hide the humanity of the condemned from the eyes of the executor, I was well and truly weeping. My shoulder shook and, exhausted, I slid upon the floor, slumped in the corner, where I buried my face in my hand to let myself cry.

This was stupid. Absolutely, abominably stupid. What was I thinking? What was I hoping for? Even if Malin were a dharmine, would he not simply feast upon my flesh and blood like any such beast from the Rift? Not being bound in the way Dinon was, what cause would he have to let me live? Love? I was a pretty little fool from the country, still clinging fast to my fairy tales, if that was what I chose to believe about a flesh-eating demon.

Yet that demon's words—his voice's palpable longing. It all returned to me so completely that I could not shake them: nor could I shake the fact that I had, after fainting helplessly in his arms, awoken safely in my bed with the true Malin at my side, my body unmarked, my blood unpoisoned. He had not harmed me, though he had ample opportunity and plenty enough reason as a natural predator of the human species.

So...if indeed Malin's dharmine lurked about these walls, I had to believe he possessed the same heart as his terrestrial prototype.

And if he was not so benevolent toward me in the end—so be it.

I would be with Malin again, either way.

When I had cried myself dry, I used the nearest counter to drag myself to my feet and, taking the candle with me, made my solemn way to the top of the stairs. With Dinon nowhere to be seen—wisely avoiding me before I laid into him for his refusals to help me in this task, whatever Malin had forced him to swear—I made my aggrieved way to that very bedroom where my husband and I had consummated our marriage.

Pain clutched my heart before I could undress. There, above the bed, hung the tapestry I wove for him during our month-long tenure in this once happy place. Red as the room that inspired it and vibrant with the eroticism of that plum-colored bedroom whose very existence evoked memory on memory, this was the only tapestry I had woven which depicted Malin and I as we were. The series I had been crafting for him certainly showed us in veiled guises—or at least showed characters whose essences had been borrowed from our souls—but only this tapestry, this half-size wall hanging, depicted us as ourselves. My figure, reclining upon the metal table of the bloody room at the bottom of the basement stairs; and Malin's, elegant and sensual even in thread, his hawklike features hovering near mine as he bent over me in anticipation of love.

Pained, I turned my eyes from it and swiftly worked open the buttons of my gown. One layer at a time, I let my garments fall at my feet; and, rather than calling on Dinon, I stepped into the adjacent washroom to start the shower. Alone beneath the hot torrent of the water, I marveled at how truly numb I felt. How quickly that hope that had been renewed in me also died in me! What a fool I had been. The absurdity to think I might find my husband a dharmine as sapient as Dinon aside, I had to ask myself why exactly I thought Malin would make that demon's home accessible from without. If my husband—or, perhaps, if the demon itself—had specifically designed that labyrinth as a home and a kind of fortress against the outside world, would it surely not be locked from inside? Would it not be the dharmine's prerogative to come and go as he pleased?

If it did not please him to show himself to me, all I could do was wait.

Feeling sorrier for myself than ever in my life, I briskly toweled off, combed my hair with a cruel intent toward my own scalp, then sank into the bed of my marriage's consummation.

How quickly I fell asleep! And how I wish I could say I received some comforting dream, some phantom embrace from my deceased husband: but, in truth, I had not dreamed of him once since his death. My dreams were empty, black, and lonely. Even that dream-loom had withheld its presence. I was hollow in sleep, as hollow as I feared my husband's entire being now had become.

It was a long sleep. I needed it. For the first time in weeks—years, in truth—I had nothing to do, and no one to obligate me into rousing myself. I would open my eyes for a few seconds, become aware that I was still myself, and roll over to immediately fall back asleep. What dreams I did have were vague and similar to one another: hints of Lescaut, something about wandering the streets of Saalast. Perfectly rudimentary symbolism that only served to annoy me when at last I came to in the half-dark of dusk, with the sinking sun provoking the darkness of my room to greater richness.

More accepting than I had felt before, yet not fully discouraged in my mission to meet with this dharmine of my husband and determine whether he was a suitable heir in love, I rubbed my face and blearily sat up in the mattress. Unable to make myself rise to my feet just yet, I pressed my cheek into my hand and wondered over my next course of action. What options did I have? What could I do to coax the blasted demon from his labyrinth?

My eye was caught again by that tapestry above the headboard—but, before I could shun it, a burst of inspirational vigor shot through my mind and sped my heart.

"Dinon," I shouted, gasping a little to turn from the tapestry and find him already standing there, his gaze intense upon my naked body.

"Oh, Matrix Thecla..." Unable to tolerate the sight of me, my unruly slave sighed with longing and stretched upon the bed. His great arms folded around me while his mouth brushed mine. "How I hunger for you when I see you in any state...but especially in this one."

"You ribald dog—you were right." Permitting my servant the liberty of trailing his lips along my cheek and down my throat, I clarified, "Sleep—I needed sleep to see the way forward. If I do that which is on my mind, will he come to me?"

"He will, Matrix...but I warn you, there will be consequences."

"There are always consequences. Consequences for everything. Consequences for the doing of deeds and the feeling of emotion. Come with me."

Still fully naked, grateful that the summer heat had settled upon the house to keep it temperate, I sprang from the bed and spent but a few seconds washing up. Then, with undisguised eagerness, I hurried back to that frightful basement so muddied by the specter of death. I admit, when my eye fell upon the table where once I had been happily strapped for love, my heart thudded with a second of hesitation; but it was nearly dark, and although I knew from Dinon's behavior that the old myth of dharmines only coming out at night was pure fiction, I nonetheless could only imagine the maintenance of a nocturnal schedule was prudent for a predator of mankind. Shuddering at the thought, I let the adrenaline it inspired push me to the table.

"There are hoods there, Dinon," I told him with a gesture, as if he didn't know better than I did which cabinet contained them. Lying back upon the table with my face resolutely toward the ceiling, my wrists and ankles fitting into the cuffs that had once bound me for nothing more than merry sexplay, I took a great breath. "When you've locked me down, cover my face. If he sees me—has even a hint of understanding that it's me—I have no doubt he'll retreat so quickly that I won't even have a note of his voice. I still won't even be sure that he's here."

"Right you are, Matrix." With an expression of great longing,

Dinon bound me down one limb at a time, his free hand sliding appreciatively over my foot or caressing along my arm to excite me for his own wicked enjoyment. "You are brave, indeed."

"No," I told him softly. "Just desperate. If I change my mind, or if he doesn't come—I'll call out the name of my old home, 'Lescaut.' That means I want you to liberate me, do you understand?"

Even as my heart ached for all the times Malin had tenderly reminded me to enforce such a limit with him if ever I needed it, Dinon smiled. "I understand, Matrix."

"But, if he does come—" I inhaled against my tense throat. "Leave me alone with him, Dinon, whatever you hear."

"It would be my pleasure. Rest assured"—the hood was in his hands, though I had not seen him turn away to fetch it from the cabinet, and that was my last vision of him as he slid it over my head—"your loyal slave lives to serve you...and Master Farrow, too."

The hood blotted out the basement lights to leave me in a darkness so total my anxiety returned, now doubled. I breathed deeply against the thick fabric and found the rough stuff made it far more difficult to inhale than I had counted on, which naturally only added to my trepidation.

But—I could not give in to it. I could not yield to the helpless animal within me, the ventil that quaked with fear to be left as an offering to the demon I was not even fully certain to exist. I had to try—I had to gain some evidence, to witness him with my own senses at any cost while in a state I knew to be waking.

Unfortunately, when Dinon left me alone with my thoughts and the hood over my head to blot out all light, I understood why Rift birds employed in hunting were often hooded to coax them to sleep. No matter how frightened I was, no matter how recently I had just awoken after sleeping all the day through, my thoughts soon wandered into dreams: moreover, that brand of dream blending so seamlessly with reality that one is indistinguishable from the other. It happened that I shifted my wrist in response to an itch and found, disappointingly, that Dinon had not properly fastened my binds: not any of them, in fact. Removing the hood, I sat up and was only about to call to him in annoyance when I discovered the secret passage into the labyrinth was open, waiting for me.

Without hesitation, without the least regard for my nudity, I made my way into the darkness. It occurred to me after a few steps that I really did need some sort of light, but when I turned my head, the silver threads of the mithrae intoxication gleamed in little hints along with their violet cousins. These streaks of thread flashed as by some unseen light source, and I marveled to find I could follow them easily, allowing their shimmer and shine to highlight the dark walls of this subterranean maze. In the dream— for this certainly *was* a dream, I am positive—I remembered perfectly the way down which Dinon had led me on that fateful night of my honeymoon; and it was this way I followed, half-running, my heart hammering in my breast as I rounded a corner I was certain would reveal Malin to me—

And I set my eye upon the Black Loom and its unreflecting mirror as I awoke to a mournful grind of stone on stone.

In a second, I was more alert than I had ever been in my life, my senses all straining through the hood. There was no question that the grating noises came from the wall behind my head, though they filled the entire basement chamber as consequence of acoustics. A shoe clicked upon the floor, nearly lost in the noise of the mechanism, and my muscles were overtaken by a tremor of anticipation.

"I thought so."

As it had been during my last visitation in this place, his voice was rough with disuse, and somehow more casually edged; something about it was musical, almost merrily light-hearted.

Yet—it was him.

Never! Never had I dreamed I would hear that voice again. I had not realized how empty my heart had become until those three words filled it, healing the void in my being and overflowing me with relief. If I hadn't commanded Dinon to bind me, I would have sprung up at once and tried to take him in my arms: my husband, this phantom of my husband, this Rift-doppelgänger whose voice was unmistakable.

But I couldn't—I could not even speak, lest my speaking back to him frightened him away. For now that he was here, I wanted only for him to stay. I would have done anything in that second if it meant keeping him with me! He could have reached his hand into my chest and pulled out my beating heart, and I would have been overjoyed to hear it thudding if it only meant I could enjoy his presence for the final seconds of my life.

Luckily, what I needed give him was not quite so vital.

"Did Charlotte send you here? She didn't call ahead."

My pulse raced so wildly that I couldn't make sense of the words. Charlotte? Did she know about him, this living shade beneath Malin's villa? What relation did they have? So much I craved to discover—so many questions bursting from my mind like wildflowers relieved by a drought-ending rain.

I held my tongue, my eyes shut beneath the hood as though even this sensory experience was too much for me to fully concentrate upon his missed voice.

"Afraid, are you? That's natural...they all are. Not all of them are brought to me in such a...*condition*, though, I must say." With a dark chuckle that revealed, in a stir of delicious fright, the true nearness of his face to mine—surely not more than six inches from the barrier of the hood—he said, "You must have been quite a rude one to be served to me thus...that, or you fought the guards a little too hard."

Even through the hood, I could smell his flesh: his aftershave was as intense as it was any morning, and I marveled at the way the iron clasp of tension around my ribs eased completely. Breathing him in even through the musty-smelling hood, I could have moaned: but I willed myself into silence, total silence, longing for his touch.

"I'm surprised you're not begging. You do know what's about to happen, don't you? Hm...I hope you haven't been drugged. Well—I suppose I'll find out."

Before I could so much as steady myself with a breath, the pressure of his mouth upon my throat stirred my body in yearning too great to permit pain. I felt only the rush of sexual ecstasy as his fangs sank deep into my artery and let loose a gush of warm blood that made him sigh with longing. It burned, that bite, but I didn't care; nor had I the least care for any consequences, mortal or medical. All I wanted was my husband, my husband—or whatever demon had taken his form closely enough that my husband had seen fit to provide him shelter and protection.

And even as the sting was intensified by the strokes of his tongue, the pleasure to feel my own blood surging into his mouth was more than sufficient to overwhelm even the greatest twinges of lingering discomfort. It almost tickled, in fact; and certainly it provoked as much or greater arousal than his former kisses along my neck, so artfully and thoughtfully applied, now clearer in memory than in a month.

I was far from the only one enjoying it too much. With a rumble of pleasure low in his throat, he raised his lips from my neck and grunted, "Delicious—sweet as you are silent. Are you mute, girl?"

My mouth opened soundlessly, panting along with the arch of my back as his lips pressed to the flowing wound again. Now, it was different. While his hand slipped around the nape of my neck to keep me still, his mouth opened and drew a great surge of blood that was so powerful and so large it was really very frightening. It caused my heart to rush strangely in my chest, hammering for a handful of rapid beats before easing down to a far slower pace than was natural; and the second deep pull he took from me repeated this effect, adding a kind of vertigo that overwhelmed me even as I remained flat upon my back. A delirium, too: I fancied my head floated, and recognized a fatigue that was far beyond even the weariness brought about by travel, or mourning, or that which had pursued my period of coma after childbirth.

"A pity you're so silent! I love it when they scream and beg— but perhaps you're just resigned. Wise...but still, too bad. At least you're not drugged...I would have tasted that by now. Ah—"

With another groan of his enjoyment, the dharmine that spoke with my husband's voice applied my husband's lips to the wound again, snatching another awful surge of my precious blood. How much more was even left in me? What about my heart, rocked by these urgent bursts of beating as my vital fluids whizzed from its ventricles and through my punctured artery? Perhaps the organ would fail before I ran out of blood to give—or perhaps I would simply succumb to the weakness enshrouding me. A complete heaviness had begun to drape like a blanket over my mind, crawling inch by inch over every neuron and stilling their functions to silence.

Yes—it was silent in my mind. Thought became futile. I felt myself sinking with each mouthful of blood the demon took from me: sinking deeper and deeper into a great, black abyss that lapped higher around me every second. Even bound, I felt only the heaviness of my limbs: the full inability of my body to obey my commands, let alone invoke them.

Abruptly, I realized I was dying. Dying! Leaving this world as my husband had already left it—to go where? Fear filled me at last: real fear, true and cold. But I am embarrassed to admit to my selfishness. My fears were not for what might become of my daughter for having lost her mother, or the fate of my country, or even concerns of Malin's legacy.

No—my fear was only that I might die without having sated the longing of my eyes for my husband's visage, even if it was only that visage as reflected in the demon that had stolen it.

So it was that, as my eyelids grew heavy with my limbs and I feared sight might already be next to impossible, I grasped through the heavy haze of my bloodless mind for the one word that I knew could save me.

"Lescaut."

Jolting as if in great terror of his own, the demon sprang back from me, his footfalls upon the floor echoing as he stumbled from the table. Then, rushing back toward it, he bent over me again. With one fast hand, he yanked the hood from my head and left me squinting, blearily trying to gaze upon his blurry form in the low light of the room.

"*Thecla,*" he cried, his voice every bit as thick with pain as my soul was with joy to savor, even a few seconds, his unsteady features, the world as it was shifting and fading with my loss of blood. Though it me ached to do so, for as weak as I was,

I produced a soft smile. "What are you doing here," he asked on, so handsome—so unbelievably handsome! Perhaps even more handsome than he had been in life. Stricken with urgency that appeared in his face, (his unscarred face! Oh, Malin), he tore his eyes from me and set at work freeing my wrists. "What on Earth is the meaning of this, Thecla, how did you—who—Thecla!"

His hand fit to my cheek and his thumb drew high my eyelid, but it was too late. Cradled by the rapture of even this one look into my husband's silvered eyes, I slipped into unconsciousness with a happy heart.

HOW PATHETIC, to be disappointed to find oneself alive! Yet, when a thick period of darkness gave way to the light of noon pouring through the half-familiar curtains of the honeymoon villa's master suite, that was my first thought—a deep weariness of the soul, of my soul which had been so thrilled to meet its Earthly end beneath the loving gaze of my husband. Or whatever of him was within that doppelgänger that wore his form, anyway.

There had to have been something of him within that creature. Otherwise, it would not have stopped. Would not have looked more afraid than I ever could have supposed a dharmine to feel.

While I lay limp in bed, nestled warm in a bundle of these thoughts and others, I became aware of two voices in terse conversation—or, at least, one voice in terse conversation with another, more melodious and amused voice. Sadly, neither one of these voices were Malin's. But one, a female's, was almost as interesting.

"Charlotte?" No matter how weak my own voice was, it was still enough to immediately halt whatever she was saying to Ba'al-Dinon. Even as her rapid footsteps and slight weight upon the edge of my bed revealed her to me, I still found myself deliriously asking, "You're here already?"

"I arrived not twenty minutes ago—oh, Thecla!"

My eyes focused with some struggle upon her face; to my surprise, her expression was lined with awful grief, and I took by her reddened eyes that she had been crying. "It's a thin line between courage and idiocy," she told me, stern even now, coaxing from me a laugh that she did not return.

"I've never felt myself exceptionally brave," I said, "so it must be that I'm stupid. Did you see him, Charlotte?"

"Yes, dear. I was just telling Dinon we need to get you to a—"

"No—*Malin.*" Frowning, her face clearer and clearer as I drew my consciousness out of that sleep which had been clearly on the cusp of death, I asked, "He isn't here anymore?"

Charlotte flicked a grim glance to Ba'al-Dinon, who approached to look down at me from somewhere past her shoulder. "Master Farrow is not in the villa at the moment, Matrix," Dinon responded, his tone more gentle with understanding than Charlotte's.

"But you did see him," I begged, desperate for the confirmation I was relieved he deigned to deliver.

"Yes, Matrix," Dinon assured me. "He put you in bed himself, and had a few choice words for me as he did."

"That makes two of us," Charlotte said to my otherworldly slave while pressing her hand to my forehead. "If Eleison were here I'd have you stripped and flayed, you worthless—oh, Thecla, you're burning up—"

"Don't speak to Dinon that way," I told her, yet unable to move under my own volition as she pushed aside my hair with a soft hiss of displeasure for the state of my throat. "He helped me."

"Some help! Go fetch a medical kit, you slug. There's one in the washroom cupboard—and water, and a washcloth."

"And a bit of paper and charcoal, Dinon," I added, earning a sharp glance of disapproval from Charlotte. "I have a template in mind. I must get started working on it at once if I'm to finish it before we go back home."

"Are you absolutely *dotty*," asked Charlotte with undisguised outrage. "Thinking of working? Now?"

"I just need a few minutes to wake up," I said weakly, trying for the first time to push myself upright and finding my body was just too heavy. "Only let me have a little water, and—"

"Look at yourself!"

Nearly choking on her words, Charlotte strode up and snatched from the nearby vanity a small hand mirror she thrust before my face. If my eyes struggled to focus on her, the act of refocusing on the closer object of my own visage seemed downright impossible: it took an unnatural number of seconds to resolve the image into a face as pale as death, the familiar hazel eyes weighed by heavy dark circles—

And my dark hair, frosty around my scalp with roots as white as Dinon's.

Lips flexing uselessly, I beheld my reflection in solemn silence as Charlotte stated the obvious through clenched teeth. "You have *blood-poison*ing, Thecla," she told me. "We must get you to a doctor, or you'll be sure to die. If we just—"

"No."

Jerking the mirror back from me, her eyes wild, Charlotte said, "What do you mean *no?*"

"I mean 'no'. I won't leave him. I won't leave this place unless my husband leaves with me."

"*Thecla!*"

Such grief I've never heard in Charlotte's voice, nor seen in her face. There was a ferality about it, like an animal whose leg had been caught in a trap—or perhaps, whose cub had been caught in one. As Dinon returned with the required accoutrements of emergency treatment, Charlotte caught my face in hands so cool they were a sweet relief in the midst of a certain clammy heat that had overtaken me.

"Thecla," she said, her voice stern, her emotions barely contained, "you are *dying*, do you understand? This is not a question or a possibility—it is a process you are undergoing right this very moment. Your organs are shutting down. If you don't receive treatment, you'll—"

"Be as dead as the girls you've been sending here to feed him, Charlotte?"

Her jaw tightening to bare her teeth, Charlotte said nothing.

"That is what's been happening all this time," I said softly, "isn't it? Brea, for instance—when you fired her, you sent her here?"

"Yes," Charlotte confessed, turning her eyes from me to dip the folded washcloth into the bowl of cool water Dinon had furnished. "Yes, Thecla, that's correct."

"Then I killed her. Oh, if I had known, I would have gritted my teeth to tolerate her better. I never would have commanded Malin to release her from our service...it's a good thing I didn't fire Nellie when Aleister and Kalypso—oh—"

The cool compress upon my forehead stilled my thoughts so completely I lost the thread, and instead lay still and silent beneath the comfort of the cloth. While Charlotte looked at me in her own silence—the grim silence of a great shame dragged newly into the open—she raised her hand from my face only to soak a second cloth. This, she used to daub at the wound upon my throat while I cringed and moaned for the pain of it.

"It isn't something I ever wanted to do," Charlotte told me, her voice measured and small as she raised the cloth to peer at the bite. "So if you think I was just being spiteful—"

"I don't think that. I only wish— I wish you had told me he was here, Charlotte."

"Do you know now why I didn't? Because I wanted to avoid *this*. Thecla, please, let me call the carriage down, and—"

"It isn't your job to keep my husband from me. It's your job to keep our house in order—our houses. And has our house not been out of order since his—since his terrestrial death, Charlotte?"

It was a whole new paradigm I barely understood. I knew only one thing—that the monster which had almost killed me contained my husband, or even *was* my husband, and therefore, either way, was the spouse to which my heart was bound. As Charlotte applied an ointment to my wound and agreed, "Yes," I let my tired eyes ease shut.

"So you should have told me the truth and let me come here straightaway," I admonished her, for whatever my admonishments were worth when my voice was so miserably weak. "Oh, Charlotte—it was him, it was—"

While my lips trembled in a sudden swell of emotion that caused tears to well from the corners of my shut eyes, Charlotte inhaled a bit jaggedly, herself. "Thecla, please—"

"I won't go to a hospital," I told her, my tone sharp. "I won't see a doctor. I won't do anything until he agrees to leave this place with me and come back to civilization as my husband. I don't care what I must do to feed him, I'll do it—I'll find a way. But he must return with me, Charlotte. I can't live without him, and Eleison can't live without me—he must surrender to us. He must."

"I've never seen him but once," Charlotte said, "with Master—with his old self. Aside from that day, he has never revealed himself to me. I doubt I will have an opportunity to pass along your message."

"If you like, Matrix," said Dinon, stepping back into my view with his hands folded behind his back, "I can pass your message along…but I am afraid it will not do us much good."

While Charlotte looked back at Dinon—then, upon receiving a glance from his eyes, tensed in a such a violent way I understood Dinon had allowed her to see him as I saw him—I demanded of my servant, "Why not?"

"He is waiting for his bride."

"I *am* his bride," I said hoarsely. "I am still his bride, no matter what."

"Yes, Matrix," agreed Dinon without elaboration. "No matter what. Charlotte appears to be nearly done here; would you like your drawing board?"

"Yes, please—prop me up, I'm not strong enough yet to do it by myself. Oh—"

Aching with dizziness as Dinon tenderly slipped his hands beneath my shoulders and drew me upright, I swooned, embarrassed at my own uselessness. With a flick of his silver eyes toward Charlotte, who had become frozen and pale upon piecing together just what my mysterious servant was—or seemed to be—Dinon asked in a kind tone, "Would you help me, Charlotte?"

Snapping into action at the sound of her own name, Charlotte bolted forward to stuff a great number of pillows beneath my back. Only when this was done, and she was free to hurry back from the bed while Dinon tenderly stroked my hair, could she speak again.

"This servant of yours is a dharmine, too," she whispered hoarsely, looking at me to see if I knew, or believed her.

"I'm not so sure," I murmured uneasily as Dinon set the board, arranged with a large sheet of paper and a few charcoal pencils, in my lap. "He is—yet, he is not. Oh...Dinon, hold the board up, please, this is so pitiful..."

"There is nothing pitiful about your dedication," Dinon told me with true reverence, holding the drawing board upright at the exact perfect angle and distance for my use. "I admire you, Thecla—I love you."

My eyes filled with more hot tears, emotion coming upon me regardless of Charlotte's eyes still fixed upon us. "But why," I asked Dinon, who smiled very gently and set the pencil in my hand.

"You'll see—I swear, you'll see. For now, Matrix, just draw your template...I'll thread the loom as you require...I'll hold you upright and push the treadles for you if I must...just draw on. Let me help you with everything."

Thankfully, I was not yet so pathetic that I needed propping up at my loom. After Charlotte, seeing her cause was hopeless, supplied me with cool water and a clear brothed soup, I had strength enough to walk with Dinon's support. The actual effects of blood-poisoning had been known to me since Rigel's death, but it was one thing to witness such misery: another altogether to endure it. I had never imagined it was possible for one to be so weak yet cling to life! It was like being sick without being sick, for although I remained feverish throughout the days of my poisoning, I had no vomiting or coughing, nor any other symptom associated with conventional ailments. I only grew weaker by the minute, and could weave in periods of no more than an hour before, finding my eyes sagging closed even as I threw the shuttle, I would have to limp to the nearby couch and doze for a spell.

How grateful I was for Dinon! Though I am sure, having witnessed me at it enough, Charlotte could have threaded the loom with enough direction, Dinon had it done in the blink of an eye and therefore provided me with nearly eight additional hours of work that day I roused from the bite's immediate effects. Indeed, I doubt he even needed me to draw the template or do the math; but that extra work, he permitted to ease my mind, because it kept in place a frame of normalcy from which the weaving benefited.

I was not certain for the first hours of work why this weaving felt so urgent—so vital. But it was, like all the other tapestries I had woven in the past years, a gift to Malin: a gesture, a plea. With this tapestry, I begged him to come to me—to reveal himself to me and leave with me, restoring himself as Gudrune's leader and my spouse. Therefore, no matter how drained I was, the need for him made me weave more quickly and doggedly than ever I had in my life. As the loom hammered and the shuttle flew, red weft interwove with the fuligin warp to evoke the walls of the basement; more ultra-black thread sewn in produced the deep, endless dark of the doorway into Malin's labyrinth, as I recalled it from my so-called dream. Ill as I was, I managed to weave a quarter of the tapestry before Charlotte, careful not to turn her back on Dinon, all but dragged me up from my seat and into my bed.

"You must let me call Eleison," she demanded while I shook my head. "Yes! Thecla, even if his nearness can't cure you, he deserves a chance to—"

She could not complete her thought and simply pinned me down to the bed with the force of her arch look. "Think how he'll feel," she said at last.

"But he won't understand. No, Charlotte—he'll take me away from here no matter what I say."

"And well he should! I wish I could. Indeed, I would if it weren't for your—footman."

"He never bothered you before, Charlotte."

"Yes, well, he ought to have. He certainly bothered the other members of the country house...I feel like a fool for not seeing it."

"I am not sure he is a dharmine in the usual sense," I told her, as if that made things better. "But whatever he is, he is loyal to me...and Malin has control of him. He is under strict orders to leave our household members unmolested."

Lips pursed with displeasure, Charlotte said nothing until I emphasized, "He has had ample opportunity to hurt us—all of us—and has not."

"And will that remain the case when you are as dead as Malin?"

"Malin is not dead," I insisted, letting my head roll back against my shoulder, the pillow too comfortable to be endured. "Good night, Charlotte."

Her unhappy mutter echoed through my ears until she snapped out the electric lights, leaving me in the dark to sink into sleep that came easier every time it met me. It eased my brow and kissed my lids so sweetly, the tenderest lover there was. Only Malin could compare for tender romance.

Indeed, it was his gentle caress that awoke me in the darkness.

I knew it—him—at once, though his touch was extraordinarily cold against my hot skin, and I swore his hand was larger than it had been. Stirring with a sharp gasp to surmise by the thick of the night that some hours had passed, I struggled to sit up and grasped for him with both hands even as he hushed me.

"Sh—sh, Thecla my love, go back to sleep—"

"No! No, oh, Malin—" Tears filling my eyes, I managed to catch hold of the fabric of his shirt and keep him from leaving my bedside. "Stay—stay with me, whoever you are!"

"It's me," he whispered, bending over me to tenderly stroke and kiss my brow. His enormous hand fit along my cheek as, yielding to my whimpers, his mouth pressed over mine to wring a dual gasp from us both. "It's really me, darling, it's Malin—"

"I know it's you," I wept, tears rolling down my cheeks while he hastened to kiss them away, each press of his lips more desperate and inciting more desperation of my own. "Oh, I know it's you. But how—how is it you? How are you here?"

"Because of you, darling. Because of you. But please, now—you're ill, you must sleep. Oh, God—"

His voice strained, overwrought with violent emotion, and he turned his face away to press the temple of his forehead against my mouth. "I wish I had known. I thought I was so clever—I thought I knew, but oh, my love—"

While his lips trembled, he pressed them to the bandage upon my throat with a low groan of devastation. I shuddered and gasped, amazed at the perverse pleasure that wracked my fever-sensitized body, and the obviousness of the ecstasy made him inhale. His cool hands, which had been cradling my cheek and stroking my arm, slid down my body and pulled back my covers. "Thecla," he cried as I lay there helpless, his gaze wandering along the silhouette his sensitive eyes could perceive through the thin fabric of my nightgown. "Thecla! Oh, more beautiful than ever my mind could recall—"

"Even with whitening hair," I whispered, having measured all day, each glance I took into the mirror, the almost luridly intriguing creep of bright silver inch on inch into my once dark locks. Malin laughed sadly, and I let myself smile while his kisses descended to focus between my breasts for a few sweet seconds.

"I'd love you with green hair," he told me, "turquoise, maroon—I love you completely, absolutely, beyond what any words could ever say. Oh—sweet angel—I must"—his hand wrapped around the strap of my gown to pull it from my shoulder, his urgent murmuring huskier by the second—"please, allow me—"

As his mouth found my breast, his lips closing around one newly aching nipple, I moaned and gladly did permit him. "You must forgive my languor," I whispered, leading him to murmur on between descending kisses.

"No, no—not at all. My God, Thecla, please, forgive *me*—"

"I would forgive anything." The fever of my body caused the one between my legs to rage more intensely as Malin pulled away my gown. Peering through the dark in a futile attempt to look upon him, I begged, "Just let me see you."

"No," he protested. "My eyes will frighten you, and my teeth, and—my face is altered from the one you know."

"I saw you." Each kiss he pressed down my stomach in the

wake of the gown he stripped from me was more deliciously intense than the last. "Just for a moment, a glimpse stolen before I slept—oh, you're more beautiful than you even were before, and before you were so very beautiful. Malin—oh, ah!"

As, with a shudder, he planted but a few quick kisses down the dark thicket before practically lunging upon the cleft it protected, I twisted my fingers in the sheets beneath me and felt astonished by the intensity of his cool tongue—and the force of it. Even that muscle was unnaturally strong now, and as it swept the length of my sex from the shameless hollow begging for his entry to the jewel that craved to be petted and kissed, the power of his mouth was a threat as much as it was an enticement. We groaned together, and while I spread my legs, he lamented against me, "Thecla, Thecla—it's been so long since I've had you, oh, my little goddess, my bride—"

As his arms folded beneath my rear to draw my valley up against his mouth more completely, his tongue set to frighteningly rapid work. The sensation was so intense that he coaxed a scream from me before I choked the noise off, afraid as I was to attract Charlotte's attention; instead, wide-eyed, I pressed my hand over my mouth and panted in astonishment, stammering in the dark, "O-oh! Ah, oh, Husband—Husband, oh, my darling, my love!"

Within a moment, his finger—broader and most certainly longer than it was before, I could now detect for an absolute fact—eased inside me, pumping into the wetness of my body to make the matter of resisting my need to cry out impossible. He cried out, himself, and quickly withdrew.

Before I could protest, his mouth was upon mine, the taste of my sex on the cold tongue that plunged into my mouth. His hands moved rapidly at his waist, a buckle jingling; I groaned in anticipation, wishing I weren't so miserably inert but happy enough to be his human sacrifice.

His hands were not all that was bigger. While he draped himself over me and the impressive weight of his manhood rested against the welcoming petals of my labia, I gasped in near fright to feel him. "I'll be gentle," he swore, his mouth against my ear, his every word a vibration of absolute pleasure that rushed through me along with the teasing of his thick cock back and forth along the track of my vulva. But I shook my head, twisting to try to look at him through the dark, then gasping as his kisses lowered along my neck and his face ducked out of sight.

"Don't be," I begged, my thighs wide as I offered myself to him as fully as was possible. "Don't be gentle with me ever—oh, Malin, Husband, my darling, don't ever be gentle. I need your strength—your vigor—"

That was permission enough. With his tongue and lips now teasing the lobe of my other ear, he slipped an arm around my thigh and rocked my pelvis upright to gain better purchase. Then, with my body in this effortless grip, he pushed down into me, his solid girth swollen such that the lacuna of my femininity strained to accommodate him for a second or two. When at last he applied pressure enough to gain full entry, we cried out together, and I had the queerest sense that we were innocents, teenagers, two peasants in a field outside Lescaut experiencing the body of another human being for the first time ever.

But he was not a human being—and somehow, my pleasure only ignited to remember that, as his penetration deepened so utterly I felt run through by a sword.

"Thecla," groaned my husband, "my angel! Oh, my wife—Thecla, oh, no—"

Hearing my sudden sob, he covered my eyes with his great hand and kissed my tears as they raced down my cheeks. "Am I hurting you," he asked, about to pull away until, with what remained of my strength, I managed to kick a leg around his hips and keep him pressed into me.

"No, I just—Malin, oh, my darling—" I sobbed deep in my throat, a wail as I had barely allowed myself to produce since his death, and slipped free of his hand to press my face against the hard stone of his fragrant shoulder. "I never thought I would feel this again! I never thought I would have this again. Oh, my husband—my joy—"

"Thecla..." Moved, his voice rich with emotion and the gentleness he showed in his kisses, Malin pressed his lips into my hair and whispered, "I'm here—I'm home. It's all going to be all right, darling...I swear to you, it will be all right."

At that time, I still could not see how. I still could not understand. It was almost unfathomable to think that my husband was here, with me—it was unfathomable to think that this was my husband at all. This should have been a half-feral beast, a danger to me and to Charlotte and all the other humans on the property. That was what dharmines were, as we had all been taught from childhood.

But even though I could tell he wanted to take me with an intensity bordering on brutal, this demon with my husband's face and voice and memories was still human enough to resist his urges—human enough to think of me, and to take me as roughly as he knew would satisfy me without crossing the boundary into what I could feel his body truly craved to give. What mine craved to experience, but, especially with the fever, was too weak to tolerate.

Yet even without crossing that boundary, the pleasure he provided was so extraordinary I felt captive to it. His hands stilled my hips to keep me in place as he drove down into me, his mouth occasionally finding mine long enough for me to get a glimpse of his eyes or his high cheekbones before he ducked back down to thrill my throat with the worship of lips and tongue. Each kiss made my body pulse and flutter around him, which only made him thrust into me with more urgent intent. However long he had been without me, and however I had despaired for loss of him, our bodies rocked together in a unity that was almost more perfect than it had been before; his understanding of my anatomy and the cravings of my soul were as preternatural as the primeval lust he awoke in me. I wished to experience the full strength of him, and thrilled to know, even as mighty as the pleasure he provided was in that moment, he still had more to give me—more I could not take, being a helpless mortal. This thought made me feel small and pathetic: ill-matched to him for the first time in my life. I had the sudden sense of being married to a god—of being descended upon by true divinity, with not even my body a worthwhile offering to submit to his pleasure.

But there was one thing I could give.

When the rising tide of the orgasm surged intensely at the base of my belly, my toes curling against the enormity of the euphoria I was about to endure, his mouth had trailed down to my shoulder and along my breasts. The scrape of his human teeth elicited pleasure as much as an instinctive cringe—but then, excited by my own fear, I raised my chin and arched my back to press my flesh into his open mouth.

"Do what you want with me," I pleaded, barely able to construct an intelligible thought in the heights of passion. "Please,

Husband, oh, let me feel your fangs again—I'm already poisoned." He had begun to lodge a protest, but the words stopped at his throat while I made my point. "It doesn't matter. It doesn't matter anymore, Malin—my love. Take my blood, oh, my darling! Renew the covenant of our marriage, take me more completely than any mortal can—Malin, Malin, quickly, please, let me feel them, now, now—ah!"

At my begging, a low groan of pleasure had risen from his body and but for a second heralded the white flash of fangs through the darkness of the room. While they sank into my breast, we moaned as one, and then those little knives slid free to let his tongue flit along my flesh so there was only ecstasy. From the first stroke, I was pushed over the edge, and the eruption of my longing into this massive tsunami of pleasure was so violent, so intense in its expression through my muscles, that it was not a second before Malin, intoxicated on my blood and compelled by the pleading of my sex, sank himself deeply into me with a few fearsome strokes that signaled the moment he let go. I shook, my legs and arms enfolding him, tears rolling down my cheeks afresh with the power of the orgasm: the glory of our love. It was, quite without exaggeration, like he had penetrated my very soul, the nature of his lovemaking so complete that I felt as I had the night before, when he had supped unknowingly upon my blood. I was quite ready to die, and to die happily if it meant my last moments were with him.

Perhaps it was not so much a readiness to die as it was the sense that I *would* die if forced to be without him ever again. When, panting his way into the afterglow with me, he gently negotiated himself out of my body, I clutched his shoulders and was hardly even past my own orgasm when pleading, "Please— please, don't leave me—"

"Thecla—"

"I can't live without you," I wept, regressed to a state of dependence by my sickness and the strength of the orgasm. Pressing closely to him, my cheek nestled into his shoulder to prove I didn't want to so much as steal a glimpse of his face before he was ready to let me see, I wept miserably for all the days I had been forced to endure with him dead to me. "Oh, Malin, my husband—my joy died with you, my soul died with you—I haven't been the same since, nothing is the same—"

"Oh! Angel, my poor Thecla—"

"Please," I summarized as, holding me with great care, he stroked my hair and kissed my head and drew me more completely into his embrace, "don't leave me tonight."

"I won't. I'll be here until you fall asleep—I promise, I'll be right here."

"And after I'm asleep?" Lips trembling wretchedly, I demanded in a tone that was a little accusatory, "Will you sneak away and leave me here alone?"

"I must," he murmured. "I must—but soon, I think, you'll understand."

"Stay up here," I pleaded. "Just stay up in the villa. Why can't you do that?"

"I promise, you'll see. But I can't—not yet. Just trust me. Do you trust me, Thecla?"

Inhaling wetly, I nodded against his shoulder and strained out a noise that was something like assent.

"Then keep trusting me. I swear, my Thecla, my doe—oh, my beloved. Soon, very soon. the day is coming you will never be alone again. We will never have to be apart again."

"Do you really promise?"

"Yes, Thecla. I really promise."

What choice did I have? With a deep, rattling breath of anguish, I wiped my cheeks: first on his shoulder, then with the heel of my palm. "All right," I said, still trembling with emotion as he kissed my tears away. "All right. As long as you promise, I believe you. Just—please, hold me for as long as you can."

"Charlotte will have to plunge a stake through my heart to pry me away," he swore, his voice lit with a soft smile as he made me laugh.

"I wouldn't joke if I were you," I said between the little sniffs with which I recovered the sad remains of my composure. "The way she was talking earlier today, I think she's sorely tempted."

"Well"—my husband pressed his smiling lips against my ear, his cool body enfolding mine completely in the dark—"let's be honest...what else is new?"

AT THE TIME, I had no idea what I was doing. Those days had the aesthetic of a bad dream, where, for instance, one is walking down a hall toward an ominous door that surely contains nothing desirable to experience or know; yet, despite oneself, one keeps walking toward it, resolutely refusing—or perhaps unable—to return whence one came.

Yet was that not life? One long march into mystery? Into the endless sleep of the gallows or the rhapsody of eternal life? When I awoke the next morning to an achingly empty bed and birds twittering outside my window heedless of my condition, I pondered this and more. My contemplation was so intense, in fact, and my mind so weary, that I did not notice until I turned over to face Malin's empty pillow that it was not entirely empty. A single mithrae flower, soft and blue as the robe of the sky, lay there in his stead.

When, with a brisk knock, the door opened to permit Charlotte's entry, I slipped the flower beneath my pillow and made a pitiful attempt to look energetic. "So you're up," said Charlotte, something shining in her hand as I tried pushing myself up. Feeling a sting of pain in my breast where the asp of love had sunk his fangs, I relented back down into the bedding. "You have a call," she said, handing me the watch while mouthing 'Eleison.'

Oh! My darling. My heart throbbed quite painfully—a literal pain, as well as a metaphorical one—and the shadow of guilt draped itself over me. Charlotte had been quite right, of course. I was being selfish by throwing myself headlong toward a death that seemed the only bargaining chip by which I might persuade my husband away from this isolated little house. Without me, Eleison would be in danger; left to rely on Stabilify once again, until and unless he could find another mate of lesser connection to look after him. My throat tightened at the thought as I raised the watch toward my face and said into it, "Eleison, oh, darling—I miss you."

"Everything okay, baby? You sound tired—and you didn't call me yesterday."

While Charlotte folded her arms to drum her fingers impatiently upon her elbow, I blearily managed, "Oh, you're right—I didn't. I'm sorry, dear, I—I'm feeling very tired the past two days. This project is taking quite a lot out of me. But—" When sitting up again engendered the sting of my breast, I pushed through it, still pressing the sheet to my chest to avoid Charlotte's judgment. Gritting my teeth, I told my beloved mate, "I think it will be worth it. I really do."

"That's good. I miss you."

"I miss you, too," I murmured into the watch, letting him hear the longing in my voice. "So much."

"And is your *pet* behaving himself?"

"Oh, Dinon has been grand—I couldn't get on without his help. And Charlotte's."

While Charlotte rolled her eyes and set about opening the curtains and straightening the room, I smiled a little—until, at least, Eleison revealed why he had called.

"That's good. I'm glad she got there safe. Say, uh, baby… now, I know what you're doing is important, but do you think there's any chance at all you might make it home a little early?"

"I'm not sure." Heart sinking at both my own endless lies and the shift in his tone, I asked, "Why?"

"Because, well—Parvati is, um—she's here."

Paled, I exchanged a look at Charlotte, who had clearly known this information on her entry considering her lack of reaction to Eleison's words. "She's in Saalast?"

"Staying in a suite in a hotel," he answered. "I've put her off by telling her you're at the Karris house convalescing and preparing for the wake, but she's, uh—pretty insistent she get a chance to talk to you. She even asked if I could persuade you to come back to Saalast before the wake, if she's not going to be invited."

Groaning, my free hand rubbing over my brow, I felt my pressures double and willed myself not to fall into the tears of an ill old woman—for that was how I felt: sixty years older than I was, and burdened by the legal and personal minutiae of impending death. Blast Parvati! No doubt, the Overseer felt she was now able to go where she wanted in Gudrune with my husband and the threat he posed her out of the way.

So far as she was concerned, anyway.

"Well…please, Eleison, darling, please keep putting her off.

I—I just can't come face her yet." At his sigh, I added lamely, "I'm sorry. I wish—"

"No, baby. It's okay. I wish you could tell me what you're doing down there, but I get it. You don't want to talk about a project before it's completed. I'm a little superstitious, too."

Grateful for my mate's empathy toward me—and all the more ashamed of my lies—I pressed my forehead down into the palm that seemed the only thing holding it upright. "Why don't you—why don't you give her a little tour, darling. And is Aleister still there?"

"He's the only one of them I didn't evict yesterday," Eleison grumbled, referring to the courtiers, "and only narrowly...only because Malin loved him."

"Then make him useful and see to it that he entertains Parvati for us. Is Arlington making any progress?"

"I have a meeting with him today, but it doesn't sound like it."

Irritated despite the increasingly altered circumstances, I muttered, "Useless—very well. Lay into him for me, Eleison, and check in with your brother about the hunt for Glenn and Rosina."

"Will do. Anything else?"

"No, nothing, just—"

Tears welled in my. I felt like a small animal, cornered. This could easily be the last time I ever spoke to Eleison, and I couldn't imagine what it would do to him if that were the case. Yet—

The world would go on without me, wouldn't it? Just as it had without Malin. This body, my body, would be interned beside him, and Eleison would weep for days, perhaps months; he would no doubt be as inconsolable as I was, or more. But then, slowly, one day at a time, he would pick himself back up. He would live on, and move on. And would he remember me, or would he try to forget? Which was better for him? What of Sable, and my stepmother? Aleister, Kalypso? How long would it be before my name was completely erased—before they, also, died, and no one was left to remember me except by reputation?

Hearing me break into weeping that made Charlotte's expression soften, Eleison asked, "Oh, baby! What's wrong? Tell me what's wrong. Is it Malin?"

"No—yes. I don't know. It's everything. I just—I miss you." Sweeping my fingers quickly beneath my eyes, I took a breath. "It's everything. I'm just overwhelmed, and I miss you. I wish you were here."

"I could always come back."

"I know...but there's so much to do, especially with Parvati there now."

"All the more reason for me to ditch this place," he muttered, inspiring a soft laugh through my tears. While Charlotte set a handkerchief in my free hand, I nodded in gratitude, then sniffed myself intelligible.

"I think I'm just crying because I appreciate you so much," I told him. "I love you so much, Eleison. I'm sorry I've been so selfish these past few weeks. You deserve someone better than me."

"Thecla...no matter what, *you're* the one I want. It's okay if you're a little selfish sometimes—I don't care. If you want to know the truth, it just makes me want you more, for some weird reason..." While I laughed again, I could hear the soft smile in his voice as he went on. "Besides...you have a right to be selfish right now. Fuck Parvati. Fuck it all. Most widows have a little paperwork and some affairs to settle; you've got way, way more. I get it. It's freaky."

"Yes—to say the least."

"Just do what you have to do and come home as soon as you can, baby," Eleison said, my gallant, my darling. "I'll be here for you whenever you're ready."

"Thank you," I murmured. "I love you, Eleison. Oh, my treasure. You're the greatest gift Malin has ever given me."

Not noticing my lingual tense—thinking, no doubt, it was the same slip of the tongue we had been making when referring to my husband since his alleged death—Eleison told me gently, "I feel the same way about you. Have a good day, honey. I hope you get a lot done on...whatever it is you're doing."

My darling Eleison! I wept over the pocket watch as we hung up, my head bowed beneath the impossible weight of it all. Charlotte watched me with strain in her features, her hands on her hips. "Let us take you to the hospital," she said again, the words formed less like a demand and more like a plea. "I can't just stand here and watch you die, Thecla."

"You won't have to," I said, pushing the sheets down. "I'll finish this tapestry, and Malin will—"

"*Thecla*!"

I paused, cringing to remember the bite upon my now exposed breast. While Charlotte looked between my bruised and bitten flesh and my consternated face, I confessed. "He visited me last night— but he had to return to that blasted labyrinth. He wouldn't stay."

"You *can't* keep letting him bite you. You're already weak enough—have you seen your hair today?" While I struggled to my feet, I let her take my arm and followed her glance to the full-length mirror.

What a funny thing to be emotionally affected by! But somehow, in my weakness and pain and my longing for Eleison, what made me cry hardest—what drove home the reality of the situation the most—was seeing that, in twenty-four hours, three inches of my hair had faded to snowy white. I burst into true tears, but while Charlotte tried to reason with me again, I shook my head.

"It doesn't matter," I told her, "it doesn't—nothing matters as much as getting him back."

"But—"

"Help me bathe, Charlotte, and let me work, and you'll see," I insisted. "You'll see."

We would both see, perhaps—I had no choice but to believe in my husband and trust my instincts. What would truly come of it all, I didn't know. I felt like a caterpillar, suddenly driven one day to spin a cocoon of silk around itself. Did that little pupa feel like I did? Was the cocoon in which it encapsulated its entire being one last stab at creation? A plea to God to extend its existence, should He look upon that little bug and see the worthiness of its talents?

Then surely that small worm was overjoyed—grateful beyond measure—when, after the long blackness of death-sleep, it broke free from the shell of its old creation to dry its new wings in the sun.

The tapestry came together as rapidly as anything I had ever made. I felt pursued into it, the hounds of Death baying after me as I worked the treadles and slammed the beam with each toss of the shuttle. My fingers trembled and my eyelids ached to close, but on and on I wove, hour after hour, singularly focused on my husband.

Would it work? Would it be too late to save me by the time I had completed this gesture for him? Would this little tapestry be enough to soften his heart? To remind him what the surface could give him, and persuade him to leave this place with me?

"Your pocket watch is ringing in your bedroom, Matrix," said Dinon halfway through that second day of weaving, looking at the wall of the workroom where he stood in case I should be in need of assistance to the couch for some rest. "It appears to be the Overseer."

"Turn the damn thing off," I told him.

"Very well. What of food? Charlotte is cooking for you at the moment, I believe."

"I have no appetite, but she'll worry for me if I don't eat. Take it from her and do something with it."

"Yes, Matrix."

"Dinon—"

At last pausing my work, I glanced over my shoulder and marveled at how this simple turn of my head irritated the wound on my throat. "You *will* deliver this to him when it is finished, won't you?"

"It will be my pleasure, Madame."

Nodding, I returned to work. I could not sing along with it as once I had, nor dream fantastic dreams. It was enough that I had the focus left for this craft of mine, however built into the very bones of my fingers and feet every little motion had become over the years. Even what was most natural seemed to require an awesome effort already almost beyond me. But I had to persevere: I had to weave on, weave quickly, before the Overseer began to make hard inquiries. Before Eleison came looking for me. Before—

Before I could no longer work at all.

There were so many pressures upon me! I had never in my life felt so overwhelmed, nor more driven to blot out all these unhappy diversions. My consciousness had narrowed to a tunnel whose end was Malin, though I knew not how. I knew only that every hour I was more tired, and every hour the tapestry was more complete, and every hour I felt more weighted down by the need to finish it and return to my duties as Matrix. Indeed, it was such that when the Extreme Rift Event was forecast for the next day, the warnings coming in on that second night, I hardly reacted: I was so burdened by all else. Why should it be surprising at all to find a Rift Event, especially an Extreme one, blanketing the villa? If anything, I was glad for it—privately, I hoped it would last five days or more, forbidding travel and buying me extra time no matter the cost to the people around me. It was a cruel thought: but, in my harrowing illness and my desperate need for my husband, my entire personality winnowed down to my most fully self-serving aspects. Anyway, I needed Malin too much. I could not afford to be anything but selfish.

On day three, the Event began. Against expectation, I felt a slight surge of energy and hoped against hope that I was getting better. Even Charlotte noted with relief, "Your hair has stopped turning white as quickly—it's quite striking, actually."

"It will be the new fashion when I've returned to Saalast," I jested as she drew a few locks back from my face and wrangled it into a simple ponytail at the back of my neck. She was right: the effect of the white, not perfectly even but instead jaggedly applied from my scalp to a few inches into my hair, resembled a starburst, or a permanent crown. Yes, a crown—a gift from my husband at which I dared to softly smile, like the marks upon my throat and breast which I had come to privately cherish.

Still, my burst of optimism was short-lived; by noon, and the descent of the Rift Event, I was barely able to function, and my heart was growing heavy with discouragement as I looked upon the tapestry. In fact, it was nearly finished—another six hours of work and it would be accomplished, a product of my single-minded focus and desperation to push myself even through the greatest illness of my life. But, looking at it now...it seemed like nothing. It was beautiful: a fuligin doorway in which I stood in my husband's arms, our faces interlocked in a passionate kiss, the entire image enclosed in a border of red and gold. Yet, it was simple. So simple! And how could I expect such a simple image to be enough to persuade him out? How could this—could any image—communicate the longing Malin inspired in my heart? I pondered over it obsessively as I wove and wove, able to turn my mind to nothing else, refusing Charlotte when she came to lure me to bed.

"Three hours more of work," I insisted, "and it shall be done. This will all be done, Charlotte. Just let me work, and then Dinon can give my gift to him, and then—we can go home."

Grinding her teeth, but disinterested in arguing with me in the presence of Dinon, Charlotte primly bid me good-night and shut the door again. Some animal howled in the Rift Event outside, not far from the house. A luptich, like Glenn. What would our daughter do after I was dead?

I worked faster than ever in my life, speeding along row after row, tears flooding my eyes and blurring my work.

And then, as I reached the last row, a new sob broke from my throat.

The futility of it all! Oh, the hubris. I was so stupid, wasn't I? How could this created thing, this object of my hands, persuade my husband to yield in a matter where not even Love could convince him?

"Sh, Matrix." As truly tender as ever I had heard him, Dinon knelt by my side and inspired me to stop working completely: to give in to the weeping that gathered in me like an unmet need of my self-mourning body. Stroking my cheeks with a handkerchief, he said, "It will be finished tonight, Thecla. I promise you that."

"But how will it ever be enough to bring him to me? If seeing me wasn't enough, I—"

Little doubts had assailed me in the prior days, but now, as the project neared its completion, they came on more fiercely than ever.

"How can I expect him to be coaxed out with this," I blubbed, burying my face in Dinon's shoulder while he slid into the seat beside me and held me in his arms. "This blasted—this *dinner napkin*—"

"Matrix...Thecla—don't insult you own work so. How can you see what it will be when it's not finished yet? You've not even added the final touches. Here, come here—"

Ignoring my small protests, Dinon effortlessly lifted me into his arms and carried me from the seat. I expected him to bear me to the couch to lay me out upon it, and this he did—but not before lying in the sofa, himself, so he might extend my body along his and allow me to rest in the comfort of his arms. "Close your eyes, Matrix," he urged me, one powerful but artfully made hand resting upon my cheek to guide me to his unbeating heart. "Be safe here: be here, in peace with me. Rest awhile, and I'll rouse you when it's time for you to finish it."

"But I feel myself running out of time," I whimpered, nonetheless finding him so comfortable to lie upon that I could not have moved had I really wanted to. "Dinon—I'm so afraid."

"I know you are, Thecla."

Shoulders trembling, tears flowing, I sobbed amid a vicious tone that came bursting from my heart, "I hate it when you call me that! Damn you—I hate hearing my name on your lips."

Those perfect lips, which curved into a soft smirk. "Is that so? And why is that, Matrix? Because you find it impudent?"

"Yes," I stuttered, going on without the ability to stop. "And because—because, Dinon—" My throat was so sharp, so taut, it felt like the muscles would snap. Without anticipation, Dinon waited for me to complete my thought, his expression arranged in one of tranquil care. Waited for me, as he had waited for me before I knew him. Cared for me, as he cared for me patiently every day since coming into my service.

"Because when you say my name," I whispered, looking into his perfect face, "it makes me long to love you—and I don't understand why. I don't understand it any more than I understand why you would claim to love me."

"That's all right, Thecla," said Dinon with an undisguised sigh of longing, his smile widening, his great thumb caressing in circles around the temple of my forehead. "You don't have to understand everything all at once. When it's time, you will."

"Then perhaps there really is still time," I whispered, shutting my eyes and heaving a wet, trembling sigh. "Perhaps. Oh, Dinon. Please—when it's time, awaken me."

"Always, Thecla—forever. For now: just rest."

'FOREVER' IS THE PAST, *Madame, as much as it is the future.*

Dinon's words rang through my head as clearly as they did the first time I heard them. They made my eyes open toward the sky of marvelous Rift indigo, yet—how different was that sky! This was not Earth's sky tainted by the radiation of the Rift.

No, indeed. My lips parted in astonishment to witness the gentle clouds of violet, the shimmering sunlight that shone in lavender beams across the brilliant cerulean grasslands swaying in the breeze. Stunned, I looked around at the endless field of mithrae flowers that sprang out in a great ocean from my feet and far beyond—and at the end of that ocean, his black cloak blowing in the same breeze that played through his silver hair, stood Dinon.

"You don't even know how you helped me," he said, looking at me without his usual wry amusement and instead only with the softness of a love so absolute it ached my very soul. "Thecla... sometimes, when I think of that, it kills me."

"What do you mean?"

"You want to know why I love you," he went on, the wind kicking up to blow fine pink petals from the trees across our faces and off into the distances. "How could I but love the woman who's done so much for me? How could I but spend a lifetime watching over the goddess that drew me out of endless sleep?"

I stepped toward him, then again, but he never seemed any closer. The longing that I always felt for him in greater or smaller amounts came surging through my body like a typhoon, aching my fingertips and face and soul with desire.

"How could I want anything more than to help you for eternity, Thecla—just as you've helped me?"

As with that dream of my two Malins—so obvious now in retrospect, what that dream had to tell me—I suddenly grew aware of the fact that I was dreaming: but this time, the dream did not respond by tricking me back into enchantment or jettisoning me into wakefulness. If anything, my awareness of it only served to real-ize it, my consciousness of every last detail increased as it seldom was in my daily reality. I felt like a bug under glass, an insect in a cup for whom the real world was on the other side of a barrier it could not understand. There, on the other side of this violet sky, was a world—my world, with my family and friends, and the great task before me.

And the tapestry I was desperate to weave.

The Weaver is the most powerful woman in the world.

The wind picked up again, petals of Rift flowers clinging to my hair and tucking into the folds of the scarlet dress that blew around me. My mouth opened and shut as I abruptly recalled the strange words of the fortune-teller. My eyes fell to the field of flowers between myself and Dinon.

When I raised my gaze again, a chill of comprehension overwhelming my senses, Dinon stood before me.

"Show them to me," I urged him. "Let me see them—the threads."

"There will be consequences," he said.

"There always are—I don't care." My lips trembled, my heart throbbing with knowledge of what those consequences would be—what they had always been, since long before I was born. "I need him too much," I insisted, my hand pressing to my heart. "Just as I need Eleison, and Glenn, and…you, Dinon. Each one of you means something to me, and even if I don't understand why, I understand that. I'll fight to have you all. I'll sell my very soul for it. I'll give my life."

"You'd give the world," said Dinon softly, "for Love."

"Yes," I answered without hesitation. "Yes. Dinon. Now show them to me. Please…show me the threads."

His cloak fluttered as he pushed it from his shoulder to extend an arm and draw me close. As if we had been true lovers for years, Dinon tipped my head back and I obliged, my mouth responding like it had been made for his. I cried out in the pleasure of it, having resisted him so long. Now liberated by the dream, I threw my arms around his neck and pressed my body totally to his. Amid a passionate stab of his tongue along mine, he slid his hand down my spine and, button by button, opened the back of my dress as though truly savoring every second. The fabric slid from my shoulders and he bent to kiss one such curve, pressing me to his chest while his hands and mine divested me of my underthings. By the time I was naked, so was he. Through some contrivance of dream or magic or both, the clothes that should have been gathered at our feet were nowhere to be seen. There were only the flowers in which he laid me down, his hands navigating each curve of my body with truly religious awe. His lips played along with them, pressing to each freckle, each mole, each little scar from my active youth. I was unwounded here, and his lips upon my neck spurred such ecstasy that they were sufficient to make me moan. Above us, the sky of the Rift seemed to spin, the dizziness of our love obliterating the stability of the environment to make it as drunk as we.

While his tongue lashed against mine, his hands glided down my stomach. One found my hip; the other tenderly stroked between my thighs, playing along my labia and coaxing me open to his gentle, impossibly well-informed caresses. Yes, there was no doubt that Malin and Eleison were well-acquainted with my body. They knew how to touch me to elicit pleasure; and Glenn, too, had exhibited great aptitude for it when we made love in Valquist.

But Dinon touched me as I touched myself, or better. Though I had never let him take me, his big fingers shocked me from the first with their expert comprehension of my sex's most sensitive nerves: I gasped into his mouth, moaning, incredulous at the gentle swirl of his finger around the bud of ecstasy. His silver eyes glittered at the amazement of my heart, and his mouth left mine only to press to my ear.

"I know just how you long to be touched," he murmured, the caressing of his fingertip resolving into lascivious petting up and down the length of my quickly slick valley. "I know how you want to be loved, to be taken—I know your every fantasy, Thecla. I'm obsessed by them."

I shuddered, unable to speak beneath the pleasure he spurred. His teeth nibbled at the flesh of my jaw and his fingers stroked on, spreading the fluid of my arousal but never quite breaching the chamber from which it flowed. Beneath these skilled caresses, I grew shamelessly soaked, the heat he kindled between my legs such an ecstasy I found myself never wanting to orgasm again—only to remain suspended upon this edge of bliss, this mountain's peak, his caring hand and the kisses he distributed from my breasts to my ears the very picture of Heaven.

Yet even in Heaven, I longed for more! I opened my legs to him, pleading, afraid to let him inside me in even a dream yet unable to live without him—and knowing, somehow, that this was necessary. A sacred ceremony. An opening of more than my body was at hand.

"Kiss me, Thecla," he murmured, his silver hair streaming around my face as he drew my head toward his. "Ah, God, I love your kisses—I love you, Thecla, oh, Matrix, Madame—my Queen—"

He knelt between my thighs, braced against me. I pressed my hungry mouth against his, swallowing his passion while my every limb quaked. Somehow, in all my days, I had never felt so naked: this man, if such a being could be called a man, saw so much more than my body. He saw the very contents of my past; my future; my mind and all its longings, sweet and profane. Dinon saw my very soul, its sins and all—and still, he loved me.

And I was helpless beneath that love. The marble solidity of his anatomy was so excellent as he rocked himself against me in anticipation of our love that I cried out at even this superficial prelude to our mating, my fingers tangling in his hair. "Dinon! Oh, Ba'al-Dinon, I'm frightened—it terrifies me, how completely you know me—"

"I promise, Thecla...I'll never abuse you. All I know about

you only makes me love you more...and I know everything there is to know about you. Absolutely everything."

Trembling so that my teeth chattered, I wrapped my legs around his hips and pressed as close to him as possible. He cradled me to his heart, his nose brushing along mine, the violet light of that otherworldly sun capturing the flyaway strands of his silver hair to create the glory of a halo around his beautiful face. My eyes filled with hot tears of awe as I was stricken by a deeper fear, more complete and overwhelming than any I had ever felt before—yet I could not look away, and wanted more than ever to give myself to him.

"I know why you're afraid," he whispered, "but you don't have to be. Thecla—I love you. I love you more than anyone...no one has ever loved someone more than I love you. No one."

His gaze pierced meaningfully into mine while his hips drew back, the hard head of his scepter nestling so perfectly against my entrance that the simple sensation was almost as unfathomable as his words. The names of my other great loves flashed through my mind—Eleison, Glenn, Malin—and Dinon rested his forehead upon my brow so all I could see were his eyes.

"No one," he said again, plunging into me an arrow of passion so mighty, with a shaft so brilliantly suited for flight into my wound, that I erupted at once with an explosion of pleasure that immolated me in a scream.

And how literal that explosion was! As though I had been struck in the back of the head, my eyes flashed with a great white spark so intense I was blinded to all things: all things except the great pleasure that throbbed in the core of me. My body was merely the interface by which he accessed something deeper, and I felt my spirit filled with what was truly the most extraordinarily humbling love I had ever encountered. I felt so seen, yet so loved in spite of how well I was seen, that I was humbled, and moved, and pained to think of the cruel ways I had spoken to Dinon in the past—all the cruel ways I had treated him! Indeed: when confronted by a love like this, I felt wicked for ever having loved others.

"Don't," he whispered as the white explosion faded, gathering into little threads by which reality reordered itself to reveal Dinon's face, and that vibrant sky—and the warp and weft I had sought to see with the mithrae, now visible with his love alone. "Don't, Thecla. The others are my gifts to you. I want your joy, I want your pleasure—your fulfillment. I want those more than I need your love."

"But—" My lips trembled and I stroked his face, almost afraid to touch him now, yet unable to resist. "Dinon—I want to love you. Oh, I want to love you so completely—"

"You will," he whispered, kissing the heel of my palm while he worked within me to stir my soul to another climb of pleasure's heights. Wrapping me tighter in his arms, his mouth finding my ear while I clutched at his shoulders and screamed for the bliss of it, Dinon murmured on. "When you're ready, Thecla, you'll give your heart to me. I've already waited for you for all Time."

As my eye followed the shimmering threads I now saw as high as the heavens above, Dinon assured me, "I can always wait a little longer."

My body vibrated with his love, and my own awe for it. As I shivered, those threads shivered with me: I panted, clutching Dinon tighter. One hand tangled in his hair as he kissed my neck, while the other hand sank my nails into the back of his shoulder. He groaned, riding me hard and fast, my pleasure his to give, my body his to command. My will, his to control.

"Go on, Thecla. Go on—open it."

His words, his commandment, echoed in the exposed soul which already understood that for which I had been destined: and still, they chilled me as he poured them into my ear.

"Take your threads," Dinon murmured through his kisses, "and open the Rift."

Enchanted by their shimmer, inebriated by the pleasure, filled to the absolute brim by his love, I did as Ba'al-Dinon commanded. From his shoulder, I extended my hand into the air and found, as naturally as a fish learns to swim, I could caress the threads of reality with my tingling fingers.

By pinching one strand of brilliant violet light, I could gently pull it free from the weaving of life, and thereby unravel the tapestry of spacetime.

Astonished, I raised my other hand to tug on another, and another; still making love to me, Dinon turned his smiling face to watch, his mouth yielding a great lover's sigh to witness the hole I revealed in the violet sky of that universe on the other side of the Rift. Stars twinkled through at us, laughing at our love from their places within the velvet tapestry of the sky with which I was more familiar: cosmic dust, the jewels of infinite planets.

The blue and green marble of Earth, where I awoke alone upon the couch of my villa workroom, surrounded by those shimmering threads.

Everything felt so perfectly clear. Even as I longed to return to Dinon, the reality of his love and the enormity of it still filling my soul, and I knew I could fly to him any time I liked.

I also knew that time was short—so very short I could feel it in the strength that had returned to me, a desperate wave of adrenaline filling my limbs to make me sit effortlessly up from the couch. The room was abuzz with the power of the Rift radiation suffusing the countryside, and though my times of headaches were long-past, I felt the urgent restlessness of the beast within me. The ventil wanted to run—to flee.

And I used that craving to push me onward. As I had in Dinon's arms, I stroked my fingers along the threads of reality, the silver and violet glory I could now clearly see made up all things. Even me, as I marveled while raising my hand before my face.

Heart throbbing with longing—longing for Dinon, for Malin, for Eleison and Glenn, for the very life that had given them to me and me to them—I trailed my finger along a silver thread in my open palm. Unhesitating, I plucked it free.

Somehow, I would have expected this self-unraveling to hurt. It did not; it did not feel like anything, in fact, except the certainty that I was making my love—truly, my soul—into an offering for the husband I wished would reunite with me. The husband for whom I had opened a hole in the very fabric of reality.

And I would show him that.

My body the spindle, I fetched a needle and threaded it with my very life: and, with the tapestry's superficial aspects finished to my satisfaction, I committed my attention to the detail work.

It was hard. I was tired. The fabric was thick enough that I had to use pliers to work the needle when I wove the streaks of silver into the fuligin of the terrestrial fabric. I sensed I was at it for hours, but I had no way to know: I had no time for breaks, and the shutters were closed against the Event that raged on all night, animals howling and audibly fighting with one another when they weren't being shot by security. When I was satisfied with the tableau's representation of the weft, I moved on to the warp. As I coaxed this violet thread from my fingers, I was beyond tired, yet I could not close my eyes: I refused to, afraid that if I so much as blinked for too long a stretch, I would sink into the oblivion of sleep. It was already more strength than I had in me to do this sewing and stay upright in the process.

But I did it. For Malin, I did it—for my husband, my beloved, as once I had woven a rope by which I fled to his aid and Eleison's, now I embroidered my being into this plea for his relent. Now, working my own new vision of reality into this tapestry of him and me, I begged him with every thread, every plunge of the needle, every second in which my life slipped away: Come to me, my beloved. Come out! Come away with me.

Come home with me, my husband.

Oh, Malin.

Dizzy—I was dizzy by the last time I plunged the needle in. Yet the sense of victory I had was so great I could not even notice it. I could only lean back, then slowly ease myself from the seat of my loom to examine my accomplishment with my failing eyes. With the sense of having just outrun something impossible to name, I laughed. My heart fluttered with joy.

"Charlotte," I called, turning toward the door of the room, "come and see!"

And I do not remember quite what happened after that.

SOMEONE WAS SITTING at my loom.

I became aware of myself only after realizing this: only after recognizing that it was *my* loom at which she sat. The mechanism was so utterly black that, against the darkness around us, it was hard to detect at first. The girl seemed floating in space, seated in it, her hands and feet working furiously with the familiar set of sounds that made me remember the word 'weave', and made me thereafter remember 'loom', and 'tapestry', and 'Thecla'. Indeed! I was Thecla—yet, was it not Thecla sitting there, her head bent over her work with such intense focus that she did not even notice me?

I raised a fist and pounded upon the barrier between us, fury rushing through my face and along my arms. Who was this woman who had stolen my loom *and* my face? Who was this with the audacity to sit doing *my* work as though it were her own? She didn't seem to hear me at first, so I pounded again the barrier, that sheet of glass I couldn't see but could feel mere inches from me.

Now, she looked up—and her face, which had been arranged in an expression of hard focus for her work, faltered. The emotion changed to shock, then animal fear: as I struck the glass in primitive outrage, unable to articulate my anger in thoughts let alone speech, that barrier between us yielded with an ominous crackling.

Paling, the thief who had stolen my identity sprang up from the loom. Without even thinking of the damage I could be doing to my own hand, I once more raised my fist and slammed the cracking glass: again, again. New cracks spiderwebbed out in all directions, the substance aching with the stress of my assault. The false Thecla stumbled back a few steps, her arms raised in preemptive self-defense.

Then, as the glass shattered beneath my hand, falling to the dark void of the floor in a rain of shards, the girl screamed. She stumbled back another few steps: then, drawing her gown high to her ankles, she turned and ran, sprinting off into the darkness with little more than one terrified glimpse over her shoulder.

I stepped forward, oblivious to the sharp cuts of the shards into my bare feet, intent on the loom—but a hand dropped upon my shoulder. I turned, my lips drawn back from my bared teeth to exhibit my displeasure for this interloper—

But Malin, nude as I was, jerked me close against his body and kissed me with such a savagery it was like I had never been kissed before. I moaned in surprise, my knees weak, and he drew back from the kiss to smile at me in twinkling pleasure—in fantastic approval.

Smiling to see him, I tried to turn away, to release him to go to the loom—but he wouldn't let me. His strong hand kept hold of me, and kisses kept coming, lips and teeth all pressing along my flesh, the power of his body controlling mine. I gasped, not frightened so much as surprised, and did not wish to yield but found I could not resist. My husband forced me down to the floor, to the glass shards in which he kissed me fiercely. Laughing in protest, I pushed at his face, and tugged at his hair, and found he responded in kind with his own devilish grin of delight. He pulled my hair, too, and took the resulting slap I doled with a pleasurable gasp of surprise; one big hand swiftly caught hold of my jaw and squeezed my mouth open so he could spit into it, shocking and arousing me. While I struggled to get away, pushing at his chest, he turned me over upon my stomach, then used that same forceful hand to explore between my thighs.

At once, I moaned, an animal tamed despite its higher desires. His name was lodged in my throat but for some reason could not come out: my brain could not make sense of language in that dark place, with his fingers testing me as though I were a fruit and he a farmer checking for the ripeness of his orchard's favorite yield.

The surge of wetness his rough treatment provoked inspired a growl of approval as never he had made. It was not even similar to the borro-growl of Eleison, who I could only half-remember in the strange, surreal urgency of that primal coupling. This growl of Malin's was unearthly, like the groan of the dead, the very sound that ran vibrating through the material of the world—the first sound of the cosmos, and the last. It made me cry out, but not as sharply as his penetration did, his hard plunge into me arching my back and forcing us both to scream with the heady pleasure. As he thrust into me, pushing himself to the root against my backside, holding my hips to keep me from changing my mind and springing away from him, I twisted at the waist and neck and flung an arm back to grip his head. Yanking his hair to make him hiss in pain, I jerked his mouth to mine and kissed him with fervor, almost angry at the passion and pleasure he inspired. I had been purely dedicated to my craft before he came along—I had not even known I was naked.

Yet here he was, my husband, derailing my attention and forcing me to love that derailment: claiming my body in a way that made me long to be obedient for him even in the midst of our play-fighting. This made it all the more vital that I remind him he was the subservient one. That without me, he would have no pleasure. His mouth was mine, his cock was mine, the very emission of his pleasure was mine. My kiss alone was enough to teach him that, and he murmured pleasurably into it, his body feeling the embrace of mine with more deliberate appreciation. This new consciousness of ecstasy made him gasp: made him groan against me the first word I heard.

"Thecla—"

"Malin," I moaned in return. "Ah—"

He pushed me harder down into the floor, the stinging glass only sweetening the ecstasy of the tool with which he claimed me. I groaned, slowly gyrating back against him, my legs splaying to beg him deeper; and the ecstasy reached a crescendo for us both when, in stroking along my sex to feel himself penetrating me, he brushed that little gem of pleasure and re-discovered how it could make me nearly weep for the severity of the pleasure it brought. My limbs tightened and his movements sped, his weight bearing down on me in the command that I let go. Eager to be obedient— to be marked by him, claimed by him—I did, a low wail bursting from my throat while my body seized and strangled his pulsating prick. As I fell to pieces of pleasure, my sex flowing, my husband responded with that low growl again: that growl I felt in the base of my body as, gritting his teeth, he pounded a few more deep, forceful times until his release dissolved his snarling into the gasps of shocking joy.

The power of his climax was so intense he collapsed upon me, his arms folding around me to keep me still while he buried every drop of bliss within. I groaned, nuzzling back against him in encouragement, re-aroused to feel him emptying himself in me, a low thrum enfolding us as if the world itself had taken pleasure from watching us. Then, with a laugh of amazement, I realized it was no sound of the environment, but a sound of my body. A purr of sorts, rising from the base of my throat: from the heights of my heart.

Moved by my laughter, made gentle and doting with the expulsion of his orgasm, Malin nuzzled and kissed me. He nibbled my ear with a few appreciative, low hums of pleasure. I laughed, knowing in my heart that we had never really been apart and now would always, always be together. I rocked back against him, the pleasure of being held as or more intense than the greatest ecstasies of sex. His cock remained within me, our bodies linked, the glow of our love so complete that I did not notice the people walking past us until one of them crunched across the glass near my hand. Still purring with contentment, I raised my head and looked curiously around us.

An endless stream of people marched past, their expressions dazed, not a one of them seeming to notice us as more than an obstacle around which they stumbled on their way across the threshold of the broken barrier.

Malin noticed them at the same time I did, and, with a purr of his own, nuzzled his nose and lips into my hair. "Good girl," he murmured, inhaling my scent, then stroking my head with a big hand in such a way I could only close my eyes with the immensity of the pleasure. Indeed, it seemed my flesh was hypersensitive to such affection—all things, even the stings of the glass into my thighs and breasts and forearms, became pleasure, and pleasure became something truly divine. I moaned as my husband petted me, this innocent caress and my helpless enjoyment of it causing him to rumble with renewed pleasure of his own. Within me, the weapon of his passion was re-forged by my heat, and the festivities of our reunited love resumed heedless of the crowd that streamed in a daze around us.

By the time we had finished again, the procession of wanderers had reduced to a trickle of those who lagged behind. Where once there had been a mass, now one or two at a time crossed the threshold and made their slow way into the darkness beyond my loom.

Where were they going? I felt as though their destination was also mine—someplace I had forgotten about, something I could not name. I turned to my husband, only about to ask him what it was these people walked toward—or to try my best to evoke this question, with or without words—when a new noise arose in our environment. Sharp and insistent, whining, a series of sound waves rising and falling in frantic demand. I frowned, my brow furrowing while my husband glanced toward the source. I looked with him—and my heart warmed with joy.

A baby lay upon its back perhaps sixty yards from us, wailing for warmth and attention.

Fascinated, I pushed myself up from my husband's arms and, a few stray shards of glass falling from my skin to rain at my feet, I wove through the mesmerized passersby to the infant they all summarily ignored. Joy filled me—I knelt beside the little boy, taking his pudgy form into my arms to cradle him to my breast. The infant's wailing ceased at once, and he gazed up at me through silver eyes shaped just like his father's.

This was *our* baby. Malin's and mine. I could not explain how I knew that—I could not explain where he had come from. I only knew he was ours. A living sign of our love, which I showed to my husband with pride while he came to my side to admire the newborn with me. Though he could speak no more than I could, I could see by the pleasurable glow in his eyes that he recognized this tiny creature as well as I did. We looked at each other, and, beaming, I offered the baby to him.

Overjoyed, he took the little boy and brushed the soft, dark hair back from his pale forehead. My husband raised his face, gentle with wonder, toward me. I smiled, the sight of my family before me stirring memories—memories of effort, of disappointment, of fear.

Oh, yes! That was where we were going—that was right. Fear made me remember it at last, yet I also remembered it was not all painful or hard there. It was a good place, in fact. A very good place in many ways. I wanted Malin to be there with the baby so we could be together, therefore I gestured toward the broken barrier with an expectant smile.

He looked at it, then at me.

"Who," he asked, looking at me with curiosity.

That was an interesting question—more interesting because I knew just what he meant. After all...I'd had a living reflection on the other side of that barrier. Someone I could replace without fuss. But my husband, now...I recalled some flaw in that, although I could not define the flaw other than with the vague recollection that his reflection had been lost. In recollecting that much, I sorted through my memory piece by piece. Who was available for my husband to replace? Whose flesh and blood could give him an anchor by which he could dock his ship in our new home?

"Rigel," I said, speaking the first name I could remember without really thinking about the man to whom it belonged. "Rigel," I said again, looking into my husband's eyes.

With an expression that seemed to indicate I had triggered some distant memory, Malin nodded slowly, then kissed my mouth. "Wife," he murmured, meaning the word as the greatest expression of love any being could speak.

"Husband," I replied, deriving the word from his in the way shadow remembers its shape from the object on which light is cast. "Baby," I said, pinching the child's cheek and feeling pleased as he laughed in a giddy cherub's voice.

Smiling slyly, my husband pressed a lingering kiss upon my waiting mouth, then carried our baby into the darkness over the broken threshold.

Pleased, I looked around myself and, seeing how few of us were crossing now, I decided it was time to cross, myself. I made my way over the glass, intent on the greater darkness ahead—

But the Black Loom, gleaming to my sensitive eyes, waited with our work half-complete.

Oh, no. I could not possibly leave the cloth of fuligin unfinished. Without thinking, I sat at the device and marveled at all the memories that came rushing back. The first time seeing this loom—Eleison in the movie theater at Valquist. Valquist, which reminded me of Parvati. How my husband hated Parvati! Hated her why? Because of the war, which had been afoot long before I was born. Born—yes, born. I had once been born! Born, as my son was born, but not quite. Born to? To Giselle. To Giselle, and—

Glass cracked softly beneath one last pair of feet. I glanced up from the cloth I rapidly wove, my hands and feet still in motion even as I followed this final straggler with my fascinated eyes. Of all my fellows who had swarmed past us and over the barrier, this man was the only one who paid me note: who met my eyes and, seeming to remember me as I recognized his thick, white-streaked beard and unkempt hair, grew grim of expression. He had paused on the threshold, unable to determine whether he wished to proceed to the other place for which we were all destined.

But seeing me already on the other side, working away to finish my business before I immigrated to our new land, my father, Rigel, turned his eyes from me and marched resolutely into the darkness.

Smiling after him, pleased I would see him again no matter what he thought of me, I hummed along with the rhythm of my weaving.

When the cloth of brocaded fuligin was completed, I left it on the loom, got up, and walked after the others.

It was perhaps less unnerving to have gone as a part of the great sea of wanderers, though 'unnerving' was not the right word for what one felt navigating that dark space alone. Disorienting—that was it. The deeper into the darkness I walked, the more disoriented I became. Though I had only marched straight ahead, pursuing some instinct buried deep within my mind, I lost all sense of direction and soon was quite sure I could not have found my way back to my loom if I had tried. The already impossible dark seemed to grow even more immense, enshrouding me so that I could not see even distinguish my own body. I could not see anything—any dimension of space—until I began to be very sure I was at risk of forgetting myself.

Then, though, the darkness changed. It was so slow a transition I did not notice it at first. But step by step, the further I walked without yielding to the urge to turn around, the more that darkness lightened. It took on a strange new hue, a tone of violet that grew more intense as I wandered into it. There was something frightening about it, but something exhilarating, too. It was the end of a great struggle, and the beginning of a new life.

I wandered on, the purple grew thick like smoke or fog—two concepts I recalled only when I felt the soft carpet of grass beneath my feet. Ah, so soft! It occurred to me how exhausted I was. The ground seemed a welcoming bed inviting me to its embrace. Smiling, all but cooing with primitive delight, I slid down to my knees and extended myself upon it, closing my eyes to rest.

And it was as I began to fully drift into the contentment of a well-earned sleep that someone bent over me.

"There you are, my angel," my husband said, weaving his arms around me to draw me to his chest. "Come on...let's get you something to eat."

HOW CAN I EXPLAIN those first few moments of consciousness after that strange dream? It was truly befuddling. Not even after the coming of the ventil and its possession for so many months was I as disoriented on waking. Indeed, I often felt as though I still dreamed: none other than Malin sat at my bedside, murmuring to me in a tone so sweet that his voice was as great a balm as the stroking of his hand through my hair. Even though his words proved meaningless, a softly babbling brook that rushed as through the other side of an impenetrable copse, I smiled just to hear him—and oh, to see him!

My eyes were blurry with the soft light of the bedroom in which I sat at the head of a bed, but despite that lack of focus I could still recognize my darling husband's face. I could even make out, from time to time, the feminine shape of Charlotte, who occasionally arrived in the sickroom for reasons of which I had no comprehension. Ironic—had I not spent so much time as a ventil, I would have suspected this half-cogent delirium was comparable to the consciousness of animals!

In those first hours, as I sat blearily striving to parse Malin's soft babble, another voice would sometimes fill my ears; soft, almost feminine, always curling up with the auditory hallmarks of questioning. Malin would turn to address this voice in as fond a tone as he used to speak to me, and would then return to his affections, fitting his hand around mine or slipping a finger beneath my chin to raise my drifting eyes back to his. I had the impression he waited for something—Dinon? Oh—where was Dinon?

I'm here, Thecla, his mysterious voice said softly in my heart, the only intelligible words I could make out in those first hours of rousing. *I'm always here for you, no matter what.*

Content with that, I rested my head back against the headboard and dozed, Malin's hand still in mine. Not even the next opening of the bedroom door could disturb my slumber; nor could Malin's glad-hearted exclamation.

Only the smell could begin to wake me—only the spoon of a rich, burgundy-brown broth lifted to my mouth could help me again make sense of the world.

The fluid, so rich and delicious my eyes fluttered open, was like nothing I had ever experienced—no meat that had ever crossed my lips before. Indeed, it awakened my palate as though I had never tasted anything, as though my mouth were a thing forgotten; and as, at the gentle stroking of Malin's knuckle down the front of my throat, I reclaimed the mechanism of swallowing, my eyes grew wild with the warmth that seemed to fill not just my belly, but my brain.

"There," Malin was saying as knowledge of speech and the interpretation of words returned to my mind. "There, now, angel, isn't that delicious...drink up, here's another, good girl—"

By the third spoonful Malin gently tendered to my lips, I found myself clutched by such an impatience that my slowly receding amnesia extended to all courtesy and manner. I caught the spoon from his hand when he tried to draw it back and, while he chuckled patiently at my antics, I bent my head to shovel the delicious stuff into my mouth. Herbs had lightly flavored the broth, but what made it so delicious was the strips of animal flesh and the supple tripe. Each bite I took of these proved such ecstasy I groaned as beneath a lover's hand. My husband smiled at me, sliding more closely to my side while his elegant hands drew my hair back from my shoulders.

"She's hungry, isn't she, Papa?"

"Who's 'she,'" asked Malin in a playfully chiding tone, glancing over at the voice I was gradually, above my fixation on this delicious soup, able to determine belonged to a young boy, "the cat's mother?"

With a slight sigh of pettish impatience kept half in reserve, the boy corrected, "*Mama's* hungry, isn't she, Papa?"

"Yes, my darling, she certainly is. You should have seen me when I came to...now, don't scald yourself, angel—"

With a wry laugh the boy shared, Malin warned me but made no effort to stop me as I abandoned the spoon and hefted the bowl from the tray I was now aware had been set over my lap. I could not hesitate in gulping the stuff down, each mouthful a bounty of energy and understanding. My eyes could hold themselves open now, and my head was no longer so heavy to raise upright. Even the room and my vision of it became clearer—so clear, in fact, so crisp and pristine, that I found myself wondering if I had always been somewhat nearsighted before my illness: for I could suddenly make out the fine-cut detailing in the wood of the vanity, or the texture of the curtains around the glass doors to the yard where I realized the Rift Event was still ongoing. Instinctively, I cringed and set the hand that did not cradle the bowl down on my husband's wrist.

"Malin," I croaked, looking furtively at the violet light tainting the landscape, then turning to plead that he pull down the shutters.

But before I could even grope for the words, I was halted.

Oh, marvelous! As scrumptious as the meal was, it was all forgotten as my eyes set upon the greater feast of my husband. My heart seized in my chest, twisting itself into knots to witness his unbearable beauty. For Malin had always been beautiful—but now I saw why he had wished to hide his face from me when visiting me at the height of my blood-sickness. He was still Malin: undeniably Malin, my same beloved husband whose very presence made me tremble with erotic anticipation for even a caress upon my cheek.

But in appearance, his proud visage was far closer to that of the haughty young man I beheld in Glenn's biography. Whatever my beloved husband had undergone in death and rebirth had washed from his face all traces of age or stress or suffering. He was without flaw, his dark eyes brightened by traces of lively silver, his hair a lustrous gold with fine reddish undertones intensified by roots now only slightly whitened with hints of his former age— and his scar, that mar I always longed to pet and kiss as though to heal the permanent pain my mother had brought him, had vanished altogether.

Suffice it to say, what I felt was not fright, but awe.

"Everything all right, Thecla," he asked fondly, a slight smile still clinging to lips that captured and held my attention.

What had I wanted to ask him? What was I even doing? I forgot it all in that instant and raised my free hand to his face, tracing my fingertips down the path where his scar had once been. His entrancing mouth opening just so, he turned to kiss my palm, then my wrist, and each simple press of his lips engendered sparks of light in my soul. The bowl of even that delicious meal now nothing but an obstacle, I dropped it with contempt, and it was only by Malin's quick reflexes that we avoided making a premature mess of the bedclothes.

His tut giving way to a throaty chuckle as I drew his face toward mine with both hands, Malin set the bowl carefully upon its tray and said without turning his eyes from me, "It may take Mama a while to come fully to her senses, Telemachus. Why not run along and ask Miss Charlotte to play a game with you? She's very good at chess—you might even lose, for once."

"But Papa, I—"

"Go on," said Malin to the boy. That name rang with significance in my ears, but only as the drowning swimmer's voice rings out below the surf. In other words, it caught some deep aspect of my attention but not so well that I could make sense of that attention, for my focus was entirely upon my husband. I could not look away from him as, with a grumpy sigh, the boy Telemachus sprang out of the chair in the corner of the room and made his sullen way out, the door swinging shut a little heftily behind him.

"You'll have to excuse him, dear," Malin told me as I more insistently pulled his mouth to mine, "he's just excited to—"

I didn't care. I didn't care about anything in that moment except my husband, who was here in the world, in the light, with me. In a strength I hardly knew I had, I jerked him to my mouth and swallowed down his lips, my tongue stabbing against his in new, more real hunger. He groaned softly, bending his head over mine, and the union of that black dream-world flashed quickly through my mind and was gone. No dream could ever compare to this—not to having him here with me, kissing me, savoring me as I savored him.

It was as my teeth sank into his lip that Malin forced himself to pull away and look me in the eyes. The degree of silver in his irises had increased: they glowed brilliantly, a predator's longing in his heart. My lips trembled. Before he could speak, as I could tell he intended, I gave in to the tears that pricked my eyes and welled along my lower lids.

"Don't leave me again," I begged, "don't leave me, Malin."

"Oh, Thecla—darling." Brow knitting, then relaxing into his soft smile, Malin leaned his forehead against mine and stroked his hand through my hair. "I won't," he swore softly. "I will never leave you. Never, ever—never again. Nothing will separate us, and God help anyone that tries."

In some way beyond articulation, the truth of these words settled consolingly upon my heart. I nodded, beating back more tears with a shaky sigh that made my husband's eyes twinkle with barely repressed tears of his own. Those eyes lowered as he spoke on, forcing himself into a sterner mode of caregiving.

"Now, angel, I know what you really need…but trust me when I say you're better off finishing your meal, first. You'll think more clearly by the time the bowl is empty. Besides…"

While, eager to obtain his consent, I snatched up the bowl to demolish its contents with truly inhuman speed, Malin watched with an amused, crooked little smile of profane pleasure.

"I did the butchering myself, so think of your first meal as a gift from your husband...and Charlotte, of course, though I could hardly imagine she would have agreed to cook if I hadn't prepared the meat."

Obviously not; Charlotte was a fine cook, but no butcher. That was a whole separate art—and where had my husband learned it? I pondered as I quickly ate, but soon supposed it was a skill he had been forced to acquire while living alone in the darkness beneath this villa.

Especially given what he was being sent to sustain himself.

Near the bottom of the bowl, the belated realization dawned on me. I opened my mouth in slight astonishment and no small amount of horror, although even as that horror came upon me, I simply could not stop chewing and swallowing the bite of meat in my mouth. When my body had swallowed against my will and I found in myself a clear craving to proceed in spite of growing understanding, I turned my astonished eyes upon Malin.

"What," I whispered, my voice hoarse, "what—is this?"

With that dark lechery, his smile tinged with cruel yet tender amusement, Malin tucked a few locks of loose hair back behind my ear while bending in to kiss my temple. "Do you know, Thecla, my love, about parasitic wasps? Even with Rift species as invasive as they are, countless terrestrial ectoparasitoids remain to prey on caterpillars and other insects; but the most fascinating by far are the wasps. There are a variety, with some preferring to paralyze larvae and inject their eggs, while others simply prey upon cocooned pupae before they can develop into butterflies. Either way...in most cases, the young wasp grows within its host and, upon eating its way out, kills its forebear while emerging as a fully-fledged adult insect. It is a fascinating form of propagation; alien, almost, in function, though it be natural to Earth's ecosystem." Seeing as I was not doing it myself, Malin took the spoon to collect another chunk of meat and raise it to my endlessly famished mouth.

"I always wonder, what must those wasps think of their caterpillar hosts? Does the new wasp consider that host its true mother, and itself merely an exotic form of butterfly? Does it perceive its sadistic form of paralytic ovapositioning to be the natural and right method of reproduction? Surely it must, as that is the correct form of reproduction for it...but, at the same time, does the stinging mother wasp look upon the poor caterpillars with contempt? As purely hapless victims with no purpose but to give life to her children? I cannot imagine she does—I think she must be grateful, as her children are grateful for their first meal, no matter how dubious a recipient of that gratitude the caterpillar is bound to be."

While I allowed him to feed me the last bite because it was the most irresistible meal I had ever eaten—even as I grew in my understanding—Malin smiled in approval for my obedience and spoke on. "How much more gratitude had we ought to show, then? For we, each one of us, have been provided individual hosts—each of us, depending on when we arrive on Earth, has the special opportunity to take a caterpillar we can replace on a one-to-one basis, making no waves and causing no suffering but our own. For you see, Thecla...we are not wasps, but butterflies. We are simply the butterflies of a newer and finer species, whose first meal is best if it is that old, dead self. Would we were all as lucky as you, my love—some of us have to make due with whatever we can remember when we first find ourselves on Earth."

While Malin lowered the spoon and moved aside the empty bowl and tray, my mind rushed like a panicked bird rather than an elegant butterfly—or even like a wasp that perceived itself as one. Indeed, as I looked at my husband and compared his words to the contents of my dream, my horror only increased.

"Rigel," I whispered as I had in my dream, searching my husband's face as he turned back to me.

"Yes," Malin said, his hands slipping tightly around mine.

"It was *you*." A great shame, almost a panic, surging up within me, I begged for another explanation even as I remembered, "Because I told you—because I told you."

"Yes, my angel." Malin's forehead rested against mine, the contact soothing even as I realized I looked into the face of my father's murderer. "Because you gave him to me. Because his existence was the one you brought to my mind before I was reborn; so, unable to consume and replace myself, I took him, instead."

And I, delayed and distracted by my weaving, had not emerged until now—the very end of my natural life, synchronized perfectly to the beginning of this new one.

"Ba'al-Dinon," I said suddenly, swallowing back my emotion with great difficulty. "Where is he?"

"I've not set eyes on him since, oh, the other day, when I brought your chrysalis upstairs after finding it in my abattoir. He was nowhere to be found when Charlotte came downstairs screaming you were dead. Hm—"

Nostrils flaring, his eyes flickering from my face to the decolletage emphasized by a nightgown slightly too tight for my altered height, Malin forced himself to look into my face again. As he spoke on, his lip curled against what I would come to recognize as an emerging fang. "Even dead, Thecla, you were—are—so beautiful to me. Butchering you was truly a great pleasure...I would do it again in a heartbeat."

I had so much I wished to say to him. I wished I could blame him for the death of my father, though I found I could not blame anyone but myself. I wished I could admonish him for feeding me my own flesh without explaining the situation to me first, though I knew the explanation would have fallen on deaf animal ears until that same flesh awakened my sapient awareness. I wished I could remonstrate him for hiding from me all this time—hiding in the world since the very death of my father twelve years before!—and allowing me to suffer such violent grief in the wake of his terrestrial death.

Yet all I could do upon hearing those profane words was to throw myself upon him and kiss him with great, aching passion, my tongue forcing its way into his mouth and slitting itself open along his sharp fang in a pain I found only pleasurable.

While endorphins flooded me, my husband groaned, sucking on my tongue and letting his hands slide along the thighs I wrapped around his hips once I'd thrashed from the covers well enough to slip into his lap. As his tongue swirled along mine, collecting the blood I felt welling from my cut, I ground my body along his and simply could not stop kissing him. Only when he at last caught my face in both hands to push me back with a little groan of self-denial did I cease, and only with a choking gasp of utter frustration.

"Just a moment, angel," he said, his words low with desire, his chuckle husky with his thirst for far more than my blood. "If you think you're impatient, I assure you, you can't imagine how badly I want you...how long it's been since I've had you freely—"

With a shudder, Malin slipped his thumb beneath my upper lip and caressed my gum, murmuring as he did, "But you might need help the first few times. Now, just relax...relax, pretty girl, let Daddy see those lovely fangs...ah—"

I moaned softly at his words, the title taking on new profane meaning; for although Malin had been at one point my wholly absent step-father, unknown to me through all my life and legally severed from me with the death of my mother on my birth, there was no doubt that the doting affection he showed for me in my first hours of new life had been equal to or in excess of the love shown by any human sire for his child. As erotically despicable as it had been of him to feed me to myself, the taboo association sparked in my loins an amorous heat that made me moan along with the invasive petting of his thumb; and with this growing arousal grew my fangs, expanding from my gums beneath my husband's slow but persistent massage.

"Ah," he said, inhaling softly, "there—Thecla, Thecla, oh, my gorgeous bride...how beautiful they truly are, yes, indeed... how beautiful you are..."

While his thumb slid down along the predatory incisor that had, I realized, relieved a peculiar pressure I had not known myself to feel, my husband's sole focus became my mouth. As the copper smell of blood rose in my nose, he slid his slit thumb past my teeth and stroked my tongue to make me moan. His lips parted, the white tips of his own fangs exposed while I moaned in wonder at the tangy, nearly sweet taste of his blood.

All the while, Malin lavished me with sensual praise. "That's it," he told me, "good girl, ah, my darling, my angel, oh, Thecla... Thecla, I missed you—good Christ, this is sweeter than I ever imagined it could be, ah, princess—"

Shivering, catching him by the wrist to draw his thumb out of my mouth no matter how much I craved to continue sipping his blood from even that small wound, I stared into his eyes.

"It's 'Matrix' now, you deceptive old lout—you're lucky I don't make good use of the title you awarded me to tie you to the bed and whip you senseless."

"Oh," groaned Malin between the heavy kisses I lunged to give him, my hands tangling in his thick hair as he pushed me down into the mattress with speed and force that served only to double my excitement, "there will be plenty of time for that later, my cruel mistress...and I pray you will be very cruel to me, for I do deserve it. But think of how beautiful it is! I have no more secrets left to hide from you, Thecla."

Catching my jaw in his hand to draw back from our impassioned kisses and look at me with wonder, his expression something like amazement even in the depths of our hostile passion, he searched my face with the glittering disks of his silvered eyes. "You know everything about me now. For the first time in our marriage, my soul is absolutely clean. I've given it all to you, my wife...you know my heart as well as I know it myself."

While his hands trailed down my body, pushing high the nightgown in which I had been dressed during my slumber, I worked open the buttons of his shirt and protested. "Yet I don't know you at all anymore—almost twelve years! Is it true, my love? Have you been here so long without me?"

"I have lived so long waiting to return to you, my wife, yes— yes, and it has been *miserably* long. Ah..." Jaw tense, he let me get his shirt open down to the ruddy trail of hair that disappeared into his trousers; then, pushing my hands away, he tugged my gown over my head and all but tore it from my arms when he beheld my body with a gasp. "Oh, Thecla! I didn't let myself look at you, really look at you, when I found you out in the storm that returned you to me...my love, oh, beloved—wife—"

As he caught me in his kiss, pressing himself down upon me to let me savor the power of his body and the pressure of his desire aching within his trousers, I found myself amazed at the feeling of this moment. Perhaps it was only because we found ourselves in the bed where we consummated our terrestrial marriage, or perhaps it was the desperate urgency he felt to finally put formal end to what, our one dalliance aside, must have been a decade of monk-like celibacy—or perhaps it was simply finding my mind born into this new body, which, though like my old body in nearly every superficial way, was without question not the body to which I was accustomed. Either way, it felt like a new wedding night: and even as I craved his touch like the wanton he made me whenever he held me in his arms, I found on each of those sweet touches that I enjoyed a virgin's sensitivity. Each contact was novel and profound, from the slide of his hand along my stomach to the kiss of air upon my vulva when he drew my underthings away to leave me fully naked for his famished eye. The new life in me was made for pure sensation, I was realizing: made for pure enjoyment and true pleasure.

And the old life, which cringed at the fangs Malin could not help but sink into my neck while his hands petted and played along my curves, quickly submitted to this greater pleasure when even the sharp sting of his teeth puncturing my flesh resolved into nearly vertiginous rapture. I moaned and ground myself savagely against the tent in his trousers, and, once more aware of that feline purr that rose from me as it had in the dream, I pulled his open shirt back from his shoulder to repay the favor while he drank from me.

Oh, what glory! No fine wine, no indulgent mithrae flower, could possibly compare to the sweet blood of my husband: a gift that filled my mouth and soul with the sheer ecstasy of his immortal life. Unprepared for how fantastic the experience would be, I groaned to let his blood fill my mouth until it ran from the edges of my lips. Only then did I commence swallowing it in great, greedy pulls. As the rhythm of my purring was joined by the almost frightfully basso of his, I found myself sinking my teeth into him again, again, desperate for a more satisfying waterfall of that instantly addictive substance. As a similar re-penetration of his fangs brought a shock of pleasure to my loins, I clutched him with every limb and moaned to know he enjoyed an identical experience of hedonistic bliss.

"Thecla," he groaned, one hand tangling in my hair while the other worked his trousers rapidly open, his mouth still at my blood-wet throat, "oh, Wife! Your blood is like honey, your flesh against my tongue pure ambrosia—"

I was barely able to register what his hand was doing, for as high as I found myself on the sheer pleasure of my husband's blood—and I was besides too busy marveling at the increasing acuity and stunning beauty with which I absorbed the world through my new senses. As my human flesh had stirred sapient thought in me, had permitted me to establish some sense of memory and context, Malin's blood surging into my mouth elevated the workings of my body and mind to transhuman heights.

As I drank, my mind grew sharp as a tack: my terrestrial memories, so fuzzy on waking, returned in high definition, with all the countless little details that naturally corroded in the march of time refreshed as if the events of my life had all just happened. Indeed, it seemed all things were happening concurrently with that moment, were always happening—and it was as I remembered and again glimpsed those shimmering threads that Dinon had laid bare for my naked eye that Malin penetrated me, with an eagerness only surpassing my own because I had been momentarily withdrawn from our lovemaking and into the astonishment of it all.

But that deep claim of my body by his snapped me back to the present, the threads vanishing for something so much sweeter. I cried out, stunned by the sharp but delicious agony of new awakening to love. Malin likewise cried out as if hurt, the sensation after such long self-denial no doubt still so intense it was quite overwhelming—especially when compared with the ecstasy of our bloody exchange, which had already left us both nearly sublingual with stupefying pleasure. Now, my toes curling, my body receiving his with the resistance of a first experience, I could cry nothing but his name, and held his head against my throat with one hand while I received him into my very soul.

The feeling of desperate famine had faded into ecstasy so complete that the room spun even when his head lifted and my mouth was forced to relinquish its hold upon his wound. "Thecla," he growled, pressing himself deeply within me and keeping one hand around my jaw to fix my eyes on his. "Thecla, oh, sweet wife—can't you see how exquisite it is, this life? Can't you see how this is the way it's meant to be?"

Groaning while his thumb raised to swipe my lips clean of his blood and smear the substance over my tongue, I asked in a pleasure-laden whimper, "Then we don't need to hurt anyone, Malin, my love? We don't need to hunt?"

"Only each other," he told me, kissing me with a passionate fury that made me cry out and arch my hips more eagerly into his thrusts. "We only need each other now. You drink from me, and I drink from you, and that is the way it's meant for us, my love. This is how our kind is truly meant to subsist in this world."

Tears filled my eyes at the beauty—and the sorrow! How many dharmines had been killed since the first Rift Events began? How many terrestrial mortals had lost their lives because the nature of dharmines simply wasn't understood? All these centuries, the inhabitants of Earth had believed that dharmines were feral animals—cheap substitutes that used the likenesses of people, living and dead, to prey upon ignorant humans.

But I was no more a substitute Thecla than my husband, the man who staked his claim over me there in our marriage bed, was a substitute Malin. We were ourselves—more ourselves than we had ever been. Which only begged the question—

"What are we," I whispered as he raised his mouth from our kiss to savor the euphoria on my stunned, flushed face as each thrust he orchestrated brought us closer to the edge.

"We're what we've always been," he told me, using my thigh to push my pelvis up and back and open me for his deeper use. "Two souls in Love—that's all that matters, Thecla. That's all I care about. And now that we're together again, nothing in Heaven or Hell could take you from my arms—I promise."

The sensitivity of my new body was too much for me to resist my climax. There were so many times I loved to cling to the edge, to extend that pleasure for what seemed like an eternity— but, as though I really were a virgin, (and wasn't I?), I shattered beneath my husband's next hard stab into my embrace. As I cried out—screamed, really—he covered my mouth with his kisses and held my bucking hips in place to hasten his strokes, driven by the gripping pleas of my body to give himself as fully to me as my muscles demanded. Groaning my name from his bloodied mouth to mine, Malin stiffened within me, against me, and I succumbed to an immediate second climax just to enjoy his pleasure. As he poured his soul out into me, I gripped his beautiful face to stare into his fathomless eyes. The silver faded, with his contentment, to the dark skies of his human irises: and, when at last the great storm passed us by to leave us purring in the afterglow, I felt more human than ever.

"That son of yours would certainly have it so." Charlotte shut the door behind her and, with an uncharacteristically telegraphed wince, swept her eyes quickly over the bloodied bed before looking instead out the open curtains of the villa's back door. Tutting, she strode over to shut them and went on as she did, "He treats me like I'm a celebrity, wanting to know everything about me. The child's been nattering on all afternoon—'Is it true you were with Papa when he did this?' 'What about *that*, when Papa was doing that, were you also there?'"

Drawn from my languid blanket of love with new intrigue, having all but forgotten the boy while Malin restored me to my senses, I sat up as my husband emitted a soft laugh. "I should say you certainly are a celebrity to him, Charlotte, or perhaps a creature out of a fairy tale. I'll tell him to badger you less, though I'm sure—"

"No, no, I hardly mind it. It's charming, really...I just wasn't expecting it." Turning back to us now with her expression slightly more braced against any flitting emotion—even as her eyes bounced quickly over the gory evidence of our love and back up to our faces—Charlotte advised, "At any rate, it's a few hours to suppertime, and I wanted to ask if perhaps you intended to do the cooking yourself, sir? After all"—she gestured to the bed—"it looks like I have my work cut out for me tidying up in here."

In other words—as discreetly and respectfully as possible, Charlotte wanted nothing to do with the process of cooking more human meat. At least, not if it was mine. Malin said with a magnanimous wave of his hand, "Of course. You take care of the room and let me handle supper. Would you like something for yourself?"

"With all due respect, sir, I haven't had the slightest appetite since finding Thecla—since finding you"—she corrected, looking at me—"stone dead in your workroom."

"I'm sure that was quite a shock," agreed Malin with a chuckle while I felt the shock, myself, having been trying, when the train of thought permitted, to work out just what had happened after I finished my work the night before. Remembering it, himself, Malin caught my chin and looked tenderly into my eyes. "Thank you for that beautiful tapestry, my love," he occasioned at last to tell me. "What a stunning gift. It seems to glow—pray, what kind of thread did you use for the detailing in the hallway?"

"I'll try to explain later," I said with an uneasy laugh, not certain I could articulate it yet. "But, about this boy—"

My throat tightened. I recalled the baby in that so-called dream and the unflinching certainty with which I had regarded him as ours. Searching Malin's face, I nonetheless asked here in reality, "Is he—how—"

"He's certainly ours." Malin's hand slid around mine and his thumb massaged the well of my palm while he drew my knuckles to his lips. "Every time I began to grow mad with isolation over the past decade, I would look into his eyes and find so much of you in him that I remembered why I was doing this, enduring this. Sometimes it was the only means to force myself back to sanity again."

"I wish I had known," I whispered, exhaling shakily. "It might have been some comfort to me these weeks."

"And it might have altered important decisions," Malin said. "You can hardly imagine the sickness and terror I felt when I realized how far into the past I had been displaced...but, I do go on. Charlotte"—releasing me, Malin slid up from the bed while our housekeeper politely looked at the ceiling with a terse little clearance of her throat—"why don't you help our Matrix bathe, and if there's time before supper, she can introduce herself to our son...I know he's just as eager to meet her as she is him. Maybe more."

"Very good," said Charlotte while Malin donned his dressing robe. "Come along—Thecla."

"See you at supper, angel," said Malin, blowing me a kiss, then adding on his way out the door, "and for many, many hours after...it's a good thing we don't need much sleep, I'll tell you that."

While my husband went merrily whistling into the halls, his scarlet robe fluttering around his bare feet, I smiled after him before turning that smile upon Charlotte.

The grim expression of her scrutiny made that smile fall just a little.

"Charlotte," I began, quite relieved when she interrupted me.

"If you're about to make some sort of apology, don't. I'm not sure I'd believe it in the first place. But tell me, honestly—*are* you Thecla?" Her shrewd green eyes flashed intensely over my face, then stared me down more firmly while she awaited my answer. I frowned, my brow furrowing as I looked down at my own extended hand.

"What is Thecla," I asked after another few seconds, looking up at her earnestly. "I mean—what are we, really? I *feel* like Thecla. I *look* like Thecla. I have all the memories of Thecla Farrow of Lescaut, Matrix of Gudrune. Doesn't that make me Thecla?"

Charlotte continued studying me with barely so much as a blink. "I don't know the answer to that."

"I don't, either. I will say—"

I tapped my chin, trying to figure out how to explain it before quickly giving up. "It's true to say I *feel* different," I allotted, my words having about them an easy-going looseness they had never had with the pressure of mortality bearing down upon them. "My mind feels—brighter, somehow. More airy. I don't feel so alone in it anymore."

You never were, Dinon's voice assured me, a shiver rollicking down my spine as his words filled my brain. Pushing his intrusion aside for now, I shook my head.

"I don't know how to explain it," I told her. "I wish I did. All I can say is, I feel like myself...I love all the people I loved before. Do I think the way I thought before? I don't know—I haven't lived this way long enough to tell. But I do know..."

Unable to help my laugh, I enthused, "Why, if that's all death really is, this movement forth into a better life, than I pray everyone may experience its fullness as I have...the world would be a healthier place if everyone could have it over with and emerge as the people the Lord must have meant for them to be."

With an undisguised shudder at a sentiment that quite understandably would have caused any mortal raised to shun dharmines great alarm, Charlotte said, "Why don't I draw your bath, Matrix, and you can sort your thoughts out to me while I wash the blood out of your hair."

And so I did, babbling somewhat like a child myself, I'm sure. The excitement of feeling incredibly fit after so severe an illness would have been sweet enough on its own; but now, for the first time in my entire existence, I felt truly lucky to be alive. It occurred to me now that, before, I had felt lucky in *spite* of being alive—in spite of being a peasant girl from Lescaut who, like her father before her, and his parents before him, and every human being who had ever lived, was doomed to die someday.

Now, however, I saw it all so differently. Mortality was not some curse: not some hateful and frightening condition of human nature. Nor was it, as I had sometimes felt while reflecting on my father, some punishment inflicted upon us by an uncompassionate God. Indeed, I now found God more compassionate than human understanding could measure—for it seemed to me mortality was not an affliction, but a treasured opportunity. It was a vessel which, correctly sailed upon the seas of reality, could reach the distant shores of eternal life. And I had thought I felt myself sinking—had indeed been drowning in the waves—but, with my husband as advocate, I had stirred from the unconsciousness of drowning and found myself upon the shore of a brave new world.

Charlotte did her best to keep up with me, but was soon reduced to making a series of interested noises at various humoring intonations ("Mmhm?" "Oh!" Mmm." "Is that so?") while I speculated loftily on the nature of existence. Quickly, I grew to find the efforts as tiresome as she. I felt as though I had returned to life with an armful of precious treasures, artifacts from an alien world which I arranged before my friend in a futile attempt to show her the brilliance of the place through which I had crossed—but, for all her intellect and all her love of me, Charlotte simply could not appreciate what I had to share. In her mind, the visionary experience I enjoyed between mortal life and eternal life—or, as I was quickly coming to think of them, between death and life— was reduced to nothing more than a literal dream, as one endures in sleep. And although I have called it a dream in these memoirs, and it bore the hallmarks of a dream, there was no doubt that the black space with its loom and my frightened terrestrial duplicate were all also real, in their ways. After all: information had been passed to Malin in that place. What I had said there had real-world consequences that rippled through time and even determined, in some mysterious way, the points in spacetime where my husband and I emerged into reality. It was therefore no paltry theatrical revue of one's day, as the mind constructs at night or in the midst of an afternoon nap; nor was it hallucination, as I have often heard called the visions of those who nearly die but return to life on the operating table or the battlefield. What I experienced was fully real and a dream at once, and gave me new, more respectful understanding of many things I had before dismissed as simple fancies.

The same could have been said, also, of that place on the other side of the Rift where I had found myself with Ba'al-Dinon—but that, I decided to keep to myself, thinking it better not to cast my pearls before swine (if, Charlotte, you would forgive me the unflattering cliche). Instead, as my thoughts careened toward my experience with Dinon and that strange and beautiful place where he had helped me to see the threads of reality, I asked, "Whatever happened to Ba'al-Dinon, Charlotte? Have you seen him at all today?"

"Not since I visited you in your workroom before I went to bed." With a displeased glance down into the reddened water of the bath, Charlotte fetched a pink towel from the cabinet and traded back in the white one she had unthinkingly grabbed. "I thought for a moment, when I found—you—collapsed on the floor, that he had done something to you. But I found no new injuries on you when I checked your pulse and—"

Her breath hitched. I glanced over my shoulder, quite astonished to find her briskly raising her hand to her eyes. "Charlotte," I said consolingly, wishing she stood close enough for me to touch. "It's all right—I swear, I'm me. As much me as I ever was—no, more."

"I'm glad you feel that way," Charlotte said, her shoulders jerking while she filled her lungs and then resolutely returned to help me from the bath. "I'm sure I'll get used to your condition in time. It was just—shocking to find you, Thecla."

"I'm sorry." Sudden awareness tarnished somewhat my joy. It was quite selfish of me to go, as she had put it of the boy, 'nattering on' when she was still strictly speaking processing my death—and, I mused, the act of cooking my butchered remains so I could eat myself. Perhaps we owed Charlotte a little vacation. "But I'm grateful to be back," I went on, "and—I'm very grateful you're still here."

With a sigh as she briskly toweled me off the way she always had, albeit with a new degree of bend to her arms for my slightly adjusted height, Charlotte said, "I won't deny it crossed my mind to abandon this blasted villa altogether and take the nearest train to the coast for a dirigible across the sea...but—let's put it like this. I've long enough served two Malins...I think I should just be grateful that my service to you is sequentially arranged, rather than concurrent."

With a laugh of agreement as she wrapped me in my robe and sat me down to brush out my hair before dressing me, I told her, "That must be a relief...oh, Charlotte—"

Even for all I had said in my effort to assure her I was still myself, I nonetheless bit my lip to ask her, "Is he still himself? Really?"

"Well...yes. But"—with a hum of contemplation as she decided how to phrase it, Charlotte untangled a few locks and stuck in a pin before continuing—"I suppose you could say he's like the self his life never gave him the chance to be. He's Malin, all right. But he's also—well, he's close to twelve years apart from the Malin you and I knew, and twelve years with only the boy to keep him consistent company."

"But you've spoken to him, haven't you? When I tricked him into coming out of his—lair, for lack of a better word, he said something about you calling him."

"Oh, yes. I've called him to tell him when I have another girl to send, or he calls me to make requests for one; on such occasions, he talks my ear off, desperate as he is for conversation with an adult." While pity filled my heart for my husband, Charlotte cut me off. "Don't feel bad for him, though. He's always had himself to speak with freely, after all."

"How queer that must have been," I mused. "I hope he'll tell me all about it sometime. Oh, but Charlotte—"

Strange anxiety plagued me—anxiety, and sorrow. I fondled my throat in my nervousness so that she paused in the matter of pinning my hair, which I noticed was still quite streaked with a crown of white. "How is it, I wonder, that the boy has come about?"

With a light shrug that refuted all knowledge of such esoteric matters, my housekeeper resumed her temporary duties as my lady's maid. "How should I know? But that gunshot did cause a miscarriage your ventil failed to resolve—perhaps he's the same child. I've heard it said, after all, that the very heart of all reality, beyond atoms and molecules and quarks and so on, is simple information. Perhaps *that* is what Thecla is—what I am, what Malin is, what the boy is. Information—and information can be salvaged, reinterpreted, transferred from book to RMS device to human mind. Perhaps even from human form to dharmine form."

Given slight pause, then letting her own thoughts settle upon her as they had upon me in that instant, Charlotte looked at me with new (or perhaps re-newed) familiarity.

"So perhaps you still are Thecla," she decided, at least at ease enough to turn her back to me as she made her way to the dressing room adjacent and snapped on its light.

"Or perhaps Thecla is only the dream of a greater information-sorter," I posited. "A thread woven by a greater hand."

"Won't you do me a favor and keep the tiresome existential theorizing to yourself," she chided me into laughter I heard reflected, somewhat muffled, in her voice. "It's hard enough deciding how I'm going to fit you into your old gowns without you filling my head with metaphysical nonsense."

Charlotte! Bless her lack of patience for all matters that were impractical to her sharp, stubborn mind. That first day back—and for quite a few days after, as my reader may be able to divine—I felt as though I floated on something far lighter than air. I might have been liable to drift away like a balloon had she not been there to bring me down to Earth. After finding a gown whose fabric and hem were both quite forgiving, and pairing it with calf-high boots that made up for the difference, she tied in my hair a bottle blue ribbon that matched and sent me on my way with a shake of her head. "That blasted dharmine footman of yours really picked a fine time to disappear," she told me while looking over the violently disarrayed bed. "If I'm to have to cope with this nightmare every day, we'd better stock up on gin."

Though I giggled on my way from the room where I left my friend to sort out her problems, the renewing anxiety very quickly caused my good humor to fade—or, at least, to reserve itself. Indeed, I felt what seemed to be a great deal of misplaced guilt, or shame; even though I had no part in abandoning the boy, the idea that I had a ten-year-old son whom I had never known seemed the most dreamlike thing about the whole affair. Wasn't this usually a male problem? Goodness. Speaking of gin—I rather longed for some in that moment!

Perhaps the child would hate me for the absence over which I had no control. Yet how could I blame him, were that the case? Had not my weaving at the Black Loom kept me from arriving on Earth at the same time as him and his father? Moreover, had it not been my ventil's failure to heal his injuries that had caused me to miscarry him in the first place? I fretted all the way to the living room to which I pursued the scent of cooking meat, the open concept kitchen being not far therefrom; and it was there, listening to the tinkling notes of piano music on the antique gramophone, (the RMS system being out of service with the height of the storm), that I first laid terrestrial eyes upon my son.

Oh, he was precious. My heart, which had possessed a curious stillness I had noticed throughout that afternoon, seemed nonetheless to almost beat to find him curled against the arm of the couch, his legs pulled up to allow his knees to support the book over which he was eagerly hunched. I was just outside his periphery, and from there I could perceive in his youthful features a distillation of Malin and myself which so excellent, so undeniable, that any doubt I had as to his heritage disappeared at once. Indeed, though his face's shape from his strong nose to his delicate cheekbones resembled my husband, I couldn't help but agree my features made up the better part of his genetic inheritance, his hair being dark and his eyes, which eagerly scanned the text before him while his finger lay poised in anticipation of the next page turn, a complex of gold and green hazel glittering with the ubiquitous silver of a hungry dharmine. There was something in the structure of his form which, birdlike, brought to mind my childhood frame, or Sable's—but when the movement of my skirt caught his eye and, in an equally avian motion, he tossed the volume aside and hastened to stand, I found him so tall for his age it amazed me. In but a few more years, I marveled, he would be his father's height, at least.

While he stared at me in an awe doubling that with which I regarded him, I remembered at last to smile. "You must be Telemachus."

Collapsing into shyness that made me forget all my own anxiety, the boy blushed and nodded, his eyes dropping to the hem of the shirt with which he fiddled to give himself something to do. "Yes, I am."

"And do you know who I am?"

"Y-yes," he stammered eagerly, looking back up at me and then, as if quite frightened to see my face, back down at my shoes. "You're my mother," Telemachus spoke on softly, the words edged with a disbelief with which I could strongly sympathize.

"That's right," I said, still smiling, allowing myself to laugh a little. At the sound, he looked up in some small relief, although his features remained uncertain until I went on. "This is all very strange, isn't it!"

"Yes," said the boy with a laugh of his own. "It's very strange. Papa, um—he's told me a lot about you."

"Goodness, how frightening!" I made my way near, sitting in the loveseat adjacent to his sofa so as to take up some nearby territory without altogether encroaching on his. "I hope he's had good things to say of me."

"*Only* good things," the boy hastened to blurt, better able to meet my eye now that I sat and, I suppose, was less imposing to him. "Papa's told me lots of stories about you. Like—like how you saved him once, when you were both from Earth; and how once you spent six months as a ventil doe before you had my little sister. What's she like?"

Less taken aback than I would have expected to hear Telemachus refer to Rosina as his little sister, (for after all, had his feet not reached terra firma long before hers were even formed?), I smiled in spite of the pain her reference caused. "Oh, she's just a small thing yet, but she's very sweet. You'll like her when you get to meet her...I'm sure it will be soon, but I can't be sure just when."

"How come?"

"Oh"—I waved away the thought away with my hand, amazed at how the fires of rage and heartbreak still burned within me when, having enjoyed resurrection into this perfected body, I nonetheless found myself ruminating morosely on Glenn—"her Daddy has taken her on a camping trip of some sort. He's quite the outdoorsman...what is that you're reading, dear?"

"It's some old love story," said the child with a little wrinkle of his nose. "Or it's supposed to be, anyway, only the people in it aren't very good at being in love. I don't like them very much."

He told me the title and I laughed. "I was going to guess that was what you meant! May I see it?"

Intent on pleasing me and visibly happy to have a chance to, the boy snatched up the old novel and scurried over to thrust it into my hands. I took it from him and leafed through its pages to discover where he'd hastily tucked the marker. "Oh, goodness! You're not yet even halfway through—don't worry, it gets much better from here on, although the people in the second half are still dreadful...this is quite an advanced book for a boy your age to be reading."

"Is it? Oh." Looking a bit shy to do so, Telemachus sat beside me and accepted the volume when I handed it back to him. "Well, Papa thought I might like it, so I'm giving it a try. He gives me lots of books to read, and lots of lessons."

"I can tell he must. You're very well-spoken."

"Papa says proper rhetoric is the cornerstone of a successful man's existence," Telemachus recited, quoting what, I can only presume, had been inserted into thousands of lectures from as far back as the boy could remember. While I smiled to imagine what it must have been like to have my hyper-ambitious husband as not just parent but tutor, the boy went on. "I like to play with Pauline sometimes, but I don't feel like we have very much in common. She's just little, and her parents don't educate her as they should. Ought?"

"Either works," I said with a shrug and a smile. While the boy looked grateful for my lack of correction, I asked, "Pauline— is this the vineyard keeper's daughter?"

Telemachus nodded. "Papa gets quite nervous when I spend time with her, because he's worried I can hurt her, but I'd only do that if I wanted to, and I don't want to."

Ah, yes—what a strange reminder, a reawakening to my own nature as well as to this boy's! It was no doubt true that his intelligence was due to three sources—his upbringing, his pedigree, and then, of course, to his peculiar condition. With a smile that was surely just a hair uneasy, I told him, "I'm sure you're a good boy, and very mindful of your strength."

"I am." In the next instance, a hint of true personality showed through the anxious child who considered it important I find him smart and well-bred. "I like playing with Pauline," he elaborated, "because I can show her how strong and fast I am, and nobody believes her!" With a giggle of wicked delight that had me laughing, too, he said, "She gets so frustrated when she tells me about it—I think it's funny. Papa tells me I shouldn't tease her, but I can tell he thinks it's funny, too."

"That's because it is funny," agreed Malin, entering the room in trousers and a fresh shirt. Animating with a combination of relief and delight, Telemachus darted to his father with a speed that made me reflexively wince—though after but a second I unbound my muscles, chiding myself with a smile as Malin lectured the boy. "But just because it's funny doesn't make it right, dear... we mustn't exploit the neighbors, especially not a nice child like Pauline. What do you think of Mama? Isn't she lovely?"

"She is," agreed the boy, clinging to his father's waist and suddenly bashful again. "She's nice, and smart."

"Well, you must have gotten it from somewhere, eh? I'm sure you two will get on famously...now do Papa a favor and go wash up before supper, there's a fine lad."

While Telemachus, obedient as only a child raised in near-total isolation could be, trotted off to do as he'd been told, Malin strode to my side and passed me one of the two glasses he'd been holding in his right hand. With the left, he furnished a wine bottle he poured out only once he had settled in beside me, an arm around my shoulders.

"Hello," he said very softly, the density of the word containing all at once the entire history of our love and the enormity of the afternoon we'd spent together. I blushed beneath his gaze, beaming up at him as he bent his head to brush his nose against mine.

"Hello," I returned, receiving his kiss with a warm, happy sigh.

"Now, I know you've only just come to, and you must be quite—hm, shall we say—"

"Frazzled," I submitted with a grin and a laugh he returned in equal measure.

"Yes, *frazzled*. However...this is a very fine wine, and since Telemachus isn't old enough to appreciate such things, I would love to share it with you, Thecla."

"Please do." Holding the glass still so he could fill it, then reach across my bosom to fill his at rest in the arm behind me, I watched not his hand but his face. "You're even more maddeningly handsome than before...oh, but I confess I rather miss your scar."

"You're always encouraged to try and give me a new one," Malin said with a wink and a grin for his own sadomasochistic swagger. While, scoffing, I batted him lightly in the chest, he leaned forward and set the bottle on the coffee table. "It might not take... but we can experiment. What do you think of the lad?"

"Oh, he's such a delight!" Smiling with pleasure as, switching his glass from hand to hand, Malin toasted with me and took a swig, I assured him, "I can tell you've done a fantastic job of raising him, darling. He's adorable—a little gentleman. And such excellent manner of speech."

"Days I don't feel like talking, I just give him a book and tell him to read aloud to me. He recites a lot of good Shakespeare... and Rimbaud, and Poe."

Though I smiled, my heart ached to think of the buried pain caused to Malin by his isolation. My hand slid along his unbeating heart and, no longer able to touch my wine, I gazed into the dark mirrors of his eyes. "I'm so sad to think I haven't been there all this time. Oh, darling—"

"It's all right, Thecla." Raising my hand to his mouth, he kissed my knuckles and squeezed my fingers, and pressed my palm flat to his chest once again. "It's all right. I know you would have chosen to be with us if you could have."

I wasn't so sure I hadn't chosen, albeit unknowingly—but there was no point in sulking about it now. "I can't fathom it. Have you two really spent twelve years living under this place?"

"Just about. I had it built for myself. It's proven an excellent investment...though it could use a feminine touch, to say the least."

"Do you come up here when the villa isn't in use?"

"Oh, yes, all the time...we must do so carefully, of course, since there's no telling when someone might wind up near enough to see a moving curtain or some such, but we certainly can't spend all our time down in the dark, and RMS reception is impossible to obtain there...I like for Telemachus to hear speakers other than me when possible, so we try to listen to news broadcasts and so forth—but I do so hate when he eavesdrops." Malin added this in a raised voice that caused me to glance in the direction of the kitchen. While, with a shy giggle, Telemachus stepped out from around the corner, Malin beckoned him over.

"I'm sure he just didn't want to interrupt us," I said, already feeling quite affectionately disposed toward the child—especially in the prolonged absence of Rosina. "Isn't that so, Telly?"

Looking pleased by the petname, Telemachus hurried over to sit at his father's other side and nodded innocently. "Yes, ma'am."

"You can call me 'Mama', dear, unless it's too strange for you."

With another little grin, the boy ducked his head. "Yes, Mama." Then, taking note of his forgotten book, he said to Malin, "Mama said she's read this book and I'm not even to the good part yet, Papa, but I'm not so sure there *is* a good part. It seems very silly to me."

Laughing, sharing a glance with me, Malin asked, "Is that so?"

"Well, for instance, the girl that it's about—she's all tangled up in knots over two men, her friend from home and the boy who lives over the moors. That's the silly part. Don't you suppose everybody would be a lot better off if she just married them both? Mama is married to you and to Uncle Eleison, isn't she, Papa?"

While I smiled in pleasure, both at the naive question and the thought that Malin had cared to include Eleison in the child's picture of our family, Malin laughed somewhat less suavely than usual into his wine glass. "Well, yes, dear, in essence—but Mama and Papa and Uncle Eleison have an uncommon sort of relationship."

"Because Mama and Uncle are altered, right?"

"That's right," I assisted, smiling on. "It used to be that there were only mortal terrestrials in the world—you know that, don't you?"

"Yes, ma—Mama."

"Well, suffice it to say that when there were only mortal humans, there wasn't much practical reason to have more than one spouse, so it wasn't the 'done thing.' Indeed, it was frowned on. Even now there are some who turn up their noses at it."

With a little frown of his own, which he turned upon the book as though it bore the blame for all matters of social exclusion, Telemachus posited, "That seems very silly. Papa says people would do better to mind their own business."

"That they would," I agreed, choking back a slight laugh as the boy went on to add, "Unless they're politicians."

"Mm! That does sound like something your papa would say." I made more wry eye contact with Malin, who chuckled guiltily and spread his free hand.

Telemachus, meanwhile, perked with greater interest, leaning around his father to look at me. "Will I get to meet Uncle Eleison soon?"

"Quite soon, I should think." Malin glanced up at the RMS readout emblazoned in the nearest wall panel, which I was thrilled to find I could read even though it was near twenty feet away. "Once Mama has had a day or two to convalesce, we'll make our way to Uncle Eleison's property for Papa's funeral wake."

"That's like a party, isn't it?"

"That's quite right, dear, it's something like a party...especially when the guest of honor is alive and well."

The sudden recognition of all the work that lay before us coming heavily into my mind, even though I yet lacked any notion of scale or import, I rested my free hand across my forehead and studied Malin's handsome face. "What on Earth are we going to do about this resurrection of yours, darling? Whom are we going to tell, and how? How can we—"

"Thecla."

His hand resting gently upon my knee, Malin stopped my fretting with a sincere look into my eyes. "It will all be fine," he told me soothingly, as though I were a Rift beast he tamed (and was I not?) while his thumb stroked me through the fabric of my gown. "I promise. Let's not worry about it now. Leave everything to me, dear wife, and all will be well. For now, just enjoy this special day. Your new birthday...the first day we've been able to spend together as a family."

In the kitchen, a timer went off.

While the boy gave a giddy clap and sprang up from the sofa, Malin rose and extended to me his open hand.

30

IF I FELT ANY REMAINING reluctance to consume human flesh, even—or especially—if it was my own, that anxiety faded away when neither Malin nor Telemachus seemed mind at all themselves. Unflinching, as naturally as though they consumed a heifer, Telemachus perched in the seat across from me while my husband served us, poured out more wine for me, then made himself comfortable at the head of the table.

How funny! This was the very house where Malin had prepared a few meals for me, and then my husband's culinary skills had been, should we say—inexpert, but charming. Now, however, I was quite amazed to find his talents rivaled Charlotte's, or perhaps overshadowed them; and although he was no gourmand, it was clear that twelve years of being forced to provide meals for himself as well as the boy had done him a great deal of good. An excellent roast had been prepared (I daren't say from where) and fantastically accented with a sauce of cilantro, parsley, and peppers from the garden. Amid the herbaceous notes of the salsa, the splendor of the wine, and the delightful conversation, it hardly crossed my mind but once that I was eating my old flesh—and when it did, it seemed so natural and so oddly comforting that I cleaned my plate without hesitation.

'Comforting.' It seems a strange word, and that comfort was perhaps the strangest thing about this autophagy. Yet it *was* comforting. My human flesh, a mere container that had borne my spirit for not yet thirty years, would be within me, sustaining me, forever a part of me—so that, even if it were possible I was not Thecla, I would, at the very least, contain her.

What thoughts! What strange thoughts crept up on me, haunting me, bringing about the blossoming of unanswerable questions in my mind. Yet my husband, sensing this, or perhaps simply recalling his own experience of re-awakening in the world, kept our conversation light and airy—mostly, by keeping it about Telemachus. Happy to oblige, the boy prattled on as Charlotte had promised he would, eager to explain to me all the lessons Papa gave him—with reading and letters well mastered, now the focus was on rhetoric and philosophy, the works of various philosophers being the procession by which Malin taught the boy various periods of terrestrial history. Perhaps owing to his name, Telemachus seemed quite fascinated by antiquity; but, as was more expected of a boy his age, he was likewise fascinated with animals, architecture, and games such as chess and cards. He expressed interest in everything under the sun, our Telemachus, (*my* Telemachus! That took more getting used to than my own transfigured nature), and seemed to have no end to his curiosity for the world, or for me.

"What is it like to be a deer," the boy asked with bright interest before chewing up his last few bites, his eyes now a more terrestrial hazel from my line.

"Oh, it's very fun. One wishes nothing but to run and run, to frolic and be at harmony with nature—to be wild and free."

With a little grin, Telemachus said, "That sounds like me. Will I be a ventil someday, too, Papa?" The boy turned his curious gaze upon Malin.

"There's no way for us to know yet, dear; you're the only little boy who's never been a terrestrial...at least, as far as we know."

"I wish that weren't so. I'd like a friend to play with—to roughhouse with, you know."

This poor child! I smiled, assuring him, "Well, we might have a difficult time finding you a playmate your own age, but that doesn't mean there aren't plenty of very fun things for you to get up to. I'm sure Uncle Eleison would love to teach you things like shooting, for instance"—the boy's expression lit very keenly at that, particularly when his father made no correction—"and Uncle Eleison has a younger brother, Kyrie, a very nice young man who I'm sure would be glad to teach you horseback riding."

"It was he who taught Mama to ride," Malin explained, reaching over to mop the boy's mouth quite mercilessly with the napkin in his hand. While Telemachus made a noise or two of protest but clearly knew there was no escape, Malin went on, "And there are a great many other things yet for you to learn— most of which, I should venture a guess, will be fun—so don't feel too badly about lacking in playmates. I've told you before, I didn't have many myself at your age."

"I suppose so...but—" Looking reluctant, his too-wise eyes distant for a few seconds, Telemachus turned to me while his father finished up his own meal. "Mama—you must remember, since it just happened for you. What is it like, being terrestrial?"

"Hm." Swirling my glass and draining the contents, I folded my forearms on the edge of the table before my empty plate. "I suppose I'd need to be my new self a little longer to make the distinction clearly...but..." That dream-not-dream of the Black Loom and the many migrant dharmines flashed through my mind. "In retrospect, it was like being under glass—in a bell jar, perhaps, like an insect on display. One can hear and see and feel and smell and taste all perfectly sufficiently to get by, and one may even be fully conscious of the experiences of those things if one applies oneself to the moment...but there is a quiet hopelessness about it, too."

My own focus growing distant, I elaborated on, "One does one's best to put Time out of one's mind, of course—to focus on the present. And that mind is full of funny thoughts. It never clearly sees itself: it sees only others. It sees others dying and says, 'That shall never be me,' while at the same time, in the back of it, the knowledge of that inevitability is always there. Lurking... waiting. Little hopes come up, little dreams of the future—and there, the thought returns again, and again...until that thought is all there is left in the world. It is so much uncertainty and turmoil, the human condition, because mortals, especially in this age of ours, cannot see the value of their own existence. At the same time, they are too self-interested to succumb to love but rarely; and even those who succumb to it, who surrender themselves to love and hope, have been willfully blinded to the mechanisms that will allow their hopes fulfillment. So...I suppose you could say it is very difficult to be terrestrial—to be mortal. But it is sweet, too. After all—"

Smiling, my hand sliding into Malin's, I told Telemachus, "If I had not been mortal, and experienced so much suffering, perhaps I would never have had the chance to get to know you, Telly, dear."

Though my brooding words had set the boy to obvious rumination of his own, he brightened a little at that, and smiled. Then, seeing more clearly my hand in his father's, he looked all the more pleased and gazed back into my face. "I think you're very nice," he said to me, and I laughed despite myself.

"That's sweet of you to say...because something tells me not everybody thinks so."

"Save your sweetness for our family," Malin said encouragingly, rising to kiss my cheek before waving the boy up from his seat. "Spare none of your affections on the world where they're wasted, but give them all to us and let the world see the sharp heart of steel that fills my own with longing. Telemachus, let's tell your mother good-night; you've had a long, exciting day, as have we all. And I think"—with a glance at me over the oblivious boy's head—"it's time for everyone to get to bed."

"Okay," said the boy with reluctance, then assessing his father for openness to negotiation. Finding something in his posture that declared he was not, Telemachus sighed and only hesitated when he stood a few feet from my chair. He looked at me with great uncertainty until, smiling, I opened my arms—then, as easily and gladly as I had seen him dart to his father, Telemachus hurried into my embrace and let me kiss him thrice upon his adorable cheek.

"I am so, so happy to meet you, darling," I told him when, with a cherub's blush, he giggled to look at me. "I've known you not even a whole day, and I can already tell you no mother in centuries has been favored with a son worth compare."

Quite gratified by my praise, Telemachus bounded from me to lead his father off to bed, hovering impatiently in the doorway while Malin bent to kiss my mouth. "Come on, Papa! The sooner we wake, the sooner it will be time to learn shooting and horseback riding!"

"You'd better learn to live with these delays, my boy," said Malin with a chuckle, telling me over his shoulder, "See you in a few minutes."

While I blew another kiss to Malin, who winked at me and indulgently permitted the boy to rush ahead down the hall, I sighed in sheer contentment and settled back in my chair. My soul as warmed as it was, I felt unwilling to rise and break the spell of such a lovely first meal as a family. Yet while I sat there, my fingers worrying the lace edging of my neckline, the spell broke itself; for it was hardly my entire family, but only aa portion of it.

Oh, Glenn—Glenn, and my Rosina! Contrary to what one might have expected of a dharmine, I found I loved them more after emerging as the self I sensed I had always been intended to become; yet I knew it would now be so much the harder to earn Glenn's consent to my love, especially as concerned our daughter. How painful it would be when we found them—yet how much more painful, their absence!

Nearly as painful as the other absence which, in the silence of the room, became increasingly apparent to me.

I am here, Thecla—I am always here.

My throat tightened for sheer agony. "Yet you are not," I chided him in the silence. "Now I realize how much I love you, Dinon—and you spite me by refusing me the embrace of your arms, the tenderness of your kisses. Oh—"

Soul aching me as though with a fever that spread down to my bones, I sat up a little straighter. "Come to me, Dinon."

I wish I could, Beloved.

"Something keeps you?"

I dare not say what.

"Do your master's commands no longer hold you? Are you a slave to me no more?"

Only by choice—but even that, I dare not be for now. For, if I presented myself before you in your current state, you might remember too soon...and you would be afraid, Thecla. Too afraid to love me, even recalling all you do already.

My hand flat upon my heart, I told him, "I would rather be afraid of you than not have you—not experience you fully and completely, as I experience the world."

Trust me, Thecla. My eyes stung with tears. I glanced aside, my knuckle pressed broodingly to my lip. *Have faith in me. All I do, I do for love of you. You are everything to me.*

When those words of Dinon's blossomed in my soul, they were not the saccharine hyperbole, the meaningless noise, that such a claim would have been from other men. It was the earnest truth: so true I did indeed feel the edges of a fright I had not expected myself to feel. While I inhaled deeply against the emotion, Dinon chuckled in my mind.

See?

"Very well," I said hoarsely. "Yes, I suppose I do. But—Dinon—"

Tears spilling over the edges of my eyes, a breath catching in my throat for the force of emotion like I never would have expected myself to feel for him, I pleaded softly, "We *will* be together, won't we? In this life?"

And the next, and the next, forever and ever, for all eternity, Thecla, Beloved—I promise.

My brisk knuckle whisked those tears away as I raised my chin. "Very well," I said again, nodding. "I do trust you. I do. But—tell me I won't wait for you as miserably long as I waited to meet you in the first stretch of my life."

Not nearly, he swore with, I fancied, the ghost of his kiss brushing over the ridge of my ear. *Have patience, Thecla. Let us take one step at a time.*

Frustrated by my longing, pained by Dinon's games with my heart, I rose from the table, intent on fetching Charlotte before making myself comfortable in the bedroom to await my husband. As usual, had I not stopped to speak to Dinon, perhaps I would have accomplished this much; but, master of synchronous timing as he was, my conversation with the entity I had once regarded as a dharmine proved sufficient to leave me crossing the living room at the exact moment the front door, some thirty feet from me across the wide space and just around a break wall, opened to let in the light of the Rift radiation.

"Thecla?"

Speaking of fear! How embarrassing that Eleison's voice, normally a balm, should ever fill me with fright—but there would be consequences to his arrival, and I was not prepared for the struggle I would surely undergo to make him see the truth. Frightfully aware of the white crown that had imbued my hair with the hallmarks of my mortal blood-poisoning, I dashed to my dressing room across the house in a speed so startling to me that, when I stopped before the vanity a few seconds later, I careened forth quite dizzily. That would take some getting used to—but there was no time to recover my senses. Frantic, I rifled through the vanity drawers for the accessories which had been stocked for my use. Pushing rapidly through boxes of jewels and hairpins, clips and lesser tiaras, I discovered with a cry of gratitude the headpiece from my wedding—gold veil still attached. Having little choice but to improvise, I affixed the band to my head, was relieved to find it still fit with ease, and folded back the veil so that it plumed about my temples and flowed along my hair, thereby hiding the immediate changes to my appearance.

My movements were so rapid that Eleison had not made it halfway down the hall by the time I was satisfied, for as much as panic could allow satisfaction—but, to my increasing guilt, Eleison's calls for me were beginning to exhibit a panic of his own. "Thecla," he shouted. "Thecla? Char—"

"Eleison?" Emerging from the bedroom as though I had only just heard him, I contrived to let my face fall into an expression of delight—made all the easier by the relief that filled his. "My darling," I cried as he hurried to take me in his arms, given pause as he found my nose nearly level with his. With nary more than a flick of his eyes down to the heels of the boots in which Charlotte had dressed me, however, Eleison drew me against his chest while I asked on, "What are you doing here? You've come early—and in this storm, oh, sweetheart, you must be barely resisting the borro."

"I was until now," he said, his tone somewhat gruff with slow-fading concern even as his eyes and jaw softened with love. "The thought of you was the only thing that kept me sane the whole way here. What the hell are the shutters doing up? This place is fully accessible—I'm glad I came. I don't usually listen to bad feelings, but this bad feeling was really bad...thank God you're safe."

"Of course I'm safe, darling," I assured him, drawing him by the hand back into the bedroom.

In perfect silence, Malin eased out of a room along the hall and made eye contact with me over Eleison's shoulder. Seeing my veil and taking stock of the quick flicker my eyes made back to Eleison's, my husband did not move; he stood in perfect silence, a statue as I guided my mate over the threshold of the bedroom and kissed his mouth.

"Your lips are freezing, baby," he told me as we parted, though he was quickly distracted with an audible *tsk* by the violet night visible through the back door. "Seriously, though, what the hell is going on with these shutters? Are they on the fritz?"

As he strode toward the RMS panel to take control of the situation, I took the opportunity to hurry to the bed and disguise my height by reclining before he could recognize it was more than just the boots at work. While he tapped rapidly through the monitoring system's screens, I hastened to find a believable lie, and confabulated, "It was Dinon—he disappeared into the night, and I've not been able to find him anywhere in the house, so I thought I'd take a chance and check outside for him."

"Yeah, well, running as a ventil in a normal Event is one thing, but an Extreme one, especially without me—you can't take it lightly, Thecla. And as to the dharmine..." With a slight curl of his lip as, beeping, the shutters audibly rolled down all around the exterior doors of the house to cut off the radiation of the Rift, Eleison hit a final button that returned the panel to its home screen. "Good riddance."

"I do so wish you wouldn't detest Dinon quite so much," I said, feeling far more defensive of him now and unable to help myself from adding, "and at any rate—I am less convinced than ever before that he is a dharmine."

"Why? Did something happen?"

Blast his protective nature. The more my darling demanded to know, the more I was forced to lie to him to preserve the peace until I could disarm him, which was the only strategy I was capable of contriving.

"Nothing *happened*—only—"

My teeth sank into my lower lip. Perhaps there was room to reveal the truth to him amid my lies. With an anxious wring of my hands as Eleison came to sit at my side, his great fingers enclosing mine—again, with a brief glance down, as if noting some difference in the shape or size of my body—he thereafter gazed with great attentiveness into my face.

"I haven't told you this," I began, speaking from my heart, "because I've been afraid of what you might think. But I—hear his voice in my head."

His dark brows flexing with a knit of confusion, Eleison clarified, "Dinon's voice?"

"Yes. And—that's not all. He can do all manner of things dharmines are not known to do."

"That doesn't mean they can't do them," he pointed out. "Just that we don't know about them."

"Yes, but—I suspect if every dharmine could do what Ba'al-Dinon does, they would already have assumed full control of our planet. For instance—"

Struggling to keep myself from sounding excited, for now I was reflecting not on some monster or my slave but rather upon the powers of a great man with whom I was in love, I sat up just slightly.

"He comes and goes without the use of doors, through walls—or, perhaps I had ought to specify, appearing and disappearing into thin air, like a bubble. And he can do the same with matter—you recall, in Glenn's house, how you destroyed his furniture during your first visit, in a storm very much like this?"

At Eleison's single nod, I tightened my hand around his. "Yet when next you saw it—albeit briefly, through the eyes of your borro—do you recall how the furniture had all been replaced? And the roses Malin had sent me, rearranged. That was all Ba'al-Dinon's doing. I turned my back for but a moment, and he had transformed the wreckage into new furnishings entirely."

Nostrils flaring even as his pupils shrank, Eleison said, "Maybe it's a good thing he's gone, then."

I shook my head, insisting, "It's not—it isn't, Eleison. I—" My throat tensed as I thought again of Glenn, Glenn and my little daughter. "I'm tired of being abandoned."

"Thecla..." With a look of pain that telegraphed his assumptions—that I was thinking of my husband, who, alive and well, listened from the hall—my beloved mate stroked my hand with his thumb. "I know you miss Malin, baby. I miss him, too."

His eyes flicked toward my hairline, to the golden wedding veil that disguised undeniable evidence of something amiss.

"We can't bury ourselves with him," he insisted, looking me in the eyes again. "I know you're suffering. And as hard a time as I'm having with this, I can't imagine what you're going through. But, Thecla—"

His hand lifted to my cheek. I ached at his tenderness, my hands stroking his chest as he bent over me.

"—you're alive," he went on. "And I'm alive. And I know that if Malin were here, he would want us to live—for our own goods, and for the good of the territory."

"I know." My words a hush as he leaned forward to kiss me tenderly upon the mouth, I shut my eyes and enjoyed this sweet exchange of love until he drew back a few inches.

"Thecla—I missed you." Drawing me forward into his arms to tuck his chin atop my head, Eleison stroked my back. "Even a week without you is too long...especially too long with this kind of storm raging outside, no way to contact you and find out how you are—no way to know that you're safe."

"I'm so sorry, darling. I wish I could have called, I—"

"Hey, that's okay. We're here now. I already feel better." With another pat, he released me, then smiled into my relieved face while he got up from the edge of the bed again. So we were still mated—the ventil doe in me lived on, and the borro still responded, and Eleison and I were still one. I was still capable of calming him.

A necessary feat.

"So how was your, uh...project?" Eleison cracked his back and rolled his shoulders from the long trip. "Did you get it accomplished?"

"Yes, I did—in fact, that was when Ba'al-Dinon disappeared. It was that fortune-teller's inspiration, you see." Fudging the truth as Eleison kicked off his shoes and loosened his tie, I got up to come around behind him—first to rub his shoulders, and then to remove his suitcoat to confirm he was, as usual, armed with his pistol snugly in its holster. "I inquired with him about my Riftborn power," I went on, whisking the coat away to hang it up before he could make any observations. "And he—Renard is his name—Renard said some cryptic, funny things, and then called me a 'Weaver'. And I thought at first he simply meant my profession, but—gradually, it became apparent to me he meant something else."

Watching me with great interest as I once more extended myself, now along the chaise not far from the door, Eleison asked, "What did he mean?"

"It's the mithrae, you see." As I spoke of it all, my eyes grew focused not on reality, but on the shining warp and weft I perceived composing it, and the threads made me smile with a pleasurable fondness I could not explain. The violet ones in particular gleamed in Eleison's lovely red eyes as he made his way to my side, maddeningly handsome while he rolled his shirtsleeves to his elbows and once more perched by my hip. "When I imbibe those Rift flowers to a great excess, I start to see these lovely threads."

As I had in the world on the other side of the Rift, I reached out and stroked them, the threads making up the air before me. They shivered and trembled as if pleased to be noticed, and smiling all the more, I explained to fascinated Eleison, "I couldn't understand their significance back in Saalast. But the more I thought of Renard's advisement, I wondered—was *that* what he had meant? So…I had to be alone and try. But I could not discern a way to make it happen on my own. I asked Dinon for his help, as it is obvious to me that, whatever he is, he is also a great sorcerer or mystic of some sort—for lack of a better term," I added with an admonishing rap of snorting Eleison's bicep. "At any rate… he agreed. He altered something in me to allow me to see these threads. Look—"

Following a violet line that streaked down Eleison's cheek and throat to a suitable point upon his chest, I plucked it as a musician plucks the string of his instrument. "Here's one that runs over your heart. Can you feel it, my love?"

"No," he said with a chuckle, his eyes crinkling beneath his languid lover's lids. "No…but I can feel how much I love you, Thecla. God! So much."

Succumbing, as he did so often, to my proximity, Eleison drew my attention fully into reality with the kiss he bent down to pour into my mouth. I moaned, the threads shifting out of my visual field and leaving him, as usual, utterly flawless. Our tongues slipped against one another and he murmured into me— "So cold"—while raising his hands, now so warm to me they made me feel like a cat curled by the fire, to caress my cheeks and throat. "How come you're so cold, baby," he asked softly, meaning nothing by the question other than fondness as he raised his mouth from mine to nuzzle his lips back toward my ear. Feeling his hand stroke back over the veil and afraid he would disorder it or out and out remove it, I smiled and nuzzled him back before, catching his hand, I slid up from the chaise to straddle his lap. "I'm always cold without you," I whispered, nibbling his ear.

How ashamed I am to think of the ways I manipulated him in these moments! But it was the only means of avoiding physical conflict, or more physical conflict than there was doomed to be. Knowing his customs, I took to unbuttoning his shirt from the collar; and, sure enough, he slid the holster, gun and all, from his shoulders to let the weapon rest upon the longue. My hips rocked anticipatorily in his lap, the fabric of my dress riding up my legs while I divested him of his shirt; then, after letting him strip off the white undershirt beneath, I rose and drew him toward the bed.

"Come lie with me and warm me up," I begged him, my hands in his only by some divine mercy not openly quivering with frightful anticipation. As I draped myself upon the bed and pulled him over my body, he took to kissing me without delay; my sighs were unfeigned, but I could not give myself fully to his love, as I was rapt with anticipation for what would happen. I wished to close my eyes and enjoy him, but I kept glancing toward the door, waiting for the moment it would open.

And, soon enough, as silent as the man who stepped in through it, it did.

"You're more gorgeous every time I see you, baby," Eleison growled softly against my lips, bending his head to kiss and nip my jaw while I made eye contact with Malin above his head. Quietly as he had entered, so too did Malin shut the door behind him. I tried not to actively hold my breath, for Eleison's kisses descended down my throat and I feared the effect would be obvious.

"It's just your imagination," I teased my sweet Eleison while, with the ultra-soft click of a lock that I had to remind myself was surely audible only to my newly honed perceptions, Malin turned his attention to the weapon left on the chaise longue. "After all the weeping I've done in your absence, my darling, I must be flush with sorrow."

"Well...you do always look pretty sexy to me when you've been crying...but maybe I shouldn't admit that."

It is funny what a man will notice. The shutting of the door, the clicking of the lock—my altered height, the cold of my hands, my insistence on wearing my wedding veil. All these things, Eleison could overlook when presented with the high probability of making love to me.

Yet the very second his gun, beneath Malin's hand, shifted from his holster, Eleison whipped his head around—

And froze.

"Hello, Eleison...oh, my loves." With a lustful sweep of his dark eye across us both, Malin turned with the gun in his hand and a smile on his face.

"It really has been much too long."

THE LOW GROWL THAT ROSE from Eleison's diaphragm was twice as vicious as anything the dharmine in the woods had produced from his borro. A more violent sound, indeed, I have not heard him make since. Yet, given his perspective—the insult of a dharmine in the house compounded by its having stolen the form of our dead love—I could not, and still do not blame him for his outraged greeting of my husband.

"Thecla," he said softly, his words too calm against the vibrations of his borro's growl, "I want you to raise the shutters and run as fast as you can to find the nearest patrol unit."

"That won't be necessary," Malin assured him in a breezy manner, glancing down with the pistol pointed at the floor. After checking the chamber, he rapidly ejected the clip, speaking as he did. "The units know I'm here, and so does Thecla...and now, Eleison, my darling, so do you. So—"

Crushing the clip in his hand as though it were made of aluminum foil, the few bullets not stuck in the metal tinkling out to roll from his feet, Malin looked back up while tossing the ruined clip and useless gun aside.

"Let's talk."

There was no stopping him. As quickly as my husband could move was as quickly as Eleison seemed to yield to the beast within him, which, owing to the nature of the Extreme Rift Event ongoing around the villa, was far more than a simple borro. Half-man, half-beast, his yet humanoid form filled out with inhuman muscles rippling beneath dark fur, my mate bared his fangs and rose between Malin and me.

"Thecla," he snarled again, now through a half-animal snout, "run, damn it."

"There's nothing to run from," I pleaded with him to see. "This is Malin, darling—"

"It's not Malin—it's a dharmine. A thing wearing Malin's form."

"More like Malin was a thing wearing my form," my husband unhelpfully teased, "but I can see why you would think that."

With a roar of rage, Eleison wasted no time lunging upon my husband, claws extended—and fangs bared, though not open for use, which was a decided handicap. Laughing, Malin caught one of the heavy, furred wrists that had been slashing down at him and—to my thrill, I must admit—succeeded in resisting the strength of the massive half-animal even if the strain made his arm shake just so.

"Hm, hm"—my husband's eyes were inappropriately heavily-lidded as Eleison's free hand managed to catch his shirtfront— "you really are a specimen in any form you take, Eleison...have you had a chance to enjoy him like this yet, my—"

With a great slam of Eleison's currently massive skull down against his, Malin was temporarily stunned into silence—though that quickly resolved into laughter as, stumbling back, Malin wagged a finger at my mate. "You naughty boy," he said. "Is that any way to treat the man who saved your brother's life?"

"That man is dead," Eleison raged while, twisting at the waist, Malin snatched up the chaise longue and swung it at Eleison as though it were nothing but a ballgame bat. The great beast raised an arm and snarled as the furniture shattered against him, splinters and cotton flying in every direction. "And soon"—he snatched up a broken leg of the chaise while I cried out—"you will be, too."

"Maybe if I were some toothless, unhoned sleepwalker fresh from the Rift, but trust me when I say, old boy, I've had quite a bit of practice since then." While Eleison jammed the makeshift steak up toward Malin's ribs, Malin caught the weapon with both hands and used it to upend his opponent. The humanoid borro raged, spittle flying from his lips as Malin quite playfully tapped him on both cheeks with the shattered leg, his body in a fencing posture until Eleison scrambled up at sprang at him. Forgetting himself, the beast snapped at Malin, who caught the maw full of teeth with the shattered leg and held him back more effectively with both hands than he had with one.

"There—now that your mouth is occupied, maybe we can talk. Have you asked yourself why Thecla isn't fleeing at your command? Maybe you should."

Only this could make Eleison release his efforts to snap through the impromptu weapon. "Thecla!" Whipping around to find I was, indeed, quite frozen to the bed, thrilled and terrified by the potentially deadly sparring before me, Eleison took a rough strike of the chaise leg against the backs of his shoulders to demand, "What are you waiting for?"

"For you to calm down, I'm sure." In a quick move even my eyes could not follow, Malin stretched his arms over Eleison's head and jerked the leg back beneath his snout to drag him closely by the throat. "Now, I know you're not causing a scene on *purpose*, but there's a child trying to get his rest elsewhere in the house, and while I've told him to ignore the clamor, I really think—"

Paying no heed to Malin's lecture, Eleison assumed control of the furniture leg and, lurching forward, succeeded in tossing Malin over his back to send him flying so far he wound up on the bed at my feet, provoking a little cry of shock and anguish from my lips. All that could soothe me was Malin's all too cheerful, "Hello, sweetheart!" and the mocking kiss he paid precious seconds to press upon my boot.

But that good humor was dissolved in seconds, for Eleison fell upon him again—this time, with far more deadly potential. One mighty, furred hand around Malin's neck, Eleison dragged him up off the bed and held him high. I screamed out, an incoherent plea for clemency that only my adoring mate could have possibly deciphered.

"It's not *him* Thecla," raged Eleison, turning upon me as his free hand fit with disturbing ease over Malin's skull. "I know it's hard to understand, but it's an imposter. A thief who's stolen Malin's form. The real Malin is dead."

"Then the real Thecla is dead with him," I cried at last, tearing the veil from my hair and marveling at the manner in which these emotional heights caused the fangs to extend from my gums. While Eleison's eyes leapt at the motion, then widened to see me better, I rose and was newly prepared to make a terrible mistake if it meant saving Malin's life. "Release him," I commanded my mate. "Let him speak to you in peace, and then you'll see."

"But—" Animal maw opening and closing in incredulous horror, Eleison remained focused on me a second too long: taking advantage of his captor's distraction, Malin managed to draw his legs up and land a hefty kick in Eleison's diaphragm, winding him so severely he had no choice but to drop my husband. While my mate careened back a step I was pained to see, Malin wisely yanked the sheet from the bed and tossed it over Eleison's upper half, not just holding it tight but using it to scale the beast's broad back. Newly enraged, Eleison howled and thrashed, his claws wildly swiping at the air and tearing at the sheet, upending a bureau in the process. His teeth clenched, Malin looked at me.

"There's too much of a man in him for me to have much sway over his animal, though I'm trying—you try calming him with me."

In testament to the influence my husband—still Riftborn just like me, no matter his resurrection—my mate produced a snarl of agonized frustration and gripped his head through the sheet as though not so much trying to tear away his impromptu hood as to blot out Malin's control of his mind. Though this sight gave me pause, I approached with my hand outstretched and trembling.

"Eleison," I said, my voice firm but calm as I could make it, "it's really me. It must be me—didn't you tell me when you held me in your arms how much better you felt after the long drive here through the Rift Event?"

Though still he growled and panted in half-insane fury, evidencing the occasional thrash as he attempted to dislodge Malin from his back, Eleison the man heard my words through Eleison the beast, and both sides of him struggled to make sense of what had happened.

"You did," I reminded him, not waiting for his answer. "You were stabilized at once by my kisses, my hands. Even if your mind can't accept it, your soul knows that I am still myself, no matter how I've changed. It's still me, Eleison. I'm still me."

As his growling lowered to a miserable whine of animal heartache, I neared him enough to place a cautious hand upon his shoulder—and even as he cringed, a jerk of muscle that made me wince, I forced myself to draw closer and nodded for Malin to dismount. Still keeping hold of the sheet, he did, sliding down Eleison's back and upon his own two feet as I gently caressed the half-beast's face through the veil of the sheet.

"You see," I whispered as he produced a noise like a choke that, quickly, I realized was the man within him weeping. "You see, Eleison—it's me. I'm really still me. And if I'm still me, Eleison—"

"Then I'm still me, too," Malin said, new gentleness in his voice. "It's me, old boy—and I would never hurt you. Willingly," he thought to add with a glance over his shoulder at the wreckage of the room.

Poor Eleison's soul had no room for a sense of humor at that moment. It was too burdened with the horrific truth that overwhelmed him as, beneath my caresses, the beast yielded to the man and faded away as though I sculpted him back into a human with my own two hands. Suddenly Eleison, in the ruins of his tattered trousers, still panting for air as the sheet slid from his face, stood between us with an expression of agony.

"But," he said, his red eyes glossed with tears such as I'd never seen from him before, even at Malin's death and funeral, "you can't be. You can't be yourselves. If you're yourselves—"

I realized what he now understood a second before he said it, and felt my face fall into a mask of sorrow.

"Then my mother—"

Eleison stopped, unable to finish the words as he looked into my face and found, indeed, I was simply still myself.

"Oh, sweetheart." It was all I could say as his lips wetly trembled. Astonished, he drew back from my husband and myself, his recoil causing me heartache that paled in comparison to what I was sure he must have felt in that awful second.

Knowing Eleison's story just as well as I did, Malin looked on him with empathy. "You had to protect your brother, Eleison," Malin said gently. "You did what anyone, any terrestrial human being, would have done. You can't blame yourself for what you didn't know."

But it was clear that he did. His hand raising to his mouth as though to contain his awful grief, too stunned to truly cry, Eleison stumbled back another step before contact with the upended bureau tripped him. His step faltered so he fell back upon his haunches. Though I cried out, Eleison did not react and simply remained where he landed.

How well I could relate to Eleison's pain! For the joy of my reunion with Malin, I had not yet had the least chance to process and reconcile—indeed, to fully accept—that, without meaning to, I had traded his eternal life for my own father's mortal one. Yet whatever of my own sorrow and shame my mate's grief evoked in me was, to me, less than nothing: his pain was all, all I knew and all I could feel, and my soul ached for him. With but a brisk glance at Malin to ensure that any superficial wounds were healing with a dharmine's natural rapidity, I hurried to Eleison's side and knelt by him.

His eyes, which had been locked on some memory, turned toward me.

I did not speak: I only gathered him into my arms, drawing him to my breast with one hand folded over his bruised shoulder and the other pressing his head to my heart.

Once, twice, his shoulders jerked. But it was only as Malin knelt to touch his forearm that Eleison truly sobbed, a gut-deep heave that seemed almost like a laugh rising from him in response to his horrific shame. Whatever its resemblance, the sound was accompanied by too many trickling tears to be mistaken for anything but weeping. I petted his hair and murmured his name, kissing him, telling him through his tears, "Oh, darling—I'm sorry, I'm sorry, I love you so," as Malin shifted his grip down to hold his hand in silence.

To the great relief of my heart, Eleison let him—even tightened his grip around Malin's like a drowning man taking tight hold of his savior.

At last, as though he realized how vulnerable he had let himself be in that moment of woe, Eleison halted his tears with a sharp breath. He asked, his face still half-hidden against my heart, "If it was her—why did she try—" He couldn't speak without risking more tears, but tried again, "Why did she—" before he fell silent.

"Because she didn't remember," Malin said softly. "The dharmine awakens with one instinct, Eleison—to consume *until* it remembers. And, by and large, it does that by consuming whomever it first remembers...if not itself, then those it loved. Trust me, darling—it may not seem like it, but you did her a favor."

Sitting slowly up from me to look at Malin through an expression that resembled a glare, Eleison waited for Malin to explain himself. "As greatly as you suffer now knowing how you hurt her," Malin said, "imagine how she would have lamented her immortality when she regained her memories to find her youngest son dead in her arms. You saved her soul a terrible burden by taking on one of your own. I'm sure, wherever she is, she's grateful to you."

His chest heaving with another strangled sob, Eleison breathed himself into an emotional equilibrium that, though tentative, was at least functional enough for rational thought. Looking at me—then, with a glance at my hair, away with a wince of pain that drew his eyes to Malin's—Eleison said, "This is a lot to process."

"I think I can speak for us both when I say I understand," Malin told him, releasing his hand. "If you need some time alone to think, I'm sure we'd be happy to send you on a little sabbatical. You could—"

"No," said Eleison quickly, gladdening my heart as he said, "not without Thecla." Then, brow furrowing as if he recalled something from the contents of a dream, Eleison looked at Malin and me in turn. "Did you say—something about a child sleeping here?"

"Our son," Malin answered, gesturing between him and me. "Telemachus. You'll love him. And trust me when I say, he's been looking forward to meeting you for a long time."

Struggling to process this, Eleison asked, "A dharmine?"

"From his 'birth', in essence."

"The miscarriage," Eleison observed with a haste that far exceeded my own earlier approach to understanding. Looking at me, now, Eleison searched my face and paid special focus to my eyes. At last, his hand raised to my cheek to let his knuckles stroke along my flesh.

"You're really you." His soft words contained as much relief as sorrow.

"I swear," I told him. "And I still love you—perhaps even more than I did before."

Eleison drew my face toward his to rest his forehead against mine. His eyes shut. It were as though I could feel a new wave of tranquility wash over him—or perhaps that was only my own renewed sense of calm. Inhaling deeply, those brilliant garnet eyes opening again, Eleison drew back and looked at me.

"I guess," he said, "if you two weren't really yourselves, you would have killed me five minutes ago."

"More like ten," Malin said merrily, a little twinkle in his eye as he pointed out, "I did have your gun."

Eleison snorted in response, his eyes averting. Then, with another contemplative look at me and a brush of his thumb across the temple of my forehead, my beloved mate leaned away to push himself up to his feet.

"I think," he said in the steady tone of someone who was, at present, feeling unsteadier than they ever had in their life, "that I am going to take a shower and...think about some things for a while."

"Take your time," Malin and I said at once, resulting in a smile I had to hide and Malin didn't bother to. Having exchanged a cheerful glance with me, Malin asked our shaken cavalier, "Can I get you some wine, darling?"

"No," said Eleison, then thinking better of it, shook his head and said, "Yes—absolutely. Or whiskey?"

"Sounds fantastic. Mind if I join you?"

"It sounds like you probably should." Eleison eyed Malin with a half uncertain air before, reassured by the sight of me, he limped off in the direction of the washroom. "I think we've got a lot to talk about."

While the door shut behind him, Malin surveyed the wreckage, looked down at me, and smiled with his hands coming to rest on his hips amid a great sigh.

"Well," he said contentedly, "that went better than expected! Don't you think?"

Despite myself, I laughed. Malin smiled more easily than ever I had seen him and, laughing, himself, extended a hand to help me to my feet. Rather than letting me simply regain my balance, however, he pulled me into his arms and pressed a sensual kiss to my unready mouth. The light of pleasure illuminating my mind, I moaned, and sighed, and was just leaning up to properly engage with the kiss when Charlotte's brisk knock rapped out upon the door.

"What the *devil* has gone on in here," she hissed, looking between us with her eyes practically glowing in fury to see the state of the room. "Is this what I'll be forced to contend with every time you two are left alone together?"

While I bit back my laugh, Malin said with a roguish smile, "Well, Charlotte, you're welcome to join us and find out—I think," he added with a glance to me, eliciting a flex of my lips and a not unhappy shrug of agreement.

Our little half-joke disarming her as much as intensifying her annoyance, Charlotte kept it professional. "The boy is getting worried—I didn't think it was wise to lie to him and blame the earthquake it sounded like, since his room has remained intact."

"It was just Eleison," Malin said with good humor, releasing me to upright the bureau with an ease that excited me and slightly frightened Charlotte. "Don't worry, Charlotte, dear. Thecla?"

Glancing over at me with a fond expression, he suggested, "Why don't you go settle Telemachus's busy mind? I told him not to mind the uproar, but he is an anxious boy...I'm sure he's up in bed, fretting as we speak. Meanwhile, I'll talk to Eleison...and we can reconvene to see where we are, eh?"

With a smile and another kiss, I left my husband, sure my mate was in more than capable hands. Then, ignoring Charlotte's slightly reproachful little huff as she announced, "If it's all the same to you, I will retire for the night," I waved her off and made my way down the hall to the room whence I'd watched Malin emerged before the brawl. Sure enough, I found the boy exactly as promised: if Telemachus had not already been sitting up, he certainly sprang quickly upright when I knocked and leaned in to the darkness of his seafoam colored chamber.

"Mama," he yelped in surprise, his eyes ringed with fright, "what's happened?"

"Everything's all right, dear." Amazed at the naturalness with which I'd come to look upon this boy as my son, I left the door ajar to let the hallway's light shine in. I swept across to his bedside, where I perched to take his hand in mine. "I'm sorry about all the fuss! It seems your Uncle Eleison has arrived somewhat earlier than expected, and, well—" I affected a breezy socialite's laugh, one which I had perfected by many interactions with the courtiers. "Adults can sometimes be difficult to reason with when they think they know everything about the world."

With new understanding that smoothed somewhat his furrowed brow, the boy nodded in solemn agreement. "Oh yes," he said, "I think that's true. Papa says terrestrial people hardly stand each other when they look a little different or even dress or walk funny, so he doesn't think they have a prayer of accepting us."

"Maybe not at first," I agreed, smiling at how soft this child's hand was in mine, and feeling a distinct pain of nostalgia for my

470

own distant youth. "I suspect it will take a very long time for most people to accept what we are, and what we represent, and what it might mean for them—some of them, anyway. But we must do our best to be patient. They've been lied to for so long…they really can't help it. The truth will seem very scary, indeed."

"I'm sure that it will," Telemachus said very grimly.

"But the good news," I told him with a pat of that hand, "is that Papa is perfectly fine, and Uncle Eleison is only a bit bruised, and the two of them have agreed to have a conversation that will help Eleison understand he has nothing to be afraid of."

"Do you think Uncle Eleison will be a dharmine someday," the boy asked, peering up at me through the slightly illuminated dark with very real interest. The thought not having yet crossed my mind, I let my lower lip protrude in a pout of contemplation.

"Hm! Interesting question. Well—I suppose I don't rightly know." Spreading my hands in admission of my own ignorance, I went on, "I suspect that will be up to Eleison, at least in part. It seems to me, after all, that altered people live really a very long time, perhaps even forever—they haven't existed long enough yet for us to know for sure."

"But they can still die in accidents and things, can't they?"

A frown crossed my lips. "I suppose they can," I agreed after a second of contemplation. "Yes. But, well—let's not worry about that yet, shall we? Such matters are concerns for the future, hopefully *far* in the future—and I'm quite sure that, by the time they become relevant, Uncle Eleison will see the value in embracing eternal life to remain a happy family with us. He's a smart man. Just like you're a smart boy!"

After sharing a smile with the lad whose hair I ruffled, I noted the book upon the bedside table and took it up with a smile. Amazing! Even with so little light, I could read as clearly as though it were noon. Pleased by this small perk of my new nature, I suggested to my son, "Why don't I read to you a while, until you start feeling sleepy; then, in the morning, you can meet Uncle Eleison, and we can all set out on the road back home to Karrisregion!"

"All right," Telemachus enthused, letting me snuggle him back down under the covers and making no protest as I sat against the headboard by his side. Indeed, while I picked up the book where he left off, the boy shyly leaned his head against my hip, the plume of my dress's fabric a preferable pillow to him in that instant. Intent on enjoying consciousness with his long-lost mother for as great a length as he could, the boy clung to wakefulness through quite a few—in my estimate—rather dull passages that formed exposition to more intriguing parts of the novel; but it wasn't long before, a charming purr of kittenish love rising from his heart, his breathing (purely to scent me, I was soon to realize, for I did not yet note I myself had no use of breathing but that and speech) soon devolved into a light sequence of easygoing snores. Quietly as I could, I shut the book and replaced it on the bedside table, then gently eased him back into his intended pillow. He stirred only a little, his eyelids twitching but failing to open.

"Night," said the child, his face slack and already half-turned away.

"Good night, darling," I said, pausing to stroke his hair and then, with only the slightest of hesitance lest I seem overbearing, adding, "I love you."

"I love you, too," he murmured as, in smiling delight, I slipped from the room to shut the door and leave him dreaming, safe and sound.

A S MIGHT WELL BE IMAGINED, given the state in which it was left, I found the bedroom empty—but, noting the shutter of the back door had been raised, I stepped into the vibrant purple night to find Malin and Eleison seated together on the poolside divan. Their body language relieved me; aside from Eleison's willingness to sit by Malin at all, both men had adopted a similar posture and, at the time of my discovery, both leaned forward, their heads close together as they conversed softly in the night. Hearing me, it was Eleison who looked up first; he regarded me with an expression that remained yet a little grave, but which grew tender as I bent to kiss his face and took the liberty of sitting in his lap.

"Hey," he said, folding my hand in his and sighing with a kind of sorrow. "Baby...your hands are so cold now. What am I supposed to do with you?"

Genuine anxiety heavy in my heart, I told him, "The same things you always do, I hope. I'm sorry if you find me less attractive for it now, but—"

"What? No, of course not—it's not that at all. It's kind of intriguing, actually." Watching his own thumb stroke back and forth along the back of my hand, my mate looked up at me with pensive eyes. "I just wish you would have told me," he said, adding with a brisk glance at Malin, "both of you."

"I recall it crossed my mind a few times," Malin said, peering out through the violet haze that obscured the yard and made the distant howls of Rift beasts all the more uncanny. "But I refrained for the same reasons Thecla refrained from telling you why she was coming here. Think of it, Eleison, darling...if I had told you that despite your best efforts to protect me, you would someday watch me die and then be among the first witnesses of my household to see me return as a dharmine, how sleepless you would be! How exhausted and anxious you would have been for the years you spent in my service. Joyless. And the better you loved me, the worse it would have been for you. So it was better to keep it from you...although I'm sorry for the pain all this caused you."

Nodding, his attention still on Malin, my mate asked, "Did you know about the motorcade before? I mean—did you know for sure that would be when it happened?"

"Hm...it was a long time ago now from my view of things, but yes, I recall being quite certain. I told myself a little bit—not enough that I could have gone and ruined things had I gotten the urge, but enough that I would be able to prepare for the day in question. When I was ready to see true movement on the Rift energy project, I would be a dead man; that was what I revealed, and no more."

What a sacrifice it must have been for him to make the decision to fund Horizon! I had never realized. My heart ached. I slid my free hand into Malin's left, gazing into his gorgeous dark eyes and recalling how I had found him praying before we were to leave for the motorcade. "I'm sure knowing even that drove you mad enough."

"Yes, well, I didn't believe myself at first—who could? But"—Malin spread his hands—"it became more and more obvious as the day approached. Especially once I met you."

An almost bashful flush crossing my cheeks, I laughed. "You told yourself about *me*?"

"Only abstractly...only to warn myself that if I didn't wind down my hedonistic ways, the love of my life would never be able to accept me well enough to be corrupted by me."

Snorting lightly, Eleison took a swallow of the whiskey in his glass, then leaned past me to set it on the low table before us. "You're nothing if not honest. Thecla..."

Both hands free now, Eleison caught my face and stared into my soul. "Promise you'll never do anything like this again. Please—both of you. I don't want to be left in the dark anymore."

"We both promise." His great hand fitting to Eleison's shoulder, my husband said from the very bottom of his heart, "Thecla has been a victim of this just as you have—this need for my secrets to be kept has maintained a barrier between us all. But it's gone now, Eleison. From now on, all that needs to be protected is our family. All our secrets can be shared amongst ourselves; let's hold back nothing."

With an uneasy nod that grew steadier to see the intensity of my gaze, Eleison said. "All right. Let's all start fresh."

"Please," I said, "yes."

"I still wish I could have been here," my mate added in a mutter while I wove my arms around his neck and pressed closely to his heart.

"Seeing her ill would have killed you, Eleison," Malin told him. "It nearly killed *me*, and I was fairly certain of how things would hash out. Ah—"

With a dark chuckle and a distant glance away, my husband murmured, "This is the first time in so long that I have found myself operating without knowledge of the future—now no presentiment of fate can give me comfort, and all is entirely uncertain. It's freeing in so many ways...I feel as if I've spent the past decade confined to a casket, and now I can once more move about."

"That's just the time you spent living underground in that maze of yours," I teased, then finding myself given pause.

There *was* still something I was not speaking of—something neither of the men knew. And that was that *I* had some presentiment of fate—some strange understanding that sat on the very tip of my tongue yet could not be spoken aloud, because it was but a vague shape of itself. The themes of a forgotten dream left to nag endlessly at my consciousness until it was recalled.

With a shudder, I looked between the men. "Since we're to keep nothing from one another, I had ought to open my heart on this matter as completely as I can. When Ba'al-Dinon helped me to see the threads of my Weaving, I realized—no, I *remembered* somehow—that he is not just some servant or slave or object of use to me. I think I'm in love with him"—while Eleison's nostrils flared with a slight jealous breath that indicated more annoyed confirmation than surprise, Malin listened with keen interest that grew only keener by the second—"and, moreover, that I've been in love with him—*before*, somehow. Whenever 'before' was."

"What do you mean, darling," Malin asked with great interest, leaving me speechless as I strained to articulate my thoughts on the subject.

"I—I can't explain it. He's always teasing me about time and eternity when he's alone with me. I never really understand what he means, but—" My lips pursed, I told the men, "I believe this has happened before, this life. Our lives. Many times before. Goodness, well—"

Looking pointedly at my husband, who had existed concurrently with his own mortal consciousness, I observed, "It *must* have happened before."

"Yes," said Malin with a deeply contemplative tone, his eyes drifting off as though in pursuit of clouds through the sky of thought. "It must have. Such things have crossed my mind in passing before, of course, but...perhaps I did not fully think through all the implications—nor want to, until now."

His eyes narrowing as he tried to absorb this with far less preparation than either of us, Eleison observed, "You were just telling me you don't think Dinon is actually a dharmine, Thecla... so what do you think he is?"

I shook my head. "I don't know. But he's—it's cruel." My jaw tightening, I glanced away, off into the Rift radiation encompassing us, feeling his interdimensional eyes upon me even though I was not sure if they watched me from without or from within. The emotion was more than I had expected, and I struggled to keep it contained as I said darkly, "The instant I realized I loved him, he stole away from me—perhaps in my death your contract with him was broken, Malin."

"Or it never was, and he was only ever interested in being close to you."

"That has crossed my mind," I confessed. "But, either way—I still feel him in me, speaking to me, looking through me. And one of the last things he told me is that, if he remains with me, I might remember what he is too soon. He thinks I'll be afraid of him... but how funny to say 'remember', as if I have ever known in my life him, or my love of him, or what he is! As if I have ever known our futures."

"Anamnesis," said Malin. "The unfolding of all Time is but a recollection of our destiny. Isn't that what you once told me, Thecla?" His eyes piercing deeply into mine, my husband said on, "Sometimes you wonder if you are not Thecla, but rather someone remembering Thecla. Thecla remembering herself, perhaps, but either way—such notions hint the viewpoint of the self may well be rooted in the future."

"This is way too much for me," said Eleison, who got along with Charlotte as well as he did owing to their similarly practical worldviews. As my husband and I chuckled together, Eleison rubbed his brow and said, "I haven't had thoughts like these since the first time I smoked mithrae flowers. Ah, shit—that reminds me—"

Hand dropping to look between us seriously, he said, "The reason I came here, Thecla—aside from the bad feeling I was apparently right to have—is that the Overseer went on ahead to the Karris house to try and speak with you."

While Malin produced a dark snort, I said to Eleison, "Then she's already *there*!"

"Seems like it...and she knows you're not. I'd expect your pocket watch to be ringing off the hook when the weather clears up."

"What liberties that woman takes..." Irritated, I ran my hand along my forehead. "No doubt she's eager to prove me weak and irresponsible...not that I haven't been."

With a tut, Malin patted my hand. "You've been in mourning, my angel. Don't let Parvati alter your perception of yourself...I think all three of us can agree she is insufferable, and only capable of forming opinions that align with her pre-existing political viewpoints."

His hand still on mine, thumb and forefinger gently massaging my joints one knuckle at a time, Malin regarded me with a leonine purr of contemplation slowly rolling from his chest like a distant thunderstorm. The sound thrilled my body and heart so that I hardly heard Eleison's breath hitch.

"But you know, my love...my darling...my delight...this is a unique opportunity for us. When was the last time, after all, that Parvati visited Gudrune? Quite some time before you were born, if memory serves; perhaps even before your mother's separation from me."

You could have heard the soft tap of a rodi's feet as it caught hold of the eave to perch and rest its wings awhile. "She does seem quite frightened of you," I observed, trying not to take too much pleasure in the notion.

"And now that she thinks I am dead, no doubt she is deeply relieved, and eager to shape Gudrune into alignment with her vision for the rest of the continent. Did you happen to invite the other territory masters to the wake, as well?"

"I invited *only* them," I said in irritation. "Parvati invited herself."

With a chuckle for my stubbornness, Malin rolled my fingers into a fist he held between both his hands, glancing away from me only as Eleison said, "That reminds me—we got RSVPs from everybody except Alberik and Elita."

"Excellent news...Elita will respond soon, surely, even if only for fear of offending Aleister and his entire duchy with him. Mm..."

Malin's dark eyes drifted off, trailing past our faces and out to the distance where they stared and nothing external. "Your face," I told him after a moment of silent admiration, "is as a dark mirror, my husband, reflecting my own thoughts but veiling all yours with strange obscurity."

"Well...one doesn't wish to say such things aloud and in so doing evoke ill fortune...but it just occurred to me if—God forbid—something were to happen to the Overseer during her visit to Gudrune...who, who could say *what* truly happened, with so great a many ambitious territories represented in one house?"

While my brain prickled with an intrigue that worked its way down my spine and excited even my flesh with its promises, I added, "And the head of Gudrune's old Hunter's Guild, Winston, succeeded in extricating an invitation from me—"

"Did he, now?"

"Oh, yes. Though it's apparent enough to me that the Guild has far more in common with Parvati than it has differences, I can't help but suggest I would be personally very suspicious of them were she to be met with an unhappy fate so soon after you did."

"So soon after I almost did," Malin said with a wink.

"Of course—such an excellent job was done in restoring your handsome visage, my husband! We shall have to handsomely reward your plastic surgeon when you're able to come out of recovery."

While we laughed softly together, Eleison looked between us with considerably less mirth—but no resistance. "It's strange to see how much you've both changed," he observed.

"No, darling," I told him, turning to brush my lips along his cheek and toward his ear. "We're just being honest now."

"How true, my lovely wife...honest for the first time, with one another and with you, Eleison. Surely *you* would have no objections to seeing Parvati killed, given how she humiliated our Thecla in Valquist."

A growl of his borro rumbling through the Adam's apple I softly kissed my way along, Eleison said, "I'd slit her throat myself if she were anything less than the Overseer of the continent...but you two are suggesting something—very serious."

Suddenly thrust into the role of Reason, Eleison studied us for a few long seconds. "There are going to be consequences," he said at last, unknowingly evoking Dinon's most recent refrain before going on. "Political, social, maybe even geographical."

"One can only hope." Malin leaned from the sofa to pour himself a finger of whiskey, then added a splash to Eleison's glass. Sitting up to raise his own in a silent cheers while passing over Eleison's, Malin regarded the amber liquid and said, "I've always thought it a pity that the territories are so disjointed—so frequently at odds in policy and practice. Amazing, how Parvati has never been able to inspire them into harmony...granted, it is quite a *large* continent, but it seems to me a sufficiently strong leader—perhaps with a sufficiently strong partner—should easily manage to keep the interests of the territory in check."

As my mind thudded with thrill, a predator's excitement rising in my breast and flooding through all my limbs, I nodded eagerly. "Yes, my husband, too true. Perhaps what holds Parvati back in that regard is her stubborn hold to conservative values— the idea of a pure continent, a pure world, where altered and Riftborn humans are consigned to the social sidelines...it's just outmoded, isn't it? The more she resists broader acceptance, the more the territories will alternately buck her control or show the same stagnation demonstrated by Valquist and its neighbors."

"I'm so glad you understand me, Thecla." Malin emitted a sublime sigh to caress my cheek with the knuckles of his hand. "Besides...well, since we're being honest, I must admit—after twelve years of fatherhood alone in a dark maze, I feel rather restless. And it has been such a long time since I've indulged my favorite game."

Extending that hand, Malin snapped his fingers as I asked, "What game is that?"

The question was barely out before a shriek rose from the sky, so shrill and sharp in my sensitive ears I cringed back against Eleison in a lifelong instinct of fear for Rift beasts. Alert, himself, Eleison sat up and seemed poised to push me in the direction of the door back to the house.

We only relaxed when the harpros which had shrieked swept down: not to attack but to balance perfectly upon Malin's forearm amid a great flapping of wings and a sharp flash of silver eyes upon all three of us in turn.

"War, of course," said Malin, smiling fondly at the bird. "And do you know what I love most about it, my darlings?"

As I shook my head and Eleison humored him by asking, "What's that," Malin turned that smile upon both of us.

"I always win."

PART III

THE NEXT MORNING, we set out as a family to Karrisregion, with Charlotte remaining behind a day to shut down the house and tend to details that could incriminate us and cause greater gossip should the family of the vineyard uncover them. "I'm going to miss Pauline," Telemachus lamented as we prepared to set out. "And she'll miss me, too—she doesn't have anyone else to play with, really."

"Well, I'm sure we'll come back all the time." I spoke fondly while fixing the collar of his shirt the way Charlotte was always fiddling with the little details of my clothing. "Once a year, at least—ah, look, here's Eleison!"

My soul breathed a sigh of relief to see him loping out with the same energy as ever, looking a little tired and a little annoyed in a good-humored way to be roused so early in the morning. Malin and I invited him to bed with us, but he had politely requested more time to process—and to rest, seeing as he had just traveled in and was set to travel back out with us the very next day. We obliged him, happy enough to spend time alone, but I nursed secret worries that we had been set back more than a year in terms of intimacy. Thank goodness, that did not seem to be the case. His hand slid around my waist and he kissed me the same as ever, even embracing Malin with a few extra seconds and an expression of relief only I was able to notice. Sighing and patting him on the back of the shoulder, Eleison then turned to regard the child.

"And this must be—Telemachus, right? Nice to meet you, kid." Offering one hand to shake while using the other to ruffle the boy's hair, Eleison smiled at his protests and glanced up at me with an amused twinkle in his eye. "He really looks a lot like you, huh...how's it feel to have a second child?"

"Goodness, I barely know yet. But I suspect we'll get on well, won't we, Telemachus, darling." At my smile and nudge of his cheek, Telly nodded with excitement.

"Yes, Mama! Uncle Eleison, Mama said you'll teach me shooting. Will you, really?"

Looking impressed I had volunteered such an idea, Eleison shrugged and said, "Sure, if it's okay with your parents. I'll teach you how to fight and gamble and get the ladies to follow you around, too, when you're older."

Looking interested at this little wisecrack, Telemachus nodded before I tittered and urged him into the auto-carriage. "Let's stick with the present, shall we...so far as I'm concerned, you're growing up fast enough already..."

In the car on the way to Karris, I sat in joy beside my husband, our hands intertwined, while the boy sat beside his uncle across from us and proceeded to interrogate him as he'd interrogated

Charlotte and then me. I watched with fondness for a time, then glanced over at Malin with a whisper.

"How are we to explain him," I asked into his ear while Telemachus was distracted hearing about the time Eleison rescued Glenn from an oris at the Torea Festival. "To the public, I mean."

"Hm..." Turning to brush his mouth across my cheekbone and hair amid the confabulating workings of his mind, Malin softly fictionalized, "Why, my little peasant girl, don't you remember how we met? In Lescaut, when I traveled through on business, and my eye fell upon the loveliest maiden I had ever beheld in all Gudrune."

With a deep blush at his improvisation to explain away the advanced age of his hitherto unknown heir, I whispered, "I would have been—at absolute *best*—seventeen, you rogue!"

"Why do you suppose we had to hide him for so long?" With a chuckle, his arm draping around me while his eyes glittered with a combination of mirth and pleasure at my embarrassment, Malin added, "Besides, this little fib would at last provide a sufficient public explanation for our relationship...you know people are always dying of curiosity about how we know one another."

That was true, I supposed. When he put it that way, it seemed better that Gudrune—and the continent at large—should see me as the victim of Malin's seduction who ascended into his favor by providing him an heir, rather than his former ward and the daughter of his dead wife. Though it may have been the case we did not set eyes upon one another until I was in my early twenties, I worried often for Malin's reputation as went the matter of my heritage, and I occasionally grew nervous that it might come out if people asked themselves too critically just why a man of Malin's stature had come to know a girl from Lescaut in the first place.

However...a racy story like the one of his concoction could content people with what they thought was the truth, keeping them from digging much deeper.

"Very well, you cad," I said with undisguised delight, smiling up into his dark eyes with impatient desire in mine. "I suppose, given Rigel's fate, it's fair enough now to say both Telemachus and *you* were born in Lescaut...so it's only a quarter of a lie, from that perspective..."

My smile fell at the still unreconciled bargain I had never known myself to make. Sensing well my twinge of conscience, Malin rested his brow against mine. "I'm sorry," he said without elaboration, looking intrigued when I shook my head in response.

"Don't be," I told him. "Please. I would make that trade a thousand times, one hundred thousand times, if it meant having you once."

Lips curling into a soft expression of pleased wonder, Malin caught my chin in his hand and tipped my head back for his kiss. As I sighed into my husband's mouth, our child produced a little scoff.

"They're always smooching," he criticized to Eleison, who laughed.

"Yeah, well, they haven't seen each other in a long time. You'll probably have somebody you want to smooch all the time someday...say, what's that behind your ear?"

As Eleison distracted the boy with a gold coin he pulled seemingly out of thin air, inciting many enthusiastic exclamations and pleas that Telemachus be taught this trick, Malin and I drew apart with a mutual laugh. He tucked me closely against his heart, his mouth coming to rest with several lingering kisses atop my head.

"I have missed you," he sighed, his arms tight around me. "More than I missed theatre, or freedom, or Gudrune, Thecla…I've just missed you."

How Malin's love made my heart sing! It was like the sun itself, that love: a brilliant glowing orb in the black tapestry of space, its light pouring through a void where all number of frightful mysteries passed by, unknown to Man. Even as his mind turned over and over with political machinations I never could have thought to devise, he was a man of pure devotion—perhaps all the purer for its contrast with his strategizing mind. To witness him interacting with Telemachus was a source of endless delight for me; as the boy peered out the window, farther from his childhood home than he had ever been in his own memory, Malin explained every feature of the landscape about which the boy inquired. He pointed through the malingering violet atmosphere to indicate cows being guarded in their pasture by a farmer and his dogs, then some time later let the lad have his watch awhile to check the weather and study the news when the device was capable of better service.

"Now—when we've reached Uncle Eleison's estate"—Malin opened his explanation as we were near enough, and I felt the twinkling of anticipation one enjoys when in the embrace of familiar landmarks—"Papa will take you in through a back way, but we must wait in the car a time, first. Eleison will park us in the carriage house and, when I decide it's safe, I'll show you how we can reach the master apartment."

Eleison arched his brow. "There's a secret entrance?"

"Are you surprised," I asked him, eliciting a shrug. Malin, meanwhile, chuckled in agreement.

"Come now, old boy…you thought I maintain that hedge maze for aesthetics? Think of the orchard we could be growing…

but I always figured it would be better to maintain something that could give me a fighting chance to flee if ever I needed to leave the house unexpectedly some night."

"You're going to have to write a list of secret entrances and compartments for me," said Eleison with a wry look and a shake of his head.

"If I can remember all of them," Malin replied, "I'd be glad to."

As happy as we most assuredly all were to be together, there was no question that fresh tension descended upon the car when, through the plum veil of the Rift, the Karris house took on form as though from nothing. I inhaled, seeing it newly as what it was: the site of a great turning point in history, and in all our lives. What my husband and I had discussed in detail with Eleison would be no easy task, but it would be greatly simplified by the illusion that Malin was dead. I would need to rely on all my charms to navigate us through the next few days, until all were accounted for at the wake and the deed could be done to great subsequent confusion. I would need, most of all, to act normal: and though the idea of having to invoke my terrestrial normalcy when I could already feel how much my immortal heart had changed was quite intimidating, I was sure I could do it. I just had to look at it critically and do as would be expected of me: had to circulate with courtiers, had to prepare for the wake, had to mourn Glenn's absence without letting on he had fled—

Had to weave, I realized, a surge of inspiration rushing through my body to the very tips of my fingers.

Yes, indeed—my darling Dinon was right. There was something magical in the threads of my weaving, even without the integration of those eternal strands I plucked from the aether of the world. And with their addition...who knew what kinds of marvelous events my tapestries could herald?

As I mused on this, Eleison and Malin switched seats. With a kiss atop Telemachus's head, my husband pulled the windows down so we were all left quite blind to our surroundings. It was therefore no small surprise when, as the carriage rolled to a stop before the house and Eleison hastened to get the door lest someone should do it for us, we discovered ourselves surrounded by the besuited security personnel of the Overseer—with Parvati herself standing atop the stairs to the front entrance of the house, smiling in the violet radiation with such a beneficent sociability she appeared for all the world to be the very owner of the estate.

"Matrix Farrow," she called, adding, "And Eleison," even as my mate dismissed her with a nod while mounting the driver's seat to park the carriage as agreed. "It's so good to finally see you," Parvati said, extending her hands to me and taking me in to kiss my cheeks in a generous show of noblisse oblige, ignoring everything from our deeply unpleasant final interaction in Valquist to the way I had unflinchingly ignored her every request (that was, command) to speak with her after Malin's death. When she drew back with her eyes flashing first to my hair's white streaks, then, by way of rapid-fire confirmation, to my unblemished throat, she said with a little gasp, "Oh, Thecla—"

"I have been under a great deal of pressure beneath the weight of this grief, Parvati," I said, assuming a brave but tired smile. "You shall have to forgive me for my negligence. I've longed for the energy to contact you but have hardly mustered strength enough to get out of bed—it's so nice you were able to come to Malin's wake all the same, without my having needed to invite you."

"I wouldn't miss it for the world," she said, her smile unflagging as she elegantly rejoined my passive aggression with some of her own. "But your *hair*, Thecla—are you sure it's not—?"

She dared not finish her sentence, lest she sound too hopeful. Marveling at my own thoughts and how they had taken such an especially hostile turn toward Parvati—whether or not she deserved it—I allowed her to guide me into the broad foyer of Eleison's house, busier than ever with the comings and goings of far more staff members than just ours. "Quite sure." My sensitive perception calculated by the clamor of this and more distant wings that over half our guests had already arrived, the usual group of clinging courtiers now accessorized by dukes, counts, and territory masters all foreign to my association. Drawing the hem of my gown a little higher to scrape my shoes, I led the way through the flowing crowd that parted for us while I assured Parvati, "It began to come in the day after the—attack, and has spread with quite a shocking pace since. Luckily, I think it's slowed by now...I may have some time yet before I'm as silvered as you."

"Silvered, or snowed," she remarked, eying me with great interest as she walked alongside me up the stairs. "It really is *bright* white—as white as blood-poisoning."

"I know it is—but hasn't my blood been poisoned, even if only by sorrow?" Rather enjoying this chance to play up my mourning now that the need for it had passed, I endeavored to look very solemn. "My heart is so heavy, Parvati. I've heard it said it's better to have loved and lost than never to have loved at all, but when I think of what was given to me and then so cruelly wrest from my grasp—oh, I can't help but pine for the simple life I had back in Lescaut."

Now her sympathy was more genuine, however briefly that twitch of eyes and mouth softened her. "I'm sorry, Thecla," she said. "I know you loved him. That's something I've always seen about you—something about you I've never doubted for a second."

"Yes, well...I have my darling Eleison, who obviously loved Malin enough to host this wake, but having two loves does nothing to ease the blow of losing one."

The same could be said of three, I mused, or four. Oh, Glenn! My Dinon, too. Would there never come a time when all four of the men I loved could settle themselves equally in the vault of my heart?

There will, Thecla.

While I forgot myself and cast a flick of my eyes in the direction of my left hemisphere, half-expecting Ba'al-Dinon to be walking with me in his footman's guise for as clearly and completely as I'd heard him, Parvati was in the midst of saying, "—Speaking of Eleison, he was there to greet us in Saalast, but I must have misunderstood him. I thought for some reason he had said you were already down here in Karris, so I and my staff came on ahead. But you weren't here?"

"Mm," I lied, "no—I tried, but it was much too familiar. Instead, I wound up visiting my relatives back in Lescaut for a few days, then returning to the villa where Malin and I honeymooned in search of a little closure."

"Did you find it?"

"I concluded that true closure will only come when my husband's killer has been identified and prosecuted to the fullest extent of Gudrune's laws. Indeed, how can I rest when my own life is threatened by some unknown conspiracy?"

"It is very difficult to lead a country with such an axe hanging over one's neck," Parvati observed as, having led her to my workroom, I opened the door and strode within. Casting a half-interested eye upon the vast collection of threads with which Malin had furnished me, she added, "Especially for someone with no political experience."

"I wouldn't say *no* political experience. Given how much time I've spent shadowing Malin this past year in particular, I feel I've already been Matrix for some time."

"Perhaps you do feel that way...but, Thecla—and I hate to sound harsh when I can see that you're suffering—"

Parvati at least had the decency to shut the door after us, her orange gown whispering around her as she leaned back against the jamb with her arms crossed.

"—you haven't exactly been acting that way, from what I understand."

"You're quite right." I affected a wretched sigh and tamped down my very real offense by reminding myself that in this, Parvati had a valid point. "I have not coped well with my sudden grief and all it has implied, and I've been relying in these past weeks on the momentum of my husband's final policy decisions. However... there's no denying that momentum has run its course and we are in need of a new push. Perhaps"—from the drawing table along the far wall, I plucked a sheet of paper and a charcoal pencil—"some new ambitions, entirely."

"Well...I'm glad to hear you're taking your responsibilities more seriously, Thecla."

She was so comfortable with me! Oblivious to how easily I could have snapped her neck right there, with her security personnel nowhere to be seen, Parvati made her way to my side to watch as I rapidly sketched the rough template of the tapestry that had come into my mind upon seeing the Karris house. "I don't mean to put extra pressure on you," she said, watching my hand and only occasionally glancing up into my face, "but the other territory masters of the continent have been eager to know my decision about Gudrune's inheritance. It's going to need a permanent leader soon, and—"

"And you are worried that my husband made the wrong decision by appointing me?"

"I wouldn't say *that*. I just wonder if you're more focused on protecting Malin's legacy than you are in leading Gudrune into civilization with the rest of the territories. For instance—and I understand this may be a sensitive subject, given it's so intimately tied with your husband's death—but Horizon Energy—"

"Horizon needs my support now more than ever," I told her, my pencil pausing in my rough illustration of the trees to frame the scene of the tapestry. "Look outside, Parvati—this Rift Event has been going on, goodness, three, four days now? I've lost track"—really, I had, my own death having muddled my sense of time for the past week or so—"and I can tell you based on the previous ones I've witnessed that Gudrune's infrastructure requires improvement if we're to survive these severe episodes without undue suffering to the people. I'm quite sure the same could be said of the other territories...perhaps the day will come when they'll thank us for what we've given them."

"Thecla—" Her jaw tight with annoyance, Parvati leaned against my desk to attract my attention back from the work I'd resumed. "Surely now you can admit the dangers of experimenting with the Rift outweigh any possible benefit we could gain from fooling with it."

How close I came to laughing in her face! How my blood boiled with ever-increasing distaste for her, Parvati, who truly thought of nothing but how her interests might be served. She was my husband's opposite in all ways: his love always real, hers always false; his reputation fearsome in spite of his heartfelt love of Gudrune and its people, hers undeservedly adored even as she schemed and grasped at power she had in no way come to merit.

"Surely you can see," I told her cooly, glancing over into her face and judging by the surprise there that my expression was now very hard, indeed, "that even after all these centuries, we still have no idea exactly *what* the Rift is, let alone how we can take full advantage of it." The brilliant amethyst sky glittered in my soul, my memory of Dinon's perfect face bending to capture me in tender kisses as I lowered my gaze and spoke to the figure of Parvati I lightly sketched in the center of my template. "Besides—perhaps if I'm the one who brings our energy research to fruition, you can accept more comfortably the notion that nothing malicious lies behind it. I'm no military strategist, hoping to make use of the Rift to supplement my skill in war...I'm just some woman from Lescaut."

"So it would seem."

The Overseer assessed me with dissatisfaction to find I was by no means the uncertain and naive girl she'd been able to bully in Valquist. With another glance at my in-progress template, too early in its development for her to parse, she stepped back and said, "Well, we can discuss all this more later. I can see you're eager to get settled back into the swing of your routine. Weaving takes up much of your time, I'm sure."

"Not really...just something I do to unwind from a long trip—or distract myself from an unpleasant conversation."

A little smirk crossed her lips, her amusement patronizing even now. "I'm sure it's difficult to think you might not be suited to the role your husband wished for you...but you know, it wouldn't be so bad if I decided to remove you from the position of Matrix. After all..."

Opening the door, always eager to get the last word, Parvati slipped out to the hall while saying, "You did just lament to me how you missed your days in Lescaut."

My workroom door clicked shut after her, leaving me alone with the thoughts she had thrust upon me. Or, rather, the thoughts she had thrust upon the human shadow within me—the shadow she still, thankfully, saw upon my face.

Really, everything she had said was irrelevant. She had no idea who I was; had no idea of Malin's condition; had no idea of what Fate and my husband's ambitions had in store for her.

All the same...I marveled at how hot my blood had run with rage. Parvati truly had a way of plucking at one's nerves. She loved identifying the most vulnerable regions of the soul and picking them open like a fingernail picking at a scab, exposing a million little sensitivities to the air and waiting for one of them to become infected.

Yet, for as annoyed as I was, it was so much easier to calm myself now. I felt a great deal more in control of my emotions than ever before. Either for having lost and then regained my husband, or for being a mother twice over, or for the new condition of my dharmine's body—but no matter the cause, I tucked all my thoughts away into the lines of the template I shaped, the figures I arranged with deliberate care. Then, speeding through my calculations for the threads, I satisfied myself the first step was done and left my workroom with the snapping off of its electric light. Gladder than ever to be back in the estate I most regarded as home, I drew my fingertips along the wainscoting of the hall and meandered to the west wing, taking stock of the servants whom I passed—and pausing as I noted one of them flirting, more or less consensually, with a highly identifiable head of blond hair.

"Aleister," I called, biting back a laugh at the visible tensing of his shoulders with a repressed sigh of annoyance. No matter how irritated he was by my interruption, however, when he turned back to face me, the Duke Montagne wore an elegant smile of sociable welcome.

"Thecla! Darling. I was starting to worry you wouldn't be back for the wake. Half the guests are here already."

"So I've noticed—yet hardly a decoration to be seen! I'll have to speak with Kyrie about that..." Slipping my arm through Aleister's, I guided him to the west wing while he eyed me with new interest. "Do you like my hair," I asked him, patting my coiffure while he attempted to avert his eyes down to mine.

"Mm? Oh, yes, your *hair*. Very *striking*, isn't it? Did you bleach it for that effect? It's so white one would almost think a dharmine had come upon you while you were off in Lescaut or wherever it was...you *did* visit Lescaut, didn't you?"

What a wily little gossip. Not a second went by that Aleister wasn't snooping around, collecting information that could be of any use in improving his status with the other courtiers. Well...I would give him all the information he could handle.

"I did indeed," I told him, beaming. "My sister is with child—married! In that order." While my voice dropped with a conspirator's stage-whisper, Aleister tittered lightly. "Not that I'm one to judge on that account...goodness knows, our dear Malin did his level best to have me in his bed as many nights as possible before the wedding."

Aleister chuckled in wry understanding, the sound of his voice tinged with that unnatural melancholy. "Oh, that old devil... it's awful. I keep expecting to meet with him in these halls—keep waiting to hear his voice, demanding to know why I've not yet been to a luncheon with you both."

As I opened the door to Eleison's apartment and stepped in to the sound of casual male banter, Aleister was in the middle of saying, "Keep thinking I'll come around the corner and there he'll be, just—"

Aleister looked up toward the sound of laughter, frozen by the voice of my child calling, "Mama! The hedge maze is so pretty, have you solved it yet? I like this place much more than our old house."

Slowly draining of all his color, the Duke Montagne looked again at my hair, then at the door I shut behind us with a happy smile; then, at last, at Malin, who crossed smoothly over with a drink already in his hand.

"Aleister, darling," he said, bending to kiss the duke's cheek, "you look dizzy! Are you quite all right?"

"I...I..."

With a look between all of us that settled, at last, on curious Telemachus, who stood in the parlor somewhere between us and Eleison, Aleister peered into his drink, threw back its contents in one fast gulp, and said with a woozy flutter to his voice, "I think I had better sit down for a moment...or twenty."

"**S**OMEHOW," ALEISTER SAID, still sounding a bit lightheaded after we explained our intentions to him, "it doesn't seem like a good sign for me that you've decided to tell me all this."

Malin, who had made himself comfortable in his preferred armchair with the expression of a tomcat who had been out roving the country and at last wandered home to find everything just where he'd left it, chuckled at Aleister. "On the contrary. It could be a very good thing for you, old boy. Look at it this way—I'm giving you a chance to decide how to react, instead of putting you on the spot. You're even being given the opportunity to be part of the game...and make a preemptive decision."

While Telemachus—who had snuggled into the couch under my left arm while Eleison sat closely to my right—watched the conversation with the keen interest of a future territory master taking mental notes, Aleister loosened his tie just slightly. "What are my *choices*, exactly? Stick around and look complicit because everyone knows you're my mentor, or—"

"Or," said Malin, "flee with Kalypso tonight and look like you were not only warned, but too cowardly to stand by us against the threat—thereby earning Elita's ire, to say the least."

"Some choice." Smoothing his hand over his brow, he then worked his well-manicured thumb against the tip of his index finger and drifted momentarily off into thought. "Say I do stay and offer you support," he began. "What are the odds that things will devolve into immediate bloodshed?"

"That depends on how the rest of the operation proceeds—but, considering the current shape of things, I would say those odds are quite low."

"What cause would anyone here have to shed blood"—I spread my hands and earned a glance from the duke—"if due process must be relied upon, and an investigation must be completed? Why, I would venture a guess that by the time it's even *begun*, most of the territory masters will have fled back to their own estates to avoid the possibility of similar fates."

"Just so." Malin nodded. "All you need do, Aleister, is remain here and support Thecla, and to help her be brave and confused. When everyone else has gone back, and you've returned to Montagne—"

"Say," said Aleister wisely, "I don't think it's intelligent to return to Montagne without an Overseer safely installed in Valquist. May I stay here?"

"As long as you like, of course. Thecla? Do I speak for both of us?"

"Oh, of course. Especially if you may still persuade your duchy to our line of thinking, and pull strings enough to convince Elita that serving us is service to their own best interests."

"That's a taller order," said Aleister with a slow, careful nod, "but I'll see what I can do. Now, to be clear...there's no chance of me getting the old—"

For lack of a clearer term, he pointed to his jugular vein with a nervous glance at Malin's mouth. Chuckling slightly, my husband assured him, "Afraid not, darling...I'm a married man."

"By God, but you really *are* still the same Malin...this is all—really quite a lot to take in."

"That's why I appreciate how seriously I can see you're already taking this, and why I hope you know how touched I am that you would treat my home as a safe haven even now."

"Not as though the alternatives are any good. Besides..." With a little drum of his fingers upon his chin, he shrugged and confessed. "I don't know—I've never much cared for the idea of becoming altered...no more than I've cared for the concept of aging. And you are looking very fresh-faced, Malin...I'm just a little jealous."

While I withheld a chuckle at Aleister's willingness to forsake his humanity, Malin smirked. "I'm sure we could discern some way to assist you once the dust has settled," Malin offered, glancing at me, then getting his eye caught briefly on watchful Telemachus. "Ah, yes—but there's just one other little matter in which Thecla will require your support..."

When, after another thirty minutes or so of planning, we were interrupted by a knock at the door, it was safe to say the conspiracy had grown by one; and although Aleister was a self-interested man, I certainly felt assured he realized his best interests were in loyalty to the House of Farrow. While Malin retreated with Telemachus into the dining room where he could listen in, Eleison got the door. Meanwhile, Aleister and I tried to look like casual mourners.

"You're going to have to tell me what the sex is like," Aleister whispered while I bit back a laugh.

Eleison, meanwhile, relaxed. "Kyrie," he sighed, stepping out to embrace his brother and engage in short conversation in the hall. Relaxing a bit myself, I assured the lewd-minded duke, "I'm a bit worried for the plaster of the wall behind our headboard here, to be honest, but I'm sure we can come to a solution of some sort...I'm so glad you're understanding, Aleister."

"What can I tell you? I know Malin when I speak to him... and, I don't know. Call me strange, but I've always found the idea of dharmines somewhat—*enticing.*"

"That's why there are so many romance novels about them," I agreed with a nod, glancing up as Eleison stepped back into the room and set eye upon me.

"It sounds like I'd better help Kyrie wrangle the staff into doing what he needs them to do about the wake, so I'll be back later. But, uh, Thecla—you've got somebody asking for you in the foyer."

Still nursing secret hopes that Glenn would turn around and come home without need of coaxing, I asked brightly, "Oh, who?"

Ten minutes later, Winston Garland turned from his study of a striking painting of an ancient saint. He approached me with an outstretched hand.

"Matrix," he enthused, the smile beneath his moustache flattening to see my hair. Already growing tired of this pattern, I swept a hand across my updo.

"Stress," I told him blandly, adding, "don't stare at a woman's imperfections if you want her respect, Mr. Garland."

"Of course—my apologies. Just a little surprising, is all...not to say you aren't still perfectly lovely."

Struggling to decide who annoyed me more—Winston, or the Overseer—I gestured toward the sofa of the tearoom into which he'd been sent to await me. "Shall we sit? I'm so glad you've made it for the wake."

"Paying my respect to your husband is the very least I can do. Beautiful painting," he added, gesturing to the oil piece of a half-nude woman in ecstasy, a skull in one arm and an open book resting upon her blue lap while her eyes rolled toward some unseen divinity. "Who's the artist?"

Very nearly, I said, 'I'll have to ask Malin,' but cut myself off with a sad look. "Oh, I can't remember—I shall have to check Malin's old records, or perhaps write to the curators he knew, if you're really interested..."

"Ah, I don't mean to trouble you. I was just wondering. So—"

Hands folded between his knees, Winston bent toward me to ask, "Have you had a chance to think about our agreement?"

"Have you had a chance to track down Glenn Stone?"

With an amused quirk of his moustache, Winston raised his eyebrows. "I asked you, first."

"I didn't realize negotiations were a quickdraw, Mr. Garland... to tell you the truth, I've hardly had an opportunity to think of anything in too great a detail. This past week has been an awful blur."

"Of that, I have no doubt." His ingratiating expression unflappable even as his eyes dulled with disappointment, (or perhaps mere irritation), Winston glanced down to his suitcoat.

While speaking on, he opened it to feel about an inner pocket. "Well, it just so happens I *do* have a little information about Glenn Stone...at least, we have a lead or two."

My heart produced a phantom beat, straining against the prison of my chest at this news of my missing family members; yet I resolved to remain neutral of interest, especially considering the way Winston eyed me to gauge my reaction. "Is that so," I asked, folding my hands in my lap while he flipped open a bit of paperwork that was presumably some kind of report. "And just where has he gotten off to?"

"That, we're not certain of just yet...but it would seem a few weeks ago he boarded a train after purchasing a ticket for Valquist—bold move, considering the guild there is so interested in obtaining him."

"Perhaps he thinks he can win amnesty from them now that things have cooled a bit."

"Perhaps," Winston agreed. "Or perhaps he thinks he'll have an easy time blending back in as a father." While a chill settled between us, the hunter sharing the davenport with me raised an eye. "You know—when I got this report, I suddenly realized that I don't think I've seen your daughter around since Malin's assassination."

"She *is* a little child," I told him darkly. "It's hardly as if the public has any business knowing what she's up to on a given day... especially when she's much too young to understand death, let alone mourn it appropriately."

"Uh-huh." Folding the report again and tucking it away, Winston studied me in silence for a few long seconds. "Let's talk straight, shall we?"

"Please, let's. I sense today marks the start of many intense conversations I'll be having over the next week, and the more straightforward they are, the happier I think we all will be."

"The paternity of your daughter and what that means for your territory aside, I can't help but notice a funny coincidence. That is—your, uh, altered nature."

My jaw tensed. In all the busyness of the past week, my public exposure during the motorcade had been the very last thing on my mind. Now that Winston had moved it to the forefront, I could not help my slightly tart tone. "What about it?"

"Well, we just found it to be a surprise, is all. At least, I did. And I can't help but think it's very interesting that you turned into a *ventil*. Because—if my memory serves—wasn't it a ventil that was seen fleeing the house of Glenn Stone after all those men were killed? And here you are...an altered woman with ventil genetics...negotiating with me to remove the bounty from Glenn's head. Like you know something we don't. Maybe even like you did something we've been blaming him for all this time."

I said nothing, my face unmoving as I stared him down.

"Just seems sort of interesting...and, might I say, an inauspicious coincidence for a new leader to sort out."

"With all due respect, Mr. Garland," I told him coldly, my mouth aching curiously, "if I were really responsible for what you implied, it would be exceptionally foolish of you to bring it up to me in this way—privately, in my own home, with no one to help you should things go awry."

The insufferable man lowered his eyes with a chuckle, ushing back the dress coat he wore to reveal a holstered gun at his hip. "Maybe it would be foolish, if I were like the men you killed in Valquist...but there's a reason I've headed up the Gudrune chapter for over a decade now. I'm known for being something of an excellent monster slayer, even of dharmines...and when it comes to my quickdraw, well—not even Glenn Stone can react quicker than I can."

Nonetheless, I could not help an inundation of violent fantasies: of imagining how, by unnatural haste, I might snatch his gun as I snatched up the gun of the veteran in Valquist. And how, like Valquist, I could shoot Winston and have done with him. I might even enjoy it this time. In fact, I *would* enjoy it. A single bullet hole through the center of his head: a fountain from which I could slake the thirst that grew with the increasingly oppressive images of the flowing blood upon which I longed to sup.

My gums itched peculiarly, and split beneath my lip in a little burst of tissue that signaled physical relief, but internal panic. In my unsmiling mouth, my fangs had extended, and I knew no way to retract them other than to satisfy my hunger.

"I will say this," I began, my words small and particularly icy as I avoided revealing my incisors as best I could. "If your skill as a hunter is in any way comparable to your audacity, you must indeed be unparalleled in your vocation."

"Those who hire me seem to think I am. But, I digress...we don't need to speak to one another on such unfriendly terms, Matrix Farrow."

After letting his jacket fall back over the gun again, Winston spread his hands. "You help me. I help you. All you have to do is let the Guild run here in Gudrune again. We can continue our operations, and you mind your business; and one day soon Glenn Stone and your child will be returned, and we mind our business. Doesn't that sound simple?"

Rising before he could detect any adjustment to the shape of my upper lip, I told him, "You drive a hard bargain, Winston.

But what you are asking—to undo the work of my dead husband and permit the return of the very guild that killed him—is quite a loathsome request to me. Surely you can see that."

"Of course. I'm not completely unsympathetic...but I'll be here until the wake, too. So why don't you give yourself time to come to your senses before you pull the trigger? Sleep on it. I'm sure you'll see working with us is the only way forward."

As much as I hated to give him the last word, I feared it impossible for me to speak further without revealing my nature. Therefore, letting him see the disdain in my eyes, I said nothing: merely turned and strode from the room, the door bearing the strength of my displeasure as I allowed it to swing shut with far greater force than necessary.

Contemptible idiot of a man! Threatening me in my own house. He was lucky he did so when it was overfull of fellow politicians, and when my husband and I had made such delicate plans for the unfolding of the subsequent days. If Winston had any idea of what I had become—well, we never would have had that conversation to begin with. It was obvious enough to me that Winston was among the many hunters who perceived altered individuals as barely human; had he known I was a dharmine, my life would have been gravely endangered.

And not just by him, I realized as I hastened through the house and back up to the western apartment. Every servant I passed, every courtier who bowed or smiled and petitioned for my attention by making hopeful eye contact—each and every one of them was my natural prey, and would have fled or fought me if they had the least idea.

Rightly so! Each human being I passed—each throbbing heartbeat that echoed even distantly in my ear—made my mouth water and my gums ache for something to sink my fangs into. God only knows the grim cast of my face as I avoided them all, hurrying on with uncontrollable fantasies of bloodlust surging through my soul until my trembling hands at last fit to the doorknob of the apartment. I found it to be locked and strangled back a whine of frustration. Hands slick, I rapped upon it, then, with a great breath, stumbled back a step to find Eleison on its other side.

"Hey," he said, starting toward me to kiss me but stopping as I raised one hand to fend him off. Embarrassed more than afraid, I threw the other across my mouth with a furtive glance over my shoulder.

"I long to kiss you," I told him, "but do me a favor: let me in and take Telemachus to see his room. The attached one where I used to sleep when Malin was first courting me."

Eyes making intent assessment of the situation as they flashed from my face to the hand that shielded it, Eleison stepped aside with a nod. "All right," he said. Yet, as I rushed into the apartment and he shut the door behind us, I gasped—he caught my elbow and held me back. While I pleaded with him to release me, he ignored me and caught my other bicep to pull me back against his chest.

"Thecla," Eleison murmured, bending to nuzzle into my hair before his cheek came to rest atop my head, "you know I would give you my blood if you ever needed it, right?" While tears filled my eyes, his grip on me tightening, his heartbeat louder in my ears in that instant than my own had ever been, Eleison went on, "I would let you poison me. I would let you kill me. Thecla—I swear, I would die for you."

While my hands went slack so his arms could enfold me completely, Eleison kissed the crown of my head, the temple of my forehead. "I love you more than life itself," he said. "You *are* life to me—and I'm sorry I wasn't there for you when you were dying."

"It wasn't your fault," I told him, unable to marvel at the curious sensation of speaking around my fangs when I was far more overwhelmed by wonderment for Eleison's love. "Darling— I'm sorry I couldn't let you be there. I'm—I'm sorry for how I've changed without warning."

"Don't be sorry," he whispered, kissing me once more, then releasing me. "I love you. I mean that, no matter what. I see now that nothing, truly nothing, can ever change that. So, when all this is over..."

I glanced back at him and felt my cold face bloom with heat to see his roguish smile, his wryly crinkled eyes.

"...I'm going to hold you to that vacation alone."

While longing of a different kind gripped my body, Eleison snapped me back to the present by saying, "I'll go grab the kid and let him look through the books in your old room. Think there's anything else I can show him?"

"Not yet, unfortunately—he can't walk the halls of the house until the release of information has been controlled."

"Fair enough...then we'll look at books and play cards for a while. He's probably tired from the trip, anyway...is twelvish too old to have an enforced naptime?"

"Much too old, I think," I said with a laugh that grew easier for the comfort provided me by Eleison's presence—by his unflagging love, which, if anything, seemed only more intense now that he had an opportunity to prove how unconditional it was. "Then again...I think you know about as much as I do. Maybe more, considering the gap between you and Kyrie."

"Yeah, but that was years ago...I'll figure it out." With another look of longing and a bold kiss he didn't hesitate to place upon my lips, Eleison strode off to fetch Telemachus and leave me to my husband.

How fascinating! Eleison's disappearance around the corner proved his stabilizing influence over me, the power of it so complete it seemed as though he carried with him a bubble of peace that vanished as soon as he was out of my proximity. It was a relief to know he was safe from me—that I could control myself around him and would never accidentally harm him in the heat of passion, or of hunger. But now that he had absented himself from me, I realized how insane my cravings had made me. How, had anyone else with a human's pulse answered that door, they would have wound up dead at my feet. Quivering, I gathered my gown in my hands and rushed through the apartment, seeking my husband in every room until, at last, I found him where I ought to have expected to find him—sitting in his desk, re-familiarizing himself with his work at the point where death had forced him to abandon it. When I burst in without knocking, he looked up sharply, then dropped the paper in his hand to see the desperate expression on my face. Without a word exchanged, he pushed the chair in which he sat back from the ornate rolltop and extended his arms to me.

Surely looking twice as wild as I felt, I flew into his arms and let my body—a stranger to me in that second—do as my muscles commanded. While one hand fit to his jaw to push back his head and extend his throat, my other gathered the fabric of his shirt collar to jerk it down. In seconds, my fangs found purchase in his flesh, then swiftly slid free so my watering mouth could press greedily to the resulting wound. Malin's breath hitched in my ears while, embracing me closely to his chest with one hand tangling in my hair and the other stroking my back, he murmured, "There, there, darling...I'm sure you must be famished! It occurs to me now you haven't had anything to eat since yesterday night...I can last far longer between feedings these days. Forgive my thoughtlessness, Madame..."

At the affectionate tone of the title which accompanied the rumbling of that great, feral purring from within him, I heard somewhere my own purr again; but I was only really conscious of his sweet blood, his gift to me, filling my mouth and rushing down my throat with every rapid gulp. The sensation was sheer ecstasy: the trembling of my body stopped almost at once, a new clarity coming upon my mind as I surged with energy. The frantic animal was once again enfolded in the shell of the human being I resembled. I moaned in soft relief, my fantasies of violence subsiding for other, far more enjoyable thoughts of the man who held me in his lap and caressed my body, his hands gradually sliding under my skirts. Somehow, I managed to reduce my greedy gulps from his throat to far more gentle, ladylike sips.

"There," Malin murmured supportively, his strong hands sliding over my thighs, one trailing around to massage and squeeze my rear while the other encouraged me by teasing between my legs. As I moaned, nuzzling my lips against his wound and smearing his blood over my mouth and cheek, my husband worked his big fingers through the lace of my undergarments in sexual reinforcement of my eagerness. "Isn't that better...what a good girl you are to come drink from your husband, instead of giving in and killing someone in the house...not that a massacre wouldn't be good fun. But...I'm so glad I can provide for you. No reason you should need to stain your hands in anyone's blood anymore, none but mine..."

Finding the little puncture wounds were naturally closing around the same moment I was truly sated, I kissed the sealing holes and raised my bloodied lips to whisper into his ear. "And Parvati's," I whispered.

With a dry chuckle, Malin turned to trail his murmuring mouth along my jaw. "I can tell the renewal of your acquaintance is going well...mm, as satisfying as it would be for me to set her head on a platter myself, I could hardly turn down such a grand gesture. Just remember, my delicious little wife..."

Effortlessly rising with me in his arms, Malin perched me on the edge of the desk and pushed my dress high around my hips. I helped him, exposing myself to his eager eye as he knelt between my splayed legs.

"You're not yet confirmed Matrix, and Rosina is both nowhere to be found and of dubious paternity. Parvati could strip the title from our family in the next three days and make our lives very annoying in the months to come...then we would have the added difficulty of coping with the political claim of some other party over our territory—and fair Gudrune, along with Azstoria, will have her resources tested enough in these next few months without fighting a war at home as well as abroad."

The silver glitter in his eyes breaking through the natural darkness, Malin drew my panties down my thighs and looked with deeply appreciative lust upon my exposed sex. "In other words," he said through the extension of his own fangs and the slow caress of fingers still eager to refamiliarize themselves with my anatomy, "you must be sure to play nice with Parvati and the other territory masters, at least until she is dead and gone. Better that she should die without approving your interim status than that she should award the title to someone else before we can reveal my existence to the nation. And I know, Thecla…"

As he bent forward to kiss the bud of pleasure that ached so acutely for his attention, I moaned and gripped his hair in my fist. His eyes contorting into small crescents of amusement for my enthusiasm, my husband brandished his fangs and consoled, "When it comes to Parvati, getting along is easier said than done… but if anyone can manage it, Thecla, my charmer—it's you."

S MUCH AS I HATED to admit it, my husband was quite right. Although when Malin re-emerged in public he would no doubt have a great deal of support—and a very valid claim to, if not retake Gudrune's leadership, at least see it remained in possession of the Farrow family—giving Parvati an excuse to appoint an unrelated successor would have made room enough for dissent that we would see nothing but domestic difficulty. Then, in addition to dealing with inevitable splits in Gudrune's political alignments, our very necessary efforts to peacekeep the vacuum of Parvati's demise would look like a mere power grab—when, of course, we were only doing what was best for the territories, and the people within them!

Therefore, after my mind was cleared by my husband and we were fixing up our clothes, I suggested to Malin, "You know, dearest, don't you suppose I'd ought to be meeting the other territory masters before the wake? This is such an excellent opportunity, and I wasn't able to greet them on their arrivals."

"An excellent idea, my love." Kissing my hand, then having his attention drawn to something on his desk as I swept past to gaze out the window, he said, "Ah, by the by—"

I turned as he plucked up the bloodied box containing his lapel pin, the intended gift to cheer him after his duties pertaining to the motorcade were finished. "Is this for me?"

"Oh! Yes, yes—open it, darling, do—"

I was so pleased to watch him unwrap it that I had nearly forgotten the nature of the symbol Dinon had selected for me— that brilliant bejeweled butterfly, the morpho with its proudly shining wings. My smile widening to see it in his hand, and do see how my husband's expression was of genuine, quite emotional delight, I stroked his chest and asked, "Do you like it?"

"I love it—if you had any idea how long it's been since I've received a gift...ah, my angel." After catching me by the chin to kiss me so deeply I nearly succumbed to another surge of passion, he asked, "Would you put it on for me?"

"Of course—oh, Malin." My throat tightened despite my joy, the murky past breaking in as, inhaling, I took it from his hand to carefully affix it to his suit jacket. "I never thought I'd have an opportunity to do this."

"I wish I could apologize enough. I really am so sorry I couldn't tell you, Thecla." His soft words were an echo of my conversation with Eleison not forty minutes before. Eyes hooded as he regarded my concentrating face, my husband admitted, "But I must say, it's a comfort to know how deeply I was missed...not just by you, either. Eleison seems much less wary than I expected him to be."

"I agree...but I think that must be the practical evidence he has. It's my stabilizing effect over him, and his over me—there's no room for doubt of his senses when we hold such power over one another."

"A lucky thing, that influence. I was concerned about the difficulties you might experience when adjusting to your new—lifestyle, shall we call it, around so many terrestrials. It was personally quite difficult for me to manage...even to the end of the first year, I found the siren song of human blood nearly irresistible."

Shaking my head, I admired the pin upon his breast while saying, "I can only imagine...I'm worried for our Telemachus, darling. How are we to feed him and keep him such a tranquil delight when he's surrounded by people for the first time in his life?"

"Don't fret, Mama." While I smiled with pleasure to hear my husband use the title, Malin smiled, himself. "When first I became aware that I had stumbled out of the Rift with a child in my arms, I, also was concerned with how to feed him, until I realized he was a very well-tempered little creature when he was surrounded by living plants. Living, and quickly dying plants."

As the biological facts of my new species clicked into my mind, Malin explained, "It's only lately that Telemachus has experienced cravings for human blood; it seems to me that we are equally designed for the passive ingestion of the lifeforce of terrestrial plants, though I have tried it myself for periods of time and have found that, in me, such vegetarianism results in extreme lethargy and a kind of general malaise. I've come to the conclusion that it's a mechanism designed to feed young and weak dharmines, and perhaps also to help us survive in times of famine. But there is no replacement for blood...and no replacement in particular, I am finding, for *your* blood, Thecla, my queen. But perhaps that's simply having you in my arms again after such a long time spent waiting...ah, you make me feel so alive."

While Malin kissed me, my heart glowed with the returned sentiment; I wanted to do anything it took to please him. To make him feel as loved as he made me feel. What a difficult task that was! Yet little was as pleasing to my husband as the notion of how I had grown during our marriage, and I could see real pleasure in his eye as I proposed a tea at which I might meet the territory masters. With his suggestion, I hand-wrote invitations to be delivered to each, including in each a little fib about some fondness of Malin's for them, or some anecdote I 'recalled' him recounting once to me—really, recounted as he stood at my elbow.

I suppose now, reader, I had ought to take a moment out to do as I have avoided for nearly three full volumes of my memoirs, and describe—as best as one can in prose—the geopolitical landscape of the continent at this time in Earth's history; for it occurs to me that, depending on how long this work survives, and how far into the future my words are studied, our continent may have taken on a very different shape, and indeed has already had its borders quite transformed since the time of which I am writing now. Therefore, allow me to detail, in brief, the territories.

As previously explained, Gudrune was a vast land stretching along the Western coast and south, to Azstoria, which it counted as a part of its holdings. In the nook of this roughly 'L'-shaped double-territory of ours was nestled the sprawling landscape of Alberik, which, in spite of its size, had never held much interest for my husband as an acquisition. This owed to its lack of either arable land or minable resources such as uranium; it did, however, serve as an important source of trade with Gudrune, which provided it with a great deal of water per annum and therefore enjoyed a friendly relationship as neighbors. North of Gudrune and Alberik lay Siegland and Harteveldt, moving west to east; both of them being snowy territories located in regions quite seasonable during the heat of summertime, I have since found. Harteveldt was the largest of these two, extending to the sea from the eastern border of Alberik and stretching far south as a cluster of great lakes north of the capital city of Valquist.

Valquist itself was nested within a handful other territories, smaller in size than either Gudrune or Alberik but more densely populated for it; sharing its borders with Harteveldt and taking equal benefit from the lakes, Dominia neighbored Alberik and formed the northern demarcation of the muggy territory of Richter, which was itself far more pleasant than the mosquito-infested swamplands of Manot—a nightmare to control during Rift Events, I had heard even then, and home to many dreary souls who relied heavily upon the Hunter's Guild to keep them safe. Of these just listed, only Dominia was a neighbor of Valquist, and only awkwardly, the tip of its southeastern quadrant resting against the Capital's northwestern edge. Then, around that jewel of Parvati's regime, were the territories of Pagaloria (directly north, curving up into the edge of Harteveldt); Krystos (the smallest of all the territories and the original home territory of Valquist, located just east); and, of course, aforementioned Elita, which sloped from the coast southeast of Valquist and up into the mountains west of it. Given it was this last territory that contained Aleister's duchy, Malin and I both found it appropriate to invite Aleister to the tea—but, as from my original guest list, I excluded Parvati, this time not out of malice but strategy. If I brought her into the conversation, even if it was merely a light social hour designed to impress upon my peers a favorable first impression as hostess, I was certain—as was Malin—that she would proceed to dominate the rest of the meeting and control all discourse to her liking.

So it was we organized our plan for the next day around the luncheon, which I increasingly regarded with real excitement and cautious optimism.

Though Malin had been right to observe we needed less sleep than terrestrials, I was still so drained from a long day of transit—and of then immediately launching into our political affairs—that I went to bed nearly as early as Telemachus. I slept at peace despite the many machinations in which I was engaged, and even more peacefully when, having thoroughly studied the contents of his old desk, my husband slipped into bed beside me and took me in his arms. We slept until dawn, when, roused by the brilliant sunrise that indicated the Rift Event outside had reached its overdue termination, we feasted upon one another's blood and bodies until all our needs were sated; then, with a final kiss, I leapt out of bed, bathed while reflecting longingly upon my absent footman, and hurried to my loom with more enthusiasm than I had felt for it since the birth of my precious Rosina.

How good it felt to feel *good!* My merry mood was self-reinforcing and had sweet results for my creative work. The calculations having been made the day prior, I ensured my door was shut and allowed my preternatural speed to expedite the process of threading the loom to my template's specifications. By then, the process was already as natural as, say, whipping the household into shape was for Charlotte—who, I was glad to see, had ridden through the night and appeared at my door looking drained but, for some sleep in the auto, at least more awake than I would have expected anyone else in her position to.

"Charlotte, darling," I enthused as I recognized her not by her knock but by some intake of breath I had never before consciously noticed, a tell that revealed her to me before she had even opened the door. As I hurried up to embrace her, a twinge of fright darted through her eyes; then, finding herself released and unharmed, she regarded me with a sigh.

"I suppose I'm to be your lady's maid again," she said, studying the robe still about me since my bath, "until your footman deigns to return...if at all."

What amazing sway my mysterious Dinon had over my temperament! Even with so much to do and think on, when his absence once more became apparent to me, my soul ached for his beauty as the lily for water. "I suppose so," I told her, bravely soldiering past the pain. "And now that you're back, perhaps we can make some real progress on preparing for the wake, too. It sounds like the most Kyrie has managed from the staff is to plan the menu—and the storm this past few days has delayed the acquisition of foodstuffs to make the menu with, so—"

"You let me handle it," said Charlotte. "And Mas—Malin," she quickly amended upon considering my continued position as Matrix, at least for now, "sent me a message that there's to be a luncheon of some sort today?"

"Indeed! Let me help you prepare for that, if you don't mind. I want everything to be just perfect. The territory masters must have no doubt that Gudrune will continue running with an attention to detail that does honor to my husband's."

"Very good," said Charlotte, opening the door again. "Let's get you dressed—"

I couldn't help but pout, looking back at my loom. "But I've hardly begun for the day," I cried, earning a tut as Charlotte slipped her arm through mine to guide me from the room.

"That is the trouble with being Matrix; it doesn't leave much time for leisure. Especially not when there's an event about. Why, before that contemptible motorcade, Malin didn't even have time to chase your skirt as usual...but once the wake is over and the house is clear of guests, something tells me you'll have your leisure time back again."

Yes—something told me that, as well. I was not certain whether I was to continue acting as Gudrune's figurehead, or if I would hand power back to Malin—I was quite comfortable with either possibility—but I trusted that when the time was right I would have the information I needed to act appropriately...and then I would be able to once more live in a way I desired. Perhaps even with my family intact somehow...ah, joy!

And bitter sorrow. Having Malin back made it difficult to act bereaved, so to evoke the emotion I did my level best to keep my mind continually upon Glenn and Rosina—and, as a result, it all too often turned to Winston and the Guild. My blood boiled with hatred whenever the progression was made. All I wanted was to find the man who had shot my husband, and the lover who had absconded with my child. Now I was being tormented, blackmailed: despised by an ignorant fool of a man who made his living and drew his fame exclusively from death. The idea that Winston had any position of moral superiority was as deranged as it was insulting, and I loathed the thought that he was strolling around Eleison's house in perfect freedom. Even respect.

But I could be respected, too. When dressed and ready for the day, I went about with Charlotte and involved myself deeply in the matter of arranging for the wake, as well as greeting new guests. Indeed, by this means I discovered the territory master of Harteveldt was the last to arrive, so he—a somewhat hefty but otherwise handsome man with a jocund energy to his genuine smile—became the first of my acquaintances among my peers. While he gladly accepted my personal invitation to that day's luncheon and expressed no small amount of pleasure at the thought of a hearty meal, the staff representatives from Horizon Energy arrived. I turned my attention to them just as soon as was polite, very aware of the Harteveldt Master's proximity while he stood in half-feigned discussion with his guards as I conversed with the scientists.

"Matrix Farrow," said Arthur, who was the only person thus far polite enough to make but quick assessment of my hair, ascribe it to grief, then focus himself on business matters in the few seconds our handshake required. "Thank you for inviting us. There's no way to express how sorry I am for your loss."

"I ache every day with the heaviness of my heart," I told him, picturing Glenn with my daughter in his arms, "but Gudrune's interests cannot wait, and neither can history. How is the new location in Saalast? I trust it serves your purposes?"

"Yes, Matrix, it does indeed. Uh—" With a glance back at his companions, a man and a woman being directed to two of the very few remaining rooms even the sprawling Karris house had to offer, Arthur adjusted his spectacles and returned his attention to me with a hopeful look. "Would it be a burden to ask for a moment of your time, perhaps in private?"

"I have really quite a lot to do today," I warned him, taking by the eagerness of his tone that the purpose of his request was something I wouldn't mind floating into the circulation of aristocratic gossip if Harteveldt over there should catch wind. "Perhaps you could abbreviate it before I must dash off to deal with other interests— Is it very sensitive?"

"Well..." He dropped his voice and said, "It's about the uranium your husband mentioned to me during our final meeting, Matrix."

"Oh, *yes*—the materials. Goodness, has my descent into mourning these past weeks delayed your research terribly? I feel simply awful."

With only the briskest glance over at the territory master who, having caught my unreduced volume, had aborted his conversation to more or less openly listen to ours, Arthur decided the matter was no longer as sensitive as once it was and said, "Well, we have a very small amount of enriched materials for our study, and that has permitted us to make some promising strides. But he did say something about more, I believe?"

"Yes, yes." As I fondly patted his shoulder, my attention was arrested in by the sight of Parvati in tense conversation with none other than Winston. In that busy foyer, the two of them were tucked into an alcove under the staircase, a bodyguard of hers standing at such an angle that they were clearly hoping to obscure their brief exchange. I looked Arthur in the eye again. "I'll see to the logistics today, as soon as I can."

While the researcher relaxed, he assured me, "There's no need to rush the matter into your schedule *today*, Matrix—I can see how busy you are. Just—"

"Nonsense, Arthur. The sooner, the better. After that awful Rift Event this week, all I can think of are the people of Saalast in need of more reliable power. Did your facility manage to maintain operation this past few days?"

"Yes," he said, looking very pleased. "We're already self-sustaining at this point; the issue is one of scaling, but I'm confident we'll have it tackled by this time next year."

"Very good! You know, Arthur, dear, I can see why my husband liked you. Charlotte"—I called to our housekeeper, who had been taking advantage of my conversation to deliver a few words of guidance (and perhaps an admonishment or two) to Kyrie, his control of the household being still forgivably inexpert—"would you be so kind as to show Arthur to the rooms where the Horizon researchers are staying? I believe his coworkers have already gone ahead."

"Very good, Matrix," Charlotte said, springing into action and glancing at still lightly eavesdropping Harteveldt, who had taken to miming the act of browsing messages on his watch so as to remain on the periphery of my conversation. "And what of the Harteveldt Master?"

"I believe Kyrie knows—but I really must—excuse me—"

With my most politely apologetic smile flashed for them all, I hurried across the room in a demonstration of employment that was by no means mere imitation. Whatever Winston was discussing with Parvati, their chat had gone on too long for my liking and needed to be severed; indeed, seeing me on my way to them while wearing an ingratiating smile, Winston summoned up one of his own and tossed aside his look of humorless intensity to say, "Matrix," in a way that was as much greeting to me as warning to Parvati. Stiffening with the look of a gossip deciding how much had been heard, Parvati turned to face me with a similar smile to Winston's, her eyes not matching her mouth.

"Good morning, Thecla," Parvati said. "You seem busy today! Was that a researcher from that firm—what is it, Horizon?"

"Oh, yes, there's so much to do. A luncheon to plan for, too."

"I heard!" Looking almost amused to say so, she asked in mock innocence, "Did my invitation get lost in the hallways?"

"Actually, no." Confabulating on my feet to get her away from Winston, I stepped closer and dropped my voice. "I was rather hoping you and I could have a private chat *before* the luncheon. I hope you don't feel rejected, I just thought—well, we know one another quite well already, and there are things I can tell you in confidence that I wouldn't share with the territory masters I'll meet for the first time today."

Now her eyes did fit to her dimpling cheeks somewhat better, as, in the same moment, Winston's moustache gave a wiggle of consternation. "Well, I have nothing on my schedule this morning. Excuse me, Winston...lead the way, Matrix. Oh—"

I had taken no more than a step when, in a tone somehow lightly testing, Parvati inquired, "*How* private is this chat? Should I leave my man behind?"

"Goodness, no, it's hardly as though there's anything indiscreet to be said—though I am always a bit strange about letting staff members other than Charlotte into the apartment, seeing as it's Eleison's, now. Would you mind if your guard waited at the door?"

"Not at all." Parvati was satisfied with my answer, going by her tone. Falling into stride, she allowed me to shepherd her upstairs while observing, "I have to admit, Thecla...when we spoke yesterday, I had the impression that you wanted little to do with me."

"Goodness, well, I had just had quite a long carriage ride, and from the site of my honeymoon with my dead husband, at that... you must forgive me if I was not feeling especially diplomatic.

Though I agree—I need to *learn* to be diplomatic in all situations and moods, no matter how harried I feel."

"You've really grown up this year," said Parvati, who, like me, glanced aside to smile and nod as we happened to pass Aleister. The duke made eye contact only with me, but Parvati did not notice; she simply went on in our conversation. "You seemed overwhelmed in Valquist...but down in the foyer just now, you looked awfully natural."

"When the water is over one's head, one must either drown or take up swimming...and luckily for me, my husband was prudent enough to provide me some swimming lessons."

At the apartment, I let Parvati in, paused only to ask her guard if he would like me to bring some tea out to him—he would not, it seemed—then set about putting on the kettle in the kitchenette off the main parlor. As Parvati defiled the very couch where Malin first kissed and narrowly avoided taking advantage of me following some nightmare—a couch I loved, and still think very fondly of—I sighed to hang about in the doorway.

"Goodness gracious, it really is quiet here in comparison! I've seen the house busy during the summer, but never like this."

"It must be gratifying to know that so many of the territory masters consider it a priority to pay respect to Malin. I can't remember the last time so many of us were all together in the same place."

"It makes me nervous," I artfully fibbed, using the fine line between excitement and anxiety to method act. Worrying my hands together before me, then fitting them against my stomach in an imitation of my stepmother's mannerisms, I glanced back at the kettle that gathered its resources for a scream. "Especially after what happened to my husband, the thought of so many territory masters all in one place seems a risk I'm glad we have the guards to mitigate—though goodness knows what could happen anyway. Especially with— Well…never mind."

As I waved my hands and turned away to arrange the tea service, (which I found I had to do conscientiously, lest I reveal the true speed of which I was now capable), Parvati—no doubt knowing the tactic—took my bait with interest as feigned as my downplaying of my thought. "What is it?"

"It's that Hunter's Guild fellow. Winston. I don't want to speak ill of him, though, since it seems you're friends."

"I wouldn't call him a friend," she clarified. "You'll find women in our position can't afford to have total loyalty to a person, anyway. I can see you want to tell me what's on your mind, so do it. I won't judge."

Smiling away my annoyance at her sustained entitlement to order me about, I dropped a diffuser into the teapot and covered it with half the kettle's contents, then left the rest to continue boiling. "Well," I said, sighing a little, "this is one of those confidential matters I was hoping to discuss with you. You see—Glenn Stone was staying here with us this past year and a half or so."

While Parvati's eyebrow arched to a theatrical height on hearing that, I whisked the service over and nodded when she asked, "With you and Malin, you mean?"

"Yes, and—I've been very concerned with his safety, since there's that price on his head. So, when Winston approached me to discuss the possibility of re-instating the Guild here in Gudrune, I told him I was open to it if he could assist me with two matters, namely: the task of identifying my husband's killer, whom I'm quite sure to be a former Hunter; and the matter of the price of Glenn's head, which I was hoping to lift."

"The price for killing those men in Valquist, you mean?"

"Yes." I set her saucer down before her and settled into Malin's armchair, placed adjacent to the couch. "It's unfair that a man should lose his life when—"

"When he didn't do anything, right?"

Beneath Parvati's hard stare, I took a tremulous breath and nodded, my expression solemn, my saucer and teacup resting in my lap as though I had not strength enough to raise it to my lips.

"I didn't think that seemed like Glenn. What happened that night, Thecla?"

"You'll think I'm lying." To summon a glaze of tears, I remembered dutiful Glenn defending me in the dark as Dinon killed the guild members; and how, while Malin cared for me in Azstoria, Glenn was always there in secret, on the fringes, waiting for an opportunity to do what he thought was right. To save me. "I'm frightened, Parvati—and I hate to think about that night."

"Try me," she said, observing with a neutrality that signified real openness.

"The conspiracy to kill Malin was far wider than merely Gudrune." The new acidity to my words was natural. "That night, the hunters there—they tried to persuade me to cooperate with their intentions to kill my husband. Even Glenn was among them."

Nostrils flaring, Parvati lowered her teacup to regard me with a somewhat more captivated expression. "Really?"

"Yes. But of course, when push came to shove and my life was at stake, he couldn't help but reveal his good heart and defend me. Likewise—when the ventil emerged for the first time that night"— now Parvati's brow eased into an expression of *true* sympathy, and I did my utmost not to sound relieved by the sight of it—"he pursued the woman he loved into the night, not thinking how it would look or what it would do to his reputation.”

“And you’ve been letting this would-be conspirator stay with you here in Karris because—?”

“How could I let the father of my child—”

I couldn’t finish the phrase. Saying those words out loud caused an abrupt deluge of very real grief. My face contorting, I covered my mouth with my free hand and thrust my teacup back down upon the coffee table, untouched. “Excuse me,” I told her with a sharp breath, “I’m so hurt by all this, Parvati, and that night—”

“Thecla...” Looking astonished, she set down her cup and slid to the corner of the couch nearest me. Her hand extended to hold mine. “*Stone* is your child’s father? Rosina?”

“Yes—and while I and the rest of my family were in Saalast, I stupidly let Glenn and Rosina stay behind here. And he took advantage of me, Parvati.” Covering my eyes to truly weep now, as I hadn’t allowed since first hearing the news of his departure, I clenched my teeth and gasped out a few heavy sobs. “He’s whisked her away, who knows to where—and Winston sees opportunity in my pain. Like I’m some fool who can’t discern that the death of my husband has been an intention of his Guild writ large, and not the ambition of a small splinter group of conspirators who have gone rogue in the absence of organization here in Gudrune.”

Taking a shaky breath to calm myself, I drew my handkerchief from the bodice of my dress and mopped my eyes. “He’s blackmailed me now, you see, holding all I’ve just confessed to you over my head in hopes it will bully me into reinstalling his blasted guild. He’s desperate, in other words—and desperate men do evil things, even if they are not themselves evil.”

Weighing those words carefully, Parvati watched me bunch the handkerchief into the palm of my hand. "And you intend to resist him?"

"With all my might. I can't sit here and pretend that the information he has won't hurt my public reputation, or my claim to Gudrune. But—"

"Approving you would be much easier," she admitted, her tone impossible to read in that particular moment, "if Rosina really were Malin's, and not Glenn's."

Still appearing quite wretched through the veil of my tears, I summoned up a great firmness of purpose and whisked the handkerchief beneath my eyes but one last time. "It doesn't matter if Rosina is Glenn's or Malin's."

"From the perspective of confirming your position with the other territory masters—"

"No," I interrupted her, "that isn't what I mean."

While she looked at me with first surprise, then slight befuddlement to have been interrupted in what she assumed was greater knowledge of the circumstances, I raised my voice and turned my head but a few degrees toward the depths of the apartment.

"Telemachus," I called, "darling, would you come out here a moment? I have someone who wants to meet you."

The delay was only a few seconds—long enough to seem to me like forever, but short enough, in retrospect, to hint that Telemachus was not the only one eavesdropping on my production for Parvati. The door from the parlor to the rest of the apartment cracked open, and Telemachus peered shyly out at me and my esteemed guest.

"You called, Mama?"

"Yes, dear," I told him, smiling bravely and extending my hand while, from the corner of my eye, a satisfying astonishment widened Parvati's eyes. I swear, it even rendered her face just a little ashen. "Come here for a moment, please. I warned you, didn't I? The time for hiding you is almost at its end."

His look of nervousness toward Parvati was genuine, but easily misappropriated into the shyness of an average child. Shutting the door behind him, he trotted to my side and bent to hug me around the neck while Parvati stared on, incredulous. "Now," I said, patting him on the shoulder, "no need to be bashful, dear—you recognize the Overseer, don't you? She and your papa used to be friends, oh, quite some time ago."

Peering back at Parvati, who at last managed to produce a smile for the child, Telemachus said, "Yes, I recognize the Overseer. Hello, Ma'am; I'm glad to make your acquaintance."

"And I'm quite amazed to make yours!" Looking Telemachus up and down and then turning to me, Parvati asked, "This is—Malin Farrow's child? I mean, of course he is. I recognize the nose, the shape of his eyes, but—how—"

Affecting a quite chastened look, I told her, "It's a long and embarrassing story with many details not fit at all for a child, but...the truth is, Malin and I first met many years ago. He came to Lescaut—I believe to find me—and—"

I smiled meekly as I let my lie hang in the air with a meaningful pause that Parvati absorbed exactly as she had absorbed the rest of my confessions; the true parts of my confessions. This, though—this calculated fiction concocted by Malin on the way back to Karrisregion—in so many ways felt like it *could* have been the truth, and it glided from my lips as easily, or more easily, than the actual truths. Besides...it was really quite a fun, naughty thought to let drop into the public ear. Certainly more entertaining for its taboo qualities and therefore even more romantic, in some ways, than the more typical manner in which proximity had naturally unfolded our love story.

"At any rate," I went on while Parvati's mind whirred with nearly audible processing, as though it were an old watch struggling to keep up with a news stream's live broadcast, "I discovered Telemachus here quite some time after Malin had satisfied himself with my existence...though I did not know why my existence had been so important to him at the time, I *did* know he would think it important that he had an heir on the way. So, I approached him."

"And?" Looking intent on the details that explained the sudden appearance of this eleven-year-old boy, Parvati leaned forward almost despite herself. "What happened?"

"Well, Malin longed for the heir, but he tried to resist his feelings for me for quite some time—propriety forbade it, and he feared, I think, my discovery of my heritage. The idea of our legal relationship, which was not made clear to me until I visited with you, Parvati, distressed him in light of his growing love. So"—I shrugged, collaging reality with truth—"he paid my family to see to my care for quite a number of years, likewise funding my education, and the boy's. But when I met his servant, Eleison, during one of Malin's visits, well...I believe that through this rivalry he saw at last what I was worth, and what might have been taken from him if he did not open his heart to love."

I owed a debt of gratitude to the romance novels Charlotte and the other maids passed from hand to hand before recommending to me. While I tried not to smile amid my silent self-applauding, Telemachus peered at me uncertainly and then perched upon my knee. As my hand settled upon his back, he relaxed, even smiling at me.

And all the while, Parvati pondered, first regarding us together and then regarding the boy.

"So, this child—"

"Telemachus," I reminded her, earning the tight flash of her smile as she pondered on.

"Then Telemachus here," she resumed, "is a third-generation altered, isn't he...it's no wonder Malin wanted to hide you both until the boy was less at risk. But—"

Looking at me more confrontationally now, Parvati demanded, "Why wouldn't he have revealed this to me sooner, to make the arrangements for me to approve you as his successor?"

"He hardly expected to be shot during a motorcade, Parvati," I told her with a scoff for her ignorance, inwardly pleased by the undisguised clenching of Telly's fists. "At any rate—he *has* been making the preparations to contact you about these matters, or he was before you called me out to Valquist. But, after first devoting a great deal of time to my condition while I was pregnant with Rosina, he came to perceive you as too greatly antagonistic to be trusted—especially since it was *your* city where I discovered the conspiracy against my husband."

Suddenly feeling as though there was something there—certainly something discernably truer than anything I had just said—I narrowed my eyes. "Indeed, the way you and Winston were talking, one would almost be inclined to see the benefits that would have come to you had the deed ended both our lives."

"Thecla, that's—that's *really* something to say when I came all the way here for your husband's wake." Her scramble was desperate, the pride of her wounded ego not arising from hurt feelings but instead the grains of truth I'd just spoken. If only *she* knew the truth! If only she knew that the boy upon my knee was indeed the motorcade's second victim—a life that had been taken by the assassin. A threat who would not be before her were it not for the Hunter's Guild and its murderous ambitions.

Suddenly, I wondered if what we planned was not absolved of all guilt by justice—but only time and greater understanding could make certain of that.

"I'm sorry," I told her, softening my tone. "I know I should not throw around baseless accusations, especially in front of my son—but I can hardly help speculating. I feel sometimes as though, aside from Eleison, my Telly and I don't have a friend in the world."

Her posture relaxing as the accusation passed on to apology, Parvati said, "I can imagine you both feel very isolated...and frustrated. Thecla—"

Focusing entirely on me, Parvati said, "Maybe I owe you an apology for the way things went in Valquist. I like to maintain freedom of the press, and I always let my people think what they want...but I could have done more to preserve a charitable view of you."

Did she say that because she meant it, or because my appointment again had a stronger argument and was therefore likely unavoidable? Indeed, Parvati went on, "He did write me a letter about this subject—that is, your promotion to his successor— and I confess, I had some...inappropriately personal feelings at work at the time, so I let the issue drop. But...aside from how dedicated I can see you are to the position...Telemachus here does make up for Rosina's, for want of a better term, lack."

"Is that a legal position," I inquired, allowing her to feel superior in knowledge for at least a moment, "or is it merely a practical, political maneuver to prevent Telemachus from reaching adulthood and deciding he could—and should—reclaim the Farrow legacy from your appointee?"

With a razor thin smile that I should say such a thing in front of the boy, who was listening with increasing interest now that the lies for which he had been coached had sufficiently justified his paternity, Parvati said, "In all honesty—both. In the event of a child, the surviving parent is almost without exception legally appointed the position of custodian—interim territory master like you—with the stipulation that their position remain untouched until the next master or matrix comes of age." While I reflected on Malin's similar explanation, she added, "The ability to approve you as a permanent leader is mine, as is the ability to strip the child of the inheritance if there's sufficient agreement among the territory masters. And if I'm being honest, Thecla, I was leaning more toward the latter when we were just talking about a baby."

With a brief glance at the true successor to Malin Farrow—the legacy of her lifelong enemy who was, if she failed to permanently approve me, the default leader of Gudrune in just over six years—Parvati told me, "But I'm starting to see wisdom in honoring Malin's wishes. After all...I do like you, Thecla"—I smiled slightly at this lie of hers, and more still at the truth she next furnished while finally attending her neglected tea—"and you're obviously a fast learner. It would be good for Gudrune to enjoy the wisdom of a female leader on a permanent basis."

How quickly her tune changed! Pleased, I stroked Telemachus's hair back from his pale brow and assured the Overseer, "I'm sure you would be able to teach me much, Parvati, if you decided to approve me to the position in a permanent capacity. But that is up to you. Meanwhile, all I can ask is—

please, do be careful about that awful Winston fellow. I don't trust him…and I don't think you can, either."

Nodding firmly, Parvati hastily swallowed the rest of her lukewarm tea. "I'll be sure to keep that in mind."

Then, setting the saucer down, she regarded us both and shook her head. "I have to say…it's incredible to think he kept this a secret from me—and more incredible still that you were able to keep it along with him. I had no idea you were a woman of such discretion."

"If you had, I would hardly be discreet, would I?"

Parvati chuckled dryly. "I suppose not. Well…goodness. No wonder you wanted to keep things quiet. Don't worry. No one will know about Telemachus but me."

That was just what she wanted, no doubt. If she really was working with the Hunter's Guild in any capacity, and really had enjoyed even the most distant hand in the assassination scheme, how simple it would have been to finish the matter if Telemachus continued existing only in secret! "On the contrary," I therefore hurried to tell her while, gently patting him, I encouraged Telemachus to rise with me and took his hand so we could walk her to the door together. My heart soaring with joy to share a smile with my son, I continued on to Parvati, "You see, now that *you* know—and now that Malin's reputation is no longer quite so at stake—I have been thinking it time to debut Telemachus here to the public eye. My Telly is such an intelligent, charming boy, anyway—it seems a shame to waste him in obscurity when all Gudrune could delight in him the way I do."

While the boy grinned down at his shoes, Parvati smiled with somewhat less relish. "So he'll be about at the wake, then?"

"Perhaps, for a few minutes before bed. It's only reasonable that he should be able to circulate at his own father's parting fete."

"Then I might see you again, Telemachus," said Parvati, getting the door for us.

And, with immaculately believable air to his very natural—very typical—flirtation with the barely responsive guard who quite clearly just wanted this borderline sexual harassment to end, Aleister glanced up from where he stood, brightened to see Parvati, then brightened further to note Telemachus. With a great sigh, the duke flipped both hands palms-up.

"Oh, thank *God*," he said as he'd been told to when we met with him the day before, "so we can all stop acting like he doesn't exist? Very *good*."

While Parvati's eyebrows worked with dynamic frustration to register this confirmation of a story she had perhaps still hoped to lack merit, the Overseer asked Aleister, "Why—*you* knew about Telemachus, too, Duke Montagne?"

"Of course, I knew! Malin always told me everything. You know we were close. Why should that surprise you?"

Her eyes closing even as her eyebrows slid up toward her hairline, Parvati shook her head. "I...suppose it doesn't. Just sort of a shock that everyone's kept me in the dark like this! I'm not usually the last to know this sort of situation."

"Might want to take it up with Ambassador Platt, dear," Aleister quipped amid a wry laugh, then pouting as the bodyguard stepped around him to follow Parvati like a loyal dog. "He's always struck me as a man more interested in kissing your shoes than doing his job...anyway, Thecla"—now flat-out ignoring the Overseer, Aleister turned to smile at me and offer his elbow—"it's nearly time for lunch! Care for an escort?"

"Certainly, Aleister! Oh, and do call on my Charlotte, Parvati... I'm sure she would be happy to furnish you with a private lunch."

While the Overseer lobbed us a tight imitation of a smile and headed off down the hall with her guard in tow, I glanced down at Telemachus to squeeze of his hand.

"Well, angel, what do you say? Care to come with Mama to meet the territory masters?"

Looking quite excited, he asked, "Can I, really?"

"Why yes, of course. If you're going to be as expert in politics as your Papa someday, I had ought to get you started now...come on!" Guiding him along with my free hand while Aleister walked with his arm linked in mine, I shot my son a sly wink. "There are some pretty flowers Miss Charlotte has brought in to arrange around the tearoom—I'm sure you'll enjoy having a look at them while we wait for our guests to assemble."

TO DESCRIBE IN DETAIL the contents of that luncheon meeting would, I fear, be a boring derivation from the style to which my fair reader has no doubt adapted, if not grown to enjoy. Therefore, let me summarize it in broad strokes so you may know how redundant it really was in the flow of the rest of my life: one by one, well-traveled Aleister introduced me to the territory masters, and one by one, I introduced to them Telemachus. Most of them expressed varying degrees of surprise, though none did so with the sprinkling of frustration that had adorned Parvati. They conversed among themselves as well as with me, the matrices of Elita and Monet in particular humoring Telemachus with fond chatter that proved my husband had learned the art of lying from his father well enough to be trusted in the maintenance of his false origin. Harteveldt, meanwhile, switched the tags at our table when he thought no one was looking, so I found he was now seated at my right hand and able to make all manner of charming and interested conversation with me—having decided, I am sure, that those territories who made themselves intimate with Gudrune's new leadership could only stand to benefit from the energy research and related stores of uranium that awaited enrichment.

Perhaps the only point of worthy note came near the end, when the Master of Alberik, who had more cause to acquaint himself with the fallout of Malin's death than anyone else at the table due to our territories' proximity, asked, "And how goes the investigation into Malin's assassination, if inquiring won't ruin the mood?"

No falsity was necessary to encourage the darkness that slashed across my face to consider my answer. "Last I received a report," I told him grimly, "the progress being made by the police here in Saalast has been next to nothing—indeed, I fear more than sufficient time has passed for the perpetrator and his conspirators to escape the territory altogether."

"Don't you have a man in custody?"

"I do, indeed—but he, like the rest of the Hunters with whom he is affiliated, is exceedingly tight-lipped. I doubt even torture could persuade him to speak: no deal we've offered has made him budge from the notion that he and the rest of his black-hearted ilk have done what is right for the continent."

Very interested in this, Harteveldt leaned forward to ask, "He's a Hunter?"

"As was the one who shot my husband and fled," I said, extending my hand to touch its back. "I glimpsed his tattoo in the seconds before my Eleison marked his shoulder and sent him fleeing off into the crowd."

Elita, at Aleister's side, frowned and suggested, "And it isn't some fraud designed to place the blame on the Guild? Anyone can get a tattoo, after all."

"Now"—Harteveldt bristled on my behalf, far more annoyed than I was as he gestured—"I'm sure Matrix Farrow has made thorough inquiry into the matter. It's Occam's razor, as they say; if the man in prison was a Hunter, and the one that shot Malin bore their symbol, it's simple enough to discern that the Guild had some involvement."

Pouring himself a glass of the wine that had liberated his lips—and that gave me an excellent idea as I beheld it flowing— the Master of Harteveldt went on. "I've never liked that blasted Guild, to be perfectly frank."

"That's because all the Rift Beasts you get up in the north migrate to their preferred climates," said Richter, quite annoyed to even need say it. "That is to say—ours." He indicated Manot, who nodded.

"Yes—it's very easy to refuse the help of the Guild when one has the weather to repel the beasts in the first place."

"You say that as though we haven't *any* Events. I assure you, we have weather up north the same as any of you in the south. But that doesn't change the fact that the Guild acts as if it feels entitled to engage in its own form of government."

"Rather hard to avoid in a freelance police force," I observed with a slight shrug. "What can we do? Their services are necessary to the *traditional* functioning of territory governance...especially in those areas with large rural populations. How can the Hunters be done without until there is some improvement to infrastructure and a way to improve our relationship with the Rift itself?"

With a short scoff, Krystos—who, given the long relationship of his territory with Valquist, was never likely to side with me—

asked, "Our 'relationship' with the Rift? You'd might as well try to take some benefit out of wildfires, Matrix, or pandemics. The Rift is nothing but a danger, and massive economic disruption."

"Wildfires serve their purpose in nature," I assured him. "And even the emergence of a new disease among the populace can motivate the modernization of medicine and hygiene, if the people are open to change."

"So it would seem you are dedicated to your late husband's commitment to progressive politics?"

At the withering tone of Krystos's question, Pagaloria's leader took up a plum and used it to gesture at me. "Of course she has a vested interest in progressive strategies—you're altered, aren't you, Matrix Farrow?"

"I am," I said, nodding. "It's was excellent luck—or terrible misfortune, I'm not sure which—that light Rift weather occurred during the motorcade where Malin died; if not for that, I might never have been able to keep pace with the killer well enough to watch him flee in an auto that clearly contained a number of other conspirators. We could have been laboring under the delusion that there were only one or two involved that day; but it seems to me that this is a much broader matter. Even in Valquist—well, I dare not detail it all here. But there were Hunter murmurings of dissent against my husband as far as the Capital, which came to me by way of my relationship with a certain Hunter of my acquaintance."

"Really quite a serious claim," muttered Krystos, looking askance. I nodded.

"Indeed, it is—quite a serious claim. A serious threat to my life, and the life of my son. So, I cannot help but take it seriously... and I cannot help but continue denying the Hunter's Guild the right to operate in Gudrune's borders, although Winston came to petition for his restoral to power."

"I'm quite sure," said Harteveldt with a scoff. "Take my advice and stick to your guns, Matrix Farrow, my dear; don't let him boss you into it. Indeed, I find Gudrune's continued smooth operation without benefit of the Guild for the past sixteen or so months very inspiring...I may look into other options for my own territory."

Although the reader may now be dozing, as I certainly was by the end of the meeting, it is important that you have read this conversation for the sake of understanding clearly what began happening the morning after the wake, when the guests awoke to news of murder—as it is important to know that, following the luncheon, I asked Charlotte to watch Telemachus a moment while I pulled Aleister aside.

"I've not seen Kalypso around, I've just realized—isn't she coming to the wake? She's still in Saalast, no?"

"Oh, yes. *You* know how Kalypso is by now, darling; likes to come fashionably late to everything, stirring up the crowd as to whether or not she'll come at all...as though anyone is thinking of her on an occasion like a territory master's wake."

At Aleister's snort for his little sister, I smiled. "Well, *I* am certainly thinking of her—and since she is lagging so behind, let me ask: Would it be possible for her to do me a great favor? I'd gladly pay her back, but—"

I described my thoughts to the duke, who arched a brow and laughed slightly. "You're going to serve *mithrae* tincture to the territory masters?"

"No, no. Only to the servants, and the guards. I can imagine no more harmless a way to put such hard workers into an easy sleep to reward their efforts," I told him innocently. "It will help them avoid hangovers...and, naturally, make the mood of the house somewhat less grim. Why—in Lescaut, a wake was always meant to be a relief after the unpleasant funeral. I'm not certain these sycophantic aristocrats will understand that, but the staff might."

After looking me in the eyes long enough to gather the intent of my scheme, he removed his watch. "I'll have her bring it down... and make sure she knows to keep her mouth shut."

"There's a good man," I said, patting his arm. Then, my hand lingering there, I squeezed it and regained his gaze from the face of his watch. "Thank you, darling. For earlier, and—for loving Malin, no matter what."

With a little twitch of his lips—a smile constrained by the falsest modesty that ever man knew—Aleister kissed my cheek and resumed dialing his sister. "You taught me loyalty as Malin never could on his own, my dear...I should be thanking *you*. Kalypso! There you are. On your way down yet? Oh, good—well, because I had a little thought—"

While Aleister strode off to find an alcove where he could conduct his business in private, I smiled in on Charlotte and Telemachus. The boy perked to see me, hurrying over in great excitement he did not try to contain. "That was fun, Mama," the boy enthused as he slipped his hand into mine, making me laugh. The corrugation of his brow and pursing of his lips speaking to pure confusion, he asked, "What is it?"

"Nothing, dear—only that you really are your father's son to say such a thing. Most children would have been asleep in their seats twenty minutes in to that tiresome lunch."

"Really? You didn't like it?"

"It was fine, of course...but to tell you the truth, Telemachus, Mama doesn't care much for politics."

Interested to hear this—having been raised exclusively by a politician, the idea that anyone could detest these games of diplomacy had perhaps never occurred to him—Telemachus peered up at me. "Then what do you like?"

"Honesty of thought," I said, "and simplicity of conversation."

"And weaving," Charlotte answered for me while slipping past us to resume the work from which I had called her to sit with the boy. I laughed and nodded in agreement.

"Yes—and weaving, as Miss Charlotte said."

His intrigue all the greater now, Telemachus stood on his toes and rocked back down to his heels in an expression of excitement. "Papa said you're a great weaver! I saw the ones in our villa— they're pretty! Did you really make them all by yourself?"

"Yes, sweetheart, and many more. It's not so exciting— anyone can do it if they've been trained and are inspired."

"I don't think *anyone* could make the kinds of weavings you do," said the stubborn lad. "Maybe anyone could weave a rug, or a towel; but that's a silly thing to say, Mama. Like saying anyone could paint that lady"—he gestured toward the same image that had captured Winston's eye the day before— "or build the kinds of buildings I've read about in Papa's books on Rome. Anyone can do anything, but only special people can do special things."

Charmed, especially by the boy's defensive consternation and his quick desire for my affection, I stroked my thumb back through his hair. "Perhaps you're right, Telly."

"May I see it," the boy asked on. "You use a, what do you call it—"

"A loom. Yes, dear, of course you may see it, if you're really interested...though I fear the process of weaving really *will* bore you."

"I still want to see it," he begged. "Please? I won't break it, I promise."

"I don't think you're going to break it, but... Oh, dear, very well." With a laugh and a pinch of his cheek, I took up his hand again. "You're such a sweet, polite child...it seems impossible to deny you anything at all."

How dutiful Telemachus was in learning about his mother! He was very interested in the loom as a piece of equipment, a great machine whose precise functions he was keen to observe; but, as predicted, he who had found politics so fascinating could not maintain much interest in watching me weave. I hardly blamed him when, after about forty minutes, he dozed off. It was simply pleasant to feel him near me, slumped against the arm of a chair with his arms folded around him and his mouth open for the occasional adorable snore.

There was truly no end to the strangeness that came with so suddenly having a son! I endlessly marveled in those early days at the naturalness and obviousness of the connection. Though not having raised him myself, we both in our hearts longed for closeness with each other; therefore, like two magnets, Telemachus and I clipped together happily, naturally, having been held apart by the fingers of time until at last we were permitted to make up for the gulf.

But perhaps it had less to do with openness of heart and our shared natures than it did with our circumstances. He, no doubt, had spent his whole life longing for a mother to go with his father; and I, having felt my heart break with the loss of my daughter, was eager to fill the void with the son who stirred in overconfident protest as, having left my loom for the day, I bent to gather him to me.

"I'm awake," he lied briskly, adding, "what is it," while I laughed.

"You snore while awake, do you...then perhaps you really *were* sleeping at the luncheon. Come, dear, let me give you back to Papa for now...no doubt, Mama is expected to circulate among her guests, and there is everything to be prepared."

"Can I help you," he asked. "I'm bored of Papa; all he wants to do lately is sit at his desk and write letters and things."

"Well, Papa has an *awful* lot to do just now, my prince— when we're through with the wake and all this business with the Overseer, he must be ready to reveal his presence and act rapidly. In fact, I'm sorry to say Papa will be exceedingly busy for the foreseeable future...not that he won't still take lots of time for us, I hope."

"Then you'd ought to let me help you," the boy concluded with a shrug. "Or I'll become very bored and play hunting games with the staff."

Repressing a laugh as the boy revealed a hint of the bratty sadism I would have expected in Malin's dharmine heir, I pinched the back of his hand and told him, "Now, don't frighten the household. They work very hard just like Papa does—and they're Uncle Eleison's staff, anyway."

"I was just kidding," Telemachus said with a naughty giggle, rubbing the back of his hand, then getting a bleak look in his eyes. "Did I do a good job with the Overseer?"

"You were excellent," I told him, "and very good at lunch, too. I hate to ask you to lie, but—"

"Why not? It's fun. And, anyway—I didn't like her. Parvati. Papa doesn't like her, either, but now I see why. She's a liar, too."

Intrigued, I studied Telemachus's face. "What makes you say that?"

"Papa told me when humans lie their hearts speed up, and you can smell them sweat and things like that, because humans aren't made for lying. And when you told Miss Parvati it would make sense if she had wanted the Guild to kill Papa, and she got all mad about it, her heart was like a hummingbird's—couldn't you hear it?"

Reflecting back on the moment, which had caught my attention also, I confessed to Telemachus, "I suppose I was so focused on her words, rather than her body—I didn't even think to listen for her heart."

"You'll learn to," said the boy with a knowing nod. "It's funny! In some ways, you're younger than I am, Mama...but I'm sure Papa will teach you a lot."

"Goodness knows, he already has."

With a smile that gradually drifted into another frown, Telemachus observed, "Papa said not many people liked him. I guess I didn't believe that—but I think he's right. Why is that?"

My lips pursed. "Well—because Papa is a strong man who does what he thinks is right, and he isn't very interested in discussing what he does with people he knows are wrong. And those people know that when he *does* speak to them, it's not generally to consult with their opinions."

"Sort of like when Papa and I disagree about something, and he pretends like he's listening to me before doing just what he said he'd do to begin with?"

"Exactly," I confirmed, laughing slightly as I took the child's hand and guided him out of my workroom. "Well, Telemachus, dear, come along then—if you really want to spend your time elsewhere today, perhaps we would do well to introduce the staff to you and get it over with..."

Better to do it when they were too busy to ask many questions, anyway!

THE NEXT DAY, there was nothing left to do except to anxiously await Kalypso's coming; I had arranged all that needed arranging, spoken to the staff members who required extra guidance, and, with Telly watching, met with the Horizon Energy team to organize logistics related to the delivery of the uranium. Malin's heir, though young, was rapt with interest for every matter to which I intended, his mind forever calculating his future responsibilities. For my own part, I was so busy I had no time to think, or even really to sit down, until I came upon Eleison and Kyrie discussing security arrangements not far from the ballroom. Eleison flicked a glance at me—then, seeing me more clearly on the second net his eyes cast across my face, exhibited an intense shift in expression that excited my blood.

"Hey, Telly," said Eleison, "this is my brother, Kyrie. Kyrie, you should tell Telemachus here about the horses while I borrow Matrix Farrow for a second..."

My mate's hand slipped around my bicep and I found myself almost afraid. Afraid he was going to back down from the plan; afraid he had some bad news to deliver, and me having already had too great a share of such things in the past month to bear more; afraid, really, that at any moment he was going to issue some formal rejection of my love, now and forever, my new condition unreconcilable to his mind even if we still shared the same soul.

Yet it was not so. Luring me into the ballroom while asking, "Let me get your opinion on these decorations," Eleison slipped the toe of his glossy shoe beneath the doorstop and let the great hinge swing closed. I did not notice, as I naively looked about the slow-growing assemblage of banquet tables along the walls and chairs at the perimeter of the dance floor. Vases of flowers had been placed in clusters here and there, not yet set in final places; and banners featuring Malin's seal, the serpent beneath the petals of a rose, had been hung floor-to-ceiling between the tall windows.

I turned, approval already on my lips while Eleison stole that and more by snatching me into a kiss so passionate I forgot to breathe. When the pleasure of his tongue's dominion became too rich to bear, I remembered at last to inhale the breath of his lungs only to find I could do nothing with it but moan.

"I just had to kiss you," he murmured, raising his mouth from mine to kiss my cheek, my jaw, my hair, my ear, his kisses darting all upon me before at last he spoke in the rough tones of love against my cheek. "You look sexier than ever, and it's driving me crazy."

I laughed. "Well, I am a few inches taller, it would seem."

"I don't think that's it." Lips peeling back from his teeth so he could nip my earlobe and produce a new gasp, Eleison rubbed his face down into the crook of my neck before raising his head to look into my eyes.

"Can I see your fangs?"

Almost embarrassed by his forward request—and all the more excited for it—I stuttered, "I don't quite know *how* to make them show up yet, darling...or how to put them away."

"Hm...maybe Malin can help."

At his significant tone—and the expectant look he delivered when he raised his head to rest his brow on mine—I bit my lip and slid my hand along his tie.

"I wouldn't have expected you to be allured by such an accessory, darling...frankly, I didn't expect you to remain so fond of me, let alone to *grow* in fondness."

"I don't know—it's strange. I feel...lighter, somehow, even though—"

Lips pursing, his crimson eyes flicking along my body and back to my face, Eleison shifted his embrace around my waist and said, "I know our problems haven't disappeared, and they've only changed. We've got more to hide from the world than ever before. But, all the same...I feel like I can relax. Like you can take care of yourself better than you could before. And that makes me feel more like—I don't know."

With a boyish laugh and a glance down at the polished floor, Eleison said, "I don't usually put my foot in my mouth like this."

He was so charming. "I know just what you mean," I assured him, smiling. "Myself, I've been liberated. I feel powerful."

"Maybe that's it. The confidence...it radiates off you. Makes me feel lucky that you would deign to love me."

The realization hit me very suddenly, and only because Malin played such games with me from time to time. It was no small wonder Eleison could not put into words quite what he wanted, or what so intrigued him: he was so used to being in charge with me, sexually speaking. He wasn't a man like Malin, who could easily suggest I take control.

Rather, he required control to be wrest from him.

"Then you'd ought to kneel and thank me, Eleison, darling, for being a kind and tender mistress when I could instead be so cruel."

His chest expanded beneath his shirt with a sharp inhalation. I half expected him to reject the invitation to the game, out of pride or embarrassment; instead, with his eyes fixed upon mine, my beloved mate knelt at my feet and made me really feel a delicious rush of that power.

"Thank you, Thecla," he murmured, his lips in a half-smile, his eyes heavy with bedroom thoughts as he bent forward, arms still wrapped around me, to press kisses along my stomach and the apex of my thighs through the thick fabric of my gown. "God, oh, baby, I love you—"

"Lower," I told him, "kiss my shoes."

While I drew my hem high enough for him to do so, my body ached to see how quickly he obeyed. How I adored Eleison and his willingness to experiment! He was a jealous and quite possessive man, it was true; but he was by no means too proud to give himself completely into play with me, so long as things progressed at a pace to which he could adapt. As his kisses migrated high as my ankle, I set my other foot upon his head to stop him.

"You're going to be a good pet for Malin and I, aren't you? We should play a fun game…something delicious and new. Something we've never tried before. After all! How many times have I been an obedient little bitch for my masters...but you, Eleison—don't you suppose you could use a bit of education on how to treat us, seeing as we are so much more than human now?"

"I suppose you're right," my mate said, the borro in his heart mingling low growls with his words. As I lifted my foot from his head and dropped my hem again, he rolled upon his back to gaze up at me from the floor. "You know how I can get, baby...you'd better teach me how to respect you."

My gums itched. Inhaling quite sharply, I told my mate, "Indeed—why wait for tonight? Let me just—hold on—"

My footsteps echoing quickly across the floor, I stuck my head out through the door whose yawn open gathered the innocent attentions of both Telemachus and Kyrie.

"Kyrie, dear," I told him, "Eleison and I have just realized we have a few details to tend to. Would you be so kind as to take Telemachus out to the pasture to *meet* the horses?"

As the boy's excitement grew, Kyrie said, "That's a good idea—I'd better check on 'em anyway. We just hired a new groom after firing the last one, so I should make sure he kept 'em calm this whole last Event. Want to see the horses, Telemachus?"

"Yes, please!"

Smiling at them both, I said encouragingly, "Go on, then. When you're back, Kyrie, find Charlotte and ask her to see to Telly's supper. Have fun, now..."

While the boy trotted off with Kyrie, both of them eagerly discussing the animals, I let my tone drop to something far sterner while turning to face Eleison. "Get up," I told him, biting back a smile as he woozily obeyed me. "You've gotten your wish, you mongrel...you've aggravated my condition with your antics. See?"

Mouth open wide, I showed him my glistening tongue, and

the very back of my throat—and the pointed tips of the pearly fangs drawn out of my gums by the arousal he provoked. Inhaling, Eleison rose swiftly to his feet and studied my mouth before daring to approach, his hands fitting to my face.

"You're so beautiful," he murmured, regarding me with the mingled awe and fright of a terrestrial human on the other side of a Rift zoo's glass. "Thecla—"

"You had better come with me this instant without trying to delay," I warned him, assuming the stern, coldly maternal tone I suddenly understood to serve him some valuable psychic purpose. "Now that you've distracted me *and* caused these daggers of mine to emerge, I think we have no choice but to talk to Malin... Come, come. Be a good boy and perhaps you'll get a treat..."

With a shudder of desire as I slipped out of his grip to lead the way, Eleison strode after me, surpassed me, held the door for me. I withheld my smile: a simple task, and not just owing to my fangs. I had so incessantly played the part of derisive tyrant with Ba'al-Dinon that assuming the appearance of feminine cruelty was by then second nature to me. My eyelids lowered and my lips slightly curled in a calculated expression of bored inconvenience, I swept through the crowded house, up the stairs, and down that hall where fewer courtiers were about.

"How lucky you are that Malin granted you this property, Eleison." I reached back to grab hold of his tie when the place was thin of servants. As, by this leash, I jerked him forward into closer step with me, I warned my mate in a tone not entirely play, "It would otherwise be all too tempting to press you into service as my pet...to withdraw you from the public and keep you locked in an apartment for my use, where you could set eye upon no woman but me."

"There are other women?"

His bleary question nearly made me lose composure, and the corner of my mouth twitched with a barely fought smile. Seeing it, Eleison grinned and glanced down at the tie by which I led him, his expression of mirth repressed only when I chided, "You cheeky man...we'll see what our master has to say about it."

In the apartment, I locked the door behind us and caught him by the collar to drag him close, where I could press a thirsty kiss to his fathomless, softly gasping lips and thereby thrill him with the proximity of my malicious fangs. When I drew back, his glittering ruby eyes were overwhelmed by sizable pupils. I told him softly, "If I didn't know better, I'd say you long to be bitten by me."

A shudder rolled through him. Despite myself, my smile widened. I had never seen him like this, my Eleison—never had enjoyed him in a state of submission to me in this way. Still with the collar of his shirt bunched in my hand, I glided along the floor and forced him to keep pace lest he strangle himself by resistance.

Then, at Malin's office, I rapped sharply upon the door.

After the delay of only a few seconds, it swung wide; and the pleased crinkle of his eyes narrowed with quick adaptation to find I was not alone, but with our compromised beloved. Eleison exchanged a meaningful look with him while I said, "Darling, our hound has agitated my senses—look at what trouble he's caused."

While my free hand gestured to my mouth, Malin caught my chin in his fingers. As his thumb rubbed consolingly over one fang and up my gum, I found myself wondering who the pet in this relationship really was; nevertheless, my husband was happy to play along with a tut.

"Poor angel! He's lucky nobody saw...otherwise, there would be fresh blood on those already bloody hands of his."

"Yet he so arrogantly expects to leave his own blood out of it." While I shoved my mate down to his knees between myself and Malin, barely restraining an exclamation of pleasure for way Eleison caught himself with both hands against Malin's hips, I tweaked my lover's ear and gazed into my husband's amorous face. "Just as he expects to enjoy some possession me—as he wants to fuck me in front of you, never being subject to the same."

"And never being fucked, himself," Malin agreed while, with a soft growl low upon his lips, Eleison glanced up at our resurrected love. Malin returned the sound with one of his own, that profoundly frightening thunder rising up from his heart to quite deafen Eleison's. While my husband raised his lip to reveal his fangs had unsheathed to glitter in the light of the office, he suggested with a contemplative look into Eleison's eyes, "Perhaps we'd ought to change that...no time like the present."

One may imagine the pleasure that rushed through my body when, with one hand still cradling my jaw, Malin fit his other hand to the back of Eleison's head. There, roughly playing through my mate's effortlessly styled black hair, my husband asked, "What do you say, Eleison? Don't pretend you don't like the idea...I can hear your heart from here. Can smell the desire of your body...or is that just from the thought of being forced to watch while I give Thecla the fucking she so obviously needs?"

With his eyes flashing in human desire and animal resistance to those human desires, Eleison lowered his attention to Malin's trousers, mere centimeters before him.

To the greater excitement of all involved, my mate leaned forward to nuzzle against the protrusion therein, then slid his hands into the motion of unzipping my husband's slacks.

"Ah, see...now there's a good boy, Eleison..." With a low

chuckle, Malin stroked my mate's head once more before raising that same hand to draw me closer by the waist. Bracing himself back against the doorway, embracing me to his flank as Eleison liberated his cock, Malin murmured to me, "Come here, wife, give me that gorgeous mouth of yours...let me relieve your needs, I'll make you feel so much better..."

While I whimpered softly, clinging to my husband's shoulders and submitting my mouth to the virile stabs of his tongue along mine, Malin inhaled sharply. We glanced down, our tongues still intertwining as we together watched Eleison swallow down Malin's cock with a greed I didn't know to be in him. He wasted no time taking two, three, four inches of that great rod, his hand working along the remaining length. As he lavished affection on my husband's prick, my mate's eyes raised toward us, absorbing us, darting across our fangs—especially mine. My predatory instincts much too aroused by the vision and Malin's delicious blood so nearby, I drew back from the kiss and sank my teeth into my husband's throat. While Eleison growled at the sight, Malin groaned, his arm tightening around me as I jerked my fangs from his flesh and lewdly ran my tongue along the punctures now surging with blood.

"That's it, angel, oh, yes...drink your fill, Thecla, ah, that's right—isn't it a husband's job to provide for his wife? Especially when that wife is so generous..."

He rocked his hips to push his cock a little deeper into Eleison's mouth, and this at last proved too much; Eleison choked a bit, drawing back to cough, a ribbon of saliva snapping from Malin's proud prick and clinging to our dear Eleison's lower lip as he laughed.

"Fuck, ah—you really are bigger, aren't you..."

As, without delay, Eleison resumed servicing my husband, that same diligent husband groaned and shuddered in the euphoric work of both our mouths. My lips pursed to suck more dedicatedly from the wounds, the taste of Malin's life in my mouth so splendid I could not stand the thought of wasting it for visual stimulation in our sexplay; but even without my tongue tickling up and down the wound, Malin seemed to be enjoying himself plenty, and responded to my eager suckling of his blood by growling, "Pull up your skirts, pretty girl, ah, fuck—let me make sure you're ready to take the dick Eleison is working so hard to ready for you..."

Moaning softly against my husband's neck, I did as he commanded, savoring the sadistic pleasure of demonstrating dominance to one lover while submitting to the other. While Malin's hand raised from Eleison's head to slide up my thigh, over my stomach, and down into my panties to provoke from me a ribald cry, Eleison watched as best he could from the rapid bobbing of his head along Malin's cock. When next he choked, he drew back to apply the vigor of his tongue—and more openly enjoy the sight of Malin's fingers, barely visible through the lace of my underthings as he teased along the soft furrow desperate to be plowed. At the sensation, I couldn't help but raise my mouth to whimperingly beg for his kiss. Malin denied me, his cruel smile a delicious accompaniment to the caresses of his strong fingertip around and past, but only sometimes directly over, the needy center of pleasure's greatest height.

Second greatest height, at any rate. For, as Malin himself marveled, I was, "A wet little bitch in heat, aren't you, angel? My God...if you like seeing Eleison suck my cock so much, just wait until you get to watch me fuck him. Down, boy."

Pushing Eleison back to make way, Malin dragged me to his

mouth for a plunging kiss that opened my lips the way I yearned for him to open the delta of love. Groaning, I stumbled at his behest into the office and fumbled my way out of my dress while Malin worked open the buttons of his shirt. "Shut the door," Malin told Eleison, who obeyed unflinchingly and seconds later only showed the slightest flicker of resistance at the follow-up command, "Strip her for me."

With a hint of jealousy even now in the growling mouth he pressed to the nape of my sensitive neck, Eleison conformed to our master's desires; expertly as any servant, he eased the work of my hands so I could focus on undressing Malin, and within moments I had been stripped down to my bodice and garters before the nakedness of my husband. Satisfied, he pulled me closely to his chest to let me feel the strain of his cock against my sex. One massive hand slid back to possessively knead the flesh of my ass while he pushed me back against the arm of the velvet sofa, arranged across the room from the desk where his work lay forgotten. It was against this desk that Eleison leaned, arms crossed, jaw tight with a profound interplay of desire and jealousy as Malin kissed his way down to my breasts and ground himself against my inner thigh; but when my husband's head lifted amid the shine of those powerful fangs, which plunged into my throat the same instant his cock stretched the aching cunt that quickly eased to accommodate him, Eleison's body language changed. Inhaling sharply to hear me moan, he gripped the desk behind him, his eyes fixed on us as Malin fucked me with truly relentless abandon.

I made no effort to dampen my expression of pleasure; such a thing was impossible, and it thrilled me to tease Eleison's jealousy into a state of hostile lust. As my husband swallowed my blood— one hand upon the back of my neck and the other upon my hip to keep me well-supported as he fucked me so hard the couch trembled several inches out of place and soon rammed against the side table—I let my eyes fix upon Eleison's. The animal intensity of his barely restrained desire only increased my pleasure; I cried out for Malin, folding my legs around his hips and gripping his powerful shoulders as his prick hammered into me with a savagery he'd no longer been capable of in mortal age.

Now, I had no doubt Malin was even more athletic than he'd been as a notorious rake in his early years; a silvery lock of hair falling out of place against his forehead, Malin raised his head from my throat with his mouth red by my blood and his fangs still visible. He stared into my eyes, our bodies working in perfect sync as I took every stroke with greater and greater incredulity. "That's right, darling," my husband said, panting as my limbs tightened and my back arched to rock my hips into an even more deliciously yielding angle, "that's right, oh, Thecla, Daddy knows how you need to be fucked, doesn't he—"

"Yes! Yes! Oh, fuck, oh, Malin—oh, Daddy—!"

"Nice and rough." My husband gripped my moaning mouth with one big hand to keep my neck extended at an angle he enjoyed. With a flick of his eyes briefly toward Eleison, then to the hand with which I gripped the cracking back of the sofa, Malin lunged down and snapped his fangs into my throat, my collarbone, my breast, inducing in me a state of ecstasy that was nearly too much to bear. Indeed, when his mouth raised to press my own blood into my mouth with his commanding kiss, his next words proved the only catalyst necessary to push me into orgasm.

"Don't worry," he told me fondly, nuzzling his bloody lips against mine as each hard pound of his cock reverberated so utterly I swore I felt him fucking his way into the back of my throat, "oh, don't worry—Eleison will come to his senses soon enough, I'm sure...perhaps seeing how long I can fuck you will persuade him to step into true immortality...and then won't you be a happy girl, oh, yes, my angel...your husband and your mate, forever and ever—"

"Yes," I screamed, my nails scratching into Malin's shoulder and splintering the sofa's frame while my eyes rested upon Eleison's hungry, haunted look of irrepressible desire, "yes, oh, sweet fuck, Eleison, darling— How good it would be to give both of you my blood, my soul, my heart, my sex! Oh, God, oh—Malin!"

Toes curling as the climax ripped through me, the swollen pressure of my sex releasing in a gush of dizzying passion amid the deep thrusts of Malin's heavy cock, I threw my head back to moan while the waves drew me out to sea. As my husband let the hard work of his rutting guide me through the orgasm, he watched my face with appreciation, his deeply lidded eyes and parted lips the face of a man enchanted.

"Oh, Eleison, look at her—look at our darling. Aren't you patient to wait your turn...come on, take her. You know how she is: one cock is never enough..."

Dismounting me to provoke a whine of desperate protest, a smile touching his lips as he bent to kiss me, Malin urged me down into the cradle of the sofa and let his lips nuzzle gently over my whimpering mouth. "Don't worry, Thecla...I'll mark my territory tonight, once Eleison has had a chance to enjoy its grounds...my God, and what an eager beast he is to enjoy you..."

I glanced over, my vision muggy through the haze of my orgasm, and gasped with longing to find Eleison already stripped to the waist and in the middle of removing his trousers to free his straining cock. Oh! What a beauty my mate is—every hard muscle seemed intensified by the lighting of Malin's office, the lamps of which cast shadows to emphasize the statuesque angles of deltoid, pectoral, abdomen, ilium. As though the gravity of a dream caught my words in my throat, I could only utter a low sigh of appreciation; but soon, when Malin stepped aside where he could watch with pleasure, Eleison draped himself over me to cover my face in kisses. I ran my tongue along my lips to clean them of dangerous blood and reached for him, drawing his mouth directly to mine. Knowing my fangs remained extended, he paused; but after a few heartbeats that thudded loudly in his chest, he pushed down against my lips to kiss me in that thorough, emboldened way of his. With a cautious exploration of my incisors, his tongue slid in against mine. I opened my mouth to him, my tongue curling and coaxing along with the hands that slid up his strong arms. Soon, he could not resist but be between my legs.

"Look," he said, drawing his kiss away with a heady glance back at Malin. "Look, I just want to be sure, because I've heard—you know—I want it to be my *choice* if—"

"Don't worry, beautiful," Malin told him, bending to catch Eleison's face and command him into a kiss the way he so often did me. While my mate groaned softly and quickly gave himself up, Malin cut it short to tell him, "You can fuck us—be fucked by us—all day, all night, and no harm will come to you, no matter what terrestrial humans tell each other to keep themselves from being embroiled in our kind."

With a sigh of pleasure for their kiss—and relief to hear this, for it had also concerned me—I arched a brow at Malin. "And how would you know this, Husband?"

Chuckling, Malin bent his head over mine to kiss and nip my ear, Eleison's pressure against my wet and eager sex nearly distracting me from comprehension as Malin whispered to me, "Where do you think your precious Ba'al-Dinon has been while waiting for you? Advising me from time to time...not very often, but certainly with information that counts."

Oh! That scoundrel—small wonder it was he who first introduced me to the labyrinth hidden in the villa. That pleasurable understanding was not long-lived before being subsumed in other pleasures, but still I enjoyed a little rush of knowledge—and of gratitude, my heart gladdened to know that Malin had not been completely alone all the time.

I told you I love you, Thecla...I told you, these are my gifts to you, these men whom I love because I love you. I would never abandon Malin to the darkness when it costs me nothing to share with him some light.

Even within the vaults of my soul, I had no time to consciously respond to Dinon's words: Eleison, his mouth covering mine with more kisses, plunged into me without delay, comforted by Malin's advice. For having been fucked by my husband so roughly, I found accommodating Eleison a simpler matter than usual—but once he filled me, plunged to the hilt in the core of my pleasure, I keened and whined to re-experience the sheer indulgence of his gorgeous cock within me. While he murmured my name and praised Malin for getting me so wet, my husband's purring seemed to fill the room.

"I have no doubt, Eleison, that you inspired her as much as I did...now, I'll be right back..."

While—after leaning briefly out to check the way was clear—Malin slipped from the office in the direction of the bedroom, Eleison raised my hips to initiate a rhythm of lovemaking that teased me after my rough use by Malin. He savored me, this sweet reunion with me after my rebirth, his hands tangled in my hair and his eyes fixed upon mine while his forehead rested upon my brow. "Thecla," he murmured, bruising my lips with kisses, "oh, Thecla, baby, I don't care—I don't care what you are. Fangs won't stop me...I'll fuck you with your antlers bursting out of your forehead, I don't care. I just want to make love to you—I love you, Thecla—"

Though his hunger for me made me giggle at first, by the end, his oath left my heart aflame with passion. Stroking his cheek and that dark hair I loved to pet, I told my mate, "I love you, too, Eleison...Eleison, my darling, my heart—I swear, I'll never hurt you."

"I trust you." He kissed his way to my ear to murmur hotly there with the slow rocking of his cock within me, "And I know that if I asked you to, you would."

Shuddering amid the purr that rose from my breast, (and, I swore, hardened his cock another degree), I trailed my fingers tenderly over his back and assured him, "Just remember, darling... the family safeword is 'Lescaut.'"

"I love to hear good communication," Malin said in a merry tone, pushing the door shut with his bare foot while striding back to us with a familiar glass bottle in his hand. "Really sets the tone for what's about to happen."

The popping open of the stopper was familiar to all of us by then, and Eleison glanced back from kissing me to make visual note of it. His grip on me, those hands which had caressed along my breasts and stomach to squeeze my ass as he fucked me, tightened in delicious anticipation. My mate braced himself against me, watching over his shoulder—as did I—while Malin knelt on the sofa behind him and set the stopper aside.

"Now, Eleison, darling, just relax. Just keep fucking my wife. Enjoy the sensation. Don't think too hard about it...your body knows what it wants better than you do."

While a glistening ribbon of lubricant poured from the bottle and along the statuesque slope of Eleison's ass, I braced my heels into the sofa at the slight sharpening of his stabs within my pulsing cunt. I groaned, drawing Eleison's attention back to me by taking his face in both hands and claiming him for my kiss—though I kept my eyes open, peering past his face to watch as Malin collected some of the lubricant upon two fingers and summarily ceased the downpour.

"Here we are...tell me if you feel any discomfort, now...I've done this once or twice before"—my husband's eyes twinkled wryly at his joke, which made me laugh against Eleison's kiss— "so I think I know what I'm doing, but since it's your first time, I want to make sure it's not the last time..."

Malin's hand disappeared from view. Eleison's breath hitched sharply into my mouth, flaring his nostrils and drawing from my throat an encouraging moan—especially at the way his cock seemed in that moment to be made of marble.

"There," Malin coached, working his fingers tenderly around, then gently just within, Eleison's virgin rectum, "there! Oh, Thecla, darling...what a nice, tight asshole your mate has. Eleison! How you've guarded your heart from me all these years, oh, pretty boy..."

While Eleison groaned upon drawing back from our kiss enough to catch his breath, his hands sliding up over my breasts and his turgid cock slowing its hammering within me, Malin carefully worked his way in, his free hand occasionally stroking his own prick to exasperate the pleasure of the moment.

"Don't worry...a few times of this, Eleison, and soon you two will be fighting over my cock...ah, I can't wait...the first time you come to beg me to fuck you, Eleison, will be a very happy day...we just have to get you used to the idea. Besides, look at it this way..."

Eleison choked on his breath, his cock pulsing within me as Malin pushed his fingers all the way in and—as I would later be informed during some educational dirty talk—lightly crooked his fingers to tease Eleison's prostate gland for bursts of intense, soul-deep pleasure apparently comparable to what I experienced when they hit that maddening little soft spot deep within my belly.

"If you let me teach you how to take a cock, Eleison, then we're one toy away from Thecla being able to fuck you...and won't that be fun? Then you can enjoy a cock up your ass and still feel perfectly straight about it...unless, of course, you feel like giving it to me as good as you're about to get it..."

Surrendered to the sensation, Eleison could produce no verbal parry for Malin's teasing; he could only kiss me, sucking love from my lips while Malin fetched up the bottle again and applied more of its contents to his own cock. Then, carefully, with the utmost love and tenderness, Malin pressed himself between the nates of Eleison's gorgeous ass and gently extricated his fingers.

"Just breathe out, Eleison, darling...a nice breath. Ah—" Demonstratively, Malin inhaled, the tips of his fangs still visible in his mouth to exponentially increase the already powerful excitement of this opportunity to watch him assert his love for my mate. Prompted, Eleison breathed in from my panting lungs, then pushed the air back out against my tongue—only for the exhalation to strangle off into a choke of incredulous ecstasy as, exerting just enough force to fit the flared glans, Malin pushed his cock into Eleison's anus and groaned at the completion of this circuit of pleasure between the three of us. Seeing how Eleison's brow furrowed and Malin's eyelids fluttered with the sensation, I very nearly collapsed into orgasm on the spot; but, as addicted to that delicious edge as I was to the celebration of the moment, I hung on, stroking Eleison's face and steadily arching my hips to work his cock inside me as he paused to let Malin mount him.

"Oh, Eleison"—Malin's voice was low and raw, his jaw tight, his chest expanding with a great inhalation as he slowly found a pace that seemed to be one our lover could take—"oh, you naughty boy, denying me this tight, fine ass for so long—ah, Thecla, what a generous wife you are to share your mate with me—"

"What a generous husband I have," I praised, still stroking Eleison's face as I gazed into his eyes, "and what a loving mate. Oh, darling...doesn't it feel good, Eleison?"

"Fuck!" He gasped, unable to help himself but say, "Yes— Yes— So fucking good—"

While Malin and I chuckled together, exchanging a glance, Eleison deemed it safe to renew the pattern of his thrusts within me. Oh, how that steely cock had hardened! I might have worried he could hurt me with it, it was so hard—but I was no longer merely mortal, I reminded myself, and my body was equipped to take (and enjoy) far rougher treatment. With a low groan my husband shared, I braced my leg up against the back of the couch to open myself as completely as I could. His eyes bright with the opportunity, Malin caught my ankle and raised my stockinged foot to his mouth, kissing the arch and sucking my toes with such lascivious expertise that each contact caused another surge of sexual pleasure I hardly could have expected to be so intense. Though I delighted in Eleison's kisses upon my shoes just a while before, and Ba'al-Dinon's worship of my feet had certainly provoked quite a strange, lewd pleasure, Malin's attentions caused my foot to transcend from mere extension of my limb to actual sexual organ. The pleasure provoked my body to flutter around Eleison, who was rapt withal, caught between us and pummeled by waves of the two sweetest raptures any man could hope to enjoy separately, let alone together.

And Malin, meanwhile, watched me as he fucked my mate, his strokes growing a little more intense each time I moaned at some powerful strike of Eleison's cockhead into that sweet spot of my center. One hand upon Eleison's shoulder, the other upon my foot—which he pressed to his heart as though in lieu of my hand—Malin watched us both and gauged Eleison's enjoyment, measuring not just whether he experienced discomfort but how close to ecstasy my pretty mate was hovering. Judging by the pitch of my moans—a proper measure, considering they were directly correlated with how hard and fast Eleison's cock roughly, eagerly filled me—Malin reached down and surprised Eleison into a new groan by massaging his testicles.

"Are you going to cum, Eleison? Go on, darling...cum in my wife. She wants it—ah, sweet fuck, and I'm close, myself. Look at our adorable little slut, Eleison...go on, give it to her. Why, hell—I have an heir already. If you want one, I wouldn't object to you trying. What are mates for? We'll have to discover if such a thing is possible for dharmine...but, worst-case scenario...our Thecla is just an eager little slave to our love, greedy for cum, desperate to be filled—ah, oh, Eleison—oh, yes—"

Teeth bared, half a growl on his moaning tongue, Eleison pounded inside me so roughly I couldn't resist anymore: my body clamped around his, the powerful squeeze of my sex roughly jerking him over the cliff and bringing about an orgasm of Eleison's that was so powerful he cried out. His tone was nearly helpless, boyish with surprise, his brow furrowed as though he had never experienced such pleasure in his life—and, having discussed it since, I'm quite sure he hadn't. Letting go completely, Eleison groaned to release in me as Malin, gasping in appreciative pleasure, let Eleison's ecstasy jettison his. Bending down, catching Eleison's hair in his fist, Malin twisted my mate's head to savagely kiss him on the mouth; then, with a shuttered stare of love into his eyes, and mine, Malin committed the second half of his orgasm to me, filling my mouth with more kisses while he emptied his balls into Eleison, my mate—our love.

As in the aftermath of a powerful storm the sea grows quiet, so fresh silence descended upon Malin's office in our pleasure's wake. All three of us softly panting, we collapsed together, Eleison's body warm with sweat and mine still trembling with the glory of such excellent, truly equitable love. Malin, it may be predicted, maintained sense enough to remain director of our affairs, sitting up slightly after a moment with the punctuation of a single kiss upon the back of Eleison's neck.

"What say," suggested Malin, "we hop in the shower and move our happy little family to the bed? There's more room there for a nap...or a second round...or a third..."

"You are truly incorrigible, darling," I said with a laugh. "Insatiable!"

"With you two," my husband said, a dark chuckle on his lips to look between us, "why should I ever be satiated again?"

"That implies you ever were," Eleison managed, clawing his way out of the depths of a great daze to evidence the wit that made me smile, and made Malin smirk in guilty agreement.

"Too true, Eleison—but isn't that just why the two of you love me? Now, come along...I don't know how much more this poor sofa can take."

HOW EASY ALL OUR HEARTS were left after that happy reunion, our true reunion: the realignment of our souls into the synchronization of our love! We rested in contentment, Malin forgetting all about his work to dwell in the moment with us, while I likewise neglected all to which I would probably have been better off attending. With my husband and mate back with me, however, both together in bed with me, I was in a paradise much too sweet to leave until the rumbling of Eleison's stomach signaled we had ought to dress so he and I could put in appearances at dinner. Human food, I had found since my metamorphosis—that was, all foods which did not contain the flesh or blood of terrestrial mortals—was especially delicious and enticing, the sense of taste re-tuned as excellently as the rest of them. I therefore had something to look forward to by going downstairs, if nothing else; though I admit, I still longed to be with Malin, in our happy apartment where the truth resided and we did not maintain a charade.

For the mask I wore was stiff, and heavy on my face; so much so that, once we retired to bed, I awoke in the darkness of the early morning with thoughts of the deed to be done nearly suffocating me.

I had killed a man before. I had even done a good job not thinking much of it, since it was in self-defense. But the fact remained that, held beneath the blacklight of God's judgment, my hands were stained just like Malin's and Eleison's; like Glenn's...and Dinon's.

When I sat up in bed, Malin revealed his own wakefulness. He tilted his head toward me, stroking my forearm. Eleison, sleeping more heavily on my other side, stirred but slightly as my husband asked in a quiet voice, "Everything all right, angel?"

"Yes," I began; but, realizing that was a lie, admitted, "I'm just quite nervous. I think I might weave awhile today."

"That sounds like a good idea." Cupping my hand in his, his fingers working along mine, Malin drew my knuckles to his mouth and kissed them. "I have no objection to doing it myself, darling," he assured me, leaving me biting back a very dark laugh.

"Of that, Husband, I have no doubt...but that would give me no comfort. Indeed, I fear I would only be worse off for standing aside while you did the deed—trying to convince myself I had been involved but in premise. Let me commit fully to our decision. And, besides—"

Our dear Telemachus's suggestion, that Parvati had been frightened by my accusation of her involvement in Malin's death, haunted me too deeply to ignore.

"—I wish it to be a gift to you," I told Malin. "A gesture. I want to prove that I am worthy of you—devoted to you, through and through."

"Thecla…" Sighing in low love, Malin slid his big hand up my arm and over my shoulder to fit his palm against my cheek. "You needn't do anything to prove that. You don't need to weave tapestries, or save my life, or offer anyone's heart."

"But I want to."

The gravely emphatic tone of my voice made him smile in indulgent affection. He drew me down into his kiss. "Then I will gladly receive your every offering," my husband told me, "and work all the harder to return in kind."

After gazing meaningfully into my eyes for an electric handful of seconds, Malin released me and patted my cheek. "Have fun weaving today, darling…do you mind if Eleison and I—?"

"Oh, of course not…I never mind. Knowing you love one another brings me such joy I couldn't even begin to express it—I love you, my husband."

"I love you, my wife," Malin told me, sliding over to drape an arm around Eleison's waist and hold him from behind as he often did me. "Then we'll see one another tonight…and oh, how we'll celebrate after."

Smiling at the sight of my beloveds together—and, wrapping myself in my robe, half-fleeing the scene before Eleison fully awakened and persuaded me back to bed—I hurried to my workroom and flipped on the light to regard the barely started tapestry. Soothed by the sight of it, I shut the door behind me, sat at the stool attached, and spent no more than a few seconds regarding the template before I resumed the work.

How my hands and feet flowed as never before! Certainly, I had enjoyed many moments of inspiration that had resulted in my hands flying through their work as with a kind of divine grace, my speed unnatural even as a terrestrial mortal. But now, with my new body born into the world from the start with a mind made for weaving, I seemed to become aware of my motions only after I had engaged in them. Indeed, I seemed only to realize I was weaving after I had been at it for two or three full minutes. Suddenly conscious of myself at the loom in a full way, I smiled and studied the progress I'd made in the forty-some minutes I'd spent weaving in demonstration for Telemachus. Given how quickly I was able to weave a full tapestry as a mortal with human dexterity, how long, I wondered, would this one take me now?

The answer turned out to be about twelve hours.

I astonished myself. Never in my wildest dreams had I imagined the creative flow could come on me so instantly, so completely. I seemed mesmerized by my own act of creation, my shuttle rocketing back and forth, my feet working the pedals without a single diverted thought. My body knew my template better than I did: it reminded me of weaving at the Black Loom, the evocation of which summoned a curious pang of longing along with the mysteries it continued to represent. Would I ever see it again, I wondered? Would I ever discern the nature of the cloth I had woven upon it?

Though I told myself that perhaps this tapestry was only so fast-moving because it was so simple, that proved not at all true when I set about embroidering details into the image. First with red threads, next with blue, I drew out the blood and then the mithrae flowers upon which that mouthwatering substance fell. The work made me long to find Malin so as to slake my thirst, but I could not justify getting up. My perpetual promises that I would take a break in five minutes were never fulfilled; nor were they necessary. I found myself more than equipped to hang on, the rapid labor distracting my mind from the least need…save for one.

In the shadows of the trees lurked the witch that haunted all the tapestries, Dinon's image captured in thread and evoked to excellent effect in previous renderings. Yet how much better could *this* rendition be if his exquisite silver hair might be captured with that sacred thread, that mysterious stuff forming the weft of reality?

The soft song used to keep my rhythm falling silent on my lips, I stared into this phantom Dinon until my eyes unfocused. It was not more than half a minute of this indistinct meditation before I noticed the shimmer of the threads. First, merely the violet warp; but by allowing my eye to follow these streaks, I discovered the strings of silver with which they interwove. My eye pursued them as my hand extended, my fingers splayed. I turned my wrist to look with awe on the dazzling glimmer now imbuing my flesh, a smile on my lips.

Never looking away lest I should lose track of them, I gently picked at a thread running along my palm and, as I had with my tapestry for Malin near the end of my mortal life, I drew these silver threads from the spindle of my body to weave Dinon's hair directly from my own soul.

My soul? Was that truly what I drew from when I slid my own marvelously strange threads into these works? I was not certain. As I had told Malin, I knew less of the soul than I knew of death; and even now, immortal, I knew precious little of what death was. I only knew I *had* been dead, I thought, while I was mortal; and with my husband's love, I was now alive.

My meditation deepened intensely. I lost track of the violet threads and soon enough saw only the silver ones: the silver of Dinon's hair, the silver of the moon I sewed into the top of the tapestry, the silver of Parvati's coiffure; and all this silver gradually blurred together, pulsing like the waters of an uncanny ocean beside which I stood to watch the mercury waves sloshing back and forth along the shore.

"Would you walk with me awhile?"

His voice was so hushed it seemed almost awed. Drawn from my self-hypnosis to find I stood, still barefoot and in my robe, upon the violet sands of an alien beach, I turned. Dinon stood all of six yards from me, his expression possessed by a new, breathless uncertainty—unveiled love, I interpreted. True love, without the amusement that so often shone from him as, like a mirror, he reflected playfully on my ignorance of our romance.

"Dinon," I whispered, falling toward him a step, then hesitating to look around and down at myself. "Am I dreaming?"

"You're weaving," he said, extending his hand. "Please, Thecla? Let's just be together right now."

Lip bitten, I dropped my eyes from his face to his offering. Having grown past the point of disguising my eagerness for him or any other lover outside of the context of a specific game, I darted over and threw my arms around his bare waist in a tight embrace. Inhaling in deep pleasure, Ba'al-Dinon slid his hands over my biceps and up my neck, where he tousled my hair as he murmured, "I've missed you, Thecla."

"I've missed you so much," I told him, although I knew as I spoke that he had meant the sentiment differently than I—on a vaster scale, incomprehensible to a mind that worked within terrestrial spacetime. "Oh, Dinon—darling—won't you come to me?"

As I gazed up at him, his brow furrowed in gentle sympathy. "I want to," he told me. "I do."

"Nothing stopped you before."

"Because you knew so much less before." The silver splendor of his eyes trailed over my face, focusing upon my mouth while his thumb drifted down my cheek. He bent and kissed me: a kiss so soft, so full of intimate longing, that I felt dizzy with the wave of pleasure sweeping over my skull. "Let me just enjoy this moment with you, Thecla," he whispered as we parted.

A real plea in his voice—his eyes. It took me aback.

"All right."

I made no further protest as he lowered his hand to mine, kissed me on the knuckles, and then by this same hand drew me along the whispering waves that lapped over my feet and his boots upon their caresses of the shore. "You seem so different, suddenly," I told him, adding by way of explanation, "I can hardly ever think of seeing you without a smile on your face."

"I want you to know who I really am."

"And that is—?"

Instead of answering me, Ba'al-Dinon asked, "Thecla—what's the worst thing you've ever done to a sentient being?"

Thrown off-kilter again, I frowned and glanced away from him. The surf receded, its platinum foam still clinging to the sand.

"The man I killed in Valquist," I suggested, adding, "or—what I am about to do."

"I have killed many sentient beings," he told me. "Many, many more than you or your mate or your husband have killed. Than you all will ever have killed in the final tabulations."

His tone was not indifferent to this—but not proud, either, as one might expect a pure predator to be. "I'm sorry," I said, earning a gentle squeeze of my hand.

"But it doesn't have to be that way. This time can be different. It can always be different, Thecla."

"This repetition…Dinon, will you tell me, please, if it's my husband's fault?"

"You don't really want to know that."

"Of course, I do."

When I looked up at him, I found him studying me with great intensity.

"It's you, Thecla," he said. "Your weaving."

"But *how*?" Annoyance bubbling up from my heart, I insisted, "Even with these threads I pull from the aether, and the way they somehow let me come to this place on the other side of the Rift— surely even they, woven into a mere tapestry, could never exert such influence over reality."

"You are so powerful, Thecla," he said. "And so wise. You know in your heart that now is not the time to know. You will paralyze yourself with gnosis if you keep up the pursuit and remember too early. That's why you're always asking me not to tell you the future…and so I don't. Even if, to me, it's all merely the past."

My teeth grinding, I stopped and gripped his hand while turning to gaze into his beautiful features. Far behind his head, suspended in the dark indigo sky, the moon betrayed a pinkish glow amid the atmosphere of that weird world.

"But you *will* be with me, won't you? Dinon—"

"Sh…Thecla."

His free hand fitting to my face again, his fingers curling

into my hair and against my ear as his figure shimmered with my tears, Dinon looked at me with such immense, complete love that I found myself longing time to stop.

"Trust me," he whispered, the words as fair as music to my ears. "Trust me—I won't betray you, Thecla. Remember the first time you met me? How you knew so little that you were afraid to look at me, thinking a glimpse could produce some accursed connection between you and what you regarded as no more than a parasite?"

"I'm so embarrassed," I lamented, my eyes falling away until Dinon's fingertips sank into my flesh to draw my attention back.

"Don't be. I only mean to say—your understanding has come so far, Thecla. So far, Beloved. Yet, as far as your understanding has come, you still have further to take it. And even for as long a time as I know you've felt this unfolding, we must yet take longer. You must not push yourself. Let me tell you when it's time to push, Thecla."

Lips pursing, I nodded, trusting him for reasons beyond my own comprehension. "All right," I said softly, captivated by his quicksilver eyes and the tender smile that at last crossed his lips. "All right—I'm depending on you."

"You always have. And I've always depended on you."

What was this connection? What did he mean, and why did I feel so close to him that I felt as if we shared a single mind—albeit one divided by a barrier I could not surmount alone? Questions surged through my consciousness the way the water surged across the beach.

Dinon looked at me with wonder, his expression softened once more away from amusement and into pure desire.

"I love to watch you think," he murmured, his free hand slipping into my robe. Pushing the fabric back from my shoulder, he slipped the garment loose and liberated my other arm so the covering fell at my feet. He smiled gently as he added, "And I love thinking about you. You're all I think about, Thecla. You're all I've ever thought about."

I trembled despite myself, my teeth chattering. "What a thing to say! Why is it that what sounds like romance from another man is frightening from your lips, Ba'al-Dinon?"

"Yet here and now, you want to know who I am," he observed, his hand raising along the column of my throat, "and what my relation to you really is. But...I suppose you like being frightened, don't you, Thecla?"

Shivering beneath his touch, his eyes, I confessed, "Sometimes," and glanced down at the grip of fabric around my neck. To my amazement, as his hand caressed my shoulder, my collarbone, my breast, a web of silver lace followed; an underdress of dark netting even appeared to accompany it, preserving my modesty for whatever that quality was still worth.

"Then I'll only frighten you sometimes," he told me, the hem of the gown pouring out of his hand to fall around my feet with a languid sway in the breeze. A twinkle in his eye, he clarified, "When you want it...when you deserve it."

Before I could remonstrate him, he gathered my hair into his hands and, with another caress, arranged it perfectly, my silvered roots host to a glittering tiara that kept my coiffure in place. "How I love dressing you," he said breathlessly. "And how I love undressing you...I will do it every day when we can be together again."

"As you did before? As my footman?"

He didn't answer. Dinon only raised his hands to my cheeks, studying my face, his silver locks framing my vision as he bent over me.

"Dinon—"

"Sh," he pleaded, his nose brushing mine. "Just kiss me, Thecla—just kiss me."

"Thecla."

The pressure of Dinon's mouth was so light and tickling at first that, agonized by longing, I pressed back with force that surprised even me. His breath hitched and his hands trailed down, gripping my shoulders as he pulled me to his heart.

"Thecla."

Moaning, I opened my mouth to feel the confident coaxing of his tongue against my lips. We explored one another's mouths, my hands trailing along his chest and down his flanks. The wind whipped up, his black cloak enfolding us both in the heavy coastal breeze—

"Matrix—"

I jumped upright at my loom, startled to recognize Charlotte's voice at last. With a somewhat delirious look—and a disappointed one—to find myself back in my workroom, I glanced over my shoulder to the door, then back down to the tapestry in my hands to see how far I had gotten.

To my astonishment, it was finished.

"The wake is about to begin," she said in the middle of opening the door. "We'd better get you— Oh—"

Her eyes narrowing slightly, Charlotte looked me over in a manner assessing, but not disapproving. "Who dressed you?"

Looking down to recognize, in an almost expected way, the gown in which Dinon had adorned me, I glanced at his face in the tapestry to find in my reverie I had sewn my silver world-threads, also, into the delicate details of his watchful eyes.

"A witch," I responded, rising from my loom. "Let's pick out shoes together, Charlotte, darling...but first"—holding out the tapestry, I smiled—"what do you think?"

HAD THE PURPOSE OF THE WAKE truly been closure for my husband's death, I would have been quite pleased with it and the manner in which it proceeded; indeed, as a means of honoring his mortal, terrestrial existence, I was glad to see those staying in the house—and those who made the long journey from other points, such as Saalast and temporarily packed inns sprinkled throughout the Gudrune countryside—were in a mood that was an excellent combination of respectful and merry. As I told Aleister, when I was growing up, wakes were considered celebrations as much as a means of processing bereavement. Therefore, while those who addressed me tended to adopt a somber tone, I noted that when talking among themselves, the guests seemed to be having a very fine time.

I daresay few had as much fun as Eleison, however. He had found me trying on shoes and, looking so handsome in his three-piece suit I could barely tear my eyes off him, I only barely succeeded in taming his kisses long enough for him to escort me into the ballroom downstairs. And that was only the start of his good time. As it was Eleison's estate, the wake was largely regarded as Eleison's brainchild; and although he had hardly anything to do with its arrangements aside from organizing security, all whom we greeted were quick to praise the fete, its stylings, and even its menu to him. Although Eleison tried early on to push credit to me, I laughed and kissed his ear when we had a moment between conversations.

"I had as much to do with it as you, ultimately," I reminded him, smiling at the way his heart sped beneath the music, the conversation, the clinking of glasses and steps of dancers. "It's Charlotte and Kyrie who are better off with the credit; these guests should all be praising them."

He turned with a chuckle, his nose brushing mine, his undisguised red eyes aglow with the fullness of his soul after having been persuaded by lovemaking that Malin and I were truly ourselves. Barely resisting the urge to kiss me, Eleison murmured, "If you really want to get right down to it, isn't Malin the one who deserves the credit? He went through all that trouble of dying, after all..."

We chuckled together, a restrained flash of mirth retained in the bases of our throats lest we raise questions by having too good a time. I felt so completely torn that night! So of two minds, two realities. It was not as though I had any hesitation about what needed doing; I simply knew the truth of things, at least in part, and knew that this fictional world where Malin was dead would be soon to fall apart.

But first, there was business to attend.

"Thecla—"

I looked up from my conversation with Eleison to find Parvati not far from us, all of two feet from my escort's back. Her gown a complexly embroidered combination of blue fabrics and gold lining, eyes and nails painted to match. She looked quite beautiful and had even eschewed a headpiece out of, I supposed, some symbolic respect for me, her hair elegant but unadorned. Taking my hand, she flashed a pleasant expression between both of us. "A beautiful wake: Malin would be proud to see it."

"I can only hope you're right. Thank you again for coming, Parvati. I know I've not been the most social animal of late, but—"

"No, Thecla, really. I understand—and, after our conversation the other day, I *really* understand. You know, I was looking for you today, but I couldn't seem to find you. Then your housekeeper mentioned you were weaving!"

With a guilty laugh, I confessed, "I get nervous before events like this—I must busy my hands or else spend the whole day pacing about, fussing over details better left alone."

"I can relate. It seemed like you were in there a long time, though! Do you often work such long hours?"

"Not anymore." Fast to laugh, I suggested, "You know better than anyone that the duties of Matrix forbid much leisure—one is busy enough without weaving added to the mix. Why don't you and I speak now, though?" Gesturing toward the doors which were open to permit the flow of guests in and out of the gardens, I smiled, then added to Eleison, "If you would excuse us, darling."

"Of course...Madame Overseer." With a nod toward Parvati, Eleison let his gaze linger on me but a second or two before he headed into the crowd, peering about to re-orient himself in the direction of the bar. While I smiled at Parvati—an expression that doubled in breadth to realize she had left her guards at the door of the well-attended fete—I slipped my arm through hers and guided her into the night air.

"You really should have your men a little closer," I advised in her ear as softly as I could while we made our way down the steps and, by our presence alone, shooed from the fountain a few chatting courtiers. "That Winston is about—he still makes me terrifically nervous."

With a soft laugh, Parvati assured me, "Well, they're watching from the doors. I don't like everyone I speak with to be intimidated by them...they should be intimidated by *me*, instead." As I laughed along with her, she glanced around to ensure we were being given sufficient space to consider ourselves in private. "Anyway...I just wanted to let you know—"

While I straightened up in eager attention, trying to keep the excitement from my face, Parvati explained:

"In light of the...new information you shared with me yesterday, and the importance that Gudrune remain a stable territory able to cooperate both with its own people and the territories surrounding, I've decided to make your position permanent."

With a great breath, I pressed my hand flat upon my heart and told her, "I don't know if it's right to thank you for such a responsibility, but—"

"It's not easy," she agreed, "and I think you still have a lot to learn; but I also mean what I said. Your territory would benefit from female leadership, both now and in the future. When your son replaces you someday, he'll have seen Gudrune ruled with what I hope will be a gentler, more cooperative hand than that of his father."

In other words—she hoped feelings of goodwill toward her and her support would allow her to make a puppet of me. I smiled on, however, happy enough to play the part of my old, rather more clueless self, and reached over to take her hand. "Thank you for believing in me. What must I do to establish this control officially?"

"Well, I've talked to most of the territory masters already, and no one expressed any particular concerns. There will be an official vote to confirm among them, but with my support you can consider it a done deal. I would like to discuss the energy program with you again sometime, though—once the dust has settled, and you feel a little less protective of Malin's will."

"No doubt we will discuss that and many other matters." Maintaining a smile, I kept hold of her hand and leaned in to whisper with a conspiratorial tone, "Perhaps—since I've become better-acquainted with the ventil since last we spoke—we might go running in the woods tonight to celebrate?"

Pleased that I should invite her as once she invited me in Valquist, she tilted her head and glanced off into the dark tree line surrounding the property. "All right," she said. "I'd enjoy that."

A look of relief—only partially affected—crossed my face. "I do so wish to be friends, Parvati," I told her, lifting my hand from hers and folding my fingers in my lap. "Perhaps it's immature of me, or unprofessional, and I would be better off thinking of you as a sheerly political associate, but—well, as you said of Gudrune and my son, one does benefit from exposure to strong female leaders. And now that Malin's dead, I think I'm at greater liberty to say...I admire you, Parvati."

How strange! I had expected more difficulties: suspicion, derision. But I should have realized that Parvati, who preferred to walk about a party for her dead rival without her guards close at hand, was too arrogant to see through my flattery when she thought of me as a naïve and easily manipulated woman from rural Gudrune. "I want to be friends, too, Thecla. I loved your mother very much—and even though I struggled to love Malin, I sort of think that, if you loved him, there must have been something about him still worth caring for. We *used* to be friends," she clarified, drifting off into a thought, "a long time ago, ages ago...but—"

"The-cla!"

The high cry of Kalypso made me tense slightly, but thankfully it was a jerk of the shoulders that simply appeared the birdlike wince of a traumatized woman unable to bear surprises. Looking at me with great sympathy, Parvati patted my hand and rose from where she'd perched at my side.

"People change...and feelings fade in time. Even bad ones. Where should we meet?"

"Back here," I suggested, "around two—is that too late?"

"That's perfect. I'll retire at midnight and get an hour or so of rest...good evening, Lady Montagne." While, looking like a perfectly adorable doll of a woman in a dress as pink as the clothes of fairies in picture books, Kalypso skipped before us and curtseyed with a dramatic depth that signaled she had been sampling what I asked her to bring, Parvati headed back in to rejoin the wake. "Enjoy the party, both of you...Thecla, I'll see you later."

"You weren't out here talking about *politics* or some such, were you, Thecla?" Pouting, Kalypso slid her arms around mine and drew me to my feet, reminding me, "Whether wake or wedding, don't forget, it's a *party!* And anyway—"

Leaning close enough to my ear that her whisper stimulated me quite unexpectedly, (so much so I wondered if Lady Montagne might not make a more entertaining bedroom guest than our

Charlotte, should I ever feel like humoring Malin and Eleison's occasionally floated fantasy to see me with another woman), Kalypso went on, "I have what you asked for, though I left it in my room to be safe. Would you like it now?"

"Not yet. I'll send Charlotte up for it soon; where is it?" When Kalypso had described the bag carrying what she explained to be roughly a dozen vials of tincture, I nodded and told her, "Then, if you don't mind—"

"Oh, not at all! Fetch away, fetch away, it's your house... well—*Eleison's* house, but you know what I mean. Goodness!" With a laugh as she lost her balance and tumbled down upon the fountain's edge beside me, Kalypso enthused, "It's *strong* stuff, Thecla, I'll warn you now! Much more than the few drops I took under my tongue, and I think even a giganturn would be napping."

Pleased to hear it, I told her, "Then I'll be prudent, dear, don't worry. Will you be staying on long after the party?"

"Mm? Oh, yes, I suppose I'll keep on with Brother until we hurry home to beat the winter weather."

"Well, we must have more time together, Kalypso, dear...it's only just occurred to me how much better I would like to know you."

While the girl beamed dimples into her pretty cheeks, nodding with great agreement if only because she, like her brother, was drawn endlessly to power, I regarded my reflection in the waters of the fountain and found it clearly visible to my eyes despite the dark night.

How incredible it was to look at myself! To look at my soul. I had hardened, certainly—there was no doubt of that. My growth was not all good. But when I looked back at the girl I had been when Malin took me in, and saw clearly how naïve, how repressed, how alone I was in the world, I regarded this hardness as the source of something far more important: confidence, as Eleison had described it. Indeed, it was a confidence that permitted me to know those soft parts of my heart that were worth protecting, and instilled in me understanding of whom and how to share these soft parts. I felt like a statue that had been carved down beneath the hand of a great artist—though whether that artist was Malin, or myself, or someone else altogether, I could not rightly say. I only knew I seemed to watch myself as I entered the wake again, and, as had been the case with my weaving, it seemed my body knew what needed doing better than my mind. I discovered Eleison in conversation with a territory master, (Richter), and, not wanting to interrupt the chat to lose the benefit of my mate's networking, I circulated on my own. Soon I found much life to be enjoyed in this party of death. The time I spent with the courtiers was not wasted: it had taught me how to have fun with people I barely knew or did not know at all; how to dance and drink and put on a great show of merriment when, within myself, I was anything but.

For even as I celebrated my husband's life with the attendees, my mind was geared entirely to the future. And, as one 'o' clock rolled around and—with the help of the staff and the guards—I began to politely ask the guests if they would require a place to stay in the house or help setting their autos for the trip home, my very molecules buzzed with my intent.

Should I not have felt wicked? I asked myself many times that night—but the only wicked thing about it seemed the deception. No matter how I endeavored to put the question of killing to myself, I could perceive it only as nature at work. It was natural for the strong to overcome the weak, and the young to supplant the old. And although it was the unique privilege of humankind to transcend nature and behave in ways aligned with civility and morality, I could not make myself believe my intent was immoral. Perhaps it was only wishful thinking—but my heart could not shy away from what it had committed to, as I would have expected had the deed been truly evil.

When the ballroom was empty, I stood with my hands upon my hips and regarded the servants who wandered about cleaning the place. Charlotte put on a wise charade of directing them, leaving me the task of catching the bartender before the open bottles of wine could be poured out into a bucket for disposal. Seeing him tip the first vessel, I cried out and hurried over to earn his pause.

"I know it was Master Farrow's custom to prefer sobriety among his staff except for holidays," I said with all my casual charm, "but this is certainly a holiday. Look—I want to be thought of fondly, so why don't you all in here split these four bottles among yourselves; Charlotte and I will take the rest to disperse to the others in the household."

Too glad to ask questions, if he had any at all, the bartender thanked me and helped me by loading the remaining bottles, including a few sealed ones, upon the cart behind him. Smiling, I waved Charlotte over to me and said, "Will you help me, dear? I'd love to be well-regarded by the guards of the other masters... perhaps we'll receive greater privilege should we make diplomatic visits abroad."

With a nod, Charlotte took up the task of pushing the cart from the ballroom as I bade the rest of the staff good-night; then, feeling the pressure of our time limit, I hurried out along with her and followed her to the nearby tearoom, where we had the luxury to work in private.

"Here," I told her, handing her the corkscrew. "You open these last few—where are the vials?"

With a tinkling of glass, Charlotte removed one such precious container of tincture from her apron, then, at my hastening gesture, proffered four more. They were small things, so much so that all five fit into the well of my palm; I shook them vigorously and cracked open the first, adding the fluid inside to the first half-full bottle of wine, then emulating the process for the next, and the next. "That is *quite* a lot," Charlotte observed, working the corkscrew with such brilliantly practiced automation she needn't watch herself at work. "How long are you planning to put them out for, exactly?"

"However long it takes," I said, snapping off the tip of the fourth vial and barely beginning to add its contents.

I had not added more than a drip or two when the door behind us opened in time with a sharp knock.

My body tensed with animal surprise; spine snapping straight, the vials hidden in my palm and closed within my fist so quickly I nearly crushed them with my inhuman strength, I whipped toward the door half-expecting Eleison, who had gone to bed ahead of me. Accordingly, my face was arranged in a smile: I was ready to tell him playfully off for frightening me in the middle of such important doings.

But how that smile faltered when Winston Garland stood in the doorway instead, his eyes crinkled with delight that matched the white of teeth more predatory than any dharmine's fangs. How that smile of his was empty, and false, and hateful to me!

"Matrix," he said. "There you are! You're a hard woman to get alone...have a few minutes to talk?"

40

My already pale knuckles grew alabaster as my fists clenched in Winston's presence.

"Of course," I told him. "Charlotte—why don't you go on ahead and share the leftover wine while I meet with Mr. Garland?"

"Careful with that," the hunter said in a humorless chuckle as Charlotte pushed the cart past him. "Mithrae doesn't agree with everybody...I'd warn them, first."

While Charlotte glanced at him with a sharp pair of eyes and a scoff of befuddlement meant to disguise her true reaction, I tipped my head back in a laugh. "Oh, Winston, aren't you funny...of course, we're going to warn them. We don't want anyone dozing off on the job! This is just a little thank-you to all the servants who've worked so hard tonight."

"Uh-huh." While the door swung shut behind Charlotte to

leave me alone with Winston, the eye of my ill-esteemed guest swept me head to foot and back again. "You seem pretty jumpy for somebody just saying 'thank you.'"

"Well, I'm not used to people walking around my house without knocking." Turning away from him to set the vials upon the nearest table—and glad that Charlotte didn't pass all of them to me—I asked, "So what is it this time, Winston? Here to blackmail me again?"

The hammer of a gun clicked.

I froze.

"You could say that."

Empty hands lifting, my fingers spread, I turned very slowly to face him and the pistol between us. With an unsteady inhalation, I tried to laugh and could not produce more than a few weak notes of a chuckle.

"Winston, now…just what's brought *this* on?"

"Desperation, Matrix. You see—"

Taking his time in making his approach, Winston kept the gun trained on my chest with each step.

"I learned at that wake out there tonight that Parvati has made you Matrix of Gudrune on a permanent basis…and that's just not going to work for me."

"Because nothing you could hang over my head could possibly undo it, right?"

"That…and I don't like it when a woman lies to me."

Scoffing even then—even as he stopped with the muzzle of that gun not three feet from me—I assured him, "I may have let you believe I would think harder on your proposal than I actually did, Mr. Garland, but I assure you—"

"Not *you*," Winston said in undisguised disgust. "You idiot— Parvati. Though I can see why she decided to approve you…kind of a dumb bimbo, aren't you." My face burned in barely contained fury as Winston's tongue navigated within his mouth, a protrusion that traced beneath his lower lip as he regarded me. "I'm sure she doesn't see what a threat a brainless bitch can be when in power with no goals other than serving a dead man's legacy."

"Are all the Guild members such misogynists," I asked, my expression flat with disdain as I looked into his eyes, "or is it just you?"

"Now, Matrix Farrow, I don't *hate* women...I love to fuck 'em. And I don't mind a smart woman like Parvati, who knows what's good for the continent—"

"And who cooperates with the Guild lockstep."

"I do admit...that is a favorite quality of mine. She's a wise woman, most of the time—she sees the wisdom in working together. In working with me, specifically. You know, you still have time to learn a thing or two from her."

"Do I?"

"If I came here just to kill you, Matrix, I'd have pulled this trigger and gotten out clean by now."

With an amused twist of my hands at the wrists in substitute for a shrug, I at last successfully laughed. "How, exactly? This place is crawling with guards."

"Don't worry about me...I just mean to say, if you want to live tonight, there's a way out of this."

"That way being?"

"Abdicate." Eyes never leaving me, Winston jerked his head in the rough direction of the stairs to the second floor. "You walk out of this room, go knock on Parvati's door, thank her for the opportunity, and politely decline. That's all you need to do; and I'll never bother you again."

"What makes you so certain the next territory master will be obedient to your whims and reinstate Guild operations?"

"I like to think I'm fairly trustworthy in that regard."

I was so shocked that I could only make sense of his words after a few seconds; by then my eyes were surely wild. "*You* were her next choice?"

"Maybe you're not so stupid after all." His smug little smirk infuriating as the way he felt at liberty to speak when on the other side of a gun, Winston studied me through eyes as dead and hateful as I have no doubt mine were in that moment. "Sure, I was Parvati's next choice. She and I go way back...it's how I know your boyfriend. Going back and forth to Valquist, I got to know the Hunters there damn well. Well enough to be sure our interests and Parvati's are sympatico."

"You can't know that for sure. Parvati is among the most self-interested people I've ever met. Be reasonable, Winston... she doesn't look it, but Parvati's old. She's set in her ways. More importantly, she's had control long enough that you can be sure continuing her reign uninterrupted for as long as possible is foremost in her mind. If she appoints you Master of Gudrune and senses the slightest deviation—or sees the ambition I can detect in you so clearly right now—don't think she'll hesitate to move against you. You may be an expert hunter...but I doubt you're even half the military strategist Malin was."

With a mocking laugh, Winston worked his eyebrows. "You seriously think Parvati would make a move against me? You don't know how well-aligned her interests are with ours. Where do you think we've been getting the funding to continue skeleton operations in Gudrune since your husband dismantled our chapter?"

As I absorbed this new verbal blow while trying not to exhibit the loathing that raged in my heart, my adversary shook his head. "That's why I'm pissed, Thecla, and why I think it's best you abdicate. That way, everybody can get their heads on straight without fuss. Whatever you told Parvati, or promised her, or bribed her with to get her to change her mind about putting her support behind me—it's clearly made her forget the importance of working with the Guild."

Resisting the urge to look down at the gun that remained almost unnaturally steady between us, I smiled. "Or perhaps it made her realize the more intelligent play was keeping Gudrune from dissolving into political strife."

"Oh, she's still going to get political strife—especially if I have to put a bullet in that pretty head of yours to get what she promised me. So, I suggest we wrap this little chat up and you take the chance to tell her all this responsibility is too much for you. Don't worry...I'm sure she'll understand."

What a pathetic person. Surrounded by such worthy specimens of masculine love, I had almost forgotten how base and wretched a man could be when he hated womankind; yet I knew, too, that such hatred was often motivated by jealous lack, as Eleison's sullen behavior during the early days of our love had in retrospect been the singular indicator of that deep attraction. Whatever Winston felt was not love, of course, but a kind of dehumanizing lust in which he projected his inadequacies out upon the women to whom he was attracted...but he did not consider one important fact:

I was already inhuman.

"*Now* I see." With a soft laugh and a shake of my head, I took a step not in the direction of the doors, but toward Winston. As my hands lowered despite his protests, I told him, "It's one thing to long for Gudrune's throne—but to speak to me with such disdain made no sense to me until this moment. Poor Mr. Garland..."

His nostrils flared, his dark pupils somehow all the darker as I suggested, "If you wanted to fuck me, you just had to ask. Why—if you had showed me you really know how to use that fat cock of yours, I might have given you Gudrune without your having to hold a gun in my face."

Slowly, slowly, as though I were petting a rattlesnake or a wild luptich, I extended my hand forward and stroked suggestively along the barrel of the gun and over Winston's hand. He made no move to lower the weapon, but did risk a glance away from my face to watch my fingers slide down over his wrist—then, he took in a few other parts of me.

"I've always heard you were easy," he said, "though maybe I didn't count on *how* easy. But if you think I'm going to let you disarm me and just—"

"Winston...I don't think *you're* stupid. I wouldn't try to disarm you."

My hand tightened around his wrist and his eyes flashed up to mine as, with a vicious wrench, I crushed his hand around the crumpling gun and smiled at the snap-pop of his dislocating shoulder joint. While my other palm flew up to slap across his mouth and muffle his screams, I showed him the fangs that his agony had summoned out in an instant.

"Just dislocate," I suggested, smiling as his efforts to work the trigger of the severely bent gun were either too weak or too futile to open fire. I sprang forward, my exposed teeth snapping around the flesh of his neck and pushing past muscle to reach the surging artery with its rapid, happy surge. With the pounding of his heart, blood gushed from the wounds and into my mouth the very second my fangs lifted away; I drank greedily, focused entirely on his death, gripping him tightly enough that I was overconfident in his imminent demise. Moreover, I was famished, having not fed since the night before; and as the rich substance flooded my throat, his blood thinned and enriched by the same wine that had no doubt emboldened him in the attempt on my life, all I could think of was satiating my own appetite. I drank and drank, my hand bruisingly tight over his mouth, his gun no longer a threat—

Which caused me to discount the possibility he had other weapons, such as the knife he plunged into my side with his still good left hand.

As I cried out in surprise and stumbled back—amazed at how the brief sting engendered a kind of physical excitement, as had the broken glass in that dark space between life and death—Winston cursed me while yanking a handkerchief from his pocket. "You fucking bitch," he gasped wetly, pushing the cloth against his throat to staunch the spurting wound. "You dharmine whore! Now I see. Now I get it. The rumors about Malin were true. And you—you probably wanted us to get him out of the way so you could take power from him."

"That's all you can think about, Winston." I grit my teeth so tightly my fangs slit my lower lip in two places. Thus braced, I jerked the knife from my side with a gasp for the nearly erotic sensation of the weapon sliding out of the wound. As my flesh knit across my lip as well as beneath the torn fabric, I regarded the pitiful little blade while I went on. "Power—all the power you want—all the power you don't have. It doesn't occur to you that others might have different motivations in this life. That some of us could be motivated by things like love."

Spitting his own blood upon the floor with total disgust, Winston sneered. "What the hell could an undead cunt know about love?"

"More than a soulless man like you," I told him, advancing with the dagger in my hand.

Teeth bared, Winston looked rapidly around, then leveled his gaze with mine. His chest heaved beneath his bloodstained suit as he did precisely the last thing I could have expected.

He took what seemed to be a step toward me—and altogether disappeared.

41

THE WORD FLEW THROUGH MY MIND in Dinon's voice, emerging so organically I nearly mistook it for a natural thought.

Riftborn.

Fangs still bared and all the rest of my teeth showing along with them, I whipped my eyes wildly around the room and unfocused my attention to draw into relief the threads: hoping, somehow, they might divine the means by which the conspirator had fled. There was nothing, however. No trace, no disruption, had been left in the fabric of reality so far as I could see it. Hatred blazing in my heart, I tightened my grip on the dagger while Charlotte's brusque knock rattled the door upon its hinges.

"Thecla," she called, "are you all right in there?"

"I'm fine now." I stared down at the blade in my hand, then up as she let herself in and paused uncertainly on the threshold.

"Take this," I urged her, turning it around to pass it to her by the handle. "Clean it quick as you can; then, if he hasn't left already, give it to Malin."

"As you wish. Are you sure—"

"Don't worry about me, Charlotte." Though I was flushed and somewhat breathless, my fangs no doubt a frightful sight, the wound in my side had fully healed. I swept a hand over the lingering blood to show her not so much as a cut lay beneath. "I'm lucky—I got the drop on him. But it would seem that Mr. Garland has more in common with Parvati than mere common interests... they're all blasted hypocrites. All of them thirsty for control of peoples they despise and yet are part of—damn them."

I wanted to stay and rage; wanted to enjoy Charlotte's validation of my opinion while I vented all my upset upon her. Instead, I waved. "Go on—hurry. If you go now, you may catch him. When you're through, finish handing out the wine, and be sure to drink some yourself to allay suspicion."

Without further delay, Charlotte whirled about and hurried across the foyer to the grand staircase. I caught my breath. The clock on the wall read 1:55—how fortunate for Winston! Fain would I have stuck around, hunting him out or perhaps even seeking a means by which I might enter the world on the other side of the Rift, where I sensed he had fled to escape me with his life.

Yet this opportunity would never come again. All things had been perfectly arranged, and Malin, certainly, would not wait for me to hunt one of our enemies when he had a clean chance to slay another. Therefore, mopping the blood with a doily I tore from a nearby table, I hid the tear in my dress with the position of my arm and hurried back to the ballroom which provided the most direct exit to the gardens. The external doors slammed a little hard beneath my rushing hands, but I didn't care: my goal lay close enough for me to smell on the breeze, quite literally. As the light wind bore into my nostrils the coarse, wild musk of an animal, I glanced in its direction and whispered, "Parvati?"

A nearby hedgerow rustled and, from its manicured depths, an ertiz's fiery orange head appeared amid the twitching of four attentive ears. She came slinking out, her long ermine body seeming to ripple as she revealed herself, then sat upon her haunches. With a sigh of relief, I smiled at her and reached into my hair to remove the pins Dinon's magic had placed.

"I'm glad I didn't miss you," I told her, enthusing on, "what a wake! If it were anyone else's, I might have almost had fun...I hope you enjoyed yourself."

She looked at me oddly, and I realized my mouth still had a tinny taste. "Do I have lipstick on my teeth?" I laughed and rubbed my finger along them, cringing at the hint of Winston's blood there. "Goodness...it's been such a night! I hope that hasn't been there long. Ready to run?"

Her tail swirled and wagged, but those keen eyes next slid down to the hole in my side. I waved a hand at it while contorting my arms back to unbutton my dress, telling her through the locks of hair that had poured around my face, "That's the cost of pride...I haven't been exercising as intensely as I'd ought, not since Rosina's birth." Aching to think my new rivalry with the Guild may have cost me quick discovery of my lover and our daughter, I sprang free the final buttons and wiggled out of my dress. "Yet here I am, still trying to fit into the same old dresses...I'm glad this one lasted most of the night before the seam gave way."

I had not attempted to transform into the ventil, with or without the Rift, since my rebirth as a dharmine; but to be nude in the night, the sweet scents of the forest richer on the wind than ever as they blew into the garden on the lightest wind, I stepped out of my shoes while comfortable in the certainty that the stirring in my breast was the Rift beast residing in my soul.

"My Eleison and I know the most beautiful little pool," I told her, or her ertiz, anyway, quite certain she understood me whatever the case. "Let's go there—it's not a long ways, but it's very fun. Come on!"

Laughing like a girl, my feet bare as they pounded across the grass, I let the ventil take control of my limbs as I urged the Overseer's Rift beast, "This way! Just wait until you see it!"

In seconds, my torso had collapsed forward, and what sprinted along the ground were not hands and feet but perfect hooves.

How exhilarating a sensation! Had there ever been a dharmine ventil in all history? I supposed there must have been; yet, as strong as I normally felt to be that liberated Rift beast, my borrowed body coursed with a new energy...especially after a recent meal. I could have run all night, and then some—could have even outrun Eleison, I realized with delight—and struggled to resist the urge to give in when already I galloped so fast the little ertiz rushing after me could hardly keep up. As was so often the case with Eleison's means of humoring me, I paused to look back and await Parvati's proximity; then, off I would bolt, my hooves thundering across the forest floor while I made my way through the estate's woods and toward the pond where destiny awaited. More deftly than ever, I ducked and darted around the low branches while nimbly springing over rising roots; and it was not long at all before the Overseer of the continent and I reached that clearing, where a spot of grass had died beneath the body of the beheaded dharmine that had since—whether by our own staff at Eleison's command or some wild animal making a grave mistake—been borne away.

Oblivious to this dark spot in the grass, my ertiz companion gave her tail an elegant shiver of approval. She bounded forward a bit before striding in a more tranquil manner toward the water's edge. I cantered up behind her, coming to a stop just as that sweet night breeze kicked up again.

This time, it brought with it not the aromas of the woods, but an aftershave of sandalwood.

The ertiz's head jerked toward the scent—then froze. I watched every survival instinct ever identified in human or animal cycle through Parvati's mind.

Before she could decide whether to run or investigate, I stomped my hoof down and only by the narrowest margin missed her instinctively dodging spine.

That little beast glanced back at me with an equally small yelp, an expression of annoyance and insult rather than condemnation— the command of a human to watch where the other was going. She assumed it was an accidental misstep, perhaps supposing me as distracted by the scent as she.

But that changed when I brought another hoof down, this time succeeding in pinning my heavy weight down upon her tail.

Crying out, the animal wheeled around and nipped the ankle of my ventil, which snorted and stumbled back a step. I lowered my head, brandishing my antlers while the ertiz reclaimed its tail and turned to growl at me. Seeing, however, that the size difference was too difficult to surmount, and that my antlers were a formidable weapon to face as a creature smaller than a fox, two of her four ears pinned back. Parvati wheeled about with a feral snarl, rushing to the tree line with an expression that, even in an animal, was one that communicated dawning recognition of the depths of its mistake.

But that expression was not as haunted by error as the one the ertiz wore when it reached the trees and skidded to an abrupt halt at what it found there.

Sparing no more time, my husband stepped into the open.

His dark eyes crinkled handsomely with his smile for me. Malin then studied the ertiz at his feet, his tongue clicking in a patronizing little *tsk*.

"What a pity, Parvati," he said, stepping left to block her way while she growled and bristled. "You're quite charming this way... you might have lived longer if you spent more time as an ertiz."

I delayed no longer, the opportunity of her fright too vital. She was between us. Her back was to me. Snorting, I charged.

At the rapid clatter of my hooves, the ertiz whirled around to face me—

And her eyes widened as the spire of one antler, its flowers wilting with summer's imminent expiration, impaled her through the heart.

In seconds, we were both humanoid again. I recognized it only when my eyes parsed the shape of my forearm plunging into Parvati's chest—only when I realized I felt the wet pumping of her heart in the palm of my hand. Her eyes still wide, her lips slack with shock, Parvati stared into my face.

As I squeezed her heart tight in the grip of my fingers, I smiled.

Those delirious eyes fell upon my fangs, hanging there for but a second of strained comprehension.

Blood and muscle bursting around the fingers that crushed her life away, our continent's Overseer died.

EPILOGUE

I LOOKED OVER THE CROWD that had been stunned into paralytic silence before turning my attention to the camera lens. Behind me, Malin's dark eyes made careful progress from face to face, taking stock of who was there and who was not.

"I hardly think I need explain every detail of why I have decided to address you today," I said, having practiced the words sufficiently that I required no more than the occasional glance at the prompter running smoothly on a screen just behind the camera's lens. "Nor do I need to justify why Malin Farrow has been in hiding since the attempt on his life. With the tragedy of Overseer Parvati's death, we can all agree the problem is broader than anyone ever could have believed."

From the podium before me, I raised my prop: the blade shone in the light as I emphasized, "This is the dagger found not far from the Overseer's body on that fatal morning two weeks ago; her throat had been slit and, in a hideous insult, her heart removed, though this latter mutilation did not seem to be caused by the weapon I now hold."

Once more setting down the knife, but still gripping it with the same hand I used to clutch the edge of the podium, I eyed the crowd. "This dagger belongs to Winston Garland, the leader of the terrorist group once known in Gudrune and abroad as the Hunter's Guild; and while they maintain license to operate in territories other than this one, I have it on excellent authority, based on conversations had after the morning of Parvati's assassination, that many other territories from Harteveldt to Evita will be following in our footsteps and disbanding their chapters. This sounds like good news—and in many ways, it is. It is a sign of the future: a sign of progress into truly modern approaches to dealing with the Rift and the beasts it brings us.

"But in other ways," I warned gravely, allowing my stare to pierce the camera through, "I fear this change will represent the beginning of a truly dark period in our continent's history. The Guild has already shown they do not lightly accept challenges to what they perceive as their special brand of martial law—a shadow government that feels entitled to circumvent the true laws of the land."

"Mama's good at speeches," Telemachus whispered while Malin, showing the boy the recording on the pocket watch as I tried to blot out the sound of my own voice by weaving all the more furiously, gently hushed him. As I chuckled despite myself, my past self upon the little screen still managed to reach my sensitive ears.

"I have no doubt that Gudrune will continue to be punished for setting such a powerful example for the rest of the continent," my old self was reciting. "And I likewise have no doubt the people of Valquist are, on the other side of our great land, suffering deeply with the loss of Parvati. We, as a territory, have experienced such grief. We have all known what it is like to be widowed by the death of one's leader; but, sadly for Valquist, they will never know the ecstasy of freedom that comes with a kind of resurrection."

"I can't stand the sound of my own voice," I complained, earning another of Malin's shushes, this one rather amused.

My recording continued, the rhetoric's passion rising as the speech reached its natural conclusion. "The people of Valquist will require our support during this trying time," I insisted, "as well as the support of many other territories while our continent grapples with the matter of a replacement Overseer. Given the involvement of the Hunter's Guild in both Malin's attempted assassination and Parvati's successful one, there is very real concern that continental control will fall into malicious hands. Hands that will try to strip Gudrune of its advancements such as Horizon Energy, advanced alteration procedures, and the free movements of registered Riftborn throughout our noble territory.

"That is why Malin and I have decided to reveal his presence and address you all today. While he requires yet more time to heal and must carefully allocate his energies, it is obvious to us both that we cannot rest—either as a territory or as a continent—until the Hunter's Guild has been fully relegated to the annals of history. No doubt, they provided great support in reconstruction in those early centuries of our adjustment to the Rift: but we have outgrown them as a people, and if we do not fully shake free of their influence, we will suffer the consequences for many more years to come.

"For this reason and others, Malin has requested I remain Matrix of Gudrune, the position to which Parvati permanently appointed me in what was possibly her final political decision ever made. This is to respect the late Overseer's wishes, in part; but it is also to allow my husband's undivided attention in the matter of aiding our allies in the complete eradication of the guild and its primitive ways. While I tend to the needs of Gudrune as the mother to her child, my husband—*our* husband, my people—shall be serving our continent with that same great strength of will that allowed him to survive being shot in the throat by treacherous Hunters during that evil motorcade." The angry tears that glazed my eyes then had been as real as my clenched teeth, and as I wove ceaselessly, my eyes watered just slightly again. I glanced over my shoulder at the chair where Malin sat with Telemachus crowded close, their heads bowed to witness my speech.

"By that will," I heard myself assuring the people, "Gudrune has the opportunity to step into a new epoch of human existence... and where we lead, the continent will follow. Thank you all for coming out." I stepped from the podium and bowed my head to the people, adding, "And God protect the territory of Gudrune."

While the crowd burst into thunderous applause giddy Telemachus imitated, I shook my head indulgently and eased up on my weaving. Malin tucked his watch away.

"See," he said to the boy. "Fairly short, but deeply stirring, and memorable as all good speeches are."

"That was a really good speech, Mama!"

"Papa wrote most of it," I told him, still throwing the shuttle. "I just read it."

"But you read it well, my darling...and anyway, most speeches read by politicians are written by at least one other person. Often, by whole committees."

"I suppose," I said in simple return while, patting Telemachus's head, Malin urged the boy up.

"Why don't you go play for a while, now," he said warmly, "and we can save your history lesson for later. Papa has business to discuss with Mama alone."

"Oh, fine." Telemachus sighed, but—glad to have a break from the near-constant schedule by means of which Malin contained a source of energy otherwise boundless as the Rift—he wasted no time scampering off while calling behind him, "Bye, Mama! See you at supper!"

"Good-bye, dear," I responded, smiling to myself while slowing further the operations of the loom. As the door shut, Malin rose behind me, his hands sliding along my shoulders and then tightening to let his strong fingers sink into my muscles.

At this, my weaving stopped altogether. I sighed, eyes falling closed as my husband kneaded my stress away amid his thoughts.

"You're embarrassed about that excellent speech," he observed after a second, "but I just want to know when I'll be able to get away without wearing that blasted neckerchief in public."

"It could be much worse...you could have been shot in the face. Then you'd have to wear a mask, like the fellow in that musical you took me to last year."

Laughing, Malin asked, "Why do I have the sense you would like that? Mm...perhaps I'd ought to be wearing one already. Would be easier than having to falsify all those plastic surgery records."

"What's the point of having a doctor on our staff if not for just such occasions? Besides...a scar treated with the right surgery should vanish quicker than a recent wound, I should think."

"Too true," he said, his mirth drifting off into a chuckle, his massaging hands slowing to simply hold my shoulders as he bent to kiss my head. "You seem preoccupied, darling."

Unable to help my sigh, I glanced out the window of our Saalast townhouse. My spirit pined after a simpler time for only a few seconds—only until recalling a night of that simpler time spent weaving a rope with my own two hands to flee through this very window. Shaking my head, I resumed the movements of the loom, assuring him, "It's nothing I can control. Don't mind my moods."

"Your moods are my moods, my love. I can't stand to see you in a state of longing...when I see you wishing for something, I want nothing but to present you with the object of that wish."

Sitting in the bench beside me, his back to the loom so he could look into my face while the sunlight caught the blue shimmer of the butterfly on his lapel, Malin said softly, "If you think I don't remember her well enough to feel her absence as acutely as you do, you're wrong."

My lips pursed. I raised my feet from the treadles, inhaling very sharply, the pain such that I struggled to look into Malin's face. His compassion made me too emotional, so I instead studied that butterfly. "I miss her so much, Malin. And—Glenn, too, oh, that bastard! I hate that I miss him—"

"I know, Thecla." His arms folding around me as hot tears surged into my eyes, Malin drew my face to his shoulder and pressed his hand over the back of my head. "I'll find them for you—I swear it."

"If that blasted Winston finds them first... I'm so afraid."

"As hard as it is to avoid"—he released me to take my face in his hands and train my gaze upon his—"I would encourage you not to worry about such things. They haven't even been found yet, so far as we know—and if they are found by the Guild first, I would predict them more likely to be kept healthy and used as some sort of bargaining chip in another pathetic attempt at negotiation."

I nodded, my throat tense while Malin's soothing thumb gently rubbed along my cheek to wipe my tear away. "I just hope we find them before she forgets me," I whispered, feeling absolutely wretched.

"I don't think she could ever forget you, Thecla," my husband told me, his forehead resting against mine. "Nobody could."

Someone—Charlotte, I could tell—knocked upon the door. At once, Malin and I urged, "Come in," and shared a smile despite my morose attitude. "Why don't I fetch us a little tea," Malin said, kissing the corner of my mouth. "Or fetch someone to fetch us a little tea, at any rate...hello, Charlotte!"

Anticipating she might want a moment of my time alone, Malin stood while our housekeeper entered. "I'll be back in a jiffy," said my husband, far more independent in these matters after a decade of surviving on his own. "Don't worry, darling, cheer up...something tells me that, between Eleison and me, we'll find them sooner than you'd think."

While Malin slipped into the hall, Charlotte watched him go with an expression that was, for her, quite fondly amused even if it remained implacable as ever.

"He really has changed for the better since becoming a dharmine. Not that he was ever as unpleasant as everyone seems to think him...but I wouldn't have expected his humor to seem so bright after undergoing death."

"That's just it, Charlotte...as a dharmine, you have a chance to find out death's really not so bad. That it's not really *anything*, in truth. Is that for me?"

"Yes." She passed me the letter at which I hardly glanced, though the slanted handwriting rang the most distant of distant bells in the back of my mind. "The only thing of note for you; I put the rest on Malin's desk, but this looked personal."

"Thank you." She nodded; then, seeing her eyeing my in-progress tapestry, I smiled. "Do you like it?"

"I do. It's good to see you taking a break from that interminable series you've been toiling over for Malin's apartment upstairs."

"'Interminable!'"

While I laughed, Charlotte spread her hands. "It's practically the definition of the word—you've been working on those tapestries since you came here."

"Yes, well...I think they're almost done. The walls are practically filled up with the last one, anyway...soon, the new pieces I weave will have to go to the Karris house, which would make them gifts for Eleison."

"Well, whatever the reason, it's very nice." Her scanning eyes pausing, then narrowing, she snorted and spared me a rather more critical look. "Very odd decision to include that Dinon fellow in a family portrait," she told me.

I frowned. "Why's that? I've included you, too, haven't I?"

The edge of her mouth twitching until she turned so as not to reveal her smile, Charlotte said, "Yes, well, who am I to judge? I kept a pet mouse when I was in my thirties...we were quite fond of each other. He rode about in my apron two and a half years."

Laughing, I told her, "Thank you again, Charlotte," and bade her leave the door open for Malin's return while I remained alone with the tapestry. My smile softening, I let my eyes trail from face to familiar face.

It really was quite strange to represent myself so clearly in these threads of mine! This was the same conundrum I'd had when regarding the honeymoon piece at the villa. While I had inserted myself and Malin and Dinon—even Parvati—into the series now lining the dark wood panels of Malin's apartment foyer, I had never depicted us truthfully: never as ourselves. Now, as this pretty portrait of my family took on greater life with every thread, I seemed somehow exposed, yet also dissociated—as though I was and was not the woman whose image I captured along with Malin's, and Eleison's, and Dinon's—and Glenn's. Soon I would be down to the children upon the sofa with us, and to the hands with which Charlotte would be forever embroidering in a seat beside the greater group.

And if God was really good—really the force of love so natural in the universe that Dinon did not even need to believe in Him—perhaps, not long after I beheld the images of my Rosina and Telemachus seated side-by side, my aching heart would be relieved by bearing witness to the real thing.

Soul heavy with longing, I resisted the urge to look too long at the threads emulating Glenn and instead tore open the envelope which I now noted was just slightly deformed. As I turned it over to slide the letter out, something small and metal—an oval, half the size of my palm—dropped into my lap. Curious, I picked it up to examine it in the light.

And a polar chill swept through my every molecule as I recognized first its design, then the photograph I hastened to confirm within. Unable to bear too long the sight of it, I snapped it shut but found I could not put it down.

As I unfolded the letter with trembling hands, the photograph of my mother remained in my palm.

Dearest Thecla,

I must not make this letter long; it is nothing I have wished to write, no more than it is something you wish to read. The only thing that has caused me greater pain than finding myself thus (and knowing what I am!) is seeing how you have been swept into the machinations of Malin Farrow: perhaps even while knowing his was the hand—or the fang—that took my life.

It would be wrong of me to act as though you are the only one who has changed. Moreover, knowing you only as you were, I think of you as wise and good-hearted. I therefore must assume that the greater proportion of your changes have been to the benefit of your soul. But I cannot remain idly by when my daughter is in the thrall of evil influences. If there is indeed a reason I have been forced to endure this hateful rebirth now, at this time so far from the last date I can remember living, it must be to offer some intercession in your moral life.

Thecla, I urge you to find me in Valquist. Leave all your sins behind. There are people here who can help you, so long as you help them—so long as you renounce your mistakes and resolve to deviate from the evil path down which your husband leads you. If you do not do this, I cannot help you, and I will be forced to reckon you among my enemies. Perhaps an enemy worse than Malin Farrow himself; for it is obvious to me you have let yourself love him, and love is a force that inspires us to do dangerous, often foolish things. Trust me: I know.

With great hope to see you in Valquist,
Your Father,
Rigel of Lescaut

IN THE FINAL VOLUME OF
THE RIFT BRIDE

Our continent is divided: and so is our family.
With the power vacuum from
Parvati's death threatening to eat Valquist alive,
My husband, Malin, has no choice
but use his military prowess in the name of peace.
Yet as my husband goes to war, my heart is tangled
in conflict of its own.
It would seem my father, Rigel,
is a dharmine like myself.
Returned from the grave,
he pursues vengeance for his stolen life:
And to wreak that vengeance upon my husband,
Rigel has, in his turn, stolen
something infinitely precious to me.
But he has no idea of Dinon, the ally watching from the
shadows of my soul—
And neither, for that matter, do I.

VISIT ADA'S SITE
FOR RELEASE UPDATES!

http://www.adadartromance.com

OTHER WORKS
FROM PAINTED BLIND PUBLISHING

REGINA WATTS

INDUSTRIAL DIVINITY (2020)
WILD GIRL RUNNING (2020)
DOTTIE FOR YOU SEASON 1 (2021)
THE BURNINGSOUL SAGA (2021-)
I WAS AN OP DEMON LORD (2021-)
BE MY BULLY (2021)
SEDUCED BY SABINE (2021)
MAYHEM AT THE MUSEUM (2021)
IDOL (2022)
TEXAS CRUEL (2023)

M. F. SULLIVAN

DELILAH, MY WOMAN (2015)
THE LIGHTNING STENOGRAPHY DEVICE (2017)
THE DISGRACED MARTYR TRILOGY (2019-2020)
CLEAR LIGHT (2023)

FINN VANDERGRIFT
SKINSLUT (2023 - with REGINA WATTS)

ABOUT THE AUTHOR

Ada Dart is an author of reverse harems and romances with undercurrents so dark you'll only want to read them at night. Her brooding, intellectual heroes defy boundaries and straddle conventions: whether older or younger, commanding or sensual, the men Dart writes are sure to keep readers' imaginations going long after the final page. In addition to writing other pulp genres under the pen name Regina Watts, Dart enjoys spending time watching opera with her cat and her real life age-gap partner of over half a decade.

ABOUT THE PUBLISHER

Painted Blind Publishing and its erotic imprint, Painted Blue Publishing, are the brainchild of M. F. Sullivan. Founded in 2015 while Sullivan resided in Tucson, PBP is a house dedicated to bringing readers the finest in consciousness-expanding fiction. Be sure to check out the wide variety of essays available for free at paintedblindpublishing.com to learn more about the company, Dart, and Sullivan.